Gabrielle Lord is widely acknowledged as one of Australia's foremost crime fiction writers. She is the author of fifteen adult novels, and her stories and articles have appeared widely in the national press and anthologies. Her psychological thrillers are informed by a detailed knowledge of forensic procedures and are set in contemporary Australia. The seventeen books of the award-winning 'Conspiracy 365' series for young adult readers, published by Scholastic Australia, have been sold into twenty-four countries and have been made into a television series. Gabrielle Lord won a Ned Kelly award for *Death Delights*, shared a Davitt award for *Baby Did a Bad Bad Thing* and was awarded a Lifetime Achievement Ned Kelly award in 2012.

www.gabriellelord.com
facebook.com/GabrielleAuthor
twitter.com/gabriellelord

Also by Gabrielle Lord

Fortress
Tooth and Claw
Jumbo
Salt
Whipping Boy
Bones
The Sharp End
Conspiracy 365 Series (for children)

Jack McCain novels
Death Delights
Lethal Factor
Dirty Weekend

Gemma Lincoln novels
Feeding the Demons
Baby Did a Bad Bad Thing
Spiking the Girl
Shattered
Death by Beauty

GABRIELLE LORD
DISHONOUR

All characters and events described in this publication are fictitious and any resemblance to real persons, living or dead, is purely coincidental.

Published in Australia and New Zealand in 2014
by Hachette Australia
(an imprint of Hachette Australia Pty Limited)
Level 17, 207 Kent Street, Sydney NSW 2000
www.hachette.com.au

Copyright © Gabrielle Lord 2014

This book is copyright. Apart from any fair dealing for the purposes of private study, research, criticism or review permitted under the *Copyright Act 1968*, no part may be stored or reproduced by any process without prior written permission. Enquiries should be made to the publisher.

National Library of Australia
Cataloguing-in-Publication data

Lord, Gabrielle, 1946– .
Dishonour/Gabrielle Lord.

ISBN 978 0 7336 3245 7 (pbk.)

A823.3

Cover design by Christabella Designs
Cover photograph courtesy of Trevillion
Author photo courtesy of Borys Rudko
Text design by Bookhouse, Sydney
Typeset in Adobe Garamond Pro

*To Dr Ida Lichter and Dr Eman Sharobeem –
two of the countless women who are working
to give voices to the voiceless*

CHAPTER 1
GARRALONG, 1992

I heard later that 16 April 1992 was the coldest April night in Garralong since records began. It was the Thursday before Easter, and the northwest section of the state of New South Wales was shrivelling in drought.

It was the night my father, Sergeant Peter Hawkins, aged forty-four, was murdered. I was twelve years old.

It was the night that God and I parted ways.

That day, after school, I'd walked to the Convent of the Holy Family where Sister Mary Aloysius taught me piano in the nuns' parlour, beneath a painting I loved which hung on the wall above the piano. Sister Mary Aloysius told me it was a reproduction of Raphael's *Tempi Madonna and Child*. The sister, who'd been at the convent for years, was famous for knowing everything about everyone in the district and surrounding towns, Catholic or not. We were in-betweens – my father was Catholic and my mother came from a Protestant family.

After my lesson I headed to my best friend Kiera's place where we raided the fridge.

Instead of doing our homework, I taught Kiera the new dance moves I'd learned from Miss Kimberly last Thursday night and then we watched television. Later, I headed off to the library where it was warm. I changed into my dance gear – my short-sleeved black leotard over the pink tights with the hole behind the left knee – and then put my school tunic on over the top, ready for my father to pick me up. I realised I'd left my jacket back in the front parlour of the convent, hanging over a chair. Funny how I can remember all those little details, as if that night were imprinted on my mind.

—•—

Twenty minutes later, I was sitting in the front seat of the car beside my father. We were driving to the older part of town, to the Soldiers Memorial Hall where Mrs Rita King played the piano while her daughter Miss Kimberly taught dancing.

'Dad? I'm freezing.' The car heater wasn't working.

'Where's your coat?'

'I left it at the convent.' There was no way we would go and pick it up now; it would be unthinkable to disturb the nuns in the evening.

Dad frowned across at me. 'You can't walk around dressed like that in this weather,' he said, his voice irritated. 'Now I've got to drive you home so you can pick up something to wear. I'm already running late as it is.'

'Sorry, Dad,' I muttered. I knew he was really tired. He'd been called out in the morning to a car crash on the highway and now he had to go straight to work because there wasn't anyone to cover his shift. I also knew that something at work was worrying him, something to do with a visit by his boss from Newcastle; this morning I'd overheard him say to Mum, 'It has to be done, Claire. And if it's not done tomorrow, it'll be too late and an innocent man could be convicted.'

Dad slowed then swung the car around, the tyres crunching on the gravel at the edge of the road. He drove back to our house and pulled into the driveway.

'Just run in and grab my jacket. I might need it later. In the kitchen,' he said, his voice softer now. 'Or I might have hung it on the back of the door. Make it snappy – Gavin's away on a job and Fonzy can't leave till I get there.'

With Gavin Bailey, my father's friend and partner, away in nearby Derby investigating a suspicious fire, and Fonzy – Alfonso Delgarno, the detective senior constable – leaving for Sydney this evening for his rostered days off, Dad would have to be at work all night on his own. There were only four police officers at Garralong, and the only female, Constable Carleen Gilder, a quiet young woman, was on some kind of special leave, which meant the station was understaffed. They were a tight-knit group, and occasionally got together with their partners for picnics along the river and barbecues (when the fire bans permitted), burning sausages and talking shop.

I ran up the drive and through the front door – we only locked it late at night – and looked for Dad's jacket hanging on the hall stand just inside the door. 'Mum?' I called. There was no answer; she must have been out, maybe doing some last-minute shopping before the shops shut for Easter. The jacket wasn't behind the door and it wasn't in the kitchen. I noticed Mum's shopping list on the kitchen table. She'd be annoyed that she'd gone out without it.

Then I spotted Dad's dark blue jacket draped over the banister near the foot of the stairs. I gratefully wrapped it around myself and ran back to the car.

We took off again, heading back to town and my dance class, Dad driving faster than usual.

'Have you been using perfume?' I asked, sniffing the collar as I tugged the jacket closer around me. It had a pleasant woody fragrance.

Dad glanced across at me, his heavy eyebrows drawn together in a frown. 'Perfume?' For a second he looked puzzled, staring at me sitting there all rugged up in his jacket, and then something weird happened to his face. Maybe it was only the streetlight falling in wavy streaks across his features as he stopped at the red light making the dark shadows around his eyes and mouth, but I was suddenly aware of the change of atmosphere in the car – the air felt different, hard and even colder.

On the rare occasions when my father became angry, he would go quiet and still, as if he were crouched down, just waiting for the best moment to pounce. It was frightening. 'Dad?' I said uncertainly.

But the light changed and he drove on in silence, gripping the wheel.

The drive back into town seemed to take a long time. Something had happened that I didn't understand, that I didn't have the words for. The silence between us grew wider and deeper. All I knew was that I had angered my father and I felt very bad about it.

I was relieved when we finally pulled up outside the Soldiers Memorial Hall and saw the sandwich board that announced: *Kimberly King – Modern Dance Academy – jazz ballet – ballroom.*

I took off the jacket to leave it behind for him and opened the door. 'Thanks, Dad,' I said, trying to make things better between us. 'Sorry I held you up. Hope all the criminals have the night off tonight, eh, Dad?'

He didn't answer. He didn't even look at me. The minute I stepped out of the car he took off, heading for the police station.

That moment too is frozen in my heart – a sharp, glassy ice splinter that will never melt. It is the last memory I have of my father – his stern profile as he pulled away from the kerb.

My memories of that night and the following days come in horrible jagged shards as if that section of my mind had been dropped and had shattered into dozens of pieces. Although I've tried lining up the broken bits, they never quite fit together properly. Some of those memories may not even be mine but rather fragments of what the neighbours told me, or they might even have been created from crazy things my mother said in her grief and pain.

On Friday morning my mother's friend from next door, Jenny Trainor with the amazing woolly golden hair, the retired principal of Garralong High, came in with the police officer from Mount Margaret, and they sat my mother down and told her what had happened. My mother jumped up and ran out of the house, screaming, '*No no no*', running onto the road in the direction of the police station. The detective and Jenny Trainor ran after her; they eventually stopped her and half-carried her into the front room of a kindly stranger's house nearby, some streets away from our place. I don't recall where I was during all this. I have a memory of someone giving me a glass of milk and a biscuit – it might have been the kindly stranger – but other than that, all I can remember from that morning is seeing my mother, watching her shocked and contorted face, and wondering what would happen to us now that my father was dead.

I remember Gavin, his face grey and drawn, his fiancée, Amy Sheffield, waiting in the car outside, coming around over the Easter weekend looking for my father's appointments to take back to the police station, throwing things in a box – Dad's webbed belt and handcuffs, his baton. With my mother upstairs, unable to see anyone, he turned the house upside down looking for my father's sidearm. Gavin found a box of ammunition with four rounds missing on the top shelf of the walk-in pantry. But Dad's police-issue .38 Smith & Wesson pistol, serial number 67823, was nowhere to be found. The police station too was turned inside out, I heard later, but the gun wasn't there either.

—•—

I hated the funeral, people I didn't know staring at me or trying to be nice to me while I stood close to my mother and tried not to cry. The long, polished box heaped with flowers and messages in the centre aisle near the sanctuary and my father's police cap; Father McElroy raving on about how we should thank God for the gift of Peter's life and me bursting with tears I would not release, wanting to jump up and yell, 'Thanking God for his *life*? God's just taken his life away – away from us! Away from him! I hate God!' But of course I couldn't do that at my father's funeral. And especially not in a church.

Despite the honour of a police funeral for an officer KODed – killed on duty – I overheard snippets of conversations concerning my father, quickly hushed if people noticed me standing nearby; some man I'd never seen before hinted at Dad's stupidity in walking straight into a hot incident without sufficient cover, while another gossiped about the mysterious loss of his firearm. I wanted to scream in rage and pain, 'You people didn't even *know* my father but you're tearing him down! And he can't say anything because he's lying dead in that polished timber box.' But I was only twelve, and good little kids such as I was kept such thoughts to themselves.

Four local men, plus two police officers from the neighbouring town of Derby carried the coffin out past a straggly guard of honour of whatever police personnel had attended from other stations in the local area command. People stood around the entrance to Mary Immaculate Catholic Church, built in 1898 and officially dedicated by Monsignor Eamon McManus a year later, according to the faded gold lettering on a granite stone which was at my eye level and at which I stared fixedly while my father's coffin was slid into the back of the black hearse.

The adults thought it best that I didn't go to the cemetery with my mother and Jenny and some locals for the last dismal service at the grave. I was determined not to cry in public and my throat ached with the effort. I stood pressed close to my half-collapsed mother, held up by Jenny. I wondered where my father had gone – that loving, funny, sometimes stern man who had always been there, a huge presence every day of my life. We rode together through the bush on his trail bike, we camped out and swam in the river while my mother relaxed on the bank with a book and billy tea, waiting for us to come out of the water to grill sausages and toast bread over the campfire on a toasting fork made of twisted wire. What would I do now without him?

Some big fat senior sergeant from Altona patted my head and told me I would have to be brave and look after my mother. But who, I wanted to ask, will look after me?

—•—

The following days blur in my memory – trying to entice my mother to eat something, watching her shrink from a healthy size twelve into a tiny, hunched eight. Anything she did eat she immediately threw up again. I sat by her bed as she lay prone and silent, staring at the ceiling. Trying to interest her in something, anything, I dragged the television set into her bedroom and set it up where she could watch it. She wouldn't see anyone from the police, not even Gavin Bailey.

One day when he rang I heard Jenny say to him over the phone, 'That child needs to know the truth. It's important she be told exactly what happened. She shouldn't be left in the dark.'

So a detective from Newcastle called Gary came around to our place, and while Jenny held my hand, Gary told me what had happened at the Davidsons' farm that night. Old Frank Davidson had shot his wife, Gary said, then he'd shot my father, who'd arrived at the scene, and then, sometime later, himself. It was a dreadful, terrible business, he said. I just sat there, blank-faced and listening.

I was bewildered. My father would never have gone into a dangerous situation unprepared, I knew that. He was the type of man who noticed *everything*. He was the one who always knew where things were or when they'd been moved. He knew when I'd helped myself to one of his favourite chocolates, which came in large boxes, five rows of ten. He noticed the first shoots in spring, the sound of a bird new to the district. Whenever I'd lost something, I'd always ask my father – not my mother – where it might be. On top of the pain of losing my father was the knowledge that he had lost the respect of the township he had served.

A card arrived from the cousins in England a few weeks after the funeral, from the only relatives we had, with grey doves and white and green lilies on the front and, inside, flowery print saying, *Deepest sympathy to you*, signed by two people with indecipherable names.

Towards the end of the second week after my father was murdered, Jenny called Dr Phil Burgess, who visited and spoke to my mother in a loud jolly voice about how we couldn't have this sort of thing going on. My mother had lost seven kilos already from the vomiting. He gave her a thorough examination and that's when she discovered she was seven weeks pregnant. Dr Burgess told her she had to pull herself together for the sake of her unborn baby. Jenny held her while she wailed over and over, 'I don't want this baby. I don't want this fatherless baby.'

Dr Burgess left a prescription for some tablets for my mother, and I ran down to the chemist and ran back with them. I brought Mum one with a glass of water and then waited eagerly for the result, hoping that in a short while the tablet would make her better, that my kind and loving mother would be restored to me. But the tablets only seemed to make her sleep.

I lay awake worrying. How would my mother cope with a new baby? The thought of a new brother or sister arriving should be exciting. But not now. Not this way. The worry about my mother compounded the grief for my father. I felt as though I had lost both parents.

Then one morning, about a fortnight after the doctor's visit, Jenny said quite loudly – and, I realised later, quite deliberately – in my mother's hearing, 'If this goes on any longer, Dibs darling, you're going to have to go into care, and so will the new baby when it comes. I'll call Community Services about this.'

These words filled me with terror. I couldn't be sent away from home and live with strangers. Jenny saw my distress and hugged me. 'Could I go next door and live with you?' I asked. 'I'd be really good and I could just run in here and help Mum and the baby every day. Don't let anyone take me away.'

Jenny hugged me tighter, kissing the top of my head. 'Hold on, Dibs,' she whispered. 'Just hold on. I will never, ever let that happen.'

Although my mother showed no response to Jenny's words at the time, the very next day she got out of bed and showered and had some toast and Vegemite, which she managed to keep down. I was so happy to see her out of bed and eating something. Once, she put her arms around me and said, 'I had a bad dream, a nightmare, about what happened out there at the Davidsons', and I think my dream was telling me the truth.'

'What, Mum?'

My mother hesitated. 'I can't quite remember,' she said at last and took her arms away from me. I knew then that she *did* remember the nightmare and didn't want to talk about it with me. Perhaps she was protecting me.

— —

Gradually, over the months and years that followed, my mother returned to something resembling her old self. But she was never the same. Something in her had broken. I think even back then I understood that.

I had changed too. I dreaded going out anywhere. I'd hear the whispers: *. . . father murdered. Shocking really . . . poor kid . . . mother completely devastated. He walked into a killer . . . unprepared . . .* People turning to stare at me in the street, the girls gossiping at school. The artificial attempts to be kind to me. I knew they meant well but I wanted to scream, 'Just stop it! Just go back to how you were with me before it happened. When I was just another daggy kid.'

Once, just outside the supermarket, I came face to face with Craig Davidson, Frank and Betty's eldest son. For a few moments we stood in shocked acknowledgement of each other. Craig was a big man with a red face, powerful, thick hands, and thin ginger hair on a sunburnt scalp. After what seemed like a long moment, he shook his head helplessly and hurried away. I think I knew what he was feeling.

Later, it seemed that the grief over my father had been so completely eclipsed by the fear of losing my mother as well, and by the need to stay strong against the gossip of the town, that as my mother partly returned to me, the loss of my father moved further away, ungrieved and fading. But one thing never disappeared. It stayed with me in the bedrock of my memory – the sense that something *else* happened at the Davidsons' farm on the night my father died.

CHAPTER 2

Brad's birth in October brought some happiness, and for a while Mum seemed calmer and more like the mother I knew before my father's death.

When I topped the district in chemistry and maths in my final year of high school, my science teacher, Mr Heffron, visited our house waving a copy of my HSC results. 'You must go to university and do a science degree. You have a fine mind, Debra. You're up there with the best. And you've got that quality that makes for a good scientist. I'm sure you know what I mean.'

I nodded, smiling. 'There are facts and there are presumptions . . .' I began quoting.

'That's right,' Mr Heffron said. 'You're a doubter, Debra. A born doubter. That's what a good scientist needs to be. Believe nothing, question everything. That's why you must do something in applied science.'

I nodded again, not wanting to contradict him. But all I'd ever wanted to do since I was a little kid was join the police force. That was my first priority. Maybe later I'd do a science degree. I'd told the careers adviser at school, 'I don't want to marry and have a family. I want a career. I want to join the police force.' My mother wasn't at all happy about it, wanting me to do science or law – anything except policing. But my mind was made up.

A few days before I left Garralong to take up my first posting, there was a knock at the door. A heavily built man with thinning ginger hair stood there holding a bunch of yellow tulips from Melinda's Florist in the main street. For a moment I didn't recognise him. Then it dawned on me who it was. I hadn't seen him since that awful time we'd bumped into each other outside the supermarket.

Craig pushed the flowers at me. 'These are for you,' he said finally, his face reddening even further. 'I'm really sorry about it.' Although he didn't say exactly what 'it' was, I understood that he was expressing deep regret over his father's behaviour and the resulting death of mine.

We sat together on the old cane chairs on the veranda with the flowers lying on the table in front of us. Despite the huge differences between us, we were bound by the violent loss of a parent – in his case, parents. I offered him a cup of tea but he shook his head; however, the offer seemed to loosen him up and he started talking.

'I never thought my old man would do anything like that. Well, he was a real tyrant at home but sweet as pie everywhere else.

He used to go fishing with your father sometimes . . . I couldn't have known that one day my father would – would *kill* your father. He was a cranky old bugger, and Tim and me were scared of him. He used to get stuck into us when we were kids. But he'd never picked up the gun before except to put down injured animals. He bullied and yelled and swung the leather strap on us until we got too big. Tim left to work in Canada not long after the shootings.'

'Where's your brother now?'

'Not sure. We don't really stay in touch. We're not a close-knit family.'

Obviously, I thought.

'You know,' he continued, 'I still blame myself for not doing something to stop the old bastard going whacko with the .303.'

'What could you have done?'

'I could've shot the old bastard myself.'

I looked hard at him. He was dead serious.

'I used to go to sleep thinking that one day I'd come back when he least expected it, and shoot him. And our bloody mother, too. For not protecting us kids when we were little. Tim and I used to talk about it.'

A memory from my Goulburn Academy days flashed into my mind: a fellow student had confessed that his main motivation for joining the cops was to get hold of a weapon and go back to his home town of Dorrigo and shoot his brutal father dead.

'That night I was supposed to go over and have dinner with them,' Craig went on, 'but I had to cancel at the last moment.'

'I'm surprised you wanted to see him at all. After what you've said he put you and your brother through.'

Craig grunted. 'He was an old man by then. I could've picked him up with one hand. He couldn't threaten me anymore.' He paused. 'I should have gone over. They mightn't have had that last fight if I'd been there.'

The *if onlys* again. I thought of the pain I still carried: *If only* my last memory of him had been happier.

'I don't think those sorts of thoughts are helpful, Craig. Not to him. Not to us. At least, that's what I tell myself.'

Craig looked away, blinking. Along the fence line of our front garden, the climbing rose was going crazy, the pink and white clouds of flowers. 'I'm just so very, very sorry for what happened,' he said again.

We made awkward conversation for another half hour or so, connected by feelings of helplessness and sorrow, both of us haunted by the events of that night.

'I liked your father,' Craig told me. 'My old man was always in a better mood if he had company when he went fishing. Once your father brought that young constable with him, Colleen or Carleen somebody or other. And she fell in and couldn't swim. Your dad had to do the hero act.'

'I don't remember it. I wish I did.' Any additional memories about my father were precious.

'I heard what he'd written on his running sheet that night – that someone called from the public phone box at the little post office shop near my parents' place and said they'd heard a man yelling and a woman screaming.' Craig's face crumpled and quivered until he managed to still it once more. 'That was the pattern. My brother and me hated it. Sometimes we'd hear them as we walked up the drive from school, and instead of going home we'd go to a friend's place. I used to want to live there, at my friend's house.'

After a long silence I said, 'It was good of you to come and visit.'

I watched him walk down to the roadside and get into his dusty Holden. 'Good luck in the big smoke,' he called and drove away. I took the tulips inside.

——

A couple of days later, I drove to where my father was buried in the local cemetery, four kilometres out of town. It was a warm day, the air fragrant with eucalypt vapour, bees buzzing in the flowering gums and ants busy along trails in the baked, dry soil. The cemetery dated from the 1860s, and the names and dates engraved on some of the earliest headstones had been completely obliterated by weathering.

My father was buried at the northern edge, near a clump of eucalypts, next to several Websters from my mother's family. I leaned against a tree, looking at his black granite headstone: *Peter Abel Hawkins, 1948–1992. Killed on duty. Beloved husband of Claire, loving father of Debra.*

Whether it was seeing that phrase *loving father of Debra*, or the fact that I was leaving the town I'd grown up in and everything I knew to move out into an unfamiliar world, sudden grief hit me in a shocking, dumping wave. Harsh sobs shook me. Eventually I managed to push down the tears, angry at the intense return of a grief I thought had been put away a long time ago. I snapped off a spray of creamy flowering gum blossom and laid it on top of the headstone, then I stood back, rereading the words.

Silently, I addressed my father. *I'm sorry, Dad, about everything. I wish your life hadn't ended as it did. But I do know this. I might never know exactly what happened that night, but I'm making this vow at your grave that I'll be the best cop the state has ever seen. I'll do it for you, for both of us.*

CHAPTER 3
SYDNEY, 2014

I sprawled on the floor in my living room, a gin and tonic on the rug beside me. My boyfriend, Mark, was away in Western Australia and wouldn't be back until next week, so I had the place to myself. Mark had a two-bedroom unit in Mascot, but he mostly stayed at my place when he was taking a break from his job out west. I leaned back against the black leather lounge, my legs stretched out with my drink in easy reach. During the day, sunshine fell through the floor-to-ceiling window in the sandstock brick wall opposite me; the geometric wrought-iron bars over the window had been added recently. Now, backed by the darkness of the night, the glass reflected the living room with its warm timber tones and bright red wool rug. The books I'd collected over the years stood in coloured ranks along the southern wall, arranged in the old cedar bookcase I'd taken when the Garralong home was cleared out and my mother had finally moved to Sydney.

On one wall hung a painting I'd bought on impulse from a nearby gallery.

I'd been slowly renovating the small, old inner-city terrace since I'd bought it six years earlier. 'Two up, two down and a horror show out the back,' was how my best friend, Cecile, had described it when I bought it. It now had a new bathroom, polished Baltic pine floorboards, and exposed sandstone on one wall. An almost identical house next door was home to a family with two boys and I often heard them playing in the backyard. Sometimes I heard family quarrels, but mostly they were good neighbours; I'd watched the boys grow from toddlers into fourth and fifth graders.

When I came downstairs in the mornings, on my way to the kitchen beyond the staircase, and saw the sun making slanting shapes on the timber floor and filling the living room with light, it always lifted my spirits. Just as it did hearing Mark singing in the kitchen as he made the tea or coffee, or cooing over his seedlings in the built-up garden beds out the back. Even my brother's drawing of my mother, me and himself, a happy piece in bright crayons done when he was five, could usually still make me smile when I took the time to look at it properly: my mother with her slim figure and neat dark hair; me, around seventeen and Brad in his old shorts and favourite T-shirt with what was supposed to be a dragon on it but which looked more like a snail. But as Brad grew up, he had caused tension in our small family, hanging out with a gang of older kids, wagging school, and as we later discovered, drinking and smoking dope with them at age eleven. As Brad's behaviour worsened, and he went from truancy and defiance to drug-taking and petty theft, my mother's fragile happiness began to disintegrate once more, and the tension in our family grew. We had tried countless times to help him – my concern not just for him but for my mother – but these days he was a heroin user and someone I almost never contacted.

On the floor beside me that evening was a newly printed police manual concerning the recently designated police unit I'd been appointed to lead, set up to deal with hidden family violence, particularly violence against women. I picked it up and rested it against my knees, staring at the cover as I recalled the words of my father's old friend and now my mentor, Gavin Bailey, who was acting assistant commissioner. The time was right for this new focus, he'd said to me, even though the New South Wales police already had similar units dealing with these problems. 'Domestic violence is in the crosshairs at the moment. Especially violence against migrant women who might not have much of a voice in their patriarchal communities.'

Our new unit, RED-V – religio–ethnic domestic violence – together with local community centres, a graphic television advertising campaign, and a tougher stance on enforcing bail conditions, apprehended violence orders and apprehended domestic violence orders was focusing on making inroads into this subterranean world. We particularly wanted to connect directly to women who might need our assistance.

Acting Assistant Commissioner Gavin Bailey had re-entered my life. We'd lost touch as he was promoted not long after my father's death and transferred to Tamworth. I'd heard he'd married Amy Sheffield from Garralong.

It was Gavin I had to thank for recommending me for the promotion to head up RED-V after discussing my progress with my then superiors. He'd recognised my name and contacted me while I was working with MEOCS – the Middle Eastern Organised Crime Squad. We'd made it much harder for the car rebirthers and the ATM raiders in their hotted-up Subarus. Instead of being weekly events, these crimes were now only sporadic. But criminals adapt quickly, and the crimes simply morphed into new areas – more cooking of amphetamines, and the importation of chemical precursors; more drug dealing; the importing and dealing of arms; and the establishment of seemingly legitimate tattooing and other businesses where drug and extortion money could be laundered. There were still a number of cases I needed to finalise from MEOCS; somehow I was going to have to find the time to do this while working in my challenging new position with RED-V. Still, I knew the work and sacrifice would be worthwhile.

When Gavin had approached me about the appointment, I'd asked a lot of questions. 'I don't want to be driving a desk,' I said. 'I want to be hands-on. I want to be out on the street talking to people, talking to the women involved. Checking up on them. Listening to any whispers. Using other arrests to get intelligence on what might be going on in certain families. My feeling is that the women who most need our support will be those least able to approach us. And they're the ones I really want to find.'

'You can work this however you want,' he'd said. 'That's the whole point. We need intelligence-led policing in this area. Since we started putting the pressure on the outlaw gangs, they're turning on each other. They're pulling in debts that might have once been allowed to run for a few months – it's pay up *now*, or else. You'll need to have your ear to the ground regarding communities where violence against women goes unreported. You do whatever you need to.'

'Sounds good. What sort of budget have we got?'

'Don't worry about that. That's my problem. The commissioner has announced a big reshuffle. State Operation Command have restructured things to bring other local area commands and groups like the Serious and Organised Crime squads under one umbrella. The budget will be allocated accordingly. You just need to do your job. Leave the budget to me.'

With that reassurance, I had thrown myself into the new unit, determined to run it as well as I knew how. But I was also aware that my connection with Gavin didn't mean he would cut me any slack, so I'd have to manage any problems as well as I could. He would demand the best of me and I was determined to give RED-V everything I had. I knew that Gavin was under a lot of pressure competing for the assistant commissioner position in which he was currently acting. The competition was fierce. Any wrong move on his part or any stuff-up in RED-V could cruel his chances.

My phone rang, interrupting my thoughts.

'Detective Debbie.' Mark's voice down the phone was deep and warm. 'What are you doing?'

'Sitting in a dark corner weeping over your absence. What else would I be doing?'

'How's your new team shaping up?'

'Okay,' I said cautiously. 'You know what it's like. A new unit is created – that's what you read in the press – but there's no extra time created. It just means that people are pulled from their other work to do something else. They've still got to keep up with their court appearances. We don't get any extra staff. What about you?'

'Same same. Hot hard dusty work but there's plenty of it – well, for the time being. Things are slowing down. I'm not sure how much longer I'll be here. Another six months, a year? I don't know why more young people don't come over here. I talked to a kid straight off the farm today – finished his HSC last year – and he's over here earning ninety grand a year driving trucks. His plan is to work here for five years, save four hundred thousand and then go back to his rural township, buy a house and start studying. Nothing like I was at his age, drinking myself stupid every weekend. Man, the drinking over here is unbelievable.'

'Doesn't surprise me. What else is there to do?'

'Well . . .' he trailed off delicately.

'The working ladies?'

'There's always the working ladies. For those who want to spend their money in that particular way. Me, I'm a faithful soul.'

I smiled. Mark's optimistic nature and high spirits usually lifted mine, which were too often weighed down with dull police routines or the vicious cases I sometimes dealt with. We'd been together for seven easy years, and I couldn't imagine my life without him.

'And I'm a faithful woman,' I said. 'I love you, Mark Spicer.'

'You wouldn't have loved me, when I was a drinking man.'

'You often say that. I can't really imagine it.'

'I was a dead-set, first-class arsehole. You would have run a mile.' He paused and his voice lifted. 'I'll be home soon. I'll drag you out of that dark corner, wipe away your tears and we'll go dancing.'

'Liar. You hate dancing.'

'Okay. How about dinner and a movie? Or maybe a walk through the museum and a stroll through our beautiful city?'

That was another thing I loved about him. Mark actually understood my interest in the primate section of the Australian Museum in College Street, finding a similar poignancy in the story of our nearest relatives and the extraordinary branch from which we humans had descended. 'We still have a long way to go,' he used to say as we stood looking at the evolution exhibit.

I was about to ring off when he asked, 'Are you looking after my broccoli?'

'Oops. I forgot to water them today.'

'Bad detective.'

'Good detective. I'll do it now. Before I go to bed.'

'Sweet dreams, sweet woman. Hope I feature in them.'

'Always,' I said. 'Can't wait till you're home.'

I hung up just as the late news announced that there'd been another fatal shooting in a suburban street. I listened briefly and thought about tomorrow's headlines. People in southwest Sydney had had enough and were leaning on their local members, who in turn were turning up the heat politically. The airwaves were full of anger at the way criminals who seemed intent on re-creating the violent street scenes from their families' countries of origin – shooting at each other's houses, murdering their enemies' relatives – were shattering the relatively calm and peaceful streets of particular Sydney suburbs.

I went into the kitchen and unlocked the back door, then stepped out into the cool darkness of the night. The sensor light came on; the garden seemed densely black and mysterious outside the circle of light. A timber deck opened onto a paved area with a table and two chairs under a shade sail. Beyond this was Mark's kitchen garden. Past the vegetable beds was a wide concreted area at the end of the garden where I parked my car, accessed from the back lane and protected by a remote-controlled security gate.

In the kitchen garden, rows of young broccoli plants, surrounded with heaped-up moats of sawdust to keep the snails at bay, were growing new leaves. I grabbed the hose and sprayed them gently, watching as the water soaked in and their small leaves shivered under the drops.

Mark had taken up vegetable growing not long after getting sober. 'All those hours in a day that I used to spend down at the pub with my mates,' he explained. 'I had to fill them somehow, and an older, sober member of AA suggested I take up something healthy, like sport or gardening. So I hung around his garden watching what he did and helping out. Then I started with planter boxes. Then Dad's backyard. Tomorrow, the world!' Over the years, Mark's garden had produced untold kilos of zucchinis, lettuces, capsicums, chillies, tomatoes, shallots and herbs.

I finished the watering and stood awhile, looking out into the darkness beyond the diminishing sweep of light. All was still and silent in my garden, with just the sound of traffic from the main road some distance away. I'd been threatened by criminals in the past, but on this peaceful, fragrant night, menace seemed a world away.

At seven o'clock the next morning, after breakfast, I walked through the kitchen in my high-heeled boots and teal linen suit, carrying my briefcase, and out to the courtyard, past the broccoli plants and the fading tomatoes, down to my car. An aqua flash caught my eye – a Blue Triangle struggling in a large web attached to the back fence and the jacaranda tree. I hurried over and took a few moments to free the pretty butterfly, gently pulling the sticky threads from her body. I watched as she flew crookedly up and away, disappearing over next door's mango tree.

I drove out of the lane and turned into the busy main road at the lights, heading southwest. I was a little nervous, but spent the drive going over the salient points I wanted to get across to the team. It was imperative that we all understood what we were doing – and why.

RED-V had been allocated some space in the southwest upstairs corner of a police building in Bankstown. It was a soulless space that would be cold in winter and blazing hot in summer, because the smartarse who'd designed it had decided that the western wall should be mainly glass. There was a walled-off area with a lockable door away from the western wall that I'd grabbed as my office because it had a north-facing window; nearby was another, larger room the team used for meetings. It was windowless and the air-conditioning was inadequate, but it would be useful for when we all got together for briefings and feedback. We'd been given six computers and three cars, one for me and the other two for the rest of the team.

Now I nervously followed Acting Assistant Commissioner Gavin Bailey into the meeting room. The small group got to their feet as he walked in. There were six of us in the team – three women counting myself and three men. Between us, we had more than half a century of shared experience, investigating gang violence, sexual assault, child abuse and domestic violence.

Gavin looked around and smiled. 'Please be seated.' He paused as they did so with a scrape of chair legs. 'I'm here to officially launch a new program to combat an especially sensitive area of domestic violence which all law agencies have found difficult to tackle because of its religious, cultural and ethnic character. I'm referring to the widespread oppression and ill treatment of women and girls in certain communities which goes un- or underreported a lot of the time. Victims and also witnesses find it extremely hard to complain, because the consequences can be extremely dangerous for them.'

I looked at the team's faces as Gavin continued. 'You are the inaugural group for this program. As you know, the name RED-V stands for religio–ethnic domestic violence and this title is to distinguish you from other agencies that deal with more general garden-variety domestic violence, often caused by drunkenness, brutish personalities, and longstanding domestic disagreements. But in this unit you could well be dealing with people whose deep belief is that males are superior to females and are their lawful custodians, and that they are quite within their rights to deliver physical punishments even to the point of death if they decide that a woman has been "disobedient" or brought dishonour and shame to the family.'

Gavin turned to me and I stepped forward as he formally introduced me. 'The RED-V unit will be headed by Detective Inspector Debra Hawkins, who was chosen because of her broad experience with Middle Eastern organised crime. Her selection was approved by the commissioner himself, and I have every confidence that Detective Inspector Hawkins will train, guide and direct the unit optimally in this new, hitherto uncharted area of policing.

'Before I hand over to Detective Inspector Hawkins, let me sound one cautionary note. As you must have noticed, the press have not been invited to this launch. There will be no press release. We have kept it deliberately low-key for reasons all of you are intelligent enough to understand. Discretion, sensitivity and utmost care with your public utterances must be combined with just enough public awareness to make your availability known in the community. With that, I now hand you over to Detective Inspector Hawkins.'

The team clapped dutifully. Gavin turned to me, whispered, 'Good luck,' and ushered me forward as the clapping subsided. He then left the room.

A little murmuring, then all was quiet. I cleared my throat. 'Good morning. You've all been hand-picked for this unit. Our aim is to extend the protection of Australian law to communities that don't always share our values and who often view us with suspicion and even hostility. As agents of the Crown we are professional and apolitical, but we must always be mindful of the delicate political environment in which we are currently operating. One injudicious comment from any one of us could see our program shut down before it really gets going. You understand the need for sensitivity and discretion. What's said in this room stays in this room, unless you're told otherwise. Right? Just to be sure there's no electronic recording or transmission of this discussion, I want everyone's mobile phone up here in this box. Now, please.'

Some muttering about paranoia was to be expected, I thought, as they slowly came up and placed their phones in the box I'd provided. But I'd known too many individuals and organisations brought down by leaks of sensitive material to be complacent about security.

When they were settled again, Charlie asked, 'Mightn't we be on a collision course with anti-discrimination laws?' I'd picked Charlie for the team. She'd been my partner when I was investigating a series of ATM ram-raids some years back. I'd noticed her dedication and diligence, especially with the paperwork, never my favourite part of the job. She had deep-set eyes in a wide face, and cheekbones to die for, and her thick dark hair naturally fell in a stylish bob, rain or shine.

'Good question, Charlie. But there's only one law in Australia and it doesn't cease to apply at the edge of an ethnic enclave. And it doesn't stop at the front door of a person's home. We're not targeting ethnic groups or religious communities, we're targeting criminal behaviours. Okay? That's always been the job of policing. It's nothing new.'

I pulled out the folder with the mission statement for RED-V I'd devised in consultation with my friend in the Domestic Violence Squad and after discussions with people from several migrant women's health services. Gavin had also contributed to it. 'Might be easier if I just run through our statement of duties.

You can have copies if you want them.' I cleared my throat, aware of their close attention.

'Okay,' I said. 'There are four main sections here. Our brief is to respond to allegations, tip-offs, and calls for assistance regarding women of non–English speaking backgrounds – NESBies. Women in fear of, or experiencing, domestic violence, including coercion, intimidation and threats relating to personal behaviour, dress, association and arranged marriages.' I looked up from my reading. 'Arranged marriages aren't a problem if both parties are in agreement. It's when coercion is used against the young girl that it becomes a forced marriage issue.'

I continued with the second clause. 'We are to investigate breaches of the law especially pertaining to underage marriage within New South Wales, arranged overseas marriages reasonably suspected of being coerced, and cases of female genital mutilation arranged by residents living in New South Wales irrespective of whether the procedure is performed in Australia or overseas. We compile and refer evidence of such transgressions to the Director of Public Prosecutions.' I paused. 'Any questions so far?'

None. I continued. 'Thirdly, we liaise with ethnic community leaders with a view to explaining RED-V's purpose and to engage their cooperation in disseminating an understanding of the law, and Australian norms and expectations regarding gender equality, relations between the sexes, and personal choices relating to religious observance.' Again I paused, looking around at the group before continuing. 'Finally, we provide advice, support and practical assistance to NESB women in fear of, or seeking protection from, violence and/or threatening domestic situations arising from the culture and/or religious beliefs of their community. We must always be aware of cultural sensitivities and the fact that a woman seeking to report domestic violence may be seen as betraying her family and her community. So discretion is essential. Okay?'

I picked up a page I'd printed out earlier and started reading. '*A recent World Health Organization study has found that physical or sexual violence is a public health problem that affects more than one-third of all women around the world. In the UK, domestic violence kills two women every week. In Australia, twenty-four per cent of women will suffer physical or sexual violence. The problem is worst in Asia and the Middle East . . .*' I paused. 'In Australia, a woman is killed by an intimate partner almost weekly.' I looked around at their listening faces and put down the paper. All of them except one had their eyes on me. The exception, Nadine, had her head down and was fiddling with her blonde hair, patting the knot at the back of her neck. 'The stats are included here if anyone wants to note down the exact figures, okay?

'There's nothing racist or unfairly discriminatory about trying to stop domestic violence or forced marriage, or the genital mutilation of little girls,' I went on. 'In fact, the state government has just increased the penalty for this crime from seven to twenty-one years for anyone involved in this abhorrent practice. Any more questions?'

'I don't enjoy being called a racist,' said Nadine, without looking up. 'And that's what's going to happen for sure.'

Nadine hadn't been my choice but Gavin's. She came highly recommended by him from an inner-city police station where she'd impressed him with her adaptability and legal knowledge.

She was studying law part time and hoped to become a prosecutor. I hoped she wasn't going to be a problem.

'Crap!' Flash jumped in. 'Who cares what they call us? We're called worse than that often enough. Playing the racism card is just another way of trying to close down the debate. If the enemy can control what we say about them, then we've already lost the war.' Nadine shot Flash an angry look.

I'd pestered Gavin until he promised me Eric 'Flash' Hastings as investigation manager for the new unit. Flash had come over with me from the MEOCS, where he'd been a liaison officer between MEOCS and the Gang Squad. An experienced detective with almost thirty years on the job, he was a big man, his fair hair cut very short in military style. His mouth turned distinctly downwards – someone had mischievously stuck a picture of a blobfish near his desk, and there was definitely a resemblance. The nickname Flash had stuck from an incident when young Hastings was a student at the police academy, and which he never disclosed. Today he wore one of his signature novelty ties, patterned with lines of dancing giraffes.

I nodded at Flash's statement. 'There's something like war now playing out in the streets of Sydney. Tribal loyalties, religious hatreds, violent young males and criminal turf disputes are making our communities more violent. This in turn must impinge on the women involved with these men. The war in Syria has reignited some of the local hotheads. Queensland police are dealing with a new gang called Soldiers of Islam, made up of ex-soldiers from Iraq. We don't need that sort of thing growing on our turf.' I pulled out some notes I'd taken at a recent symposium on directions in policing. 'Police need to be – *we* need to be – and

I'm quoting here: "flexible, nimble, innovative, collaborative, networked and global". Because the criminals are.

'In the old days, the crims knew the rules of the game. There was the police team and there was the crims' team. Their job was to commit crimes, our job was to lock them up. You do the crime, you do the time. But things are very different now. We've had to adapt fast. There've been over three hundred shootings in the southwest of Sydney in the last two years. That's just one more reason why we've recently bought another BearCat.' I was referring to the nine-tonne bullet- and blast-proof armoured riot vehicles equipped with battering rams that were now available for use. 'And it's why the Riot Squad guys are training in military-style situations, terrorist incidents and multiple hostage-taking. New styles of criminality require new styles of policing.'

Everyone there knew what I was talking about. 'We've all experienced the odd death threat, but people from the public gallery following us after we've given evidence and taking down our car rego is a fairly recent development.' A shiver went through me as I recalled an assault outside the courts that had left me bruised and shaken. I pushed the memory of Adam Massoud's violence away and continued.

'Even though our job is to assist women rather than deal with street violence, in this role you might very well encounter similar threats directed at yourselves. No one gives up power over others willingly. The bullies and the criminals are going to fight like mad to keep their slaves and drug empires. That's another thing,' I said. 'It's not just altruism that's driving this new unit. Of course we want to help women caught in family violence, but if we hear of any other crimes in the process of assisting these women, naturally we'd hand the information over to the relevant investigative bodies.

'Right. You've all been hand-picked as investigators with brains.'

'Even Socrates?' Alex asked. Alex was the youngest, a graduate from the country, sharp and sarcastic, with a narrow face and dark, good-humoured eyes. Because of his Algerian mother, he spoke fluent Arabic which could be helpful to the unit.

'Especially Socrates.' I grinned. 'Socrates is our crime analyst. So be nice to him.'

Heads nodded. Socrates Toulakis, a tall, quiet man in his late thirties, just smiled at the teasing. He brought with him the analytical skills our team needed. His strength was putting together seemingly disparate connections. His programs could reveal patterns that we didn't know existed – networks of phone calls in diagrams that looked something like puffballs, except each radiating line was a mobile number connecting criminals to each other, opening up multiple avenues for us to pursue. Besides, I thought, someone who'd dealt with being named Socrates all through the Australian public school system would have developed qualities not found in the native born.

I looked around at their faces, expectant, engaged. 'I want best-practice standards here. I'll be detailing the investigative strategy plan and Flash is the SIO.' As senior investigation officer, Flash would be my second in command. 'I want him to be able to compile the critical incident log, and that means detailed record keeping from each of you. I want every twist and turn of anything we investigate to be available for inspection at any time.' I leaned back against a desk. 'You could be dealing with extremely sensitive cases – politically speaking – and extremely dangerous people as well. Let's not warn the targets that we're after them. Any bright ideas you might get, check with me or Flash first.'

I looked around. 'Remember the rules, be suspicious, be informed, listen carefully. Abandon stereotypes. Avoid contextual bias. That is, keep an open mind.' I couldn't help adding in a smart remark I'd picked up from a senior detective. 'But then again, don't be so open-minded that your brains fall out. Okay? Any final questions?'

They exchanged glances as they gathered up their pens and notebooks. Nadine smoothed back her hair above the tiny pearl earrings and said, 'MEOCS and other drug and gang units are putting a lot of pressure on the thugs at the moment. Let's see what we can squeeze out of them, too.'

'Okay, if that's all, let's get into it.'

I watched as my small team left the room. So far I hadn't noticed any friction between them but it was early days yet. Some teams come together smoothly and cohesively; others never meld and the constant bitching isn't just wearing on team members but can also interfere with investigations.

I knew that managing this team and assisting the people we were sworn to protect would be a challenge, but I was ready for it.

CHAPTER 4

I pulled my chair closer to my desk and opened COPS – the Computerised Operational Policing System that is the 'nervous system' of police intelligence. The database logged all incidents attended by police, charges, convictions, and any victim statements, as well as listing persons of interest who might be connected to reported or detected crimes.

My phone rang. When I picked up, a voice whispered, 'Got something for you.'

'Speedy. Talk to me.'

Speedy was a registered informant I'd been working with for several years. He mostly survived as a low-level dealer and we had an agreement whereby he provided information and I'd take that into account whenever he was picked up. He understood that if he ever did anything really bad the deal was off. I'd called him some weeks ago and asked him to concentrate on any street talk he might hear about women in danger. I was pleased to hear from him.

'Gotta talk to you,' he said. 'Right now. Meet me.'

'Usual place?'

This was a large supermarket nearby where we'd each grab a trolley and Speedy would whisper a few words as we passed each other in the aisles. He was paranoid about being identified as a 'dog' and refused to ever pause near me, let alone sit down with me. Occasionally a talk on a public phone was possible, but he was too scared to ever come into the police centre.

Alex looked up as I came out of my office pulling on my jacket. 'Great suit, boss,' he said. 'Love that blue. Matches the earrings.'

I fingered the earrings I was wearing today. Blue topaz drops. Earrings were my weakness. Ever since joining the strongly masculine brotherhood of the New South Wales police, it had seemed imperative that whenever I wasn't in uniform I should wear something of beauty, and gemstones, forged in the furnaces of creation, exquisite and mathematically perfect, had always fascinated me. The gemstone and crystal rooms were my second favourite place to visit at the museum.

'I'll be out for forty minutes or so. Have to see a dog about a man.'

—•—

I hurried down the street, glancing in passing at the words that had been written with a stick on a replaced section of footpath when the cement was wet. I checked them out every day, like some sort of compulsion. *You're beautiful*, they read. Every day the street complimented me and anyone else whose eyes strayed down to the two small words under their feet. It always made me smile. I also liked the correct use of the contraction – little niceties that are being lost in the world of shortened text.

The street was lively with people from all over the world. Asians and Caucasians mingled with a few women covered in the black robes of the Arabian desert, or more usually in brightly patterned hijabs, pushing prams. Specialist grocery shops sold brilliantly coloured spices in towering piles, weighing them in polished scales, lending notes of ginger, cardamom and cinnamon to the combined smells from the unceasing traffic and the asphalt roadway. Amid all that, I caught a delicate whiff of hyacinths. Garralong was never like this, I thought, and I wondered what my father would have made of it all. Would he find it colourful or would he be politically incorrect and make embarrassing remarks? As usual, he seemed to be hiding somewhere in my mind, just behind and under the dailiness of routine mental work.

I walked quickly towards the wide arcade opening to the mall, passing several smaller shops on the way, including a florist with buckets of roses and gerberas – as well as the hothoused lilac hyacinths I'd smelled earlier – standing in small pots at the front; further along was a takeaway hot food bar and a busy chemist. At the supermarket I grabbed a trolley. Thinking I might as well do a spot of shopping while I was there, I picked up some cereal and cheese biscuits from the shelves.

A trolley banged into mine and I looked up to see a woman in full black burqa, with a veil or niqab covering her face, black-gloved hands wresting her trolley away from mine. I had no way of gauging her reaction to our small collision, as I could see nothing but the hint of obscured eyes through the narrow slit. I wondered if the limitations to her peripheral vision had caused our collision. Her small children looked up at me with their large brown eyes. 'Oops!' I said. Neither child returned my smile, and the black-robed woman fluttered away, steering her trolley along the aisle, trailing black fabric, reminding me of the ancient retired nuns at the convent I'd attended in primary school, who – despite all the changes in the Church – still wore their medieval habits.

I spotted Speedy's gangling figure hanging around the freezer section at the end of the aisle and walked down to meet him. As usual he was wearing grubby jeans and a T-shirt with a faded lager advertisement, and his beard and hair needed trimming.

'Adam Massoud,' he whispered as I passed him.

My heart chilled. *Massoud.* Of all the criminals in all the cases I'd been involved in, Adam Massoud was by far the most evil man I'd encountered.

Doing my best to regain my composure, I parked my trolley beside Speedy without acknowledging him in any way, and frowned at the bags of minted peas in the freezer, pretending to be deliberating over which brand to select. Then I walked away towards the frozen desserts, keenly aware of Speedy moving in behind me and his whispering voice. 'He's in the Supermax in Goulburn, and his trial's coming up. He's putting out to have his witness killed. The chick who was with him in his car when he shot that guy? He wants her gone. He's looking for Skitzo Clarke to knock her.'

Skitzo Clarke too? This was serious. 'Got it,' I whispered, reaching down to pull out a box of frozen mango and icecream bars.

I sensed Speedy moving away. As I steered past him on my way to the checkout, he was examining a packet of Tiny Teddy Tots, a wistful expression on his prematurely lined face. I hoped he had enough money to buy them. If I hadn't heard the name Adam Massoud, I might have been in a lighter mood and slipped him five bucks.

I paid for my groceries and strode back to the office, barely noticing a couple of Drug Squad detectives I'd worked with some years ago coming in the opposite direction, young and casually dressed in jeans and T-shirts.

'Doing good, Debra?' the young man asked. I tried to smile back.

The girl winked. 'Looking good, Debra.'

Normally, their light-hearted comments would have made me smile. But not today.

Back at my desk, I sat blindly staring at the New South Wales police logo screensaver, my mind tormented by memories of Adam Massoud. One year ago, outside the court where he'd just been sentenced to a long prison stay, largely on evidence collected by me and other team members of MEOCS, Massoud had somehow, incredibly, broken free from the Corrective Services handlers. Before I knew what was happening he was on top of me, clubbing me with his manacled wrists. 'You're dead, bitch,' he'd hissed as three men raced to pull him off me. 'I'm even bigger in Goulburn. You hear that, you dog? You think you're safe because I'm inside?' Just before I'd kneed him and he'd been dragged away, he shoved his face into mine, his black eyes blazing murder. 'You're dead, you filthy cunt!' Hot spittle hit my face. He hadn't been able to say much more after my knee connected hard with his groin.

For months after that, I'd been paranoid, checking doors and windows, sometimes feeling sure I was being followed. 'Death threats are part of the job,' my old boss, Detective Chief Inspector Malcolm Ireland, had told me. 'Mostly they're bullshit,' he reminded me, 'but be vigilant and observe usual security measures.' During that time, I slept with my Glock lying in the top bedside drawer, ready to go. Mark was fearful for me and patrolled the house and garden, armed with his pickaxe. I upped my weapons practice, aiming for a perfect chest cluster on the man-shaped targets in the police firing range. The bars went up on all the windows, including the floor-to-ceiling window in my living room. I had discreet camera security installed over the front door as well as the back and sides of the house. No way was I going to make it easy for anyone unauthorised to visit me.

As the last year had passed uneventfully, I started to believe that my old boss was right, that Adam Massoud was just full of venom and bullshit, and I became less vigilant. But the memory of his hatred and threats never completely faded.

Now a renewed wave of horror and revulsion shook me at the memory of him spitting in my face, and I got up from my desk and went out to the toilets. I splashed cold water on my face, then patted it dry with a paper towel and returned to my desk, where I logged on and pulled Massoud's file up onto the screen. Staring at his photograph, the drooping, hooded eyes under heavy brows, the vicious mouth above the straggly beard, I could almost sense evil pulsing out from his image.

If Adam Massoud was looking for Skitzo Clarke, that woman was in real danger. Skitzo, as his nickname implied, was an unstable, violent criminal; he'd spent most of his life in prison, but when he was outside he was capable of anything.

Although I didn't really need to remind myself of his criminal curriculum, I scrolled through Massoud's history. He was the founding member of Massouds Boys, a formidable and dangerous group of aggressive young men who had graduated from street crime and dealing into armed robbery, major extortion and murder. He'd been arrested many times, charged often, and had three convictions for grievous bodily harm and other violent assaults by the time he was twenty. He was also a devotee of al-Qaeda. As I pulled up another photo of him, taken when he was younger, his face pouchy, its sullen expression revealed a mix of ossified resentment, contempt and brutality.

I looked at the latest charge agasint him, the murder of Andre Cevak, a member of the Khaybar Riders motorcycle gang; his trial was due to come up next month. Cevak had been shot four times at almost point-blank range some time ago, but it was only recently that a witness had come forward. I leaned closer. The witness was Massoud's then girlfriend, who'd been in the car with him as he fired the rounds into Cevak.

I pulled up the latest filed intelligence report from Goulburn prison. It appeared that imprisonment had barely interrupted Massoud's vigorous criminality. 'Holy hell,' I said out loud. He'd made over three thousand phone calls while in the super-maximum security prison.

I walked to the door of my office and called Flash over. 'I've just been given a tip,' I said. 'This guy, Adam Massoud. He's already inside but he's awaiting trial for another murder.' Back at my desk, I scanned Massoud's charge sheet, reading bits out to Flash. 'He set up a meeting with Cevak, an associate from another gang, allegedly to discuss a misunderstanding between them, and as the other man approached his parked car, Massoud shot him four times out of the window.'

'Poor bastard walked straight into it,' Flash muttered.

I flinched at the words. My father had done that too. I made myself refocus. 'According to Massoud, Cevak owed him a lot of money.'

I skimmed through a witness statement. 'Seems that some time earlier they'd been together organising a drug deal, but while that meeting was in process a third party did a rip, invaded Cevak's place with a couple of heavies, grabbed the suitcase with the drugs and got away. But Massoud refused to believe this – and who knows if it's true or not? Massoud claimed Cevak had ripped the drugs himself. But Cevak believed that Massoud was cheating *him*.'

'How would you know who was cheating who with that bunch?' Flash said.

'Massoud demanded that Cevak pay him the value of the ripped drugs. Cevak refused, said if it wasn't Massoud himself who'd organised the rip, then he – Cevak – was a victim of this unknown third party and it wasn't his responsibility.'

'Massoud didn't believe him?' asked Flash.

'Would you? Cevak paid with his life. Now Massoud's looking to remove the only witness, his ex-girlfriend, who's come forward and made a witness statement.'

'She's a brave girl,' said Flash.

'She's a dead girl,' I said, 'unless she disappears.'

I came to the most recent entry in the file. 'He's suspected of having ordered a violent assault on her from prison last year. After they broke up, she started dating a guy from the enemy gang. She didn't understand how inflammatory that was for a guy like Massoud. Massoud wanted her taught a lesson. According to this report, she was seriously injured. On crutches for months.'

I opened her witness statement. Kylie Jane Mifsud's photo showed a pretty woman, heavily made-up and with her hair piled up and studded with frangipanis.

'Looks like a party outfit,' said Flash, and pointed out the cake on the table and the young crowd in the background.

I glanced through Kylie's statement.

> I was sitting in the car with Adam Massoud, who was my boyfriend at the time, when the man I heard later was known as Chenko Cevak came over to the car. When Cevak came up to the open car window, Adam Massoud pulled out a gun and shot him four times through the window before driving away. I was in the front passenger seat and saw it clearly because of the headlights of the other car and the streetlights. Adam Massoud threatened to kill me if I ever told anyone about what I'd seen. He said I was an Aussie slut and that no one would miss me if I disappeared. He said he'd killed people before and got away with it. I was really scared that he would kill me. I promised not to tell anyone but I can't live with what I saw. I got real scared and that was the last time I saw Adam Massoud. That night I visited a girlfriend and she helped me pack some things and then we went to

stay with her friend. But I'm scared because Adam might find out her address.

I looked up at Flash. 'This is a truly evil guy. So . . . let's make sure he's put in touch with exactly the right man for the job.' From the depths of my unconscious mind, an idea flew in: *Get a hit man yourself, girl, and finish this evil man forever. Too easy to do in the prison system. Get Massoud moved into a shared cell with someone who hates his guts. It'll just look like another fatal prison brawl . . . it's happened to other men in prison on several occasions already . . .*

'Is your guy reliable?' Flash asked, bringing me back to my senses.

'Speedy's about ninety per cent accurate,' I said, blinking away the unsolicited homicidal thoughts. 'I've worked with him for several years now.'

After I'd filled him in on the rest of Speedy's whispered information, Flash asked, 'What have we got on Skitzo?'

'Let's take a look.'

I pulled up another set of records on the computer and Flash dragged a chair over and started reading with me.

Rodney 'Skitzo' Clarke had a long record, dating back to the time of his first conviction in the juvenile system when he was just fourteen. He'd worked as a runner for one of the Kings Cross drug dealers; then, as he grew bigger and uglier, graduated to more proactive crime. From his record, it looked as if his special talents lay in intimidating, threatening and assaulting people in the pursuit of bad debts or, in some cases, just for the hell of it.

'Thought to be responsible for the 2008 contract killing of Bernie Hassell and girlfriend Linda Hatton at Canley Vale,' I read out. 'Charged but released. Lack of evidence. Currently bailed on an aggravated assault charge.' Why magistrates bail people like this is a mystery to me. And to most of my colleagues. And, increasingly, to the general public.

'Okay,' I said, making a note of his last known address. 'Let's pay him a visit. Check on his bail conditions. We've got to get him off the streets.'

We jumped into one of the squad cars. Flash took the driver's seat. My job was to recognise Skitzo, and as we sped to the address I reviewed the mugshots on the police car's monitor screen.

As we approached the boarding house where he lived, an old silver Ford pulled out from the kerb with a screech and took off down the road. I'd only had a brief glimpse of the driver as he pulled out, but his ears gave him away.

'That's him!' I whacked the blue light on the roof and Flash activated the siren as we charged after him down the narrow suburban road. Skitzo was clearly considering doing a runner, as he accelerated suddenly around a corner, taking it on two wheels like a stuntman. But we easily kept on his tail and within minutes he pulled over.

Flash parked the police car behind Skitzo's in the protective position some distance out from the kerb so that its bulk was between us and passing traffic. I stepped out and gestured for Skitzo to wind down his window as I approached. Flash came with me to keep an extra eye on proceedings.

Skitzo had the shady eyes and compressed lips of a career criminal – too much suspicion, too many betrayals and too many drinks. His ears seemed larger than ever. 'What is it?' he asked, belligerent. 'What do the cops want with me? I haven't done nothing.'

'Licence, please, driver,' I said, giving nothing away. 'Nice and slow now.'

Skitzo pulled out his wallet and triumphantly showed me his up-to-date licence. He must have been well into his fifties, and although he looked fit enough, I noticed a slight tremor in the hand that held his licence. Glancing inside the car, I saw that it was packed with cardboard cartons and bulging plastic garbage bags. A navy-blue suit was hanging from a hook above the nearside back seat.

'What's in the cartons, Skitzo?' I asked.

'I haven't done nothing!'

'It's what you're going to do that worries me. What's in the cartons?'

'My stuff. Is there any law against moving?'

'You're supposed to inform the police of any new address.'

'I was going to.'

'Sure you were. Why are you moving? Where are you heading?'

'None of your bloody business. Anyway, who are you?'

'I'm Detective Inspector Debra Hawkins. And it's very much my business, Mr Clarke. Come on, let's take a drive to the police station. You need to talk to us.'

'Why? I don't have to talk to you. And what about my rights?'

'You're in breach of your bail conditions, I'm afraid,' I said, 'and that means you haven't got any rights. Hand over your keys, please.'

'Jesus. You bastards never stop, do you. I haven't done nothing.'

'Yet.' I put out my hand. 'Keys.'

With great reluctance, Skitzo pulled the keys out of the ignition and shoved them at me. 'You've got no right,' he muttered.

CHAPTER 5

Back in the interview room, Skitzo sat opposite Flash and me. He hunched over the table, fiddling with the takeaway coffee we'd provided. The video recorder was running as we continued our conversation.

'We've heard something that makes us think you were on your way to carry out a job,' I said. 'Care to comment?'

He hadn't been expecting the question and it hit him before he could cover up. I didn't miss the slight wince around his eyes. 'What are you talking about?'

'Your name has been mentioned in connection with a young woman. A young woman Adam Massoud wants dead. We have it on good authority that you've been contacted to carry out the murder of this young woman. What do you have to say about that?'

Skitzo was frightened now, I could see it in his eyes. I recalled his packed car, put a few things together and followed my gut instinct. I turned to Flash, who acknowledged my glance with a nod. He was getting it, too.

'You're doing a runner, aren't you, Skitzo,' I said. 'You've taken Massoud's downpayment and you're about to disappear. Is that right? You're about to double-cross Adam Massoud! Oh naughty!'

From somewhere in Skitzo's murky consciousness, moral outrage surfaced. 'That arsehole can keep the rest of his money. I wouldn't touch that girl. Poor kid's still hobbling around with a walking stick. What do you think I am?'

'Mr Clarke, I think that's been well established, don't you? But we do understand that you might be in a big hurry right now because you're taking Massoud's money and running. Massoud is serving time for killing another man who did exactly that. And we're doing our best to convict him of putting four bullets into another man he thought double-crossed him.'

Skitzo looked away. I let that sink in for a long moment.

'So here's the deal,' I continued. 'You tell us everything you know and we'll overlook your bail breach and you can be on your way. Or we charge you right now with breach bail and throw you back in prison. I'll release a statement to the media about how clever police work prevented the contract killing of a young woman – my boss will love that, and so will the premier and the mums and dads – and I'll also mention how Rodney "Skitzo" Clarke is providing very helpful intelligence to the police about Adam Massoud.' I paused for effect. 'And you'll be in the prison system too. Some of those exercise bikes have very heavy metal parts. They can be used as a weapon, as we know.' I paused again. 'So, what do you say?'

Skitzo looked from me to Flash and then back again, clearly defeated. 'Listen, Inspector, I'm not admitting nothing. But that scumbag Massoud had already got her beaten up. Broke both her legs. He wanted me to finish the job. I said I would but I had no intention of doing it. Never. I just wanted the money. I'm getting too old for prison. I've got twenty grand in my account now. There was another thirty coming afterwards.'

'So what did you tell Massoud?'

Skitzo looked at me as if I were crazy. 'I said I'd do it. Massoud's not the sort of man you say no to. I heard what he did to Danny Malik.'

I recognised the name, that of a gang member who'd vanished some time back.

Skitzo's expression shifted into genuine appeal. 'I've gotta get out of town. You understand that? I've got a chance to make another life. Find some little place on the coast. Do a bit of fishing. I've got a daughter somewhere near Wollongong. I've been meaning to look her up for years.'

'Sure,' I said. 'Family reunion. Okay, Detective Hastings. Let's charge this guy right now.'

'No, please. Let me go. Honest, I wasn't going to lay a finger on that little girl. On my mother's grave I swear. Can't we do a deal?'

'You're in no position to make a deal with me, Mr Clarke. I don't think you fully appreciate how much danger you could be in if word gets out about you ripping off Adam Massoud before you've had a chance to find a nice big rock to hide under. And then telling the cops all about it. Talk about a dog's life.'

'I'm thinking dead dog.' Flash nodded, looking gravely at Skitzo, now sweating heavily.

I looked at Flash and tilted my head towards the door, and we left the interview room together. 'I'm inclined to believe him,' I said in a low voice once we were away from the door. 'What do you think?'

Flash nodded again. 'Find out what he knows – and then wish him luck and a safe journey.'

'Mr Clarke,' I said, as Flash and I settled back down opposite him in the interview room. 'Our problem is this. We just don't know what to do about you. We catch you red-handed breaching bail, we have it on good authority that you're on a mission to murder an innocent woman for Adam Massoud —'

'No. It's not true. I swear. I was just getting away. You'll never have any trouble from me ever again.'

I brooded in silence as Flash escorted Skitzo Clarke out of the office. I sat thinking for several minutes. We'd given Skitzo back his keys and I didn't think we'd be hearing from him again – one way or another. But I wasn't taking any chances with Kylie Mifsud's life. Criminals can make up the most fantastic stories if they think it'll serve them. Although I believed what Skitzo had told me, I had to be completely sure and have all bases covered.

Stepping out of the interview room I went over to Socrates. 'Will you liaise with the guys at the Supermax? We need whatever you can get your hands on in the way of the most recent intelligence reports on Adam Massoud. It's important we move fast on this.'

Socrates picked up his phone. Silently, I prayed that the authorities would prevent Massoud from running his crime empire from his Supermax cell. I snatched up the printout with Kylie's last known telephone number and address and called Nadine over.

'I'm going to talk to Kylie Mifsud,' I said. 'I'll check that she's okay and can stay out of sight for a while longer. See if she can give me anything more on Massoud. Not sure how long I'll be out for. I'll be on the mobile.'

'I could go,' said Nadine, in her bored, super-cool drawl, smoothing her hair. 'I'd like to get out of the office, too.'

'Thanks, but I'll do it,' I said. 'Anything comes up, see Flash.'

Nadine gave me a long look and I noticed the fine line of pearl-grey eyeliner running the length of her top eyelids. 'Something I've been meaning to ask you,' she drawled.

'Ask away.'

'How come you got this position? I have more experience than you, more runs on the board. Even if I don't have the rank yet.'

'I just follow orders, Nadine, like you do.' I smiled. 'I was appointed – it's as simple as that.'

Nadine made a little face, almost a pout, before turning away and heading back to her workstation.

Now I could focus on Kylie. I thought about how scared the young witness must be. But just now, she'd had a very lucky break.

—◆—

At Kylie's last known address, the anxious woman who answered the door wiping her hands on a tea towel identified herself as Kylie's mother.

'She's staying in the mountains with a friend. As soon as she heard the trial was coming up she knew she had to lie low.' Mrs Mifsud tossed the tea towel aside and peered closely at my warrant card. 'You'll protect her, won't you, Detective?'

'We'll do our best,' I said with what I hoped was a reassuring smile.

Back in the car, I called the number Mrs Mifsud had given me. 'Who is this?' asked a young woman on the other end of the line. I introduced myself.

Just under two hours later, I was talking with Kylie in her friend's timber cottage overlooking the Jamison Valley. The famous Blue Mountains shimmered in the distance, and a flock of parrots flew past in a flash of colour.

'I can't stay here much longer,' Kylie was saying, her black mascara smudged from crying, her straw-blonde hair in tangles, as she surveyed the quiet street below. 'Roger Hammond – one of the policemen who interviewed me about Chenko Cevak – told me that the case was coming up for trial this month. But now my friends want their lounge room back without all my gear and me in it. Tanya has her own problems with Blake. They don't want me hanging around all the time. And I haven't got any money until my cheque comes through.' Her eyes filled again. 'I hate him. I wish I'd never met him.'

'He's a dangerous man, Kylie,' I said.

Kylie looked down at her black-painted nails, trying to hide the tears that ran down her cheeks. 'He had me bashed before, last year when he heard I was going out with another guy. I only just got off the crutches last month, and I have to use a stick most of the time.' She lifted her long floaty skirt and revealed her legs with their angry red surgical scarring, then dropped it again. 'I need police protection.' She blew her nose and wiped black streaks from her cheeks.

'We'll keep you safe during the time you'll be giving evidence. Don't worry about that, Kylie. You can do it via video link.'

'That's not what I'm talking about. I want a bodyguard.'

I took a deep breath. 'We can't actually provide that, I'm sorry.'

'What do you mean? I thought you said this new unit of yours was set up to help women like me. I've heard of people getting police protection.'

'If you're talking about witness protection, that's a federal matter. Not run by New South Wales Police.'

Kylie's mascaraed glance said: And I should care who runs it?

'Witness protection is a very serious matter,' I explained. 'It would mean never going home again, having no contact with your family or friends, except for very infrequent meetings organised and supervised by the police in secured locations. You'd have a different name, you'd have to live as a different person. You'd have to lose your whole past life. Move far away. It would be extremely lonely for you.'

'He's destroyed my life!' Kylie howled.

I waited till she'd calmed down a little and then said gently but firmly, 'You mustn't let him destroy your life. Is there somewhere else you can go after you've given evidence? Friends or family in another state? Once you're settled somewhere else, you'd be given a mobile with police phone numbers on it in case you need urgent assistance. There's a new app, too, that goes on your mobile phone, and one or two presses gets you help.'

'I don't want a new app! I don't want a new identity! I just want my life back!'

'Look, Massoud is safely in prison —' I started to say, as much to convince myself as Kylie. She didn't need to know how he was continuing with business as usual from the Supermax.

'I just don't know what to do!' she sobbed. 'The police are no fucking help!' She bumped her right arm against the coping of the balcony and her embroidered shoulder bag spilled its contents onto the balcony floor. 'Oh shit!' she swore.

I bent down to help her pick up her things, and frowned. 'Two mobiles?'

'That black one's not mine. It belongs to that arsehole Massoud. It fell out of the car that night and I grabbed it. He thinks it fell out onto the road after the shooting when he was getting away. He was going apeshit about it, thinking the cops would get it. I thought maybe it was something I could hold over him. But then I thought again. I just carry it around for some reason. I should chuck it in the river.'

I picked it up and slipped it into my pocket. 'I'll look after this for you, Kylie.'

We walked together down the steps leading to the front garden, and paused at the bottom. 'Let me know of your plans, Kylie,' I said. 'My urgent suggestion is to relocate interstate after Massoud's trial. He's a vengeful man. As soon as you get your next cheque, do what you can to change your appearance. I know it's tough but you must do everything you can to keep yourself safe. You have to take responsibility for your own welfare. You could regard this as a second chance. It's your life. Look after it.'

Tears welled in her eyes again. 'I thought that's what the police were supposed to do.'

I pulled out my wallet. 'Here. Take this.' She blinked at me through her black-rimmed eyes as she took the fifty-dollar bill. 'Payment for Massoud's phone,' I explained. 'I'll alert the local police and they'll keep an eye on this address for you.'

'Like what? Drive past once a month?'

'Just keep low, Kylie. Stay away from your old haunts. You'll be okay.'

As I drove away I hoped that I was right and she would be okay.

I was pleased to have Adam Massoud's mobile in my keeping – that was worth a lot more to me than fifty dollars. *Prevent, disrupt, detect* – the three aspects of my work. Massoud's old mobile might well help give us the winning trifecta.

On the way back to Sydney, I visited the local police and spoke briefly to the boss there, asking him to keep an eye on a certain address. I didn't say much more than that we had a young woman who needed to disappear, because although I hated to think about it, it was always possible that Massoud had police connections. Such things had certainly happened before.

—•—

I went to the gym in the basement and did circuit training and a lot of weights. I liked keeping fit and strong and used my hundred-and-seventy-centimetre height to advantage. In heels, I found myself eye to eye with or even taller than a lot of the men I'd worked with over the years.

After a shower I headed back to the office to find Socrates hovering over the printer. He looked up as I approached. I grinned at him, lifting the bagged mobile out of my briefcase. 'I've got something you're going to love. Adam Massoud's mobile from last year. It got mislaid during a high-speed police chase but the ex had it all that time. She's been carrying it around ever since.'

'This could be a goldmine,' said Socrates as he took it from me.

I watched as he logged the mobile. 'Log it as coming from my informant – no need to mention a name,' I said.

'Sure thing. I'll take a look at what's inside and let you know.'

Socrates' program, Cellebrite, would extract the contents of the mobile, turning the digital data into a report that would give us every call Massoud had made, and to whom and for how long, as well as text messages, any photographs it stored, and any websites he might have accessed. We could then cross-reference this information with other programs. Massoud, the big spider in the middle of this web, would inadvertently betray all his contacts and we could move in and clean them up. I silently blessed Kylie Mifsud.

'While you were out, some transcripts came through from Goulburn.' Socrates passed the printed pages to me.

The prison system has ways of surveilling phone conversations. It's a funny thing, even when the crims suspect that the police might be listening, they still just can't help themselves. They use silly code words that are supposed to have us scratching our heads. As one of our senior guys said in a briefing when I was a young apprentice detective, criminals as a rule are not and never have been much good at self-discipline. I'd used the line myself in other briefings and it usually got a laugh.

I glanced over the information from Goulburn and then looked up, calling to Charlie and Nadine. 'Take a look at these transcripts.' They left their desks to come and look at the printouts.

'I'll email it to all of you,' Socrates said.

'What a charmer,' said Charlie, reading over my shoulder.

Massoud: Find someone to knock this piece of Aussie slime. Someone who'll make her suffer. Can you do that?
Name withheld: No probs. I'll get (indecipherable). He's good.
Massoud: I want her knocked. I want her cut into a hundred pieces. I want it done now. Now!
Name withheld: Sure, man. Skitzo will do it. I'm on it, okay?
Massoud: Get the piece of shit off this planet. Do it!

I looked up as Flash joined us. I've almost got used to the fact that there are people in the world who will kill another human being, or organise them to be killed, if they present a problem. Even a small problem, like standing between the killer and a handful of dollars. Or even, in some cases, no problem at all.

'This is good,' said Socrates. 'We've got him on conspiracy to murder. That's what we need. Strong primary evidence. His voice. Our tape. Our star witness. No matter how much he pays a smart QC, he's gone.'

Nadine nodded. 'When I was with the Gang Squad we usually only had lots of circumstantial evidence. Nothing that could pin down a conviction. That was often a problem. Getting the evidence wasn't easy.'

More recently, both the Gang Squad and MEOCS had been looking for other ways to secure convictions, following the FBI's method of bringing Al Capone to justice – getting convictions on less serious charges such as tax evasion.

'I've just come back from an interview with Kylie Mifsud,' I said to Alex who'd joined us. 'She's in hiding from a contract killer ordered by Adam Massoud —'

'Massoud? I know that name. He's already been sentenced for a previous. Isn't he waiting trial for that shooting murder?'

'Correct,' I said. 'He's looking for someone to knock the only witness – a girl who was in the car with him at the time of the murder.'

My heart was racing. We had him now on multiple charges. This is personal, Massoud, I silently swore.

—•—

It was time to call it a day. The effects of Adam Massoud's clear and present re-entry into my consciousness had taken me by surprise. I felt keyed up, angry. I grabbed a sandwich from the cafe down the street and ate it in my car before driving home.

There were two places that always had a calming effect on me, a secular and a sacred space respectively: the Australian Museum and the nearby St Mary's Cathedral. Even though I wasn't religious, the dim gothic interior of the cathedral with its jewel-like stained-glass windows and banks of candles left by the faithful to light their prayers was still a quiet, cool refuge. I liked to just sit there and listen to the busy city outside the huge Norman doors. But today was a museum kind of day.

Some years ago I'd worked in Goulburn Street, at the police station adjacent to the big police centre. During this time, I'd developed the habit of going to the museum when things got rough. I'd either grab a cab to save time or, if the day was fine, stride up the hill to Hyde Park and across to College Street. The museum too had a cathedral-like ambience. There was something about the wide sandstone spaces and high ceilings, the silent displays and dim lighting that settled my soul. I could spend hours in the primate section with its poignant diorama of our ancestors from three million years ago, a family of hominids who left their footprints in volcanic ash. This later hardened into sedimentary rock, preserving their footprints. Looking at it, I often felt overwhelmed by a sense of the huge sweep of time. It helped me to keep my own problems in proportion and not feel defeated by the cases I was working on.

I got there just in time to be admitted and hurried to the primate display. I found myself staring at the case containing the hominid skull with the two big holes in it where the great fangs of the sabre-tooth tiger had seized him. Or had it been a leopard, lying along the bough of a tree, dropping its ferocious weight on the unsuspecting victim who'd passed underneath? I hoped now that the brief against Adam Massoud would be so powerful that it would force a guilty plea. It's often easy knowing who the criminal is, and what the crime was, but finding that linkage that locks them together is the investigator's place of rejoicing.

CHAPTER 6

The next morning, I opened the door to my office and threw down my jacket and briefcase. The wood veneer surface of my desk was almost obscured by mounting paperwork that needed attention.

I kicked off my heels and logged on, then checked the Eaglenet, the police internal site, and my email. It took half an hour to go through the information about the other squads' activities, particuarly checking out what was going on with MEOCS and the Gang Squad; I hoped information received by these squads might spill over into useful intelligence for RED-V.

Afterwards I made a call to Chris Everingham, a friend of mine at Strike Force Raptor, the specialist squad set up to deal with outlaw motorcycle gangs. So far, Raptor had arrested over two thousand people and laid more than four thousand charges; they'd seized firearms, huge amounts of prohibited drugs, and millions of dollars in cash. Raptor was ongoing and kept on its toes by the misbehaviour of too many criminals.

'What have you got for me today, Chris?' I asked when she answered her phone.

'How much do you want?' she laughed. 'I could offload heaps and still have more than we can handle. Raptor's now been combined with two other operations, Apollo and Spartan. They're all coming under the direct control of the deputy commissioner. Ever since we created the "direct-to-detective" dob-in line, we've been swamped with information.'

The Mafioso-style code of silence enjoined by outlaw motor-cycle gangs made it very difficult to enlist informants, so the online tip-off facility made it safer and easier for people to pass information to the police. Sometimes it was misinformation, lodged by rivals, but sometimes we received very good intelligence, especially from rival gang members, trying to undermine their opposition.

'I'm particularly interested in any cross-over with family violence,' I said. 'Gang members who might be committing violence against women.'

'I'll let you know if I hear anything,' said Chris. 'Although the ladies who hang around with outlaw bikies are pretty tough. And they almost never complain. But I'll keep you in mind if we get anything like that coming in. It's mostly male-on-male stuff over here – drive-by shootings, kneecappings. There used to be some sort of code about leaving women and children out of it, but that's all changed now. Female relatives have been copping fatal shootings. A kid was shot in his bed.'

'Really?' I hadn't heard that.

'It was in South Australia,' she said. 'And a teenage boy was murdered here in Sydney in a revenge shooting. Bikies are getting worse every day. We also discovered links between Middle East–based terrorist organisations and some Sydney outlaw gangs. Funds are being sent overseas to assist in jihad operations. We closed down a tattoo parlour that was being operated as a money-laundering hub. And you should know that women have been victims of reprisal drive-by shootings.'

'Right. I'd like to get our team involved before anyone else dies,' I said.

'Promise I'll call you if I hear anything that might interest you, Debra.'

I thanked her and then checked in with the senior programs officer for the Domestic and Family Violence Squad. She gave me a breakdown of the various cases they had running and I explained the workings of RED-V. 'We're interested in any case but especially those where neighbours or family members might have given you the tip but the victim is too scared to make a complaint,' I reminded her. 'Someone caught up in the relationship bond and who's been so psychologically battered that she doesn't believe she has any power at all. We're especially interested in any woman from a migrant group where there is a cultural fear of the police, for instance, and a strongly patriarchal family structure. Goes without saying it's got to be handled very discreetly.' In some countries, being pulled in by the police meant torture, disappearance, and your family opening the door one morning to find your battered corpse on the doorstep, eyes gouged, limbs missing. Policing by terror and horror.

I quickly checked my personal email on my laptop. There was one from my friend Cecile asking how things were going at RED-V, another from Amazon trying to tempt me with some green tourmaline earrings similar to a pair I'd purchased a few months ago, as well as some feeds from sites I followed. My eyes stopped at an email from an unfamiliar sender, someone who called themselves Smiley. The subject line read, *There's more to this than meets the eye*. I clicked on the email and found myself staring at a scanned black and white photograph. My initial surprise quickly turned to bewilderment, then disbelief and finally shock.

I stared at the photograph, my heart racing and mind going into overdrive as I tried to make sense of it. I had recognised it straight away as a crime scene photograph. And even though I'd never seen any of the still photographs from the night my father was murdered, I knew almost immediately that this was one of them. The first thing I had noticed in the image was my father's 1990 station wagon.

How the hell had someone who called themselves Smiley got hold of this photograph? And who the hell was he? Or she? Only police personnel handled these pictures. They were sensitive pieces of evidence, and photographs from old cases such as this were stored in secured premises in police records.

I reread the subject line: *There's more to this than meets the eye.*

I stared into the black and white picture, trying to see something more.

The photograph showed my father's car in front of the Davidsons' house, driver's door open, part of the station wagon's interior visible. At the front of the vehicle, and largely hidden by its chassis, I could see the outline of my father's head and shoulder slumped over on the passenger side. Beyond the station wagon and my father's body, the front door of the Davidsons' farmhouse stood half open, allowing a glimpse through to the hall that I presumed led to the main living room where the bodies of the Davidsons lay, out of sight.

From deep inside me, and shocking me with its intensity, a sob rose up, and I had to force out a cough to cover it. I cleared my throat and straightened up in my seat, trying to regain my poise.

My mobile rang and I picked it up. 'Yes?' I said, still staring at the photograph.

'Am I speaking to Debra Hawkins?' a man's voice asked.

'Correct.'

'Andrew Bell here, ringing from St Vincent's casualty. We have your mother here. She's asked me to call you.'

'What's happened?' I asked, immediately alert.

'She's had a fall,' Andrew said. 'She's fine now but she has a nasty gash on the shin. It's being stitched up and she's had a local anaesthetic. We don't want to send her home by herself. Could you pick her up, please?'

'Of course. I'll be there in half an hour.' I stood up, grabbing my things.

Flash was looking at me with concern. 'My mother,' I said. 'She's had a fall. I have to pick her up.'

I threw another glance back at the puzzling email on my laptop with its shocking photograph. I'll deal with it as soon as I get back, I thought, closing it down before leaving my office.

CHAPTER 7

I found my mother sitting on a chair in the recovery room, her left foot, the shin heavily bandaged, resting on a footstool. She was wearing one of the sober dark suits and white blouses she usually wears to her work at a health clinic in a quiet street in Newtown. It had taken me longer than I'd thought to drive from work to the hospital. Now I rushed over to her. She looked up at my approach and for a moment, her face lightened, the anxious frown gone, but she didn't greet me.

'What have you done to yourself?' I asked. 'Why didn't you call me as soon as it happened?'

'Because I was flat on my back,' she said, rolling her eyes and putting down the magazine she'd been reading. 'Down the garden path.'

'What I meant was, I could've run you to the hospital. If you'd called.'

'I thought you'd be too busy. And it's a bit of a drive to Maroubra.'

I could see it was going to be one of those days with her. 'Would you like to go home now?' I asked, carefully.

—•—

'What happened?' I asked as we drove back to her place.

'I was going down those bloody back steps near the laundry,' she said, 'and for some reason I missed the step and ended up head over heels on the path. I think I must have caught my shin on the edge of the lower step.'

My mother lived in a beachside Sydney suburb in a small weatherboard house that had been a fisherman's cottage about a hundred years ago. With my father's death insurance and the help of a police fund set up in Garralong after his murder, she'd been able to buy the place not long after I'd moved to Sydney. Since then, on either side of the small three-bedroom house, tall townhouses and villas had grown up, overshadowing my mother's home in winter when the sun dipped low in the sky. In front of the house, the land fell away to the coast and the blue of the ocean could be glimpsed in gaps between the taller houses across the road.

She'd made a cottage-style garden which struggled to grow with limited sunlight, planted with rosemary and different types of salvias and sages, as well as heartsease and pansies. Near the front fence, a series of small semicircular white headstones attested to the final resting places of the last four dogs in my mother's life, Doggie, Ralph, Cribbie and Felix, their names reminding me of one of the larger legal firms in the city. Felix had died over six months ago and I wondered when my mother would track down a replacement at the Rescued Dogs Home. Usually she got a new one within weeks of the demise of the last resident dog, unable to bear the thought of a dog without a home.

I opened the front door and helped her inside, my arm around her bony rib cage, feeling the fragility of her slender body and wishing we could talk openly with each other. Over the years, I'd noticed how different our relationship was from other people's. I envied Cecile, who chatted away to her mother and whose mother responded with warm interest and conversation of her own. By contrast, it felt as if my mother had somehow taken cover from life and never really come out again.

'Sit down,' I said, 'and I'll make you a cup of tea. What have you got in the fridge for dinner tonight?'

'Lobster, Beluga caviar, truffles. Possibly even the truffle pig himself. With an apple in his mouth. It's all in there.'

My mother thinks these sorts of remarks are funny. Maybe they are. I left her propped in her favourite chair in her comfortable living room while I hung up her suit coat, handed her her old, much-mended fawn Pringle cardigan, then made tea and checked the fridge. 'There's half a cooked chicken here and some salad,' I called back from the kitchen. 'What's the bread situation?'

'Stop fussing.'

'I'm not fussing. I'm asking a simple question.' I answered it myself by looking in the cupboard, where I found the remnants of a sliced sourdough loaf wrapped in plastic.

I put the teapot on a tray with two mugs and the milk jug and returned to the living room. My mother was sipping a small brandy from one of the cut-glass tumblers that stood in a row along the top of the low 1960s-style sideboard. I placed the tea things down beside the decanters. 'I would've got you that if you'd told me you wanted one.'

'So how's work?' she asked.

'We're just starting to hit our stride,' I said, tacitly accepting the change of subject. 'But it's a good team. Although we haven't been stretched to our limits – yet.'

'I suppose you've heard that the Hells Angels have opened a new clubhouse at Bondi. And there was that shooting at Eastlakes with the Comancheros warning the Angels not to move into their territory. That used to be your business once?'

'I should have you on the team, Mum,' I said, smiling. 'So how's your work going?'

My mother leaned back in the chair. 'Draining, in a word. Bereaved people need very gentle handling. Sometimes I wonder if . . .' Her voice trailed off. 'I'm not even sure how I got into this line of psychology. I don't think I'm very good at it. And yet people keep coming back. They say it's helping.'

My mother, having acquired a Psychology degree, worked three days a week at the clinic as a psychologist specialising in bereavement counselling. She worked with a team of alternative therapists grouped under the business name Life Force, and I knew she was highly thought of because her colleagues had told me so on different occasions. On her sideboard there was always a collection of cards from grateful clients, especially at Christmas.

'You know,' my mother said, putting down the brandy glass, 'I have a client who reminds me of you.'

'Oh?' I poured tea for us both, wondering what was coming next.

'Most nights she drinks too much while she watches all the family videos about her daughter. Who suicided eighteen months ago.'

I winced at the suffering she described, then asked, 'How exactly does that remind you of me? You think I'm drinking too many G and Ts?'

'Not so much the G and Ts. But don't you have that old crime scene footage somewhere? Do you ever watch it?'

Years ago, I'd had the old Beta tape digitally rendered onto a CD. 'Occasionally. Why is that an issue for you, Mum? You don't have to watch it.'

'It's unhealthy. It keeps you stuck in the past. It indicates what we call complicated grief.'

'I'm not even going to ask what psychologists mean by that. Surely all grief is complicated?'

My mother shrugged. 'Complicated grief is grief compounded by a lot of other baggage around it.' She sounded as though she was repeating something she'd said a million times before. Her voice was colourless and almost mechanical as she went on. 'Factors like guilt, shame, resentments, unresolved emotional issues . . . things that should have been said, things that were said that are now regretted, things that I wish I hadn't —' She collected herself but I'd noticed the slip. 'Simply put, complicated grief results in holding onto the past, endlessly reliving it. It's like an old-fashioned tape loop that never comes to an end, just recycles. The normal pattern of grief – if one can ever use the word "normal" in this case – is to move through stages, however long it might take, and finally let go of the grief, the suffering, but not the loving memories.'

'Have you?' The question was out before I could stop myself.

My mother finished the brandy, put down the glass and picked up her teacup. 'Let's not go over this yet again.'

'Hang on,' I said, my sense of justice stirring at her infuriating habit of bringing up a topic only to then shy away from it. '*You* started this conversation about the client who reminds you of me and the lesson on complicated grief. As if I'm the only one who hasn't let go. Dad's been dead now for twenty-two years. How come you've never married again? Or even had a long-term relationship?'

'I prefer dogs.'

'And it's not as if it's something we've talked about endlessly,' I went on. 'We've never properly talked about it. On the few occasions I've tried you always refuse to discuss it. You do the equivalent of clutching your chest and calling for your heart pills, like a character in a 1930s melodrama.'

'Now you're being ridiculous.'

'It's true. Any time I try to bring it up, you close it down. Why, Mum? We're the two people in the whole world most affected by a tragedy we can't talk about!'

My mobile rang. I snatched it up. 'Yes?'

It was Flash. 'Where are you? You're supposed to be here for a meeting.'

I jumped up, dismayed at forgetting. 'I've got to go, Mum. There's enough food in your fridge for lunch and dinner. I'll drop by in the morning and see what shopping you need. Okay?'

'I can make myself some toast.'

'That sounds pathetic. I'll bring round some eggs. You'll probably need to have the dressing on your leg changed too. What did they say at casualty?'

'That I should go to my doctor and have it checked tomorrow or the next day.'

'I can drive you . . . if you like.'

'I'll let you know.' She smiled. 'I can manage.'

'Managing sounds a bit grim,' I said, patting her shoulder. 'I'm happy to help out.' It wasn't quite true – the happy part. Being with her always made me tense.

'I noticed in the paper, that Massoud character – that brute who assaulted you outside the courts. He's coming up for another trial soon. I hope you keep right out of the way.' My mother had seen the footage, repeated several times on the evening news, of the scramble as Massoud was hauled off me.

'I won't be anywhere near him,' I said. 'Don't worry.'

She looked up at me as if I were insane. 'Not worry? I googled him. He's a monster.'

'Okay,' I said, leaning down to kiss her. 'Promise I'll be careful.'

I left her with another cup of tea and she waved me away in a familiar gesture. I closed the front door behind me and walked down the path, past the four small white headstones.

—•—

I was almost back at the office when my mobile rang again. Gavin – my boss.

'Where are you? You're needed back here, Debra. The assistant commissioner's just called me expecting a briefing on your directions and goals. Okay? She's on her way. I'd like to hear about them too. And the rest of your team might as well avail themselves of this opportunity.'

'Sorry, Gavin, something unexpected came up. I can put some material together for that.' It was important to me that I vindicate Gavin's faith in my ability to lead the team and gather intelligence. I wanted him to see that we were already on the job, that I'd already visited Kylie Mifsud, that I'd been on the phones, trawling for leads from other squads and divisions. 'I'm on my way. Be there in ten.'

—-—

'Okay, everyone,' I said, addressing Gavin Bailey and the rest of the team gathered in the windowless utility room next to my office.

'First point,' I said. 'I want to stress the fact that in this unit we take all reports of domestic and family violence very seriously. Last year the domestic violence helpline had twenty-two thousand calls in New South Wales alone. Domestic and family violence causes more deaths among women aged forty-five and under than any other factor. Another thing to remember is how much of this family violence probably goes unreported.' Gavin took a call and left the room.

'This unit must practise intelligence-led policing. We must be proactive. Treat every complaint we receive as genuine. Assess the incident, and once you've established that a domestic violence offence has occurred, take action.' I paused. 'Okay? Any questions so far?'

No one spoke and I looked around to see that Gavin had returned, bringing with him the assistant commissioner. Jackie Sunderland was a tall woman with fair hair neatly pulled back, lively eyes, and pale pink lipstick on a disciplined mouth. She and Gavin stood near the door.

I nodded to acknowledge her entrance and continued, 'We aim to collect as much information as possible about any incident, and that includes information about the victim, any witnesses, and of course the perpetrator. We ask around to find out what's been going on – neighbours, relatives, anyone who has any information at all.'

Charlie took this down, then said, 'Boss? What if it's a couple who've been fighting for years? There's one couple in Daylesford Avenue where I worked before who've been trying to kill each other since I joined the police. We'd get a call from one of them, or from a neighbour, but by the time we get there, they're kissing and making up. Or the old bloke's gone to the pub. They're a real waste of time. They've been at it for years and it's always the same pattern.'

Her words touched a hot spot in my memory, and I felt my shoulders tense. Frank and Betty Davidson had been fighting for as long as anyone could remember too; they'd been 'at it' for years before Frank finally snapped. 'It's got to be followed up,' I said. 'Because one day the report we get might be the time one of them actually does it.' I looked around at the group. 'And remember that a report can come in from anywhere – any source. It could be from one of the children, a referring agency or maybe a neighbour or friend. It might have come from a triple-0 contact. Someone might have reported to their local area command or a local police station.'

I reminded them of the new app, Aurora, launched by the Minister for Immigration and Family Services for use on smartphones. 'It's a one-touch method for contacting police or friends. When women run from a potentially violent partner, they generally just grab their keys and their phone. Aurora provides a "call-for-help", and a GPS system so that police know where the call is coming from. The app also lists contacts that may be useful – refuges, counselling services, that sort of thing.'

'It's going to make a hell of a lot more work for us,' said Nadine, tossing her shining head.

'You bet,' I said. 'And we have to be up to it.'

I spoke for about twenty minutes, going over operational safety principles. I reminded them that family violence is not only an ugly crime, usually against women, but also one of the worst forms of child abuse, and that our work was as much about child protection as about taking violent offenders off the streets. For the benefit of the assistant commissioner, I repeated that the government was very committed to addressing violence against women.

'Very committed to being re-elected,' someone muttered.

'Violence against women is a crime that injures individuals deeply in every way – physically, psychologically and emotionally,' I went on, ignoring the comment. 'It goes on injuring by creating generational damage. Children who've witnessed violence against their mothers grow up with that wound and often become perpetrators themselves. In families where no one deals with conflict except through violence, children grow up without the necessary skills for a decent life. They resolve conflict with biffo instead of reason, intelligent negotiation and compromise.' I could hear my mother's voice in my head. She'd taught me a lot. She was excellent when it came to teaching me about other people's difficulties. 'We're pursuing a policy of zero tolerance of offenders. We're committed to working in with NGOs and other referral agencies to do all we can from a police perspective to decrease family violence. When I say "family violence" it's almost always violence directed against women and children. It can be almost impossible for some women to make a complaint. Over the last few years we've discovered around one thousand incidents of forced marriages and attempted forced marriages here in Australia because of the diligent work of school counsellors, teachers, school friends, and police. And they're just the ones we know about.'

I noticed that Nadine continued to take notes as I spoke. 'That's where the multicultural liaison officers can be of immense assistance in gathering further information. As you know, these are people drawn from the migrant communities who are bi-lingual and help with communicating and explaining the law and other potentially difficult issues. Of course, in cases like these, sensitivity and discretion are essential. And a great deal of caution as well. With minors, remember that the first contact should be treated as the one and only contact – the only chance we have. If we fail at that stage, a young girl could be facing a lifetime of sexual assault, physical violence and suffering. Her life is over. Many of them suicide in horrible ways.'

I wound up with another reminder. 'So be prepared for any situation. Make sure you know what you're doing before you go into any situation. We need to identify hidden violence against women, contain it, investigate it, evaluate it, negotiate if that's appropriate, then wrap it up and prosecute. The conviction is the icing on the cake. And that's what we're all aiming for, guys. Convictions. The endgame. Okay?'

Jackie Sunderland nodded at me with a smile as she and Gavin quietly left the room. I felt relieved. The meeting had gone well.

—•—

I grabbed a coffee from the kitchen before returning to my office, where I closed the door. Even though the meeting had been a success, I could feel a headache gathering in my temples. Throughout the briefing, the crime scene photograph had kept flashing through my mind. Who was Smiley? What was their purpose? What were they trying to tell me? As I clicked on the email again, I wondered how Smiley had got hold of my email address.

Probably from one of the many business cards I'd handed out over the years, I reminded myself. I'm going to trace you, Smiley, I thought. Find out who you are and what you want. And most of all, what you mean by sending me this.

I emailed my girlfriend Cecile Springer. Cecile now worked as a solicitor for the legal firm Aspery and Barton but she'd spent nearly fifteen years with a government department in Canberra. The way she tells it, she was 'private secretary to someone in Defence', but I've never believed that; I think it was ASIO or ASIS, one of the intelligence agencies. Of course Cecile could never tell me such a thing, and I'd never put her on the spot, but she had a wealth of knowledge of terrorist and other violent organisations, including the international outlaw bikie brigade, which she claimed came from wide reading of academic and law enforcement publications. She was also a whiz at IT matters and had helped me on a number of occasions when I'd needed some extracurricular assistance.

I sent her a copy of the email header with a request: *Seal, I need your help. Can you please tell me who and where Smiley is? Urgent.* Within a minute, Cecile responded with one word: *Piggy*.

I smiled. Cecile was on the job. We'd met during an early case of mine not long after I'd become a sergeant. We had a special shorthand, derived years ago. The term came from Edward Lear's 'Owl and the Pussycat' – "Dear Pig, are you willing to sell for one shilling/Your ring?" Said the Piggy, "I will."' We'd used 'piggy' to mean 'affirmative' for years now.

Flash put his head around the door. 'I'm going to the pie shop. Any orders?'

I quickly shut down the email and shook my head. 'No, thanks.'

'If anyone calls, tell them I'll be back in fifteen minutes.'

'Expecting a call, Flash?' I asked, trying to sound normal.

'She can always leave a message.' I knew there was a woman. Flash, divorced for years and seemingly uninterested in getting back into the dating game, had been talking about someone he'd met a few months ago.

I sat staring at the wall opposite, once again trying to make sense of why someone would send me this photograph. Was it someone's idea of a joke? Or were they being malicious?

I looked up as Gavin gently pushed the door open. 'Deb,' he said, 'I'm going out for lunch. Want to join me?'

'Sure,' I said, feeling just a little nervous. I thought I'd covered everything in my briefing and wondered why he wanted my company just now.

CHAPTER 8

There was a Turkish kebab place on the corner across the road which offered fast service and decent food. I followed Gavin inside and the owner greeted him like an old friend. We ordered flatbread and kebabs with salad, and Gavin ordered his Turkish coffee, and then we slid into one of the small benches and tables attached to the wall.

'Good work, that briefing,' he said, and I relaxed. 'I think you're across the job, and Jackie Sunderland was happy with it. It's not like you to be late, though. Are things okay?' Gavin notices everything, I'd realised some time ago.

'Just a slight emergency,' I said. 'My mother had a fall and cut her leg quite badly. The hospital called me to drive her home. She's okay now. I left her with a brandy and a cup of tea.'

'Sorry to hear that. Give her my best wishes for a speedy recovery.'

'I will,' I said, wondering if I should add 'sir'. I didn't.

Our shared past with its legacy of grief and pain allowed these odd shifts of gear from formal interactions between a senior police officer and a subordinate to more intimate, casual conversations. Naturally, it had led to misunderstandings, and I recalled a period when there were rumours that Gavin and I were having an affair. The gossip in police circles can be very destructive. I glanced out at the people walking past the kebab shop, and wondered who might spot us having lunch together and arrive at the wrong conclusion. Anyone who knew me well, of course, would know such a relationship was impossible. And it wasn't only because Gavin was my boss. On graduation day at the academy, an old sergeant had taken me aside. 'Want to hear some advice, girlie?'

'Yes, sir!'

'Never, ever sleep with a cop. If you sleep with one of them, you have to sleep with all of them.'

'Yes, sir – I mean no, sir. I never will.' And I never had. It had turned out to be good advice. I'd seen other policewomen fall into the trap of sleeping with a colleague, and very soon the rumour mill made their lives miserable. Their reputation went ahead of them to new postings, and male officers made crude remarks to them and often made their working lives unbearable. The brotherhood could be merciless.

Quite early in my career, an older policewoman, highly respected, had taken me under her wing. Without her support, I'm not sure I would have got to where I am today. She'd taught me to be friendly without flirtatiousness, and modelled how to be a woman in a man's world without losing my femininity. Too many women tried to be one of the boys, but it never worked.

Earrings and smart suits were essential. I was also very careful never to swear on the job. I wasn't concerned when other people did, but I didn't. That was extremely hard sometimes.

'Apart from that, how is your mother?' Gavin's question interrupted my wandering thoughts. 'Overall, I mean.'

I hesitated, wondering how much I should tell. At that moment, Gavin's coffee arrived in a tiny cup. As he went to take it from the serving tray offered by the owner, Gavin's fingers slipped. The cup struck the table and overturned, a muddy pool of Turkish coffee oozing across the table. 'Oops!' I said, pulling my jacket away as it dripped off the edge in front of me.

'So sorry, Debra! Clumsy of me.' Gavin was already wiping down the table while the owner fussed, promising another cup without delay. Soon the mess had been cleared up and Gavin sipped at his replacement coffee. 'Where were we?' he asked.

'My mother,' I reminded him. 'You were asking. She's okay, I think. Her work is a bit depressing – you know she's working in the field of bereavement counselling.'

Gavin looked away briefly. 'She's well qualified for that. They say only someone who's been there can help other people who are facing similar problems.' He took a cautious sip from the small cup of coffee, clenching it tightly.

'You know,' I confessed, 'when Charlie mentioned that old couple who'd been fighting for decades I couldn't help thinking of the Davidsons.'

He surprised me by saying, 'Me too.' He put down the cup, his eyes lowered, making sure of no further mishaps. 'I know we don't talk about it, but I often think about that night. I sometimes think that if I'd been tougher on Frank Davidson the week before the shootings, I might have been able to prevent it from happening.' Our food arrived, briefly interrupting our conversation.

I frowned. 'How so?'

'I'd been over at the Cusacks' – the neighbours to the west of Frank and Betty Davidson's place?'

I remembered the Cusacks well. They had two older sons and a daughter, Helen, who was in my class at school. Their property adjoined the Davidsons' and on the other side, the huge holdings of the Sheffield family. The Cusacks owned a couple of horses that Kiera and I were allowed to ride from time to time on the weekend. Dad would drop us off in the morning and pick us up later in the day. I remembered how we'd dawdle when he arrived to pick us up, the hours having flown too quickly, petting the horses before reluctantly walking down and getting into the car, envying Helen, who could ride whenever she wanted. I blinked, surprised at the pricking of tears. Remembering Taffy and Ringo and those happy hours was making me want to cry? What was happening? I hadn't thought of the Cusacks and the horses for years.

'They reckoned Frank Davidson had deliberately cut through their fences and their cattle had got out,' Gavin was saying. 'One was hit by a car along the Brindie Road. I talked to old Frank about it, and he completely denied it. But he was really riled up, threatening revenge for what he said was people telling lies about him. I think that whole incident must have played on his mind. He was always a difficult customer but obviously he became suicidally murderous a few days after that. I could have taken his gun away for a while.' Gavin looked closely at me. 'You okay?' he asked.

I nodded, trying to smile. 'We drive ourselves crazy with the *if onlys*. If only the last image I had of my father alive had been happier.'

Gavin knew exactly what I was talking about. Over the years, I'd mentioned this particular corroding regret a couple of times. 'You mustn't blame yourself for that, Dibs,' he said, using my childhood nickname. 'I'm sure your father had other things on his mind.'

The hot tears threatened again, bewildering me. I had not been expecting this ambush. To distract myself, I tried to focus instead on what Gavin had just said about the Cusacks. I hadn't heard about that incident before. I cleared my throat and tried to sound casual and relaxed. 'I'd really like to have a look at the crime scene photos from that night, Gavin. Could you requisition them for me?'

Gavin paused, then leaned across the narrow table. 'I can do that, Debra. But are you sure you want to see photographs of your father in that condition?' I briefly considered, then rejected the idea of telling Gavin about the Smiley email. I'd wait, I decided, until I knew more about it – and Smiley.

'They couldn't be any worse than the old crime scene video that I've watched a few times over the years, and I've pretty much made my peace with that.' I'd pulled in a favour years ago to get hold of the video, and I hoped Gavin wasn't going to ask me any awkward questions about how I had come to have such a thing in my possession. I hurried on, 'The question that haunts me is why? Why did my father have to die that night?

He had nothing to do with the forty-year-old battle between the Davidsons.'

'Wrong place, wrong time,' Gavin said gently. 'It just happens that way sometimes. I know it's a cliché and no comfort, but in our line of work, sometimes you go on a callout and you never come home.' He paused again. 'What's brought on this sudden interest?'

I tore some flatbread into strips, not hungry anymore. 'It's not really sudden,' I said. 'It's just that I haven't yet talked to anyone outside the family about it. See, I've got this idea about a muddy mark on the floor just inside the front door and on the front steps – it only appears in a few frames on the crime scene footage. My theory is that old Frank comes inside and clumps over Betty's clean floor in his workboots one last, fatal time, she has a go at him about it and the whole thing blows up from there. Because it's not about dirty boots on a clean floor, it's about a lifetime of frustration and mutual misunderstanding. I feel that if I knew how it had happened, it might somehow be easier . . .' I shrugged at the futility of it. Is this what my mother meant about complicated grief, I wondered, grief mixed up with a little girl's remorse and the need for an answer to an impossible *why*?

'But even if you do satisfy yourself that that's how it happened, what difference does it make now?'

I looked into Gavin's olive-dark eyes. 'A big difference, sir. I want to know the truth. I want to know what happened the night my father was murdered. I want to know what led up to it in that house. I want to know why my father was so unprepared. Why he lost his service pistol. The only thing people remember about him is that he stuffed up covering the incident he was called out to deal with. That's what I think of too. Try living with that. If I can put together a clearer picture of what actually happened that night in 1992, I might get some, you know, what the social workers call "closure". Is that crazy?'

Gavin looked hard at me. 'Closure,' he repeated. 'It's a popular word at the moment. But you of all people must realise that there are a lot of things we will never know, no matter how much we might want to. Our files are filled with cold cases, mysteries that will never be solved.'

I knew he was right. There was a whole room at the morgue stacked with cardboard boxes filled with scraps of unidentified bones and rotting leather and poignant wisps of perished fabric, all that remained of a whole vibrant human life ending up in a cardboard box with nothing but a date and a place written on the label. There was no such thing as closure in the bone room.

'My advice, as harsh as it sounds, is to drop it,' Gavin said. 'Rule a line under it and get on with your life.'

'You sound like Mum,' I said. 'Only calmer.'

'She's right. It's almost a quarter of a century ago now. It's finished.' He paused, thinking. 'I will requisition the photos for you, but let's get this really clear: any work on this old closed case must take place in your own time. Okay?'

His mobile rang. He answered, listened for a few moments, then said, 'Sure, I'll be there.' He hung up, meeting my enquiring look. 'There's been another drive-by shooting out west,' he explained. 'Gang dispute, apparently. Between two outlaw motorcycle clubs – Warlords and Khaybar Riders. No one was hurt this time. I'm heading out there now.'

'It's going to take a long time for MEOCS to clean up all that drive-by craziness,' I said, following him to the counter as he paid.

'There was a woman in the house,' Gavin added. 'She could have been killed.'

Violence and a woman. My territory. 'Gavin,' I said, forgetting my rank for a minute, 'I'm coming with you.'

Thirty minutes later we were cruising along the streets of Daylesford, once an old working-class suburb. These days the 1930s and '40s bungalows and the even humbler fibro and weatherboard shacks squatted alongside enormous McMansions that were built right up to the boundary. We turned into the street identified on the radio, and immediately saw the commotion around a large two-storey double-fronted brick house.

As Gavin's car approached, several young guys on the corner before the crime scene turned to deliberately spit in the direction of our car. One gestured obscenely at us. Gavin ignored them.

'At least they're not shooting at us,' I said.

'Yet,' he said. 'It's when they go from jeans and designer T-shirts to beard, belly and nightshirt and attend certain bookshops and mosques that we tend to get anxious – as does much of the local community. They don't want trouble either.'

Not long after leaving MEOCS and about to take up the secondment to RED-V, I'd attended a meeting with community elders deeply concerned about the direction some of their young men were taking. Having come to the country themselves seeking peace and stability, they weren't at all happy with some of the young hotheads. A few days later, at a lunch organised by women from the Middle East and Africa at the community centre, I enjoyed their warm hospitality, delicious dishes and listened to their fears and concerns. I explained to them that as police officers, we were completely uninterested in religious doctrines and theology, but that we were tasked with protecting women from violence and responding to criminal behaviour wherever we might find it. This policing didn't target particular communities, but those breaking the law – criminals. I was impressed with their sense of family and community but I understood also that this very same closeness and strong commitment to community could also make it difficult for anyone breaking its rules. 'We go where the crimes are,' I assured them, 'that's our job.'

Out on the street, spacesuited members of the Forensics Services group were focused on the front windows of the house. Several angry-looking men milled around on the footpath near the gate, or stood, hands on hips, arguing with the local uniforms. A young female SOCO was marking where shells lay on the footpath and in the gutter, her blonde ponytail swaying from side to side as she moved around, logging the details.

Gavin parked across the street and we strolled over. I flashed my warrant card to the uniforms on the perimeter, but I didn't need to; the presence of Gavin Bailey was a sure entrée. I didn't want to get in the way of the workers so I stood well back, looking at the three large bullet holes, arranged in a rising arc, that had shattered the tough glazing of the largest front window.

'There's a girl living in there too,' an excited neighbour was saying. 'She could have been killed! These gangsters have no respect! I've got kids!'

'This house belongs to the al-Sheikly family,' Gavin said as we walked over to join the local detectives. 'They're on our radar. I hear ASIO has an interest in them too.' He discreetly indicated two men. 'Those could be the two brothers – they returned to Australia from Iraq last year.'

I'd already heard mention of the al-Sheiklys. I glanced past the detectives to get a better look at the two heavily built men standing close to the house. One appeared to be in his early thirties, the other a few years older. They were involved in angry conversation with a uniformed police officer and the plainclothes detective standing beside him. I couldn't hear what they were saying but I caught the belligerent edge to their voices. Both of them, but the older one particularly, had an intense, angry energy that showed in his narrowed eyes and closed face. I couldn't imagine either of them ever smiling. Real funsters, this pair, I thought.

'What's going on here, Barry?' Gavin asked one of the detectives, middle-aged, with a permanent frown and the beginnings of a beer gut.

'It's the al-Sheikly brothers, sir. Talal and Samir. They're yelling at us to do our job and lock someone up but they won't tell us who did it. They know all right. But they're not saying.'

'What's your latest on them?' I asked.

'They've already been linked to credit-card fraud and drug dealing,' Barry replied, 'and there are suspected links to arms dealing, but so far we haven't been able to get enough usable evidence. We're still trying to track down those rocket launchers that were reported missing last year.'

I'd heard about the rocket launchers – Chris from Strike Force Raptor had mentioned them to me when I was still with MEOCS. Frankly, I wasn't all that sure they existed. We hadn't heard any chatter about them.

'The Gang Squad busted the clubhouse of the Khaybar Riders last week on an anonymous tip-off,' Barry was saying, 'and seized amphetamines, cannabis, ecstasy and bulk precursor chemicals, plus over two hundred thousand in cash. No rocket launchers though. We reckon this —' he indicated the three holes punched in the hardened plate glass, '— is payback for something the al-Sheikly brothers did. It's possible the tip-off might have come from them. There's a lot of rivalry around, and eliminating the competition is good strategy. The brothers run an engineering shop and garage a few kilometres from here where they reckon they do legitimate mechanical repairs. But our surveillance records show they've recently been dealing with some of the Warlords. They've also been linked via phone calls to members of the Khaybar Riders.'

'The Warlords wouldn't like that one bit,' I said.

'Plus they've been mentioned in connection with clan-lab activity,' Barry continued. 'We've closed down several labs, but there are always new ones popping up. One of the new recruits to the Khaybar Riders was silly enough to resist arrest when we went in with the warrant. When we took him in, we discovered that he hadn't really adopted the KRs' code of silence. Especially when a Livescan check showed that he was wanted for a serious assault outside the local RSL club. Not to mention breaching bail conditions.' Barry grinned. 'He ended up being pretty keen on staying out of gaol. We got some good info.'

Sensing someone looking at me, I glanced towards the house. Standing just inside a smaller, intact window further along the frontage was a young woman. She had drawn aside a gauzy curtain and her right hand was pressed against the glass like a child's. Our eyes met and a shock went through me. In the split second before she lowered her hand and let the curtain drop, her large dark eyes conveyed grief, despair and defiance all in one searing glance. Then she was gone.

'Who's the girl?' I asked Barry, as Gavin went to speak to the forensics team.

'The sister.' He consulted his notes. 'Rana. We've interviewed her and she doesn't know anything about anything. I could barely get a word out of her. You know how it is.'

'What does she do?' I asked.

He checked his notes again. 'She goes to university. Studying Pharmacy.'

'She's smart, then.' I paused, considering. A chemist in this family would be an asset to clandestine drug manufacture. 'When you spoke to her, were her brothers present?'

Barry nodded.

'Of course she's not going to know anything about anything if her brothers were there.'

Barry sighed. 'The brothers are always there. That's the problem.'

I could see Gavin walking back across to the car and signalling me, so I hurried over.

—•—

All the way back to the office, I couldn't get that young woman out of my mind, kept seeing her hand pressed to the glass and the dread and grief in her eyes. I guessed being the sister of a couple of criminals who derived their income from clandestine labs cooking up illegal drugs, and who were being targeted by a rival outlaw motorbike gang would give anyone who wasn't also criminally inclined a sense of deep concern. But this woman's haunted eyes seemed to hold a deeper anguish, a plea for something that perhaps I could never fathom.

'The Khaybar Riders,' I said to Gavin as he negotiated the heavy traffic near the office, 'are fairly new on the scene. They're a feeder club and they've been caught importing precursor chemicals. They're muscling in on territory held by an old and established gang, the Warlords, who don't like this at all. Then the Riders' boss, Danny Malik, disappeared from outside his house earlier in the year. His family got a call on Danny's mobile and all they could hear was some heavy metal music and a man screaming.'

'Was it Malik?'

I shrugged. 'That's the best guess. He hasn't been heard of since.'

'So that's where the al-Sheikly brothers come in? Dealing with the Warlords' vacancy?'

'Correct. Sami Allen of the Khaybar Riders told MEOCS that Talal and Samir have thrown themselves into a hard-working life of crime. But that meant poaching in other established criminal territories, cutting out other dealers. And that means making dangerous enemies. They've been living in Iraq the last ten years but now they've come back.'

'I don't blame them,' Gavin said, 'when you think of the footage from Iraq on the television news night after night.'

'Life's much quieter here.' I agreed. 'I wonder what it's like being the smart sister of a couple of thugs like that?' I continued.

Gavin looked across at me with a grin. 'You could always find out.'

'Let's give their tree a good shake,' I said, as Gavin drove back to our unit's HQ and into the underground car park, 'and see what falls out.'

I was keen to get a fresh case of my own, not just an ongoing one like Kylie Mifsud's. One that I could handle right from the start. I liked the cleanness of being involved from the beginning, staying with a case right through to the end. As this thought formed in my mind, it resonated with something deeper. Something bigger, my intuition flashed at me, would also begin to unfold in the course of these investigations.

—•—

The first step in breaking up a criminal group – the tried and tested strategy – is to disrupt them. It's like poking a stick into a bull ants' nest, then standing back and watching to see where they go as they all run out. Call around the local police stations to get a list of names, then listen in on phone conversations. Put undercover people on the street. Compromise criminals with links to the others so they turn informer; pull people off the street on violations of parole conditions. Listen in again after this and watch who calls whom and what they talk about. Pull some more members off the street, create vacuums and see who seeps in. Leak disinformation. Then, when the gang starts to regroup, refilling the vacuum and the positions made vacant by arrests or convictions, disrupt them again. With the kinds of bull ants we were dealing with, I knew we'd have to be very careful not to get badly stung.

I hoped that it wouldn't be long before MEOCS and the Gang Squad discovered exactly who had been responsible for the three bullets shot into the al-Sheikly house – and why.

Before going into my office, I brought Flash up to date with what had happened at the al-Sheikly household. Then I went into COPS, wrote up today's action and checked up on Talal and Samir al-Sheikly. It was clear they'd been very busy since arriving back in Australia, with lots of entries in the system. But so far nothing had stuck to them.

I realised with a jolt that I hadn't thought about the Smiley email and the crime scene photograph all afternoon. I carefully put it out of my mind again – I had enough to deal with right now, and besides there was nothing I could do about it until Cecile had worked her magic.

Before preparing to go home, I called my mother. 'How's that leg?' I asked.

'Okay,' she said cautiously.

'Have you made the appointment with your docor to get the dressing changed?'

'Not exactly.'

It was the kind of answer that frustrated me. 'What exactly does "not exactly" mean?'

'Exactly what it means,' she said.

Always the edge between us, I thought. It never flows. 'Come on, Mum. Explain, please.'

'It means that I didn't make an appointment with the doctor. I plan to rebandage it myself.'

'I think you should definitely make an appointment and let your doctor take a look at it. Those injuries to the shin can take a long time to heal. People sometimes get ulcers there that give a lot of trouble.'

'You're fussing again,' she said.

'I'm being realistic, Mum.'

'I'll see what it's like in a week or so.'

'Just don't neglect it,' I said, saying goodbye and ringing off.

CHAPTER 9

'A call's come in that I think you should take,' Flash said just as I was about to leave the office. I glanced at the note. *Jamila Khan*, he'd written. 'Especially considering where you were earlier,' he added.

I picked up my phone, curious. 'Jamila Khan?' I said. 'It's Detective Inspector Debra Hawkins.'

'You're the person I want to talk to!' It was a young woman's voice. 'I've just got off the phone from my girlfriend. She thinks she saw you today. At her place – the al-Sheiklys' place. With the other cops? Bright pink suit?'

'Go on,' I said, trying to keep the excitement out of my voice. The girl with the haunted eyes wanted to connect with me!

'You're part of some special police unit, aren't you?' Jamila's voice ran on eagerly. 'We heard about it from a multicultural liaison officer. She talked about you too, said you stand out from the other police because you're so tall and stylish – beautiful suits and high heels. My girlfriend is sure it was you she saw outside her brothers' house. Are you the right person to talk to?'

'What's the problem, Jamila?'

'You won't tell anybody that I rang you about this?'

'I don't know what it is yet. But if it's a police matter, I would treat it as confidential.'

After a pause, Jamila continued, 'Like I told that other cop I spoke to first, it's about my friend Rana. I'm really worried about her. Look, could we go somewhere and talk about this privately? I feel awkward talking on the phone like this. To a stranger.'

'You'll need to tell me a little bit more so that I can judge if it's a police matter.'

'What about bashing someone? Locking them in their room for days on end? Not letting them leave the house? Because that's what they're doing to her. And worse. I can prove it.'

'Right. That's criminal behaviour. Where are you calling from?'

'I'm at uni. Sydney Uni.'

'You know the Courtyard Cafe?'

'Sure.'

'Tell me a time that suits you and we'll meet there.' I made a new entry in COPS. Jamila Khan.

'My last tute finishes at four tomorrow. I could be there around four ten, four fifteen?'

'I'll be there.'

'How will I know you?'

'I'll find you,' I said. 'Till then. Courtyard Cafe around four.'

The next morning, I left home early so as to drop by my mother's place on the way to work. I picked up some food from the local deli – three different cheeses, sun-dried tomatoes, some smoked salmon, fresh bread. But when I got to her house I saw that her car wasn't in the carport. She must have driven to work today instead of taking the bus.

I let myself in with my key and walked through the familiar living room with its neat furniture and a large pot of maidenhair ferns translucent green in the sunshine. I felt the strange and lonely sensation that I always experienced when visiting my mother's empty house. After putting the wrapped bread on the breadboard and the other food in the fridge, I went back to the living room and stood a moment, taking it in. Then, idly I went over to the desk in the corner. My mother's laptop was closed and piles of books and papers stood in orderly ranks. A printout on top of one of the piles caught my attention and I smiled – Mum had printed off an interview I'd done with a journalist for the weekend magazine of the newspaper she didn't get, complete with photograph.

Feeling guilty, as though I was intruding, I turned away from my mother's workspace and went over to the elegant china cabinet. On top of the polished cabinet stood some old photographs from Garralong days. I looked closer. In one of these, the three of us stood in a line against the back fence near the lemon tree, squinting in the sun, the contrast sharp on the shadows of our faces. In the photo, I had my head cocked to one side as I awkwardly held our tortoiseshell cat, Maisie; my mother was staring unsmiling at the lens while my father wore his good-natured half-smile and also gazed directly at the camera. I wondered who the photographer had been. Maybe Jenny Trainor from next door. I couldn't tell exactly what year it was, but it wasn't long before my father's death. I felt the haunting sadness that always arose when I looked at images from our past – a mix of sorrow, regret, and something else that I could never quite pin down, a feeling now sharply reawakened by Smiley's email with the crime scene photograph. Something unresolved, unforgiven; a silent cry from deep inside me, that I can never completely ignore.

In my office, I found I had a lot of paperwork to do. Bringing my COPS entries up to date, signing off on jobs done prior to my elevation to this new unit, responding to emails. But my mind kept drifting back to Smiley's email and that strange statement: *There's more to this than meets the eye.*

With a shock I realised that yes, I'd always thought that, too. Smiley had articulated one of my deepest, hidden thoughts.

I emailed Cecile: *How are you going with that Smiley email? I want to know how someone who knows that I'm Peter Hawkins' daughter got hold of a crime scene photograph and sent it to me. And I want to know why. I want that email traced back to its sender. I want that IP address.*

Next I called Newcastle police head office and asked who was best to contact regarding records of police service. I was put through to seven different phone locations until someone finally accepted my query, a Sergeant Daniel Rose. He listened as I explained what I was after.

'It's going to be difficult to locate the exact personnel who went out to a particular crime scene. Not impossible, but it could take time. Give me the location and date of the crime?'

I did so.

'That was the murder of a police officer, wasn't it? Double murder–suicide?'

'Yes, that's right,' I said, feeling more hopeful. At least he'd heard of it.

'We always remember when one of our own gets killed. There've been too many more since then.'

'So you might be able to find out?' I asked.

'Leave it with me.'

'I don't like that phrase, Sergeant Rose. Too many times that's exactly what's happened. The request has just been left there – on someone's desk.'

'Hey, ma'am,' he said, using a title I dislike, 'you can trust me to follow through.'

'It's important.'

'It must be, if you're calling about it.'

Mollified, I left my number with him.

CHAPTER 10

The strong afternoon sunlight of a perfect late-winter day slanted shadows across the lawns as I made my way past the neo-Gothic buildings of Sydney University. Among the students in their jeans, boots and T-shirts, I felt out of place stalking along in my faux-crocodile-skin heels, my aqua suit and fluorite necklace – rough-cut egg-sized chunks that looked like green Arctic ice. Feeling too warm, I pulled the scarf from around my neck. Students hurried to lectures or sat in groups on the lawn, chatting. Three Indonesian girls, wide faces under their hooded hijabs, passed me, laughing.

I found the Courtyard Cafe and picked Jamila Khan immediately. She sat alone at a table, fiddling with her phone, a slight frown on her strong handsome features, flicking back glossy dark hair. With her long legs in tight jeans, a tight striped sweater under her coat and outrageous mauve patent-leather platform heels, she could have been a model. She looked up as I approached, and I noticed her remarkable eyes – large and dark with golden streaks, like highlights on brown velvet, enhanced with black eyeliner. Sitting down opposite her, I introduced myself, passing her my card. She glanced at it then slipped it into her jeans pocket.

'I wasn't sure you'd turn up,' she said, tossing back her thick black hair. 'And I'm really pleased you don't look like a cop.' She made a general flourish in my direction. 'That, and that,' she said, possibly indicating my earrings, suit and chunky necklace.

'What should I have looked like?' I asked, smiling.

Jamila shrugged. 'I sure didn't want anyone I know to see me with a cop. Although the people I'm worried about – well, they'd never come to a university, but they have friends who do. Everybody minds everybody's business around the clock.'

She turned, checking out the other people nearby us. Frowning, she returned her strong gaze to me. 'Can we go somewhere else? Like your car? As long as it's not a cop car.'

'It's not,' I said, standing up. 'Let's get a couple of coffees, and then you can tell me the whole story.'

—•—

As we walked to my car, which was in a lane behind the back of the engineering buildings, each of us carrying a lidded coffee cup, Jamila kept turning to look behind her. When I unlocked the doors she slid into the passenger seat, her long legs in their platform shoes pushing her knees up. After another glance up and down the street, and a swig of coffee, she started to talk, quickly and nervously.

'Rana is my best friend. She's been my best friend since primary school. She's a really great girl. Kind, generous, she'd do anything to help you. But suddenly, I don't see her anymore.'

'Go on,' I said, taking notes.

'Where to begin?' Jamila said. 'It's a long story.'

'Begin at the beginning. I've got the time.'

'Okay,' Jamila said. 'I've known Rana for nearly twelve years. Her father, a brother and an uncle were murdered by Saddam's police. Her mother is still living in Iraq with the other kids. Rana came out here when she was eight with an aunt and two cousins and she's been living with them until last year. But things have changed. Two of Rana's brothers arrived back here early last year.'

I recalled the two men arguing with the detectives outside their damaged house. 'And that's when things began to change?'

'That's right,' she said.

'The brothers started leaning on the girls in the family. That's how it is in Iraq – especially in her family. Men are superior to women. It's in the law and in the religion too. Girls are legally worth only half a male and are raised to be servants to men. To please their husbands. And the women do what they're told, usually.' She laughed. 'Except for girls like me!'

She was suddenly serious again, glancing around, the defiance slipping to reveal the fear that lay beneath the bravado. 'I'm just lucky that my family isn't religious – apart from a few celebrations. My family escaped during Saddam's days too, because the authorities were demanding that anyone employed by the government had to be a member of their Ba'ath party. My father joined up to keep the peace, but it didn't help. One of his brothers was arrested for some offence – we never found out what – and he just disappeared. My father knew it was time to get out. Once a member of a family came to the attention of Saddam's police, the whole family was marked and watched. He managed to bribe the right people and got us all out. Once we got to Australia he commanded my mother and me not to wear hijab. He says he doesn't want any of that primitive religious nonsense in his house. He's almost a total atheist. At first I thought Mum would be relieved not to wear the scarf, but lately I'm not so sure. She's taken to wearing hijab again. They've had a few bad fights about it . . . Dad's still very bossy, ordering us around. But compared to most of them, he's okay.

'It's different for Rana. From the moment her brothers came back, they started heavying her – "protecting her", they called it – and her aunty Sarah and cousins too, telling them what to wear and what not to wear, to stop using make-up, wanting to know everything about where they were going, who they were hanging with. Rana wasn't used to that. She's a good girl – never does anything wrong. She studies most of the time and still manages to do the cooking and washing for the household. She's a great cook, by the way. But once Talal and Samir started in on the family, her aunty Sarah became very nervous and worried about going to hell. She got really religious then and began to cover – you know, wear hijab and all that – and the brothers said that Rana had to do the same as well as leave her aunt's house and come and live with them. They wanted a housekeeper.'

Jamila suddenly ducked further down in the seat, hiding her face behind the dashboard.

'What is it?' I asked.

'Someone who knows my family. She mustn't see me,' she said, slowly unfolding and peeping out. 'She's gone now. If she saw me sitting in a car with a strange woman, she'd want to know what I was doing, who you were.'

'She'd make a good cop,' I tried to joke.

'You wouldn't believe the gossip that goes on. Poor Rana. There were people in our community talking, saying why is that girl living with her cousins and aunty instead of under her own brothers' roof? Why was she cooking and washing for her aunt and her cousins when she should be cooking and washing for her brothers like a good sister? It was shameful for her to be carrying on like that and not under the protection of her brothers.'

'Protection?'

'That's right. Even here in Australia, a lot of the males in our families think they're in charge of the girls. And if the girls look like they're getting too Aussie then everyone starts saying things to the men of the family, like "What's wrong with you? Why can't you control your women? You're letting them run wild! Is your sister a whore!" It reflects badly on them and they feel shamed.' She looked down. 'It's hard for you Aussies to understand. You look at things so differently. Even I can't get rid of some of the religious stuff, and the feeling that you Australians are, well, *inferior*.' Jamila paused and sighed. 'Everything has to look good from the outside. I know you get that sort of thing in a lot of Aussie families too, but it's not like in our families. Not like some of our men. If they feel dishonoured, it's their *women* who have to be stopped doing the things that shame the males. Do you understand that?'

'I think so,' I said. It wasn't the first time I'd had this explained to me – that the women carry the honour of the family and any perceived misbehaviour on their part dishonours all the family. I'd also heard from Maryam, one of our multicultural liaison officers, that migrant men, feeling their age-old authority slipping away in a new, secular country where the legal system was not on their side, often became much more rigorous in their control of the women in their family than they had been before. Unlike the 'old country', in Australia there are no laws concerning 'disobedient' women, nor can women be compelled to domestic servitude – although, I thought, I'd be willing to bet there'd be a lot of men here who'd welcome such laws. In Australia men can be charged with assault or domestic violence if they attempt to 'discipline' their wives or daughters. 'Some men find this very difficult to accept,' the multicultural liaison officer had explained to me. 'So in a country where there is no notion of "disobedient women", let alone a law to keep them in check, some men lose it. The law is not on their side simply because they're male. They've lost their supremacy and the only thing they can stand over are the women of their families. Oh, and you infidels!' She'd smiled. 'So they hang on, tighter than ever.' What I was hearing from Jamila was bringing Maryam's briefing to life. This was Rana's lived experience. It sounded unbearably oppressive.

'Anyway, last year,' Jamila was saying, 'poor Rana was forced to go and live with them at Daylesford. She hated it. She'd been really happy at her aunty Sarah's place and was used to having a lot of fun with her cousins. Going out, doing girlie things – going to the beach, hanging out together. Talal and

Samir started throwing their weight around, telling her what to do, abusing her and calling her ugly names if she didn't obey them. They even tried to take her out of school last year before she finished her HSC, but Rana got the principal to contact them, and one of the community leaders talked to them and they finally agreed to let her finish school.'

Jamila lowered her voice, looking around as if she might be overheard, even here in my car. 'But Rana got a beating for complaining to the principal and bringing shame on the family. The brothers couldn't stand that she was still going to school, and almost every morning there'd be a big fight. But even though all this was happening, she still got brilliant marks in the HSC and she was able to get into Pharmacy here.' Jamila twirled a silky strand of black hair between her fingers before flinging it away from her face. 'I still can't understand why they let her go to university at all.'

I could. I'd already made the connection. Having a pharmacist in the family could be very helpful indeed in the production of illegal drugs.

'But after a while, they said she had to stop going to uni too. They told her she had to study at home. Rana tried to explain to them that she couldn't study Pharmacy from home – she needed to do prac work, she needed access to laboratories. She was so torn. She loves her studies but part of her felt she had to do what her brothers told her. She complained to me about the horrible way they were treating her. She's got a really good mind and she's never been afraid to use it. Don't question, just do what you're told, they say. Rana's always dreamed of running her own business one day. She doesn't want to depend on anyone.

She's got the brains and the ability to do it. She tries to explain to her brothers but they won't listen. They can't hear her. She wants to live her life like other Australian girls, choose her own friends, decide what to wear, go where she wants to, have the friends that she wants to have, choose her studies and have the chance of a profession. What's so wrong with that?'

'Nothing,' I said. 'It's very commendable. Being an adult. Being responsible for your own life. It's called self-determination.'

'Also, there's an Egyptian guy who's been tutoring her and she's pretty interested in him. In fact, I think it's quite serious.'

'What do the brothers think of that?'

Jamila rolled her eyes. 'Oh boy! Don't ask! He's a Copt. A *Christian*. It couldn't be worse!' Taking my frown for ignorance, she explained, 'The Coptic Orthodox Church is the main Christian church in Egypt. But with what's going on there at the moment the Copts are currently an endangered species.'

I knew what she meant. There had been numerous press reports on the persecution of the Copts.

'Just like this guy will be when the brothers find him.'

'Did her aunty Sarah know about the Coptic boy?'

Jamila made a face. 'She just pretended she didn't know – until the brothers arrived. Now Rana can't see him. They've forbidden any further contact. Poor Rana was so confused and distressed. She'd run round to my place and I'd try and comfort her. But I didn't know what to say – how to advise her.'

'What's the name of the Egyptian guy?'

'I only know his first name – Eshaq. Rana was a bit shy about telling me too much. But it was obvious she was seriously interested.'

'Can you tell me anything else about him?' I asked, scribbling down the young man's name.

Jamila thought for a few moments. 'He lives somewhere in Epsom. Sorry, that's really all I know about him. She pointed him out to me once when we were walking across the lawn at uni.' She grinned. 'He's really hot!'

'What's he studying?'

'Chemical Engineering. I think. Not sure.'

'So how are things for Rana now?' I asked.

'They found out she was still attending some lectures and tutorials. They were furious that she was going against their orders. And that's why I rang you. She hasn't been coming to uni for the last few weeks. At first she started making excuses not to go anywhere with me. Before that, we did just about everything together. Finally I made her tell me. I asked, "Why are you avoiding me so much?" She started crying and told me that her brothers had forbidden her to see *me* too. They say they can't accept my family anymore. That we've gone astray, become dirty by mixing with unclean people. Now she's only allowed out to this all-girl gym. She wouldn't be allowed to go there if they knew I went there too. One of the brothers drives her there and then picks her up. I have to sneak in to the gym without them seeing. That's her only chance now to see me. She told me they called me a a whore because I don't cover. She was upset about it but she was scared of them. And that's when I noticed the bruises.'

'Bruises?'

'She was wearing this heavy long-sleeved top on a really warm day when we were working out together last week. I thought it might have been her brothers making her cover up. They were telling her she should cover, telling her that men would rape her if she didn't.' Jamila snorted in contempt. 'You know which country has one of the highest number of rapes? Saudi Arabia! Where all the women are covered in those black shrouds!' Another quick glance around and Jamila leaned back in the seat, apparently becoming more at ease.

'The bruises,' I reminded her.

'It was in the change room afterwards, I saw all these bruises on her back, on her arms. Then I couldn't call her anymore. When I rang her, one of the brothers always answered and said she wasn't there. Then he'd hang up.'

'Rana needs to make a statement,' I said. 'Then we can proceed. First we can send in one of the MCLOs —'

'What are they?'

'Liaison officers specialising in multicultural issues. We could get a female liaison officer to contact her.'

'No!' The fear in Jamila's voice was palpable. 'That would be too dangerous for her! Talal will want to know who this strange woman is coming round knocking on the door or calling her. And if she won't even talk to me, why would she talk to some woman she hasn't met before? They mustn't know I'm talking to you – to the police. That could make everything worse. Anyway, you'd have to get a search warrant because they wouldn't let anybody inside the house. You mustn't do anything like that! Don't you understand? You don't know what Talal is like. He's the one in charge – Samir just does what he's told. Together, they're bad news.'

I thought quickly. 'Jamila, we can manage this very discreetly. One of the MCLOs is really good. She knows everything about everybody. She can make discreet enquiries around the community and find out what's going on with Rana and the brothers.'

'She'll have to be careful. There's no privacy, no secrets. Everyone gossips about everyone. Everyone keeps an eye on everyone to make sure they're not having any fun. Or talking to someone they shouldn't.' Jamila's voice was bitter and her well-formed mouth hardened. Again she made her quick survey, and sinking low in the seat she frowned at a group of women students walking past. One of the group turned back and stared at me. I hoped it was because of my fabulous fluorite ice cubes. Jamila waited until the coast was clear before straightening up again.

With skilful Maryam in mind, I attempted to reassure Jamila. 'I think we can manage this in a sensitive way. The MCLO I'm talking about is very smart and I know that she'd find the right people and that she'd do it in a way that wouldn't arouse any suspicion that we were even interested in Rana or her brothers. We've done it successfully before.'

'Are you sure?'

I remembered a case from last year, when I was with MEOCS; with the help of the Domestic Violence Squad we'd been able to get a woman to a refuge, almost from under the nose of her violent husband. 'I'm sure,' I said. 'We have resources that we can bring to bear on the brothers. That way, Rana stays in the background while we gather more intelligence about what might be happening in that household. And then, when the time is right, we'll pounce. Okay?'

Jamila crushed her coffee cup and looked around for somewhere to put it. I indicated the hanging plastic bag attached to the glove box and she pushed it in, then leaned back, flicking her hair over her shoulders. 'That might work. Especially if the MCLO wears a headscarf.'

'She will. She always does,' I said.

I checked that I had all the information I needed – Rana's phone number, Jamila's address and number.

'But be careful about trying to call her,' Jamila said. 'The brothers might have her phone. If they answer it, she'll be in trouble.'

'We'll find a time when the brothers are out of the house,' I said. 'Don't worry. We'll be careful. I know how dangerous this could be for Rana.'

Jamila nodded, looking around again before opening the car door and getting out. She leaned down and spoke through the window. 'Please be quick. I think I know what's going on in that house. I'm frightened for my friend.'

'What about you, Jamila?' I asked. 'Are you going to be okay?'

'Me? I'm fine. I know how to look after myself.'

'I'll drive you home,' I offered.

'Better not,' she said. 'Arriving home in a strange car with a strange woman could raise a few questions. It's just easier if I keep to my routine. Thanks anyway.' She hurried away and turned at the corner to wave at me.

—•—

I drove off thinking about how it had taken women in our society many centuries to finally free themselves from the oppression of the Church and the patriarchy but that even now there were times when I felt its weight. Everyone spoke about self-determination as a necessary condition for human dignity, and yet Jamila had just presented me with information about a young woman whose male relatives were bent on denying her this very right – something I'd taken for granted all my life.

On the drive home, I noticed in the rear-view mirror a car that I'd also seen the previous day – a dark green Subaru. I'd noticed it the day before because of its custom-made chrome roof racks. And here it was again. Coincidence? Or someone smitten by my stunning beauty and tailing me to ask for a date? The paranoid police officer in me didn't think so. I checked the rear-vision mirror again and tried to see the driver but it was impossible to see through the tinted glass. I called Alex on the handsfree. 'Check this rego for me?' I gave him the details. 'I think someone's following me.'

He called back a few moments later. 'Car registered to George Hakan. Associate of Adam Massoud.'

A chill went over me. 'Thanks, Alex.'

I made a sudden left-hand turn without indicating and was satisfied to see the Subaru shoot straight past. I told myself it was just a bit of intimidation. Two days running. If I saw that car again, I'd get it stopped and make some problems happen for George Hakan.

With Adam Massoud again in the forefront of my mind, I walked around when I got home, checking locks and making sure everything was secured. I turned on the television after dinner and felt a small sense of satisfaction at the news of the arrest of a standover man in Bankstown. I recognised his name from my days in MEOCS. He'd been charged with extorting money with menaces – in this case a firearm – from Shia-run businesses in what he fancied was 'his area'. 'Nice little place you got here,' I imagined him saying, Mafioso-style, as he looked around the juice bar. 'Too bad if anything happened to it . . .'

Good that he was off the street. It was a start.

CHAPTER 11

When I woke up to see sunlight streaming into my bedroom, for a second I felt my spirits rise. But then everything came flooding back in – the green Subaru, Rana al-Sheikly and Kylie Mifsud, and the strange, unsettling Smiley email.

As soon as I got to work I called Andrew Jacobsen, my former colleague at MEOCS. Andrew was an exact contemporary of mine: we'd gone through the academy together. He was a family man who loved boating and growing exotic cactus plants. He had been very active in slowing down the assaults by violent gangs who had terrorised Sydney in the late '90s into 2000, when shootouts in the street created scenes that resembled Hollywood westerns. Police had arrested hundreds of people and finally broke the power of the Karam and Kanaan gangs. But there's always an understudy waiting in the wings, and other violent men stepped into the crime vacuum created when these groups were taken down. The violence on Sydney streets worsened. Police radio channels were penetrated and threats made against individual police and their families. Citizens who accidentally walked into the line of fire were murdered, including a fifteen-year-old boy whose only mistake had been knocking on the wrong door. Massive police operations, reminding residents of military actions, with hundreds of police and members of the State Protection Group supported by helicopters, finally broke up the worst of the crime gangs. But in time they regrouped.

'I want the al-Sheikly brothers,' I said to Andrew. 'I want to know exactly what they're up to.' I explained about my concerns for their sister.

'Not sure we've got much hard stuff on them,' he said. 'Their names have come up a couple of times. They've been implicated in dealing in precursor chemicals and have used their premises as a drop point for the merchandise and the deals. More recently they've been connected by phone calls to a group that's being watched on account of a terrorism link.'

'Terrorism?' I said, surprised.

'That's right. The informant mentioned a sale of weapons to someone ASIO's had on a watch list. The al-Sheiklys were visited on several occasions by this particular individual. The feds had someone in place across the road from their garage, keeping an eye on the comings and goings there, recording rego numbers. Might have just been dropping in for a cup of tea, but somehow I don't think so.'

'The feds won't appreciate us moving in on their operation,' I said. There was often rivalry between the Commonwealth and state authorities, disagreements over turf and who was responsible for various parts of sometimes very complex joint operations – especially when the honours were being handed out after a successful bust.

'I've already spoken to them about this,' Andrew was saying. 'They're not interested in the al-Sheiklys at this stage. They're focused on getting the names of the people who use the garage as a meeting and trading place.'

'So we can have the al-Sheikly boys all to ourselves? Lucky us. I'd like to pay them a visit.'

'I'll organise a car and get back to you as soon as I can,' said Andrew.

For the next hour I worked at my desk, trying to keep on top of the new information, entering data concerning Jamila Khan into COPS; the notes I'd made about Rana al-Sheikly and her brothers went into my duty book, where they'd stay until such time as we had official dealings with them, when they too would be entered into the COPS system.

Andrew got back to me an hour later. 'Are you free to visit the al-Sheikly brothers? I've got a car. I'll pick you up.'

'Great. Just a nice friendly visit, to introduce myself,' I said. 'All good PR work – the human face of policing. Getting to know our local community.'

'Oh, sure.' Andrew chuckled.

———

The al-Sheiklys' engineering shop and garage was a long warehouse-style shopfront in a narrow lane about three streets parallel to the main highway. Above the almost fully opened roller door, a sign proclaimed: *Sheikly Motor Repairs.*

We pulled over and parked directly across the road from the garage. We wanted to be obvious. People would talk, and soon everybody in the community would know that the al-Sheikly brothers' engineering shop had been the subject of a police visit. This would make everyone uneasy, not just the al-Sheikly boys. Their criminal contacts would want to know what was going on – what did the cops want? Had the al-Sheiklys said anything that might bring police interest to bear on their own underworld pursuits? Were the al-Sheiklys turning informers? It would seed disquiet.

As Andrew and I stepped out of the police car, I was pleased that I was wearing my cyclamen-pink suit and reproduction eighteenth-century Portuguese gold-drop earrings. We strolled across the road.

'Good morning, gentlemen,' I said cheerily, ignoring the baleful stare from the older man and noting with some satisfaction that in my heels I was several centimetres taller than he was. 'So how's business?'

'What do you want?' Talal asked, watching us narrowly.

'Just a friendly visit, Mr al-Sheikly.'

His face, closed and suspicious, hardened even further at that. A heavy moustache arched over a sour mouth.

'Detective Inspector Debra Hawkins,' I introduced myself. 'I'm part of the police effort to maintain positive and helpful relations with the community. Any problems, you can call Andrew here. Or me.'

Andrew passed the man his card.

Andrew, his eyes everywhere, walked slowly beside me through the open roller door and into the wide, cold space, which reeked of engine oil and hot metal. Several cars in various states of disassembly stood around, one on a hoist, and the area was littered with car parts.

'You can't come in like this,' said Talal. 'You need a warrant.'

'Is that what you say to all your customers?' I asked. 'Surely that can't be good for business.'

'So why are you here? What are you after?' His scowling features crowded tighter together in a suspicious frown.

'Just making sure everything is okay here,' I said. 'Just some community outreach.'

'That's right,' said Andrew, peering at some paperwork on a bench strewn with engine parts and tools.

'We got work to do,' said Talal, rubbing his hands on a dishcloth and snatching the paperwork off the bench. 'You can't go poking your noses in. This is private property. Got a warrant?' he repeated.

'Why?' asked Andrew. 'Do you think we might need one?'

'You gotta have a reason.'

'Just checking out a rumour,' said Andrew. 'Someone from the Khaybar Riders passed on something they'd heard about Sheikly Motor Repairs. Some unusual sales, not exactly related to motor vehicles. Can you tell us what that might be all about?'

The brothers exchanged a quick glance. 'Lies,' said Talal. 'They lie. Who is saying this?'

'That's confidential police business,' I said, thinking Sami Allen of the Khaybar Riders would be the victim of a drive-by shooting or worse if the brothers ever found out the source of our information. 'Why?' I continued. 'Are you worried that we might find something here?' I looked around the crowded space and noticed a bright red Toyota Hilux on a hoist, its bumper smashed. 'Nice ute. What happened?'

'We don't ask. We just fix them.'

'I'll make a note of its registration,' I said, jotting it down in my small notebook. 'Just in case we can assist you in any way.' I picked up a business card for the garage that was lying on a bench. 'Okay,' I said, nodding at Andrew then smiling broadly at the two brothers, 'thanks for the conversation.'

'Conversation . . .' Talal growled, curling his lip.

'Thanks for your help,' I said with another bright smile. 'Lovely to meet you both.'

I passed Andrew the business card then got back into the car. 'Nice pair of blokes,' I commented. 'They looked a bit worried when you mentioned the Khaybar Riders informant.'

Andrew was busy with his smartphone and the business card then as he began to drive back to drop me off at the office, he glanced over at me. 'I've connected to a program that'll watch Talal al-Sheikly's mobile number. It'll be interesting to see what numbers he calls and who calls him.' This program would log all phone calls made and received, and the details of those who made them, gradually building up a web of interconnected callers and businesses, revealing a map of potential and actual criminal activity.

'Let me know what you find,' I said, thinking of Rana al-Sheikly living with her two brothers, frightened, alone and increasingly cut off from any outside contacts. 'I'm going to apply for a warrant for covert listening on their home landline as well. I want to know what's going on in that house.'

Andrew dropped me back at the office, where I typed up the application that I hoped would convince a judge to authorise remote listening to the al-Sheikly brothers' mobiles, saying we had strong reasons to suspect illegal drug dealing at the address. I was entering our recent interaction with the brothers into the COPS system when Cecile rang.

'Your mate Smiley,' she said. 'I should have a result on him soon. Sorry about the delay. Let's meet for dinner. You won't be so available when Mark gets back.'

'What's up?' I asked, hearing something wobbly in her voice.

'I saw Karl today with someone else.'

'But Cecile, you broke up with him,' I reminded her.

'Only two weeks ago.'

'Male resilience,' I said.

'Male bastardry. I can't believe it. I'll bet he had her all lined up before I kicked him out.'

'It's called insurance. Sounds as though we'll be needing a drink. When do you want to do dinner?' We organised to meet that night at one of our favourite Malaysian restaurants.

—·—

With Rana al-Sheikly very much in my mind, after a quick lunch I drove to Sydney University and tracked down the office of the Faculty of Engineering. I flashed my warrant card at the woman behind the reception desk. 'I'm trying to get in touch with a young man who I believe is enrolled here in Chemical Engineering,' I told her. 'But unfortunately I only have a first name – Eshaq.'

The woman looked concerned. 'He's not in any trouble,' I hastened to add. 'We believe he can help us with an enquiry.'

'Just a moment.' She went into a back office and came back a minute later with an older woman.

'You want to see our records?' the older woman asked.

'It's important that I speak to Eshaq,' I explained. 'It's a police matter involving the safety of a young woman.'

'All right,' she said. 'I'll run a search of that name.' She disappeared back through the door and returned a few moments later waving a piece of paper. 'Here he is. Eshaq Boutros. Final year Chemical Engineering.'

'Thanks,' I said.

As I left the building I punched the supplied phone number into my mobile. A woman with a heavy accent answered. I identified myself and asked, 'Mrs Boutros? Is your son there, Eshaq?'

'No, no. Not here.' I could hear the fear in her low voice.

'Please ask him to contact me. Everything's okay. We just want to talk with him.' I gave her my mobile number. 'It's urgent.'

'Is it about that girl? Rana?'

'You know her?' I asked, surprised.

'Eshaq likes her. But she brings many problems to us. We come to Australia to get away from these people – these problems – but we find them here in Australia as well.' Mrs Boutros rang off.

So, Eshaq's family didn't like the idea of Rana and Eshaq together either. Romeo and Juliet in the twenty-first century, I thought. I hoped this couple would have a happier ending.

While I was on campus, I found my way to the students' counselling service offices and, after showing my badge, asked if Rana al-Sheikly had accessed their services. The woman checked her records and shook her head. No one of that name was registered with them, she said.

The minute I got back into my car, my mobile rang. I grabbed it, hoping it might be Eshaq. It was Charlie. 'Slight problem,' she said. 'We've lost Kylie Mifsud.'

'What do you mean, *lost*?'

'One of the local uniforms checked in on her at her latest friend's place. Kylie wasn't there. The friend said she went out yesterday and didn't come back.'

'Great.' Frustration welled up. I banged the steering wheel.

'I already checked with her family. She hasn't contacted them. They've rung around her friends and no one's heard from her.'

Kylie had vanished on my watch. She should have let me know if she was leaving town. I found her number and called it but could only leave a message asking her to call me urgently.

I drove back to the office and put out an alert to all cars and stations about police concerns regarding Kylie Mifsud, together with her description. I hoped Kylie would be all right, that she hadn't been attacked or abducted but had just found another safe place to hide.

Next I called the best MCLO on the job. Maryam, a Syrian woman who'd lived both in Egypt and Iraq, had worked for us as a multicultural liaison officer for four years now and was smart and savvy. She had a great laugh and a guileless manner that put people at ease. I could sense her listening intently as I briefly outlined Rana al-Sheikly's predicament.

'No good, no good,' she said when I'd finished talking. 'These men. They think they own us. Like their cars. Just drive around wherever they want and then lock up in the garage. "You're in a good country," I tell them, "and that is not the way to treat your family here." But of course they don't listen to me.'

'I've met the al-Sheikly brothers,' I added, 'and the older one, Talal, is a nasty piece of work. The other one seems to be his shadow.'

'You leave it with me,' said Maryam after I'd given her Rana's address and phone number. 'I'll have a talk to some people I know. I'll let you know what's going on. I work out a way we can meet up with Rana. Okay?'

'Okay. Thanks, Maryam. It's urgent.'

—

Cecile had a distinctive style of dressing that always looked very sharp on her, part goth, part Gucci. Dark colours enhanced her pale skin and large dark grey eyes. She was also quite eccentric in her dressing, often choosing clothes that reflected the state of her heart – red lipstick and a pink blouse with love hearts when she believed she'd found a good man.

It was all goth and no Gucci tonight, I noted as I walked into the restaurant and hurried across to the table where my friend waited. Her long black hair framed either side of the pale face she lifted to greet me. I slid into the chair opposite, noticing the black lace mittens she was wearing.

'Widow's weeds,' she explained, seeing my raised eyebrow. 'I'm in mourning.'

'Not for Karl, surely? Maybe a little colour would lift your spirits?' I suggested. 'I'll bet you're not hungry either.'

'No appetite. That's one of the good things about breaking up. I've already lost a kilo.'

'Tell me some other good things,' I said, nodding to the waitress to indicate that we were ready. We always ordered the same things whenever we came here – Cecile had king prawn sambal, very hot, and I had prawn laksa, medium. The waitress noted down our orders as Cecile poured us each a glass of wine from the bottle she'd brought.

'Okay, let me think . . .' said Cecile once the waitress had gone. 'Reading late in bed without him grizzling, having a bath without him trying to jump in with me . . .'

'Oh, cute,' I said.

'No. Tidal wave.' She added, 'Debs. I really miss him.'

'You want to talk about it? About what happened?'

We'd talked a lot about Karl the financier over the last few dying months of the relationship. Finally, two weeks ago, Cecile had given him an ultimatum concerning marriage and children and he'd packed his things and left.

She shook her head. 'Talking about it keeps the pain fresh. I'd rather just forget him. He's somebody else's problem now.'

'Good,' I said, as she pulled off the black lace mittens. 'Looks like you're coming out of the grieving cycle?'

'I move fast,' she agreed as our meals arrived. I spread my napkin wide to protect my suit from splashes.

'So, the mysterious Smiley,' Cecile began, after dealing with a king prawn. 'I've tracked down the computer he used. Here are the details.' She passed me some printed numbers. 'The terminal is one of the public computers at Broadway Library.'

I felt a small thrill of excitement. Smiley, I've got you. To access the internet, library users need a library card – with a phone number and a name. 'Great work, Cecile. I'll drop by Broadway Library tomorrow. I really want to know how he got hold of a police photograph.'

'He could be a policeman,' said Cecile, pulling the head off another prawn. 'That's the simple answer.'

'It's not that easy,' I said. 'I'll need to know exactly who took those photographs that morning in 1992. It was most likely someone who came up from Newcastle with the Homicide detectives. Or their photographic unit. Back in the old days when everything was shot on film.' I put down my fork, considering. 'There's another thing. Even though it's completely against the rules, some cops when they retire take their favourite briefs with them – or pinch copies of the photographs. Especially cases they've worked on, cases where they got a conviction they're particularly attached to. They feel they "own" them. One guy I knew of took his pet brief when he retired and hid it in his chook house.'

'Sounds like you'll need to find the old brief.'

I sighed. 'I could find out who was in Photographic at that time, if they're still with us. But they mightn't be around anymore.'

'Then Smiley will just have to tell you where he got the photograph from.'

I nodded.

'*There's more to this than meets the eye,*' Cecile quoted. 'Smiley enjoys being cryptic. It's intriguing.'

'It's supposed to be. Someone's pointing me towards that night, trying to make me re-examine the case, and I want to know why.'

Cecile fiddled with a prawn before looking up and fixing me with her serious grey eyes. 'You know, Deb, there's something I want to say, but it's not easy. I know this is a huge issue for you but I sometimes can't help wondering if you'll be okay . . .'

'Okay about what?' I frowned.

Cecile looked uncomfortable.

'Go on,' I said. 'Say it. I can see there's something on your mind.'

Cecile sighed and poked at her sambal. 'Debs, what if your father *did* blunder into it? Are you prepared to accept that possibility? People stuff up all the time. What if you find that your father stuffed up too? Are you going to be okay with that?'

'I've thought of that. I can live with that. But this is something else.'

Cecile waited and finally I continued, 'That night in the car, something happened – something between me and my father – and it still haunts me. He was his normal self – slightly irritated because I was making him late for work by needing to go back home and get a coat. But then once I'd got back into the car, everything changed. He seemed to look right through me, as if I were – I don't know – some grotesque changeling or something. He was furious.'

Cecile looked perplexed. 'Do you think he had some sort of premonition? Is that what you're suggesting?'

I shook my head. 'I just don't know. All I know is that I'd never seen my father in that mood before. Something was terribly wrong. And then a few hours after that, he walks straight into Frank Davidson's .303.'

I could see Cecile was trying hard to make sense of what I was saying. After a silence, she spoke gently. 'Debs, I think it's the guilt – the guilt of a little girl who thinks that she had something to do with the death of her beloved father. I think it's the guilt that keeps you hanging on. I think you should give yourself a break – let yourself off the hook.'

Complicated grief, I thought, remembering what my mother had said. 'Maybe you're right.'

'So,' she went on, 'how's work? Bet you're pleased you're out of MEOCS. They've sure got their work cut out for them. One of the partners at work was saying how the outlaw motorcycle gangs are now huge international corporations with wealth estimated at billions of dollars, and growing. Local chapters joining up with groups like the US Mongols. Whenever they're charged, they can afford to hire the very best lawyers and barristers. The fear is that they could grow as big and as dangerous as the Mafia in Europe.'

'Let's hope it doesn't come to that.'

'They're not afraid to use violence to get what they want,' she said, fishing around for another prawn.

'Violence is a great force multiplier,' I agreed. 'It tends to discourage resistance.'

Cecile had tried to change the subject, but I couldn't get her earlier words out of my mind. Was I obsessed with the past? Was my mother right about this after all?

The question teased me for the rest of dinner and all the way home.

At least there was no green Subaru around tonight.

CHAPTER 12

In the morning I called Broadway Library. A woman who identified herself as Catherine answered, and I told her who I was and that a computer at the library had been used to send an anonymous email.

'Oh, I hope it's not a criminal matter,' she said, sounding alarmed.

'I don't think so,' I said. 'It's more of a security issue. Some material was sent that shouldn't be in the public domain. I'm trying to track down who might have sent it so we can discover where the leak began. I'll drop by and have a look at your system this morning. Is there some way of finding out who used the computer to send this email?'

Forty minutes later I was at Broadway Library, tucked around a corner not far from Central. I parked in the lane that formed one side of the block and walked into the bright, spacious interior.

Catherine, a slight woman who wore her dark hair parted in the middle and whose brilliant silk patterned trousers and tunic reminded me of the way Chinese women dressed in the nineteenth century, hurried over. 'I saw you on television a month or so ago,' she said, smiling. 'Standing next to the commissioner?'

I nodded. There had been a press conference to announce new policing methods. Catherine and I shook hands and she took me to the corner of the library where several computers sat along a table beneath a sign that read, *Library card holders only, thank you.*

'Our logging system isn't forensically accurate,' she said with an apologetic smile. 'We really only keep it to ensure that nobody hogs the internet all day. I've narrowed it down to the time you indicated.' She led me to the last workstation. 'This is the computer in question. You need a card to log on, and we keep records of who's using the computers.'

'So you'd know who was using it when the email was sent?' This is too easy, I thought.

'It's not a very rigid system, I'm afraid. There's a half-hour time limit during busy times and an hour limit when the demand is less. There's a fancy way of printing off the information from the computers themselves – they record the details of the library card used. But we don't use that, we just use this stone-age booking system.' Catherine showed me the library card numbers that had been written into the time slots for 22–23 August. 'This is the person who was using the computer at that time on that date.'

'This is great,' I said, taking the booking record from her. 'You would have made a great detective.' I paused. 'So, who was it?'

Catherine turned to the computer on her desk and called up the library's record of borrowers. 'The person you're looking for is Frida Ekstrom.' She must have noticed the look on my face. 'That's right. Looks like she's a backpacker. Staying at this address.' Catherine wrote down *Beachside Backpackers Hostel* with its address near Bondi.

That couldn't be right, I thought – a backpacker with a crime scene photograph from 1992?

'I should tell you,' Catherine said, 'these kids lend each other their library cards all the time, or pass on their card to someone else when they leave Sydney.' She paused. 'I checked her borrowing over the last month. She's only taken DVDs and some CDs. They've all been returned.'

I thanked Catherine for her time and then drove away from the city towards the eastern suburbs, where I found a lucky park in one of the streets west of Bondi Beach. I hurried around to the hostel. At the reception desk I flashed my warrant card and asked after Frida Ekstrom, but drew a complete blank. Frida Ekstrom was long gone, no doubt moving on weeks ago. No one had any idea about what had happened to her library card. I called Catherine at the library and asked about CCTV. Erased and recorded over every twenty-four hours, she said.

I drove back to work with a lot on my mind. I'd wasted the better part of the morning running into a dead end.

—•—

Gavin Bailey was waiting for me. He didn't look well. I knew he was under a lot of pressure these days.

'A word, please, Debra,' he said, ushering me into my office. 'I went looking for you, and put my head around your door. I noticed this on your desk.' He indicated the crime scene photograph I'd printed off the Smiley email. 'It appears to be from the scene of your father's death.'

Damn, I thought, annoyed with myself for forgetting to push the printout under some papers. 'That's right,' I said cautiously. 'I've had an email from an anonymous source – someone calling themselves Smiley – and this photograph was in the body of it.'

'Where did they get it from?'

'I can't work that out until I find out who Smiley is. That's what I've been trying to figure out this morning. But I reached a dead end.' I told him about my trip to Broadway Library and the backpacker.

Gavin drummed his fingers on my desk as he does when he's thinking. 'I don't want you wasting time on this, Debra.' He went to the door of my office, closed it gently, and turned back to face me. 'Anonymous contacts can be helpful, I know, in our line of work. But not in this case. I think you really need to let go of this ancient history.'

He walked to the far wall of my office and back, deep in thought. 'You know what I think? Someone – probably an old retired detective with nothing better to do, and missing the glory days – has dug out a brief and wants to feel important again. So he's discovered that you're the daughter of Peter Hawkins and somehow he's got his hands on a photograph he shouldn't have, and he's sent this email to hook you in.' His voice was stern. 'And it's worked, hasn't it?'

'With all due respect, sir, that doesn't make sense. If it's someone who misses his glory days, why would he be hanging back and staying anonymous? Isn't it more likely he'd be jumping up and down saying, "Look at me!" If he genuinely thought there was more to my father's death than was discovered at the time, he'd contact me personally. He'd want to see me, talk to me. He'd want to be involved again, not hide away behind a silly nickname.'

Gavin sighed. 'I can see I'm going to have to be more brutal. I'm ordering you to stop this, Debra. It's a waste of police time. You've got a huge amount on your plate and you have to make this new unit work. My reputation hangs on it too, okay? I recommended you – I spoke on your behalf. I don't want half your mind and energy distracted by pointless investigations of a case that happened back in the past and was successfully brought to a conclusion.'

I knew he had a point. 'Okay. I'll drop it.'

'Thank you.' He walked out the door and I watched him leave. I made a cup of coffee in the poky meal room, then carried it back into my office. I pulled up the email on my screen again, taking one more look at the photograph before I deleted it.

My hand hesitated on the mouse.

I couldn't delete it.

I'd told Gavin that I'd drop it, but even if I did – even if I tried hard to do as he'd ordered me – I knew that Smiley and his cryptic statement would stay in my mind, percolating, raising questions.

Even if I dropped Smiley, I knew that Smiley wouldn't drop me.

I was searching for the phone number of Kylie Mifsud's mother when a call from Maryam interrupted me. A short time later she appeared at the door of my office. As soon as I saw the concerned expression on her face, I asked, 'Rana?'

Maryam came in, speaking quickly. 'We've got to talk to that girl, Debra. Do something for her. I spoke with some of the women in the community and it's bad. Her brothers heard about the Egyptian boy. They're going to send her back to Iraq to marry a cousin. Keep her on the right path. A proper wedding to protect her from going astray and bringing shame to the family.' Maryam shrugged. 'And it keeps property in the family. Works for everyone.'

'Except the bride.' I got to my feet. 'She'll need a new passport. She'll have to go for an Immigration interview somewhere – the brothers will have to let her out for that. We can try to get her away then.' I was suddenly charged with anger. 'Why don't we just kick their door in and arrest them for deprivation of liberty? This is Australia, not some hellhole in Pakistan!'

'Better not do that, I think. Because it will not be helpful. We need smart and sneaky.'

I knew Maryam was right. I couldn't let anger and frustration cloud my judgement.

'This needs careful handling,' she went on. 'Rana is a good girl. She wants to do the right thing, to please her family, her brothers. We need to hear from her, get her response, yes?'

'I understand,' I said. 'Once you kick that door in, there's no smart and sneaky.' Smart and sneaky sounded good.

'You'll see,' said Maryam. 'We will make a plan.'

I sat down again. 'I need to know the minute Rana is out of that house. I'll get someone to watch it.'

No sooner had Maryam left the room than my mobile chimed. 'Yes?' I said, picking it up.

'It's me.'

My heart sank. I couldn't believe it. I needed time to think about how to deal with my brother. 'Brad,' I said, 'I'll call you back, okay?'

I heard his sharp intake of breath before he said, 'Don't bother,' and rang off.

I hung up and leaned back in my seat. That's all I needed. My crazy brother.

I would ring Brad back, I decided, but not just yet. I needed to cool down.

—•—

I drove to the al-Sheikly garage and parked some way down the road. I could only see the younger brother, bending over a car engine. There was no sign of Talal. He could be back at the house or out on criminal business, I thought. I drove away, heading for the house, and within a few minutes I was parked some distance away and across the road from it. The bullet-ridden glass had already been replaced and the blinds were drawn. The garage door was closed and nothing was parked in front of it. It was possible that Talal was in the house, and Rana was almost certainly inside. I got out of the car, mentally working out the script I'd use if Talal was at home.

I crossed the road briskly and stepped up to the entrance, trying to see through the amber glass panel on each side of the front door. Nothing moved inside. Not satisfied, I walked down the narrow corridor between the al-Sheikly house and next door's

Colorbond fence. All the windows were closed and the blinds were drawn. What if Talal had already taken Rana away and I was too late to help her?

By now I'd come to the last window on the side of the house, and that was when I heard it – the sound of a girl sobbing. The window was barely open, just a small opening at the bottom and top for air. Thick bars kept thieves out and people in, but a gap in the heavy curtains allowed me to get a glimpse into the room. The sobs continued and I knocked softly on the glass. Immediately, the sound ceased. I hoped I hadn't frightened her.

I drew back as the curtain moved slightly and Rana al-Sheikly appeared at the window. My anger surged again as I saw her black eye and the bruising around the left side of her mouth. Shocked, scared eyes stared out of her pale face. When she saw me, she didn't seem surprised but quickly put a finger to her lips. She wasn't alone in the house.

'Just play along,' I whispered into the gap in the window. 'Keep yourself safe. Pretend to agree to do what they want.' I wasn't sure if she'd taken in what I said, because she vanished, then reappeared moments later to pass a folded piece of paper out through the bars. I took it just before a loud voice yelled through the house and Rana ducked away, closing the curtain.

I didn't want to risk Talal seeing me leave, so, using an upturned planter box, I climbed over the Colorbond fence and dropped down into next door's garden.

'Sorry,' I said to the startled elderly lady who was watering her pot plants. 'Police.' I opened my warrant wallet.

'Oh,' she said with a puzzled frown. 'I was expecting the plumber.'

Back in my car, I read the note that Rana had written. *Please help me. I'm locked in the house all the time. I have to marry my 47-year-old cousin in Iraq. It's all been organised. I can't. I won't. They've threatened to kill me if I don't agree.* The last scribbled sentence was heavily underlined.

I read it again, and then a third time. I was reading it for the fourth time when my mobile rang. It was Socrates.

'Just letting you know that we've sent the first lot of material from Talal al-Sheikly's mobile off to the translator,' he said. 'Some of the texts are encrypted but that shouldn't be too difficult to get through. My mate at the Drug Squad is matching up some phone numbers for me.'

'I'm actually sitting up the road from the house right now,' I said. 'And Rana al-Sheikly has written me a note.' I read it to Socrates.

'That sounds bad,' he said. 'We've got laws against this. There's no way Rana can be forced to marry against her will.'

The brothers hadn't taken much notice of the law so far, I thought.

I called a contact in Immigration. Rana al-Sheikly didn't have a passport. We had some time. I had to find a way to talk with her without her brothers knowing so we could work out a plan to get her away.

And I wanted to get enough evidence on the al-Sheikly brothers to have them arrested, no-bailed and locked up.

CHAPTER 13

We spent time doing just that. The Cellebrite program produced more connections between the al-Sheikly mobile phones and other criminal groups. Remote listening on mobile phones and phone tapping of landlines gathered yet more material to be sent to the translators. All the time this was going on, other units such as the Drug Squad, the Gang Squad, MEOCS and various strike forces had their data crunched by criminal intelligence analysts. Information started building. We almost had the goods on the brothers al-Sheikly.

I visited my mother, bringing fruit, milk and the sourdough loaf she liked, and found that her leg injury was healing slowly.

I called Jamila. 'I need your help, Jamila. To find out when Rana's immigration interview is.'

'Please, don't contact me again,' she said. 'Just don't.'

I was alarmed. This wasn't the feisty rebel I had met at Sydney

University; I could hear the fear in her voice. 'What's happened?' I asked.

'One of the al-Sheikly brothers came round to our place and threatened my little sister and my mum. He even scared my father. He said I'm to keep away from Rana or else something might happen to them . . . If he even suspected I'd been talking to you, I don't know what might happen.'

'Jamila,' I said, 'you can take action against him. We have laws against intimidation and making threats.'

'Laws! What use is a law when someone is coming at you with their fist? Or knocking on the door and when you open it, *bang*!? Laws. Don't make me laugh.'

Before I could argue, she'd rung off.

—•—

By Monday, phone intercepts revealed what Jamila wasn't willing to discover – that Rana would be going to the post office in the mall for a passport interview the next day. Naturally, one of the brothers would accompany her, but this was our only chance to get her aside and talk to her.

'It's got to be done in such a way that he'll never know that Rana and I have been talking. We need to keep the situation under close supervision.'

Charlie waited while I called Maryam and told her I had a plan. She listened as I explained what I needed from her.

—•—

Around ten o'clock the next morning, Charlie called in from where she was sitting off the al-Sheikly house. 'Nothing happening yet,' she said. 'The brothers went out briefly but they're home now. I got a glimpse of Rana in the front room.' The room in which I'd first seen her, her hand pressed up against the glass, her eyes pleading, despairing.

I had already arrived at the mall when Charlie rang, and had checked in with the manager. I now had the key to a small utility room not far from the post office. I'd checked it out the day before: it would be perfect for what I had in mind. I located myself just off the mall's wide main thoroughfare not far from the post office shop in a short passage that ran off it, housing the toilets and the utility room. From this position, I was reasonably hidden from view, but still able to see the passers-by.

As always before an operation, I was nervous, edgy. The minutes went past. What if they didn't come? What if they fled, hiding Rana, and we never saw her again?

I jumped when Charlie rang back. 'Ladyhawk and the old gaoler are on their way. Copy, boss?'

'Gotcha, Charlie. Standing by.'

Fifteen minutes later, I saw them coming up the escalators, Rana al-Sheikly standing a little behind Talal, dressed in an elegant trouser suit with a scarf around her neck, the greenish hue around her left eye a memento of the assault she'd endured before. In that moment, I hated Talal al-Sheikly, as he swaggered off the escalator, scowling around at Rana, who followed him, head bowed. I had to remind myself that I was a professional and that it was essential I keep my emotions out of this. I waited for Charlie to arrive and implement our plan.

I watched as Rana joined the long queue that reached the door of the post office shop while Talal propped himself against the counter of an eatery on the other side of the mall, lighting up a cigarette as he ordered something and talked with the proprietor.

I stiffened as I saw Charlie coming up the escalator. She threw me a quick glance and I texted her: *He's in cafe opposite.*

After looking at her phone, Charlie walked quickly towards him. She pulled out her warrant card and engaged Talal in conversation. I could see him bristling, and for a moment I thought he was actually going to push her. He threw down his cigarette and stamped on it, and I heard him objecting to 'police harassment'. His voice rose, and within moments a group of people had gathered round to see what was happening with the heavyset man and the good-looking young cop. That's when Nadine, in a nice navy suit and white blouse, moved in, on cue, appearing beside Charlie, pulling out her warrant wallet as well. Two overweight security guards now trotted towards the small noisy group.

For a few seconds, Rana stood looking around in bewilderment until she saw me, beckoning her furiously. When she realised that Talal couldn't see either of us because of the jostling group of onlookers around him, she hurried over to me. I grabbed her arm and drew her into the cramped utility room, before pulling the door closed and turning to her.

I put out my hand. 'Detective Inspector Debra Hawkins, Rana. Time we met properly. Please call me Debra.'

She gripped my hand, nodding. 'Thank you, thank you,' she said. 'Thank you for agreeing to help me. I can't stay for long. I'm supposed to be organising my passport at the post office. Talal will be looking for me.'

'You've got a few minutes,' I said. 'He's going to be caught up for a little while. Might even get himself arrested if he behaves badly enough.' I smiled encouragingly. I couldn't imagine what it must be like to be so intimidated and fearful, a prisoner of your own family. 'I need to hear it from you,' I went on. 'Tell me about what's happening and how best we can help you.'

Rana looked away, her hand unconsciously touching the side of her face that was still discoloured. She's ashamed, I realised, of her family and their brutality towards her.

'My brothers,' she said. 'Ever since they came back to Australia, they've been very difficult.'

Outside, the argument went up a few decibels. 'Difficult?' I said. 'They've obviously assaulted you. Tell me everything.'

A huge sigh told me what this was costing her. 'My brothers,' she repeated. 'They say I must marry my cousin in Iraq.' She shook her head. 'I only met him once when I was a little girl. He's nearly fifty now and he's a first cousin. I didn't like him when I was a kid. He treated his first wife terribly – I remember. I don't want to marry anyone. I sure don't want to marry him!' Rana's voice was shaking and I didn't know whether it was from anger or fear. 'It's unhealthy as well – intermarriage with blood relations. But that's not the only reason. I want to continue my studies and graduate from university. If I marry someone, it'll be somebody I choose. Someone liberated – educated. Not someone from a – a . . .' I could sense her searching for the right words. '. . . a pre-modern culture,' she finally said. 'I want to live my life like other Australian women.'

'You've told your brothers how you feel?'

'Of course. That's when I got this,' she said, indicating the fading bruise around her cheekbone. 'And some others that aren't visible.'

'How old are you, Rana?'

'Nineteen,' she replied.

'You're an adult. They can't force you to do anything. Can't you move out? Find somewhere else to live?'

Rana looked at me as if I'd dropped in from another galaxy, then turned her face away. 'I've never been alone for one minute in my whole life. I have no money. I'm a student. I have one close friend and I'm forbidden to see her. If I stayed with her, her family would be in danger too. My brothers have become even more violent since the police crackdown on gangs and drugs over the last two years. They're frustrated. They turn on me even more. I can't go back to my aunty Sarah. She would simply call my brothers to pick me up. I know, because I already tried that. She's scared of them too. And I don't blame her.' Rana's eyes filled with tears. 'I know a few people from school and university but I don't want to involve them. It wouldn't be safe for them. You don't know what my brothers are like. There is no one I can trust.'

'What about your Egyptian friend, Eshaq? Couldn't you stay with him?'

Rana blushed. 'Oh no. That would not be possible. I couldn't do that to his family. To him. It would not be right.'

'Then you'll have to trust me,' I said. 'We can contact the right agencies to find you somewhere safe for you to stay for a little while. You'd be entitled to some form of benefit. There are government and non-government agencies that can help you while you work out what you're going to do next. The important thing is that you come with me now.'

'Now? Like this? But I haven't got anything with me! I can't just go like this. No, no. I simply can't do that!'

'Your note said your brothers had been ill-treating you, locking you in the house, threating to kill you.'

Rana looked away.

'Please, Rana,' I said softly. 'Come with me now. We can help you start a new life. You live in a democracy, not a totalitarian state. Every adult human being of sound mind has the right to self-determination. You're young and healthy. You're getting on with your education. Come with me now. I'm told you want to run your own business eventually. You have your whole life ahead of you. This is your chance to walk to freedom.'

'Freedom,' Rana echoed. She looked back at me, holding me in her direct and steady gaze. 'You don't understand what freedom would mean for me. If I do this, I will have no one. My family will disown me. If I leave with you now, and refuse this marriage, I will be dead to them. My mother, my brothers, my cousins, my aunt. I will have no one at all. They are already very angry with me for resisting so far. If I went back to Iraq after refusing the marriage, I would be in danger because I would have brought shame on the family by refusing to marry the man selected for me. My mother called me *shaytan* – the devil – when I spoke to her on the phone. I begged her to help me, to speak for me.' Rana's voice wobbled. 'Instead she was screaming at me that I must obey the family or I will be cursed forever.'

My mother might be difficult, I thought, but she'd never

curse me, or call me a demon. I could only imagine the pressure Rana was living with.

'My mother said it was my destiny, just like it was hers to marry a man she didn't want, I must do the same.' Rana pressed her lips together, suppressing a sob. 'If I go with you now, I can never go back again. I can never see my mother or my sisters back in Iraq. My family's name would be dishonoured and discredited. Everyone would know about it.' She looked away again, distressed. 'I have a terrible choice. Either I do as they want and go back to Iraq and marry this man, which is the end of my life as far as I'm concerned, or I run away and leave everyone I know and love, and my whole family – the extended family, the clan – will all be dishonoured. I will be dead to them.'

I wanted to say that her family didn't deserve her love. That they didn't love her at all. That their love was conditional on her bending to their will. Then I tried to imagine what my life would be like without anyone I knew – without Mark, without my mother, without Cecile, my friends at work. Even life without Brad would seem diminished.

'I just don't know what to do,' said Rana anxiously. 'I hope I didn't make a terrible mistake in contacting you. But I can't marry that man.'

I was witnessing the awful pain of indecision. I recognised it from my own experience, the swinging between two possibilities, each of them fraught with difficulty and sorrow. I said softly, 'You're entitled to own your own life, Rana. You're a citizen of Australia. And citizens have rights.'

Rana's gaze was intense before she spoke. 'I've never thought of it like that.' She looked away again, at the clutter in the utility room – flagons of cleaning fluid and boxes of light fittings and fluorescent tubes. Finally, she returned her haunted eyes to mine. 'You can't imagine what it's like. Everyone on your case, constantly questioning, demanding to know where I've been, who I've been seeing, what I've been doing. Whether I still believe in God or not. Whether I still believe in my religion. Wanting to know why I'm smiling, what have I got to be so happy about. It's constant. They try to get into my head. They try to see what I think, what I feel.' Rana put a hand to her temple. 'All the time. It never stops.' I placed my hand gently on her arm.

'I'm frightened of everyone now,' she said, tears in her eyes. 'My mother is right about one thing: I am losing my religion. But if I go to the Coptic church with Eshaq, I'm endangering those people.'

'Look,' I said, recalling Maryam's 'smart and sneaky'. 'If you feel you can't come with me right this minute, go home now. Be a good sister to your brothers. Say that you can now see that they're right. That'll calm everything down. Look very pious. Can you do that?' The only ideas I had of piety came from my own childhood, of nuns bowed over their breviaries, of girls who draped rosary beads and devotional medals around their necks to ingratiate themselves with the nuns.

Noticing that the noise had quietened down outside, I opened the door a crack to peek out. Charlie, Nadine and Talal had disappeared and the group of onlookers had dispersed. I trusted that Charlie had things under control, and I closed the door again.

The briefest of smiles tilted the corners of Rana's beautiful mouth. She shrugged. 'I guess that could work, to pretend to go along with them. It might stop them being so suspicious all the time. But then what?'

'That will give me time to talk to my officers and others and make a plan,' I said. 'To find out what agencies can help you with temporary accommodation and some income. The Department of Immigration has facilities and access to funds for special cases such as yours. It will also give you time to consider your difficult choice. Then, when everything is in place, all you have to do is leave the house and someone will be waiting to take you somewhere safe. Do you think you can do that?' I knew that the 'someone' would probably be me.

There was a long silence as she considered. Then finally, she nodded. 'I think so.'

'Okay,' I said, 'it's safe to go out now. And the post office queue is shorter. Come on.'

I gave her my card, which she slipped into her bag. After looking around to be sure that there was still no sign of Talal, we stepped outside. I added, 'If you want to continue your studies this year, it might be wise to get advice on how you can transfer to another university . . .'

For a moment I thought I must have said something shocking, because Rana's face seized up in fear. 'Oh God! It's them! Both of them! They've come looking for me. They mustn't see me here!' Rana hurried away, clutching up the scarf to obscure her face, intent on losing herself among the throngs of shoppers.

'Tell them about the queue at the post office! Tell them to post your passport! Call me!' I yelled after her as she fled.

Some thirty metres away, the al-Sheikly brothers, Talal in the lead, an angry scowl on his face, were checking out every shop, peering inside and then moving on.

I swung round again, searching for Rana's elegant figure among the jumble of moving shoppers. She'd completely vanished. Cursing silently, I grabbed my mobile, calling Charlie.

'I've just lost Rana!' I said. 'What happened? You were supposed to keep Talal talking.'

'Deb, I would have had to arrest him to detain him any longer. He stormed off – when he realised Rana wasn't in the post office queue he ran outside. He must have rung Samir, because he turned up a few minutes later. What happened with Rana? Where did she go?'

'She bolted when she saw Talal and Samir.'

I rang off and made another call, keeping my eyes on the al-Sheikly brothers, who were now talking animatedly to a man in the nuts and spices shop diagonally across from the utility room.

'I'm calling about Rana,' I said rapidly when Jamila answered her phone. 'She needs your help. I need your help. We were talking at the mall and she got spooked when she saw her brothers. Any idea where she might go?'

'I told you not to call me again!' Jamila's voice was hard.

'Jamila, this is serious. I need to know where Rana might go if she panicked.'

The man in the nuts and spices shop was now talking – was he telling the brothers that he'd seen their sister disappear into the small utility room in the company of a strange woman?

'If she suspects that they saw her with you,' Jamila was saying, 'she wouldn't dare go home again. You could get me into big trouble too.'

'Where might she go?' I repeated.

'I don't . . . Maybe Aunt Sarah's. I've gotta go now.'

'Jamila! Just give me Sarah's address.'

―――

Seven minutes later I was driving along a suburban road, heading for Sarah's house. On my way I came up with a story that I hoped would sound plausible. I was determined to track down Rana al-Sheikly. But I wanted to do it her way, and keep the idea of the police out of it for the time being.

I parked outside the house, grabbed my briefcase and stepped out of the car. I rapped on the door and put a big smile on my face.

'Good morning,' I said, as Sarah opened the door a little way, a deep frown on her pudgy face. 'My name is Debra,' I opened with an honest gambit. 'Is Rana here? I've been helping her with chemistry at uni and I haven't seen her for a while. Is she okay?'

Before I could continue with my subterfuge, a loud male voice came from inside the house and Sarah flinched.

'She's not here,' she said, her face tight with fear. 'You must go. I'm very busy.' She quickly looked back over her shoulder.

'No problems,' I said brightly, trying to see past her. 'Hope everything's okay?'

The loud voice yelled again from inside the house. Aunty Sarah must have a male relative staying.

'Please,' said Sarah. 'You must go.'

'Where could I find Rana? Where else might she be?' I persisted.

Sarah started closing the door, then paused. She placed her thumb and forefinger on the right side of her mouth, drawing it across her lips in a zipping motion.

'Oh, okay,' I said, lowering my voice.

There was another barking yell, and Sarah, eyes filled with terror, made another, unmistakeable sign. She drew the forefinger of her right hand slowly from left to right across the black fabric under her chin in a deliberate, throat-cutting gesture.

The door slammed shut.

I stood a moment outside, stunned. I was used to threatening gestures, but the naked fear on this woman's face and her terrified charades had really got to me.

I went back to the car, and sat behind the wheel for a few moments, attempting to understand the import of Sarah's gestures. In making the throat-cutting gesture, did she mean that this might happen to her if she spoke up, or had she been trying to tell me what might happen to Rana?

Or to me?

—·—

Back at work I wrote up my notes and the information I'd gleaned from Rana. I risked calling her on her mobile, but it wasn't switched on. I called my mother to check on the progress of her leg injury but there was no answer. She must be out and about, I thought, even though it wasn't one of her work days. I took that as a good sign that her leg was healing.

I called Kylie Mifsud again. Again no luck.

I requested copies of the CCTV tapes from the mall, hoping to get some kind of a lead on Rana and to see if her brothers had followed her. Soon after, a courier dropped them off at our offices. I took delivery of the package without enthusiasm. I'd have to sift through the CCTV footage looking for the tall, elegant figure of Rana among all the jostling shoppers. I finally saw her in a few frames taken by the cameras near the double doors of the main entrance, hurrying outside. I picked her up again later, this time from the street cameras, still walking fast and in a westerly direction. I was relieved to see she was alone.

Half an hour later, taking a break from the tapes, I checked my email. As soon as I saw the name and the subject line: *You're looking in the wrong place*, my heart rate sped up. Smiley again. It was from the same address as the first one – Broadway Library. I braced myself for what he might be sending me this time.

Beneath was a photograph of a man's dark blue jacket, laid out as if in a catalogue, sleeves angled at the elbows and the long front zipper done up almost to the neck.

I leaned back in my chair. What on earth was Smiley on about now? The first photograph, shocking as it had been, had at least been relevant to my life. Now I was starting to wonder if Smiley was a nutcase.

While I was frowning over the photograph of the jacket, Socrates knocked at the half-open door. 'Hey. I think you should have a look at this. The Cellebrite results.'

I took the printout from him.

'I've highlighted the interesting bits,' he said, pointing to where he'd drawn a hot-pink slash across two names. Talal al-Sheikly and Adam Massoud were joined by dozens of phone calls, some from Massoud, some originating from al-Sheikly. The brothers keep bad company.

'I want twenty-four-hour surveillance on these men,' I announced to the group at the meeting I called ten minutes later, putting the photographs of Talal and Samir up on the projection screen. 'We can manage it in twelve-hour shifts. Charlie, please draw up a roster and count me out, unless there's an emergency. I'm not keen on peeing into bottles.'

CHAPTER 14

As I approached the back lane, I was aware of a dark green car turning the corner at the other end. I didn't think it was a Subaru but it reminded me of George Hakan and his boss, Massoud. I deliberately put them out of my mind. I had enough to think about without letting those two spook me.

I swung the car in from the back lane and parked it in the shade of an old fruit tree. As I walked up to the kitchen door I made a mental note to water the broccoli plants. But first I went up to my room to get changed. I had let my hair down and was about to take off my suit when I heard a car coming through the steel gate at the back. I looked out from the window and my heart leapt.

I ran down to greet him as he got out of the car. 'Mark! You're here!'

He jumped out, looked me up and down, grinned and said, 'I'm here and I'm having evil thoughts. Arrest me!'

I threw my arms around him and hugged him tight. 'You do not have to say anything,' I warned him, 'but anything you do say may be used in evidence and get you into a lot of trouble.'

'Like what?'

'Like being strip-searched.'

'Only if it's mutual.'

'Our unit is governed by the Equal Opportunities Act of 1975.' I kissed him again. 'So good to have you home!'

'Hey, woman. Take it easy. I can't breathe!' He grinned down at me again with his good-natured face and kindly eyes. Mark was a year younger than I was but his face had a wisdom and maturity that sometimes made me feel like the younger one. He'd been to hell and back with alcoholism and I admired him for beating it. We'd almost split up when he first went west to the mines and I found the long-distance relationship too difficult. But Mark had called and written almost daily, begging me to reconsider, saying he'd fly over as often as he could, pointing out that the big money he was making would go towards getting the home we wanted to make together. And so I had given it another chance.

'I'll get my kit,' he said, as I followed him round to the boot, watching him haul out his long sports bag, which I took from him while he hoisted out his heavy toolbox.

'Let me get cleaned up. And then,' he dropped his toolbox and grabbed me, 'let me get at you!'

'With great pleasure,' I said.

—•—

We lay curled up contentedly, my head resting on Mark's chest, listening to his steady heartbeat, returned now to its normal rhythm. I ran my fingers softly over one muscular upper arm and down to his wrist. I frowned when I saw a large, healing cut across the back of his left hand. 'What happened?' I asked, propping myself up on an elbow.

'That? A tool slipped. A moment's inattention.' He leaned over and took something out of the pocket of his cargo pants on the chair. 'Got something for you,' he said, passing me a tiny gift-wrapped package. 'I hope you like them. They told me I could exchange them for something else if you didn't.'

I tore off the paper. Inside was a jeweller's box, dark blue velvet with a miniature gold clasp. Slowly, I opened it – and gasped. Two leaf-shaped gold-filigree lozenges scattered with small pink diamonds glittered in the bedside light. I knew they were diamonds and not pink sapphires or tourmalines because absolutely nothing else refracts like diamonds. I lifted out the earrings. 'Oh, Mark! They're gorgeous! I love them. Thank you! But they must have cost you a fortune.'

'That's right. You'll have to keep me now for the rest of my life.'

I threw my arms around him once more. 'Deal!'

I put in the earrings then jumped out of bed and walked over to the mirror above the long marble bench that formed my dressing table. The two gold leaves hung gracefully from my ears, just the right length for my jaw line, and the champagne-pink diamonds winked flashes of colour as only diamonds can.

'They really suit you in that outfit,' Mark said, smiling at my nakedness. 'You should wear it more often.'

I slid back down into the bed, loving him and the earrings.

'I wasn't too sure,' he said, 'after the last ones I gave you.'

'Mmm. The less said about those the better.' Mark had once bought me a pair of cubic zirconia numbers, huge and flashy. He'd thought they were marvellous because they were big and sparkly. 'You didn't know me very well then. These are adorable. Thank you so much. But seriously, they must have cost a lot.'

'You're worth it, Deb. I know I'm a lucky man.' He sat up from where he'd been lying, arms behind his head. 'However . . .'

I waited for the qualifier, then prompted him, 'However what?'

'. . . great sex and the company of a grateful woman always makes me famished,' he said, and ducked the smack I aimed at him.

'How about I get dressed with my new earrings and we go out to dinner?' I rolled out of bed quickly enough to avoid Mark's friendly slap at my backside.

At a small Greek restaurant off Broadway, we ordered up big: vine-leaf rolls, dips, calamari, souvlakia, beans in tomato sauce, Greek salad and bread, and wine by the glass for me. I fingered my new earrings and tried to see them in the glass over the framed poster of the harbour on the island of Hydra that hung next to our table. Mark brought me up to date on how things were going in Western Australia. 'It's slowing down a bit,' he said. 'I'm not sure if I'll be needed there again next year. I might be looking for work around Sydney instead. Which would be nice,' he added, placing his broad hand over mine. 'We could do this every night.'

I looked around and noticed that most of the tables were taken. The waiter was swirling around, managing several plates in each hand, deftly laying them down, sweeping napkins onto laps, smiling the whole time.

'Okay. Your turn,' Mark said, passing me an olive. 'How have you managed to live without me?'

'It hasn't been easy.' I smiled. 'It's been a bit overwhelming, actually. We're very busy organising the new unit and looking at a couple of cases. I'm concerned about a young woman who's being monstered by her brothers to marry some cousin in Iraq. She's dropped out of sight for the moment and I'm hoping she's okay. Plus Brad rang.'

'Brad? I thought you never heard from him. What did he want?'

I shrugged. 'He hung up on me before I could talk to him. I was on the other line and I told him I'd call him back. He couldn't deal with that and hung up. I was surprised to hear from him. It was the first time in almost eighteen months.' I paused. 'I feel a bit guilty that I haven't called him back yet.'

'You never talk about your brother,' Mark said, ordering another glass of wine for me and pouring himself a glass of water.

'There's not much to tell. It's a depressing story. He's always been a problem.'

'So why do you think he rang?'

I sighed. 'I don't know. But he only ever contacts me when he needs something. Like money. Or a favour. I've learned that much. And I've got to be really careful because once . . .' I stopped, realising I'd said too much.

'Because once what, Deb?'

I waved it away. 'Forget it. It was a long time ago.' Mark gave me a long look but I changed the subject. 'I got a couple of strange emails at work.' I told him about Smiley and the short, provocative messages with each email. 'Both times the sender put the photo in the body of the email, knowing I probably wouldn't open an attachment from someone unknown,' I added. 'So he made sure I saw it and didn't automatically hit the delete button.'

'You're assuming it's a he?'

'I'm not assuming anything yet. It's just easier than saying "he or she" all the time.'

Mark was frowning. 'That is strange,' he said. 'How would someone get hold of a crime scene photo?'

'I don't know. It's not impossible. I managed to get a copy of the old Beta crime scene video tape from someone.'

'And what's with the photo of the jacket? What could a blue jacket possibly mean in relation to that crime scene?'

I shrugged. 'No idea. It's just a common dark blue . . .'

Then a sudden memory arose, and I felt goosebumps prickle along my arms. 'Mark! Oh God! The jacket!'

'Tell me.'

'I've never told you – that I went back to the house that evening . . .' I paused as the chilling memories of that night took over, '. . . and picked up a jacket, my dad's dark blue jacket. I'd left mine at the convent and it made my father late for work. He wasn't pleased about it.'

My goosebumps peaked as I tried to dismiss the weird coincidence.

'Why is someone directing you back there? To the circumstances of your father's death?' Mark had it in one. His frown deepened as he continued, 'It's obviously someone who knows your history and what happened to your father and wants to get your attention.'

'Hardly anyone knows about even the big events of that night anymore. They might know that I'm the daughter of a cop who was killed because he had a sloppy attitude to the job, but that's all. This person seems to have information – in the case of the jacket, about something only I could know about. I'll get a warrant if necessary. I want to know who this person is.'

'Are you sure you haven't told anyone else the details of that night?' Mark asked.

I looked at him in silence for a moment, thinking. 'I told Cecile years ago. But it wouldn't be her.'

'Somebody knows something,' he said. 'It doesn't smell right.'

'I don't like it either. It's like . . . some kind of ghostly hand from the past reaching out and trying to pull me back there.' I shrugged again, uncomfortable. 'I'm a rationalist. I don't believe in ghostly hands.'

I felt restless and agitated, and needed to move. I called for the bill, waving Mark's credit card away. 'My shout, Mark. No argument.'

—

We walked home through the backstreets. The sound of the busy evening traffic seemed muffled, much further away than it really was. The old dunny lanes were wet from a shower that had passed over as we'd sat in the restaurant; rainwashed foliage hung over back fences and the air felt fresh.

I jumped as a cat suddenly dashed across the lane and ran up the fence on the opposite side.

'Hey, it's okay,' Mark said, giving my arm a squeeze. 'It's only a cat. You're jumpy tonight.'

'I've got reasons to be.'

'Tell me.'

'Maybe. Later.'

After we'd taken a few more steps, Mark asked, 'Why did the cat cross the road?'

'Cats have their reasons,' I said.

'Tell me what it was that you once did for Brad.'

His question was so unexpected that it stopped me midstep. Mark halted too. Even the cat looked surprised, sitting on the fence. Then it dropped out of sight.

'You really want to know?' I asked.

'I really want to know.'

CHAPTER 15

We sat together in the living room, both of us reflected in the tall window, me curled up in a corner of the lounge, Mark leaning forward from the big leather chair he'd bought for himself and then lent to me, holding a coffee mug. Past the wrought-iron bars on the window, a tree branch shivered in the night breeze.

'When I was a young constable, quite a few years ago now, and Brad was only a kid, I had a flat in Darlinghurst. He came banging on my door in a real state. He stank of alcohol. He'd wagged school to hang around with a bunch of older boys and he'd boasted about the fact that he knew where they could get a car. Of course, that was our mother's car he was talking about. No one had a licence but they took it from the carport and shortly afterwards, they put a brick through a jeweller's window. Brad had grabbed a handful of very expensive watches. Apparently they double-parked the car in front of Thomas Piper and Sons jewellery. The whole thing was a debacle because the jeweller came after them, they panicked and bolted in the car. Brad was yelling at me, "What if they took the rego? They'll lock me up in juvenile! Mum will kill me! What am I going to do?" He told me that Mum's car was parked in a laneway a few blocks away from my place.'

'So what did you do?' Mark asked, leaning closer.

'I was as stupid as he was.' I straightened up at the memory, sitting taller in the corner of the lounge. 'I wasn't thinking clearly. Mum had been ill with pneumonia and I didn't want any more stress for her – like Brad being caught by the police. He'd already had two cautions. I told him to get the hell out of my place, wipe down the car for prints and Mum would report it as stolen.'

'What about the watches?'

'He'd dropped them all while he was getting away.' I sighed at the memory of my brother's colossal stupidity – and my own. 'Anyway, that was the end of it, thank goodness. Somebody rang up about the car that was parked across their driveway in Darlinghurst. Mum was really upset about her car being "stolen".' I paused, leaning back again into the corner of the lounge. 'Fortunately, there were no fingerprints left in the car. He'd done a thorough clean-up.' I felt a surge of anger thinking about that night. 'See, I didn't know until he told me, that he'd been cautioned twice before. If he'd been caught, he would have certainly been locked up in juvenile detention.' I sighed again. 'But Brad got away with it.'

Mark put his coffee cup down. 'And I guess you hope that you did too, detective.'

I hadn't thought of that day in ages. Now it all came flooding back, bringing thoughts of Brad with it and the fact that I'd been accessory to a crime. Four people knew about it – me, Brad, Cecile and now Mark – and a wave of anxiety rippled through me. It was a long time ago, I told myself. There was no reason anyone would reopen that old case or that any suspicion would be directed towards me.

'You're very protective of your mother,' Mark said. 'It's almost like you're the mother and she's the child.'

This thought had occurred to me more than once. 'I guess there's a great variety in the levels of competence. I've always seen myself as a practical person,' I said. 'I behaved as stupidly as he did. And I've always felt responsible for him, too. I know it's irrational, but there it is. And I didn't want our mother to know how hopeless he was. It sounds pathetic, but my motives were . . .' I groped for the right words, 'well, if not good, at least complicated. You know that the police have discretionary powers – we can decide whether or not to charge someone.'

'I guess he didn't do any really bad damage. And he was just a kid.'

'It's good to have you home again,' I said.

'Good to be here, Deb. It's funny,' he added.

'What's funny?'

'The things we continue to regret. Maybe funny's not the right word. But I did something once, too, that I'm still unhappy about. To my youngest brother.'

Mark and his brothers had grown up on an orchard at Bilpin in the Blue Mountains. I'd met his parents several times over the years. They were solid farming people who'd eventually found the combination of incessant gruelling labour, the vagaries of drought, frosts and floods, and, later, the competition with imported fruit just too much to deal with. They'd sold the orchard to a developer, who'd chopped down the fruit trees, subdivided the acreage and made a fortune. Mark's parents now lived in a well-appointed townhouse in Richmond; whenever we called in they greeted us warmly and with that famed country hospitality.

'David?' I asked. 'I thought you got on well with him.'

'I did. I do. But on the night of my twenty-first he had a fight with his girlfriend at the party. He left but she stayed on and I comforted her. Well, that's what she thought. I'm sorry to say that my intentions didn't lie in that quarter. I took her into my bedroom and while the party was raging outside, I wiped her tears away and then we ended up in bed together.'

'Your brother's girl? Mark!'

'I know. It was a bastard of a thing to do. I've never forgiven myself.'

'Did he find out?'

Mark thought for a moment before he spoke again. 'One of the things a recovering alcoholic has to do if they want a good-quality sobriety is to make amends for wrongdoings.'

'So, you told him about it?'

He sighed. 'I'm still considering it. See, one of the suggestions is that you don't make amends that will harm anyone. So a confession may not be the best way to go. Because telling Dave what happened would also dob in Juliet. And that could harm her. If she hasn't told him, should I?'

'Juliet! That's his wife's name. Now I understand why you're not sure whether to tell.'

'She may well have told him. He's never brought it up with me, though, if she has.'

'That's not an easy one, Mark.'

'Too right it's not.'

I thought awhile. 'When I was younger, I thought it was really easy to know wrong from right, to know what was the best thing to do in every situation. Now I'm less and less sure.'

Mark broke the reflective mood by reaching over and grabbing me. 'Want to play cops and robbers? I pinch your knickers and you have to pin me down and arrest me.'

'Again? But I've already arrested you once tonight. And bail's been refused.'

'I can still play up in the lock-up.' He jumped up, grasping me.

'You'll never get away with it!' I laughed, wrestling him down onto the floor and straddling him.

'The heavy hand of the law is upon me,' he intoned.

'That's not my hand, it's my bum, and it's only heavy if you resist,' I said.

'Okay, okay,' he said, reaching for me. 'No resistance. I give up.'

He looked up at me, grinning, his face flushed, and I fell in love with him all over again.

— —

Later, we lay facing each other. Mark traced my features gently with his forefinger. 'Something's bothering you,' he finally said, stroking the frown lines on my forehead.

'Genius. I've already told you about work – and Brad. And Mum.'

Mark's finger stopped moving and he regarded me closely. 'It's something more than that. Something's frightening you. It's a different energy to just plain old overwork.'

I considered my reply for what seemed a long moment before I raised myself up on an elbow. 'Adam Massoud. That's who's often at the back of my mind. Adam Massoud lurks back there.'

Mark put his arms around me.

'I hadn't thought about him for months and now he's part of an active protection case we're involved in. We were trying to protect the only witness we have against him in an upcoming murder case, but she's gone missing. And last week my car was followed by a green Subaru, and when I got a rego check, I found that it's registered to a guy called George Hakan, who's an associate of —'

'— of Adam Massoud,' Mark finished for me. 'Now I understand why you jumped at a cat in the lane.' He hugged me closer. 'I'd better finish up in Western Australia and get a job over here.'

'We're working with the prison. Massoud's under constant surveillance. He knows that. He thinks he's outwitted the screws. But they're letting him run, I believe, and this is opening up all kinds of new lines of enquiry which they pass on to my old squad, the MEOCS people. Not to mention giving us the names of the corrupt Corrective Services guards.'

'Wherever there's the temptation of big money you'll get corruption, Deb,' Mark said. 'You know that. The prison staff are only human. It just takes one to take a bribe. Or do a favour.

And then they've got him on their line for good. All the same, I think it's time for me to come back to Sydney.'

I didn't try to dissuade him. Although he wouldn't be able to earn the big money he was making over in the west, I knew I would love having Mark back in Sydney permanently.

In a little while, I heard his breathing deepen as he fell asleep. I leaned over and gently kissed the outline of his cheekbone. Then I lay back down and continued to listen to him sleep.

I seemed to do that for a long time.

—⁃—

I woke up during the night. Something had disturbed me. I crept out of the bedroom so as not to wake Mark and went downstairs without turning on a light, knowing my way round the house easily in the dark. From the kitchen, I peered out into the back garden, dimly visible in the ambient light. Was I imagining it or was there a figure moving around at the back of the yard, down near Mark's station wagon? My first impulse was to run outside and yell at them, but I knew this could be dangerous. I didn't know what – or who – might be out there. I kept staring out but saw no more movement, and eventually decided that my eyes must have been playing tricks and that what I'd taken for a figure was nothing more than the shadows of the old fruit tree moving in the light breeze.

When I went back to bed, though, I was wide awake and couldn't seem to switch off my racing mind. Even the faint glimmer of my beautiful new earrings, now lying on my bedside table, failed to soothe me. Thoughts of Adam Massoud and my concern over Kylie mingled with the latest email from Smiley and the photo of the dark blue jacket, and decades-old memories of the last time I had seen my father. How could someone else know about the jacket? And what did it mean, *You're looking in the wrong place?* Then Brad's face flashed into my mind, his wild, panicked eyes that night he'd burst into my flat in Darlinghurst. He was still a boy then, still my little brother. It's not possible to discount those blood ties, I thought.

Thoughts of my family and blood brought my mind back to Rana. Where had she gone when she ran away from me in the mall this morning? Her eyes had been so desperate and so fearful. I had to find her, had to keep her safe.

—•—

I must have finally managed to drift off to sleep at around 5 a.m. I woke again at seven, to bright sunlight, and the worries of the night before were further dispersed by Mark and the coffees and croissants he'd bought from the cafe down the street.

I was washing up the breakfast things when Mark, who'd been outside watering the neglected broccoli plants, came back into the kitchen. As soon as I saw his face I knew something was wrong.

'What is it?'

'Come and see for yourself.'

I didn't like his grim tone one bit. I followed him outside and down to where our cars were parked next to each other inside the automatic gates. He pointed to something lying in the grass near the fence that divided my property from the neighbours'. I walked over.

'Oh shit!' I swore, staring down at it in shock. I felt Mark come up behind me. 'Don't touch it,' I said, thinking of fingerprints.

Nestled in the grass was an almost empty glass bottle with a rag stuffed in the top. I could smell the petrol.

I spun around. 'I heard them last night! I must have woken up when they threw it over the gate. But I couldn't see anything.'

'The petrol must've come out too quickly to vaporise, and that's extinguished the wick. It's a one-in-a-hundred chance. You're a lucky girl to still have a car.'

We looked at each other for a long moment. 'I'd better get to work and report this,' I said.

'Who do you think did it?'

'God knows. Could be the green Subaru guy.'

'What about the person from the email? Smiley?'

'That doesn't fit,' I said, shaking my head. 'Smiley wants me to *do* something. This is someone with a grievance. You tread on a lot of toes during fifteen years in the police. It could be someone who's been stewing away for years about an arrest I made or a sentence they got.

'We'll get fingerprints from that bottle, I hope. That rag jammed into the top might be helpful too. They would have been so sure all traces would be burnt up and destroyed in the fire that they mightn't have been too careful. Let's get the crime scene people to bag it up and see what the analysts can get off it.'

We went inside and reviewed the CCTV footage. It wasn't very helpful. All it showed was a murky projectile coming over the gate. We already knew that. 'I'm hoping for prints,' I said, resetting the security camera. 'And then I'm hoping that there's no match.'

Mark nodded. He understood. If there wasn't a match, it was a cleanskin. If there was a match, it was someone with a history . . . with me. And a criminal record. I prayed the prints wouldn't belong to George Hakan. If they didn't, I had a new problem.

Death threats aren't uncommon in my line of work, but they're never pleasant, even when delivered by amateurs. I recalled the days after Massoud's assault on me outside the courts, when I had slept with the Glock next to me and ready to go. This new threat had reawakened my fears.

I left Mark pottering in the garden, and drove out of the backyard, the steel gate sliding closed behind me. There was nothing I could do about my gritty eyes, red-rimmed from lack of sleep.

On the drive to work, I reported the incident and then talked to an inspector I knew in Forensic Services.

'I can send someone over to bag it this afternoon,' he said. 'Or come over myself.'

'My partner will let you in,' I said, giving him the address and Mark's name. 'He'll show you exactly where it is.'

As I drove, I put my own fears aside to find fears for Rana hiding underneath. The would-be firebombers could have been the al-Sheikly brothers, warning me to back off.

I barely had time to consider this possibility when my phone rang again. I picked up, hoping it would be Rana. It wasn't. My heart sank when I heard his voice.

'I've gotta talk to you. You said you'd call me back.'

'What is it, Brad?' My own voice was wary and unwelcoming.

'C'mon, Dibs. I just need to talk to you.'

'Okay, so talk.'

'Not like this. Meet me somewhere.'

I glanced at the time. 'Look, I should be at work. But there's a Turkish kebab place not far from the office. Be there in an hour.' I gave him the address.

'What if I can't make it?'

'Make it,' I said.

CHAPTER 16

As soon as my brother walked into the kebab shop, I could see that life had got a whole lot worse for him since the last time I'd seen him. He'd lost a lot of weight. His grubby T-shirt and jeans hung on him. He plopped down on the bench opposite me and pulled out a small round tin, selected a half-smoked cigarette from a collection of similar relics, repocketed the tin and lit the second-hand fag end. He coughed and blew the smoke away as I ducked away from it. I studied him.

'Nice earrings,' he said, squinting at Mark's gift to me, and a strange grimace briefly contorted one side of his face.

Anger rose in me as he appraised my jewellery with his thieving eyes. 'I won't ask how you are because I can see that already,' I said. 'So what do you want?'

'Don't be like that, Dibs.'

'Like what?'

'So unfriendly. As if the only reason I want to see you is if I want something.'

'And this time you don't?'

'Look, it's just a temporary stage I'm going through. This time, I'm really going to clean up my act. Promise. It's just that a whole lot of things have kind of happened at once.' He scratched at a scab on the side of his face and his hand jerked sideways in an uncontrollable swipe as if he'd touched a hotplate.

'I've heard it all before,' I said, already wearied by his latest excuses. 'So what is it that you need to talk to me about?'

He looked down at the table, his face suddenly so miserable that I thought he might be about to cry. Remembering the beautiful baby I'd once adored, I softened. 'You look like you need something to eat.'

He nodded. 'Something soft. My teeth and gums are giving me a lot of trouble.' He pressed the side of his face and winced, the grimace deepening into a series of blinking tics. Some side effect, I guessed, of his drug using.

I ordered him the $9.99 all-day special, a wrap of flatbread and thin slices of kebab, tomato and a smear of hummus, which came with coffee, and got a glass of water for myself.

When his food was delivered, Brad tore a small portion off the flatbread, dipped it in the oil on the table and put it tentatively into his mouth as if it might hurt him. It was obvious that he was eating as some kind of physical duty – he clearly had no appetite. The drugs had taken that from him as well.

'I need your help,' he said. 'I'm going to Bangkok to get clean and straight.'

'*What?* Why Bangkok? Why can't you do it here?'

'I've tried that. And the good places here are too expensive.'

'So a return flight to Bangkok and rehab there works out cheaper?' I couldn't keep the sarcasm out of my voice. Cecile had flown to Thailand a year ago and the return airfare was around a thousand dollars. 'It's called doing a geographical,' I said, remembering something Mark had told me about his drinking days, how he was always moving somewhere else, always trying to find some place where things would be 'better', never realising that the interior baggage went with him wherever he moved. 'Wherever I'd go,' he'd said, 'I'd take my alcoholic self.'

'No, listen,' Brad was insisting. 'It'll work. I've got a mate – well, I can't say too much about him, because he works as a cook for some of the clan labs . . .' My brother gave me his lopsided smile that had once been charming; these days, because of whatever was going on with his teeth and jaw line, it simply made him look sinister. 'I don't want him being picked up by the cops,' Brad went on. 'You might dob on him.'

I rolled my eyes. My concern right now wasn't with a cook working in clan labs.

'And,' Brad continued, '*he* told me how he'd got off a bad ice habit by going to a Bangkok drying-out place.'

'So why is he working cooking up drugs? He obviously hasn't distanced himself very far from the whole business.'

A couple walked into the shop and Brad turned anxiously to check them out.

'And where are you going to get the money from?' I asked.

He looked back at me. 'You.'

'Me?' I could see from his level stare that he wasn't joking. 'No way, Brad. We've had this discussion too many times. Mum's bailed you out over and over and you've never paid her back.'

'One day I will, I swear it. I'm going to a Buddhist temple. They have a really good success rate. I only need a one-way ticket. Plus about thirty bucks a day to stay at the temple. Then I'll stay on and work in Thailand for a while to get some money. That's my plan. I only need about a grand, two grand max.'

I finished my glass of water and gathered up my bag. 'I have to go to work now. There's no way I'm giving you money, Brad. Save it out of your taxpayer-funded benefits. You've been bludging off us taxpayers for years.'

'I don't think you understand, Dibs. You've got to give me the money.' His right hand flew across the table and I flinched, thinking he was about to hit me. He quickly pulled it back. 'You've just got to!'

'Got to? I don't think so.'

'Otherwise I'm going to the police.'

'And what? Have me charged with being a mean big sister?' I jumped up, flinging a ten-dollar bill onto the table between us to pay for his food. 'That's all you're getting from me. If you want to get clean and sober there are plenty of places you can go in Sydney. Get real, Brad.'

I walked out, my heart racing. Every time I connect with Brad, I thought, my stress levels go through the roof. Glancing at my watch, I hurried to work. For once, the sight of *You're beautiful* etched in the concrete did nothing for me.

Sitting in my office, I went over in my mind the unpleasant scene with my brother. Over the years my mother and I had made excuses for him – the fact that he had never had a father, that my mother was adrift in a universe of grief when he was born, after a difficult pregnancy during which she'd been tormented by the misery of abnormally violent morning sickness. We'd tried to help him for so long. But gradually, both my mother and I had come to realise that we had to let him go. He was never going to grow up with the two of us 'managing' him, trying to fix him.

I went into the bathroom and distracted myself by admiring the pink diamond earrings while I washed my hands and splashed water over my face, washing away the uncomfortable encounter with my brother. I dried my hands and walked out, straight into Nadine.

'We've been looking for you,' she said. 'Rana al-Sheikly called here about ten minutes ago. She wouldn't talk to anyone except you. Where were you?'

'Did she leave a number?' I asked ignoring her question. Nadine shook her head. I swore inwardly, cursing my brother. If I hadn't met up with him I'd have been here when Rana called. Whenever he appeared he managed to stuff things up. I wondered too why she'd called the office and not used my mobile number.

'Oh, by the way, I heard a rumour that someone lobbed a Molotov cocktail over your fence last night,' said Nadine. 'Is that right?'

'I'm afraid so. I was just very lucky that it went out before it went up.'

'Any ideas as to who it might have been?'

'There are a few possibilities. It's a bit like "join the queue" at the moment.'

'I had a stalker once. It was horrible. Ex-boyfriend – well before Alistair. But never anything like an attempted firebombing.' I'd heard from Charlie that Nadine was dating a journalist called Alistair.

'Let's hope you never do,' I said with a smile, before returning to my office.

Next I tried calling the house of Eshaq Boutros again. This time I was lucky: his mother said he was at home.

He came to the phone. 'This is Eshaq. Who is it, please?'

I introduced myself. 'I've been trying to help your friend Rana al-Sheikly. Do you know where she might be?'

'Rana? You've heard from her?' His voice was excited and hopeful.

'I was hoping you had.'

'She called me last night,' he said, sounding deeply concerned. 'Said she was scared. I told her to come to our place, but she said no, it was too dangerous. For me, for my family.'

'Can you think of anywhere she might go? Anyone she might talk to?'

'There's her friend Jamila Khan.'

'We've checked that. She's not with Jamila.'

'There's a young minister she's been talking to,' Eshaq said after a pause. 'He's an Egyptian like me.'

'A clergyman?' I asked, surprised.

'Yes. He's not my priest, but I introduced them. She might have contacted him. I know she was thinking about accepting

Christianity. We spoke about it and I told her I didn't expect her to do it for me. But she wanted to.'

This girl is really sticking it to her brothers, I thought. Refusing to obey them, then thinking about joining the opposition. 'Did the brothers know about that?' I asked.

'I hope not,' said Eshaq. 'I don't think so. She had a Bible and I told her to get rid of it. It's too dangerous for her to keep it anywhere in that house.'

'Where can I find this Egyptian clergyman?'

'I'll call him and get him to contact you, if that's okay?'

'Sure,' I said, and gave him my mobile number. 'If Rana contacts you, will you please tell her to call me? We can help her. I don't think she really believes that.'

'I will tell her. And thank you. Thank you for caring about Rana.'

'It's my job, Eshaq.'

'We've talked of running away together,' he said. 'But it's not so simple. My studies are almost completed. If we moved to another state, my parents would be very distressed. I would be in danger and so would they. We've spoken about leaving Australia altogether. But that also brings problems. I'm doing everything I can to make it possible, but . . . it's complicated.'

It sure is, I thought, after he'd hung up. Still, at least Rana had one man in her life who seemed to care about her happiness. And he seemed level-headed and trustworthy. Yet I felt restless and keyed-up. She could be anywhere, aimlessly wandering or hunkered down somewhere. I called the students' counselling service at the university again, just in case. No, she hadn't contacted them. I stood up and walked out into the larger office and then back into my own again. I rang around the women's refuges. No one of that name or description had contacted any of them.

Right. Next step. I couldn't wait for the Coptic padre to call me so I logged on to my laptop, intent on combing through the internet for the contact details of the Coptic church at South Bayview. My mobile rang and I grabbed it.

'Sergeant Rose,' a man's voice said. 'I might have something for you.'

For a second, I didn't know who he was, but then I remembered. The follow-through man from Newcastle. The one who said, Leave it with me. 'Daniel, wasn't it? So what have you got?'

'The name of the police photographer who did that job. That double murder–suicide out at Garralong in the early nineties.'

'Great work, Sergeant.' I grabbed my pen. Already, my mood was changing for the better. I felt at last that I was getting somewhere.

'Okay. The guy you need to talk to is retired detective Martin Patterson. Out of the job now.'

'Any address?'

'He's moved to the Central Coast by the look of it,' said Rose, and gave me the Gosford address.

'That's very helpful, Daniel,' I said. 'I owe you.'

He chuckled. 'I won't forget.'

I rang off and my email alert chimed. As soon as I saw the subject field I leaned closer, my heart jumping at this synchronicity. It was from a gmail account.

Hello, Smiley.

I clicked it open. Another crime scene photograph filled the page. I almost choked and tears sprang to my eyes. I found myself stupidly touching the screen as if I could get into the image and help him, stop the bleeding and call an ambulance. This time Smiley had sent a far more confronting shot of my poor dead father. He lay near the passenger-side front wheel of his vehicle, his head hanging down over the black mess on his chest, hands flopped uselessly open beside him. I knew with a .303 at such close range, death would have been instantaneous. At least he wouldn't have suffered. There would have been a moment of bewilderment, shock, perhaps a nanosecond of fear, and then the impact, throwing him backwards against the wheel.

Even though I'd studied this scene from the video footage over the years, this full frontal *still* photograph seemed somehow more shocking. Beyond his body was the veranda and the smear mark on the front step leading to the half-open door of the farmhouse.

Smiley had written a typically cryptic message in the subject field, but this time he'd posed it as a question: *What's missing from this picture?*

I stared at the image on the screen, and swallowed back the sob that threatened to break through the stricture in my throat. Goddamn you, Smiley, I thought. Stop playing these cruel games with me. Just tell me what's going on. My father's *heart* is missing from this picture, his chest destroyed by the violence of the shot. Is that what you mean?

I jumped up and paced around the room, distressed and frightened. Now it was getting ugly. For the first time I wondered whether Smiley was threatening me.

I went back to my desk and opened up all three emails, rereading their short messages.

There's more to this than meets the eye.

You're looking in the wrong place.

What's missing from this picture?

I read them over and over, trying to find a meaning in them – a final statement that would answer the three of them. Who was the 'you' in the second email – was it the police in general or me in particular?

I called Cecile. 'I've just had a third Smiley email. It's awful. He's sent another crime scene photo. It's my father, showing his chest wounds.'

'Hey, hey. Slow down. A third email? Your father's chest?'

I took a couple of deep breaths and made myself speak slowly. 'Smiley. He's just sent me a third email.' I described the photograph and read out the message.

'That's horrible, Debs. I'm so sorry. Who is this arsehole?'

I was silent. I had no answers. 'I'm forwarding it to you now.' I hung up and forwarded the third email to Cecile. I would tell her about the attempted firebombing later. *Do everything you can to find out where this was sent from and who sent it. Please.*

Within a minute, Cecile pinged back: *Piggy.*

I leaned back in my seat and continued to focus on my breathing until my heart rate slowed to almost normal again.

Socrates tapped on the lintel of my door and I nodded for him to come in. He was carrying a swathe of computer printouts. 'Are you okay, boss?'

'I'm fine,' I lied, marshalling a smile. 'What have you got for me?'

Socrates dragged across a chair and sat beside me. 'A lot of it is just conversations between Adam Massoud and relatives in Australia and overseas. But these are the links that we should be looking at.' With a pen, he traced the links between numbers, criss-crossing the paper with his fine red lines. 'And these are the *really* interesting connections.' He pointed with the pen at a number that was frequently repeated. 'This number is the al-Sheikly brothers', and these numbers belong to Khaybar Riders members – all known to the police.'

'Don't tell me,' I said. 'George Hakan and Sami Allen?'

Socrates grinned at me. 'Love those telepathic powers of yours. George Hakan is correct. The other number belongs to Freddie Besic of the Warlords.'

'Do we know him?'

'We know him and we've got him. He's currently remanded in Sydney. GBH.'

'That's great, Socrates. We need warrants to listen to some of these characters.'

'I'll talk to Gavin about it,' he said, and was out of my office within seconds.

I hurried to the door and called after him, 'Let me know when the techs are going to do the job?'

'Sure,' he said, looking up from papers on his desk. 'And you should have a look at this. It just arrived.'

'What is it?'

'It's from the Supermax. A security analysis of Adam Massoud.'

'Show me.'

Five minutes later I sat beside Socrates, his laptop open on a desk in front of us. 'He's had a record since he was fourteen.

He's been quite busy inside. The prison authorities tell us that he's attracted a following of other extremely violent young men. Some of them even kneel down in front of him and call him "Sheikh". They kiss his hand.'

'They *what*?' I was shocked. 'Sheikh?'

'That's right, boss. And it's not only men who've fallen under his spell. Recently a woman working in the prison system had to be sacked because she'd formed an inappropriate relationship with Massoud.'

'Anything else?'

'Take a look at this,' he said. 'The prison CCTV picked it up some time back.' He switched on his laptop and a frozen, grainy picture appeared. Socrates indicated what appeared to be a row of doors, obviously the heavy doors of prison cells. 'That door second from the left is where Adam Massoud is locked up,' he said. 'I'll start the footage now. Watch this.'

I was riveted to the screen as something appeared on the lower left-hand side; at first glance it appeared to be a small animal such as a rat, creeping across the corridor that separated the cells lining either side of it, until it disappeared under the door of Massoud's prison cell.

'I'll play it again,' Socrates said, 'and slow it down so you can see what it is.'

This time I saw that the object was actually a mobile phone, being drawn along by an almost invisible thread and sleek and thin enough to fit easily under a prison cell door. 'An associate of Massoud's, who's not under such strict surveillance has acquired the mobile from somewhere and organised the delivery. At the same time, someone had put several thousand dollars in his bank account.'

'Who said crime doesn't pay?' I said, watching as Socrates replayed the footage again.

'After seeing that CCTV footage, the prison authorities had a discussion with the head of Corrective Services,' Socrates continued, 'and they decided against raiding his cell and confiscating the mobile. They let it run and monitored all his calls.'

'Thanks, Socrates,' I said, as he packed up his laptop. 'I know I don't have to tell you how important it is to keep quiet about this. This information must stay in this room. We don't want any leaks getting back to Massoud.'

I returned to my desk picturing Adam Massoud in his prison cell, sending out his instructions. Had one of those instructions included sending a Molotov cocktail over my back fence? And if so, I wondered which of his minions had carried that out. I remembered what Socrates had said about the female prison worker who'd become involved with Massoud; it's a strange phenomenon how many women – often smart and highly educated – are drawn to violent criminals.

As I mulled over the latest information, I stared mindlessly at my desk, and a piece of paper gradually came into focus: retired detective Martin Patterson's address, scribbled down earlier during the conversation with the trustworthy Daniel Rose.

I thought about ringing Martin Patterson, but then decided against it. I wanted to surprise him. I tidied up my desk and put the finishing touches to the leave roster then walked to the door. Charlie and Socrates looked up from their work, Nadine was talking on the phone and taking notes. Alex was out of the office, on surveillance of the al-Sheikly house, and Flash was at court to give evidence on a case alleging a serious assault by a police officer from our days in MEOCS.

'Everything under control, guys?' I asked.

'That depends what you mean by control,' Charlie laughed. 'But we're coping.'

I knew I shouldn't be doing this but I couldn't wait any longer. I had to find out if Patterson knew anything about Smiley. Maybe he *was* Smiley. I grabbed my jacket.

'Going out for a while,' I said to Charlie as I hurried past her, feeling like a kid wagging school. I checked my wristwatch. 'Should be back by around five but I'll probably go straight home. I'll be on the mobile if anyone wants me.'

Within minutes I'd punched in the coordinates and was driving out of the car park and onto the road, heading north.

—•—

An hour and a half later I pulled up outside a newish two-storey brick house in Maas Parade, Gosford. I wasn't quite sure how I was going to run this but I had planned an introduction that I hoped would be revealing. I was pleased to see that a car was parked in front of the double garage – someone was home.

I stepped up to the front door and knocked. Bingo. The door was answered by a man who would have been in his mid-thirties twenty-two years ago. He had the weatherbeaten face of a man who likes fishing and more than the occasional beer. I smiled brightly, flashed my warrant card and said, 'Smiley?'

'What?' He glanced at my ID and then back at me. 'Who do you want?' He peered closer at my warrant card and then drew back. 'Is this how the police introduce themselves these days?' The genuine bewilderment on his face was unmistakeable. My hopes of a quick resolution in the matter of Smiley's identity faded.

'Mr Martin Patterson?' I asked.

'That's me. What does a Sydney detective want with me?'

'How do you know I'm from Sydney?' I asked.

'I know just about every cop and ex-cop in the area. And you look Sydney. What's this all about? And what's with the Smiley business?'

My opening gambit hadn't given me the response I'd been looking for. 'May I come in?'

Martin Patterson looked doubtful for a moment, then stood back for me to enter.

CHAPTER 17

'I remember that night very clearly,' Patterson said.

We sat on cushioned bamboo chairs placed around a low table on the patio at the back of the house. A green wall of tropical plants, ferns and bromeliads rose from the ground beside a small swimming pool, a vertical garden that enclosed the southern boundary, ensuring complete privacy from next door.

'The double murder–suicide out at Garralong.' He nodded.

While Martin made coffee, I pulled out my mobile, wondering why it had been so quiet over the last hour and a half since I'd left Sydney. No signal.

Martin saw me slip the mobile back into my bag as he came outside again. 'Ah, you've noticed my quiet life,' he said, placing a tray with two mugs of black coffee, a jug of milk, a sugar bowl and a plate of Tim Tams on the table. 'People complain about not being able to call from here, but I love it. Landline only. Those damn things are the curse of the modern working man – and woman,' he added. 'They can get you any time of the day or night. There are no more boundaries between working life and private life.'

Once he was settled back in his chair, I told him about two of his crime scene photographs coming through to me in the body of three emails.

'It's a long time ago, but I'll never forget.' He picked up a Tim Tam, looking sheepish. 'The wife's out shopping or she'd never let me have this,' he said with regret, closing his eyes as he bit into it blissfully.

'It was a very cold night, I remember,' he went on. 'We had our first baby then and my wife was upset that I had to leave to drive to Garralong so early that morning. She was new to being a police wife at that stage. And then I got lost – missed the Garralong turnoff the first time.' He looked up and off to one side as people often do when recalling events. 'By the time I got to that farmhouse, the local boys were standing around and the flies had come. Not as bad as they would've been in summer. But pretty bad. I spent the rest of the morning doing that crime scene and then the contractors came out from the hospital and took the bodies away.'

'And your photographs?'

Martin shrugged. 'I developed them, and a day or so later, copies would have gone off to the boss at Garralong, who would have then handed them on to the investigating officer.'

'Do you know who that was?'

Martin shook his head. 'Could've been Barney Sinclair – but he died years ago.'

'Because there were no suspects to chase, there wouldn't have been much more to do on this job?' I suggested.

'That's right. Except wrap it up and file the photographs away. They'd have been kept at Garralong for a while and then packaged up and couriered to police records.'

'So someone from Garralong might have got hold of some of them?'

'It's quite possible,' he said. 'You know what it's like when a local police officer is murdered. The police station would have been in an uproar for a while. It takes time to settle down. Those pictures could've been lying around on someone's desk – anyone could have picked them up and flicked through them. And kept a few. I doubt if anyone would have noticed. It was a solved case. NFAR.'

No further action required. Smiley seemed to be trying to tell me something, point to something.

Martin put his cup down. 'I'm sorry I couldn't have been more helpful.'

I smiled. 'You've been eliminated.'

'You thought I might have been Smiley?' He frowned.

'I was hoping. Now I have to keep searching.'

'I thought you were some crazy woman selling something when you first knocked and greeted me with "Smiley"!' He grinned. 'Tell you what, it would have spooked the real one though, calling him straight out like that.' He frowned again before continuing. 'What do you think those comments mean? About something missing from the photograph?'

'You were there,' I said. 'I know it's a long time ago, but do you think something might have been removed from the scene?'

'You mean evidence tampered with? Evidence removed?'

I considered. 'I don't really know what I mean. It's just that my father's service pistol went missing too. It's confusing. Smiley's indicating that there's something wrong with those photographs – something missing. I'm just fishing around in my mind, trying to imagine what he might be trying to point me towards.'

Martin shrugged. 'I just did what I always did. Observed the protocols about shooting crime scene photos, measured out the correct distances, took my pictures and went back to Newcastle. I suppose you've already considered the possibility that Smiley *is* just a nutter – a time waster. He might have found the photos while going through someone else's stuff – maybe he's a thief? Or they might have turned up at the tip. I met a lot of time wasters while I was in the force. Anything to get a bit of attention.'

'Martin, even if he is just a time waster, I'm still curious as to how he got hold of photographs from the scene of my father's death. I don't like that. I want to know who he is and why he's doing this.' My throat contracted and I swallowed hard. 'He's getting to me. And I don't like that either.'

In the distance, I could hear the chiming of bellbirds sounding the perfect background to this peaceful garden and pool. 'Was there anything about the scene that puzzled you, or that caught your attention in some way?'

Martin leaned back in his chair, frowning. 'It seemed like an open and shut case. Double murder–suicide.' He paused, as if remembering something. 'When I went through detective school, I remember one of the lecturers saying that the quality of an investigation depended on the quality of the investigators at the scene.'

'Are you suggesting that the investigation was incompetent?'

'Look. Specialist crime scene examiners were thin on the ground back then. You know there've been massive advances in technology and training. A lot of the scientific analyses are outsourced now with private practitioners.'

I nodded as he continued. 'And if the local detectives had formed the opinion that there was nothing further to do on this case, except wrap it up, there'd be no need to examine photographs or other exhibits closely.'

'There are some marks on the floor inside the front door and on the front step. Do you remember shooting those?'

Martin shook his head. 'Sorry. It was a long time ago. I would have photographed anything that the detectives brought to my attention. And if I saw something interesting, I'd make a record of it.'

'Thanks Martin,' I said. 'You've been very helpful.'

As he saw me to the door, and we said goodbye, I was thinking I had to get to police archives at the earliest opportunity. I wanted to examine the rest of the photographs closely.

—•—

My mobile rang a few minutes after I'd driven away from the house, after taking my leave of Martin Patterson and the Tim Tam plate. Three messages from Charlie were now showing in my voicemail box and two missed calls. 'Boss, where are you?' Charlie's voice. 'Gavin's looking for you – you're supposed to be here for a briefing —'

'Oh hell,' I swore out loud, then called her back on the hands-free. 'Charlie, I'd completely forgotten about that.' I'd arranged this meeting weeks ago. 'That inspector from Domestic Violence? Greg somebody?'

'It's finished now,' Charlie said. 'And to be honest, you didn't miss much. Just another list of facts and figures about rising domestic violence. I can fill you in. But Gavin's in a foul mood. Thought I'd better warn you.'

'Thanks, Charlie.'

'And there's someone else here who wants to talk to you. Some guy from Goulburn Street. He's driving over soon.'

'Who?'

'I don't know. But he should be here in the hour. Get back *now*.'

I swerved the car into the underground parking station, locked it and ran to the stairwell, checking my watch. I'd been out of the office for almost four hours, and now I'd have to cop the flak. I started taking the stairs two at a time, dreading Gavin's disapproval.

And then I crashed straight into it.

'Where the hell have you been?' he yelled, as we almost collided on the staircase. I jumped back to a lower step, breathless, as Gavin teetered above me, fumbling for the handrail. Seeing that he might fall, I ran up and grabbed his arm, helping him right himself. He angrily shook off my assistance and loomed a step above me, roaring, 'Where have you been? Why didn't you respond to my calls? I've been looking everywhere for you!'

'I was in a dead spot —' I started to say but he yelled over me.

'No one knew where you were. You embarrassed me by your absence! I didn't know what was going on!' He blinked furiously.

'*You* set up this meeting with Greg Masters from Domestic Violence, he comes over expecting to talk to you and the rest of the team and you're a no-show! You've made me look like a fool! He could tell I didn't know what the fuck was going on or even where you were!'

I'd shamed him, I realised. And he was furious about it. I took a deep breath. 'I was following a lead,' I said, unwilling to add fuel to his fire by admitting that it related to my father's death. 'I apologise for my absence. It was very unprofessional of me. It won't happen again.'

'Where were you?' He wasn't going to let me off the hook.

'Gosford.'

'Why?'

'I was talking to an ex-police officer.'

'What about?'

I could tell he was onto me. My reluctance was a dead giveaway.

'You've been out wasting time, chasing those damn ghosts of yours, haven't you?' he demanded.

'The guy I spoke to was very much alive.'

'Don't be a smartarse. You know exactly what I mean. You've been out on your private crusade – some nonsense about crime scene photographs. Sent to you by some idiot who wants to waste police time.' He paused, breathing deeply, and I could see him struggling to quell his anger. 'Debra, I understand that you have been disturbed by this – this reappearance of a past, personal tragedy. But you can*not* use the police force for personal matters! This unit does not operate as the Debra Hawkins personal investigation squad!'

'I know! But I —'

'Get into your office. Now!' He turned and headed back up to our level, stamping up the stairs. Pushing the door open, he stood back to allow me to pass him. I could almost smell the sulphur. Gavin indicated my office and I went in. He closed the door and watched as I sat down.

'In future, Detective Inspector Hawkins, you will give me a report of *everything* you do,' he said with cold fury. 'Consider yourself to be under close supervision from now on. Every evening you will present me with your next day's work outline. You will report to me every callout. I want to know the exact nature of every scene you attend and the precise time you spend there, from the moment you get here to the moment you leave. I want to know where you are and what you are doing every damn second of the day. Understood?'

'But sir, please —'

'You have abused our friendship. Because of our longstanding acquaintance, I've already taken the trouble to speak to you, to warn you in a friendly fashion not to waste your time, and police time – *my* time as supervisor of your team – on your personal mission. But you refused to get the message.' His frown deepened. 'I want you to know that this is a formal admonishment. I'm putting you on paper.'

My heart wilted. Putting me on paper . . . This would be an indelible black mark against me. Once an entry had been made on my file, it was there forever, for every future supervisor to see. My dereliction would go before me to any new posting. Whenever I went for a promotion, that black mark would be seen by any future boss.

'Gavin, I was sent a third email and photograph,' I appealed. 'It *is* a police matter! I was checking out what amounts to a security breach in the custody of crime scene photographs.'

It was as if I hadn't spoken. 'This entire interview goes into your personal file. You just don't get it, do you?'

I could see from the hard set of his mouth that there was no point in further appeal. After a few moments of silence, Gavin spoke again, his tone slightly calmer. 'I can't tell you how disappointed I am in you, Debra. I even thought – and I wasn't alone in this – that you had the makings of a possible future assistant commissioner. I've had to revise my opinion. Your actions reflect badly on you – and on me, too. But you didn't bother to think of that.'

I decided that a dignified silence was best. Finally, Gavin shook his head and turned to leave. 'Now go out and see what that chief inspector wants with you. You've already kept him waiting way too long.'

I headed towards the interview room feeling that things couldn't get much worse.

Boy, was I wrong.

CHAPTER 18

As I walked into the room, a dark-suited man in his forties, with a receding hairline and a chiselled, aquiline nose, rose from his seat behind the small table where he'd been working on a laptop. He had the air of a senior investigator or even a prosecutor. I put out my hand and we shook hands even though I could already feel something bad in the atmosphere. He adjusted the knot in his dark grey tie, then straightened it against his blue striped shirt and motioned me to the chair opposite him, reseating himself as he did so.

'Detective Inspector Hawkins, I'll get straight to the point. I'm Detective Chief Inspector Ignatius Fitzgerald from Police Internal Affairs, and there's a matter I've come to discuss with you.' As he spoke, Fitzgerald pulled out a large envelope from the briefcase on the floor beside him. I stared at it, wondering what was to come.

Internal Affairs. A jolting shock went through me. Every police officer dreads the man from IA. It always means trouble.

'What's this about?' I asked, my heart racing, my mouth going dry. In my mind I whirled through possible omissions and misdemeanours that I might have committed over the last few years but could think of nothing serious enough to warrant this sort of investigation. Surely Gavin hadn't lodged a complaint about me already? No, that was crazy, I told myself. Gavin didn't seem to know what Fitzgerald was here for.

'A serious complaint has been made about you,' Fitzgerald continued.

'*What?*'

'I have some questions to put to you, Inspector Hawkins. But before I do, I'm obliged to caution you that anything you say will be recorded and may be used in proceedings against you.' He paused, his expression stern, leaning forward. 'Do you understand this?'

I nodded, unable to speak, my brain spinning in disbelief. He proceeded to switch on a heavy police-issue recorder and intoned the date and time clearly for the microphone, continuing, 'Interview between Detective Chief Inspector Ignatius Fitzgerald from Police Internal Affairs and Detective Inspector Debra Hawkins of the RED-V unit.'

Fitzgerald focused his shrewd eyes on me for a second before glancing at a piece of paper he'd taken from the envelope. 'Inspector Hawkins, we have received an allegation that you have perverted the course of justice and given material assistance to someone involved in a felony. Are you aware of such an event?'

I closed my eyes. Oh no. Bloody Brad.

That night when he'd come banging on my door and I'd been stupid enough to help him and his delinquent mates avoid the consequences of their behaviour. And I'd been stupid enough not to think ahead about the consequences of my own behaviour.

He'd dobbed me in out of spite. Because I wouldn't give him any more money. I closed my eyes in despair, my mind spinning into the future. If I denied this, it would be his word against mine, and I would very likely be believed whereas my brother's claim could be dismissed as the jealous lies of an addict, intent on destroying the career of a police officer, as hundreds of others had tried to do in the past. But if I *did* lie and this was later proven, I could be charged with perjury on top of the original charge of perverting the course of justice, and this could only make matters worse for me. If I refused to answer and asked for a lawyer, that would be tantamount to admitting guilt. Yet if I told the truth, I was admitting I'd betrayed the justice I had sworn to uphold. My oath would be dishonoured. I could never again give evidence in a court of law and be taken seriously. If I survived at all in the police – and that was unlikely – it would be giving traffic safety and stranger danger lessons at primary schools.

I couldn't believe my brother would do this to me. I briefly thought of how my mother would take this. Another kick in the guts for her. Another disgraced police officer in the family, another screw-up of a child. Somehow, in a sickening way I didn't understand, and despite my intense desire to be a success, I was following in my father's footsteps. Like father, like daughter, people would say. A dud cop father. An addict brother. The whole family rotten to the core.

A black pit seemed to open up beneath me as my mind scrabbled around for a possible way out of this, or at least through it, one that might keep my career intact. I had to make a bid for time – time to consult, to get some advice. Time to think this through.

Chief Inspector Fitzgerald was watching me closely. He must have noticed my stricken face because he said in a gentler voice, 'Believe me when I say this gives me no pleasure. But it's my job and I must do it.' He paused and then asked, 'What do you have to say about these allegations against you?'

'What exactly are they?' I replied, my voice feeble, hoping against hope that it was all some terrible mistake and I'd be able to say with relief, 'That had nothing to do with me. I wasn't involved. You have the wrong person.'

Fitzgerald cleared his throat and began. 'On the evening of the twenty-sixth of November 2004, after a robbery attempt on a suburban jewellery shop in Newtown, it's alleged that you advised the offender on how to avoid arrest by suggesting to him a series of actions; furthermore, it's alleged that the offender carried out these suggestions, including making a false report to the police regarding a stolen vehicle, and thereby avoided detection.'

He flashed a warning look at me. 'Before you say anything,' he said, 'I believe you should hear this.' He reached into his briefcase and pulled out another, much smaller recording device, of the type that journalists use. He switched it on and I stared mesmerised at its tiny red light. 'Tell me if you recognise this conversation.'

The recording began, a few jumbled words and then: '. . . *just don't you ever ask me to do anything like that again!*'

It took me a few moments to realise that I was listening to *me* – my recorded voice from years ago, angry and harsh, sounded oddly unfamiliar on the tape. Shocked, I gripped the sides of my chair, staring at the small recording device. As Brad's younger voice began to speak, I realised when the recording had been made. A few years ago. Brad had called in unexpectedly, wanting, as I'd then thought, to talk over his earlier petty crimes. But now I realised that he had had a far darker motive. My brother had been thinking ahead, looking for a way to gain an advantage over me.

Brad's voice: *'You told us to dump the car and we did. We left it in a lane in Darlo. We wiped it down like you said we should. I made up this story about Mum's car being stolen when I got home. She reported it as stolen to the police. She was totally convinced.'*

Now I felt sick as I heard him laughing at his own cleverness. *'My sister,'* he was crowing on the tape, *'the ace police constable. My sister in crime!'*

My younger voice responded to his taunts. *'Shut up and grow up! Now go! Don't you dare come near me again wanting a favour. Never! Now get out of my house!'*

Fitzgerald leaned over and switched off the recording. Then he sat watching me across the table, awaiting my response.

I desperately needed time. Time to think this through, to work out a strategy. Survival instincts kicked in. 'Chief Inspector, I think you can appreciate that this is a great shock. These events are alleged to have occurred years ago and I really need to think – to examine the ramifications without the pressure of a formal recorded interview. Could I ask for an adjournment while I consult with a member of the Police Association as to how I should best proceed with this matter?'

There was a moment's silence, then Fitzgerald nodded and spoke into the large police recorder. 'Suspending record of interview with Detective Inspector Debra Hawkins of the RED-V unit at 5.34 pm.'

He even looked slightly relieved, I thought, as he put the printed sheet back into its envelope, and returned the envelope and the smaller recording device to his briefcase. 'Forty-eight hours should be enough,' he said. 'We'll continue this discussion here again on Friday – at 2 p.m.?'

'I'll need more time,' I said. 'Please make it for next week? At the moment I have special leave requirements – family illness.'

Fitzgerald hesitated, then finally nodded again, making a note of it. 'I will expect you to have everything completed by then,' he said, 'your legal representative organised and anything you might want to bring to the interview. There can be no more adjournments after this.'

With the whirlwind of confused, angry and frightened thoughts currently going through my mind, I would have agreed to almost anything at that point, short of being executed on the spot.

We stood up at the same time and our eyes met across the table. It was hard to read what Fitzgerald was thinking. He was just a man doing his job, as he'd said. I was thankful for the fact that he had warned me not to say anything before he played the tape. He didn't want me perjuring myself recklessly. He hadn't been trying to trap me and I was grateful for that.

He walked out first, leaving the door open, and I stood there a moment wondering how I was going to deal with all the questions that I knew would be waiting for me outside this room. I took a deep breath and followed him out, then closed the door behind me, fixing a smile on my face. It didn't fool anyone. Socrates looked up at me and then glanced towards the retreating figure of Detective Chief Inspector Fitzgerald.

Charlie hurried over, concern on her face. 'Are you okay?'

I nodded. 'No questions, please, Charlie. This is a confidential matter.' I hoped it might satisfy the others if they thought there had been some confidential investigative procedure under discussion in the interview room.

'Sure,' she said. 'But isn't that guy from IA?'

I looked around, wondering where Gavin was. Charlie saw my glance and said, 'He's gone. It's okay.' She put a hand on my arm. 'We could hear him yelling at you from out here.'

'He had a point,' I said. Once he'd heard Brad's allegations, Gavin would be even more angry with me. I swallowed hard as I realised he'd sack me from RED-V for this. He couldn't have a tainted officer in charge. Nadine would probably get her chance after all, I thought bitterly. 'I was out on another matter,' I tried to explain. 'One that is not an official police matter.'

I looked at my watch. 'I have to go out. Family business.'

'Your mum,' Charlie nodded sympathetically.

I didn't correct her.

Charlie gave my arm a squeeze. 'Whatever it is, Deb, I'll do anything I can to help.'

Tears stung my eyes. Her kindness had momentarily halted the whirling storm in my brain. I stood for a moment, seeing the questions on the faces of the others, then turned and went into my office. I closed the door firmly behind me and walked to the window, staring sightlessly across the buildings to the murky skyline. I had just over a week to get hold of Brad and make him retract his allegations. My career was in the chamber, just waiting for the trigger to be pulled.

I raced out of the office again, hitting Brad's phone number as I ran down the stairs to the car park. He wasn't answering his phone so I drove to my mother's place, and walked around to the back door, which was usually left open; as I stepped inside, I could hear her voice. It sounded as though she was on the phone.

'Hi, Mum,' I called out as I walked through the kitchen into the living room.

She stood in the middle of the room, holding the phone, and as she turned around to nod to me I was struck by how thin she was. Her dark trouser suit seemed to be hanging on her. She walked away to her desk and continued to speak into the phone. 'I don't want to talk about it. In fact, right this minute, I can't,' she said defiantly. I was immediately curious about who she was talking to – and what it was they'd been discussing.

She terminated the call and put the phone back on her desk, next to her laptop, looking back at me with a half-smile. 'Debra? This is a nice surprise. What brings you here at this time?'

I thought I detected a new note in her voice, a softer expression, and for a moment I felt like telling her everything – about the trouble I was in, how Brad had betrayed me, how I was possibly about to lose my career. The words were almost on my lips, but I just couldn't bring myself to speak them. No wiring had ever been laid down to connect us in personal matters such as this, and I didn't know how to create a bridge now. There was nothing she could do about it, anyway.

'I need to talk to Brad,' I finally said. 'I was hoping you would have an idea where he might be.' I glanced down at her trousered leg. 'How's it going?'

My mother walked carefully over to me then lifted her left trouser leg to show me her shin. 'See? It's still nicely bandaged up and it's not giving me too much trouble. What do you want Brad for?'

'I have to talk to him about something – it's nothing for you to worry about.'

'I'm always worried about him. Where he's living, if he's eating . . . sometimes I worry that he's not even alive anymore. I'm always worrying about him,' she repeated, rebuking me.

While she was speaking, I'd taken a break from mentally cursing Brad to look at what was in front of my eyes. 'Mum, speaking of eating – when was the last time you ate something? You're not going anorexic on me, are you?' There were deep shadows around her eyes, and her face with its high cheekbones had a gaunt appearance.

She gave a bleak smile. 'In my practice, I've never known an anorexic mother. It's almost *always* the daughter.'

'You don't look well. You're too thin.'

'I've always been thin.'

'Not this thin. Let me make you something. A sandwich, or cheese and bickies.' She protested but I didn't take any notice. Making a snack for her might also help me come down from my rage with Brad, I thought. There's always something soothing about preparing food.

I went to her fridge and found a sharp cheddar cheese, and there was an unopened packet of crackers in the pantry. I washed and sliced a tomato from the fruit bowl and soon I'd made up a plate of cheese and tomato crackers. I took them out to the living room together with a couple of plates.

'Here, have some of these,' I said, putting them down on a small table near her usual armchair.

My mother took one of the plates and put a cracker on it. 'I really have no idea where Brad is,' she said, after taking a small bite. 'He hasn't called me for a long time. Not that that's any surprise. He knows I won't give him any more money. And that's the only reason he ever calls me.' She sighed as she picked up her diary. 'I've got his most recent address though, if that's any help.' She read it out to me, and I noted it down.

My rage against my brother was subsiding. On the way over to my mother's place I had resolved to find Brad and make him withdraw the allegations against me, to claim that he had lied and that it wasn't my voice on the tape. I would find a way to force him to do this – I could threaten to make life very difficult for him. He knew that I knew how to do it. At the same time my conscience was whispering, *Don't do this. Go to Chief Inspector Fitzgerald and tell him everything. He is a good man. There's a slight chance he might not continue to press this. But you must tell the truth. Even if it means the end of your career. How will you live with yourself if you lie about this? Your whole police life would be a fraud from that day on. It would eat away at you. Every time you took the oath in the courtroom, it would be there in your mind, reminding you what you are – a liar and perjurer.*

I chewed my way through one of the cheese crackers without really tasting it while my internal debate continued to rage. Then I deliberately brought myself back to the present moment, sitting in my mother's living room, just a couple of metres away from her. 'You didn't finish your biscuit.'

'I'm not really hungry,' she said, 'although it was kind of you to make them. I might have them later.'

'Not too much later. They'll go all soggy if you leave them too long.' I stood up, preparing to go. 'You really need to take more care of yourself. I'm going to keep an eye on you from now on and make sure you're eating properly.'

'You're fussing again. You know I can't stand that.'

'I'm not fussing, I'm concerned. I care about you.'

My mother looked up and I was shocked at the depth of anguish in her eyes. Was this something new or had it always been there and I'd never noticed? I'd become so used to her unhappiness that I'd failed to notice this new level.

'Thanks for your concern, Debra.' She made a sound, part sigh, part sob, but recovered herself quickly, taking the plate with the half-eaten cracker out to the kitchen. She called back in a brisk voice, 'But you mustn't worry about me.' She returned to the living room, wiping her hands on a paper towel. 'And now, I really do have things to do.' She indicated the papers on her small desk.

'I'll call you soon,' I said, pausing at the front door, glancing back at her, so thin and hunched, looking as if she was keen to get back to her paperwork. I wanted to run back and hug her, comfort her, tell her I loved her. But I wasn't sure that I could do that. And I feared that if I did, she'd only push me away. Instead I waved from the door. 'If there's anything you need, just call me. Bye, Mum.' I closed the door behind me.

Outside, I sat in my car for a few moments, recovering from whatever it was that invariably afflicted me after any interaction with my mother. As if I don't have enough to deal with, I thought bitterly. And I couldn't tell my mother that I was probably facing the end of my career in policing. I couldn't risk it. Because for as long as I didn't tell her, for as long as I kept quiet about it, I could still hope that if I *did* tell her, she might actually care.

I drove to the address she'd given me for Brad. It turned out to be a neglected one-storey terrace house in a backstreet in Enmore; in the front yard, long grass grew up between crates of empty bottles. I banged on the door. Even from outside I could smell the cloying odour of marijuana and of the incense that had been burned, presumably to cover it. There was no response, so I peered through the narrow front windows, cupping my hands around my eyes to cut down on the reflection. I couldn't see much, just piles of old takeaway food containers on the floor, overflowing ashtrays, broken and threadbare furniture, and stained and peeling wallpaper. I went around to the back and easily forced the dodgy back door, then stepped inside gingerly, reeling at the stench of old food, stale tobacco and alcohol, marijuana and incense. I walked through a kitchen piled high with dirty dishes and burnt-out pots, almost tripping on the torn-up vinyl floor covering. The place felt empty and I was sure it was a squat. No one owning this place could have the temerity to charge rent, and no one living here would have the wherewithal to pay it.

I went from the kitchen into a dark and filthy bedroom where someone had tried to repair a broken window by taping clear plastic sheeting to the frame. This now flapped in the wind, spreading dust and dried insects along the windowsill. I glanced down and my breath caught with shock. A man lay on the bedroom floor, face bruised and covered in blood that had pooled and congealed on the dirty shag pile carpet beside him. A grubby coverlet half covered him, as if he'd grabbed it as he fell, dragging it from the messy bed. I pulled out my mobile to call an ambulance, instinctively looking behind me just in case. But there was no one else in the house.

I stepped closer, about to bend down to check for a pulse, and that's when I recognised the battered face as Brad's.

CHAPTER 19

I rode with Brad in the ambulance, and waited while they admitted him, giving the hospital his name and date of birth, and putting myself down as next of kin to spare my mother this new blow. We waited for a while in the receiving bay; a young man groaned occasionally on the next trolley, although I couldn't see what was wrong with him. Eventually, the triage nurse came in and expressed her concern about Brad's head and facial injuries, which she cleaned up as well as she could. I told her as much as I knew while a young Asian doctor checked out Brad's vital signs.

'No point in you hanging around,' she said, straightening up. 'It'll be some time before he's wheeled away to x-ray. We'll get in touch with you when we know a bit more. Okay?'

My mobile rang and I excused myself, hurrying out into the corridor as I answered, 'Deb Hawkins.'

'Please,' said Rana al-Sheikly in a whisper. 'Please come and meet me. I'm willing to make a statement about my brothers.'

I reeled with relief at the sound of her voice. Rana had called in! Finally, something was going my way. 'Where are you, Rana?'

'I'm at church,' she said, and gave me the address in South Bayview. 'Father Joseph is helping me.'

'I'm on my way,' I said. 'And Rana – thank you. Thank you so much for calling me.'

— • —

Following Rana's directions, I drove to the church. As I parked on the street I looked over at the large, long building, its Byzantine dome topped with decorative crosses. Normally, I would have taken much more interest in the architecture and the design, but right now I was too preoccupied. It took me two circuits of the church before I noticed some lights in an annex under a walkway linking the church and the church hall. I hurried over and pushed through the glass doors, following the light and saw an open door on the left of the corridor. Finding the door half open, I knocked, and an accented voice said, 'Come in!'

I stepped inside as Father Joseph stood up and came out from behind his desk. A vigorous man in his thirties, he had a full beard and wore a large cross hanging from a heavy chain against the black fabric of his soutane. He greeted me warmly and ushered me further into his book-lined office. 'Would you like a cup of tea?' he asked.

'Very much,' I said, grateful for the offer.

Father Joseph spoke with his back to me as he switched on an electric kettle and lifted two cups out of a cupboard. 'I've spoken to Rana already,' he said, placing a tea bag in each cup then turning back to me. 'You do understand that she could be in great danger from her family or even other members of her community.'

While in MEOCS I'd heard reports of death threats issued by hardliners to people who'd wanted to change their religion, of garbage and dead animals thrown into front yards, of broken windows and vandalised cars endured by the 'apostates'. It seemed unbelievable that something like this could be happening in Australia.

The water boiled and the priest filled our cups, then produced a bottle of milk from a small fridge in a sideboard. I looked around his office, noting the gilded saints in their frames, unfamiliar from my Roman-Catholic childhood apart from a Byzantine icon of the Christ. As I looked at this, I spoke a question that had been in my mind. 'I hope this doesn't sound impolite, Father Joseph, but why does Rana want to join your church? Don't you think she would have had enough of religion by now?'

Before he could answer me, a faint sound made me glance towards the door leading to the interior of the building. It opened, and there stood Rana al-Sheikly, wearing a pretty dress and light jacket. Her gleaming black hair – which had always been covered on our previous encounters – streamed down around her face and shoulders, and I was reminded of the old-fashioned notion that her hair is a woman's crowning glory.

'I couldn't help overhearing your question,' said Rana shyly, stepping into the room and bringing with her a soft floral fragrance. 'But unless you've been raised like I have, you probably can't understand that I must have God in my heart. There is a hole in my soul without God, and here I find a God of love.' She threw a shy glance at the priest. 'And Father Joseph is not like the older priests. He understands. The old priests are fearful – not for themselves but for the safety of their flock. They don't want to make things worse by confrontation.'

'I understand them completely,' said Father Joseph. 'They know only too well what can happen. They see what's happening back home in Egypt. They practise discretion.'

Rana's face appeared more tranquil today; she seemed less the anxious, fearful girl I'd met in the mall. She must have been recalling our last meeting too, because she came over to me, putting out her hand. 'I'm so sorry I ran away, Debra. I know you are trying hard to help me. But if Talal had seen me talking to you, I don't know what might have happened. As it was, it took me some time to convince him that I'd been held up at the post office. The other policewoman had taken him down into the underground car park to check out his car. He was very angry because she found some defective things that he has to fix. Then Samir arrived. While they were fighting, I tried to get away, but only got as far as the next block.'

I remembered the surveillance sequence of Rana hurrying through the doors of the shopping mall and then disappearing from view. 'But they saw me before I could get on the bus and forced me back into the car. I was sent to my room and told not to come out until they gave permission. They were furious with me. They said my behaviour had dishonoured them – shamed them.' She paused, lowering her eyes. 'I heard them talking about me in the front room. My brothers don't realise that I remember a lot of Arabic from my childhood. I can't speak it, but I can follow a conversation. They think I don't understand if they speak Arabic.' Her arched brows contracted and an expression of despairing sadness shadowed her face.

'I'm just so pleased to see that you're safe,' I said. 'You should know, Rana, that your brothers already know who I am.'

'But so far, they've never put us together,' she said.

'And I'm pleased that you're willing to make a statement, because then we can act more easily and speedily.'

'I now have evidence of them plotting my death. That's why I ran here. I overheard them planning how to make it look like an accident. They talked about drugging me, putting me behind the wheel of the car and then pushing the car into a dam in the country. A father and mother in Canada murdered their three daughters and a disobedient first wife by doing something similar. They almost got away with it.'

'We'll have to find you a safe place to stay,' I said. 'I'll talk to Maryam about —'

'No, no. No Maryam,' said Rana, grasping my arm. 'She might be okay but I don't want anyone – anyone at all – connected to the community to know where I am. It's not just me. It's Eshaq and his family. I mustn't do anything to put them in danger.'

'Okay, okay,' I said, alarmed at her distress. 'No Maryam. I promise.'

'Father Joseph is asking to see if I can stay with a family he knows who are friends of the Coptic community but not part of it – just till I get myself on my feet. But I don't have any money to pay for board.'

'We can assist a little,' Father Joseph began. 'And your student allowance will help.'

'But I can't stay at university. I wouldn't be safe there. Too many spies, and my brothers would watch for me coming and going.'

'What about Eshaq?' I asked. 'He'd surely be willing to help.'

Father Joseph shook his head sadly. 'He is. But he has to make a huge decision. If he wants to be with Rana, they'll both have to relocate. He will have to leave his family, his studies and everything else and move interstate with her. His family, too, could be in danger of reprisals. Things are not simple.'

I nodded, thinking. 'I've heard this from Eshaq himself. Rana, we can help you transfer to an interstate university. But just for now, we'll keep you safe until the appropriate agencies can take over.' I turned to Father Joseph, addressing the concerned expression on his face. 'There are government agencies Rana can utilise. She's an Australian citizen and entitled to all the support that's available.'

I felt a pang. There really wasn't a great deal we could do for women like Rana. We could give her some assistance with the installation of a security system in her new flat, when she got one; provide a police mobile with a number to call in emergencies and set up with the Aurora app, which was supposed to bring fast support and assistance; and possibly also organise a small amount of money and food packages from one of the government agencies. An apprehended violence order would be a waste of time – her brothers would pay no attention to it. The best we could do was help Rana get away and make a new life for herself in a new state or city. With or without Eshaq.

'I'll leave university and get a job,' said Rana. 'I'll work hard to support myself. I can do part-time university studies later. I want to learn to be independent.'

I nodded, hearing her youthful words. 'Let's get that statement done, Rana.' I opened my notebook, ready to take down her words, and Father Joseph discreetly left the room.

Rana took a deep breath and squared her shoulders. I could tell that this was one of the most important decisions in her life. She wasn't just leaving home, she was betraying her tribe – leaving the known world. Far more so than I was, she was aware of the dangers of what she was doing. Her voice wobbled a little when she first started speaking, stating the approximate time and the date of the incident, but then became firmer and stronger as I occasionally helped her with the usual witness statement style.

'My name is Rana al-Sheikly and I live in Daylesford, Sydney, with my brothers, Talal and Samir al-Sheikly. For over a year now, my brothers have been putting pressure on me, including by hitting me, pushing me around and locking me in my bedroom. When they heard I was friendly with a Coptic boy at university, they forced me to watch DVDs of the torture and murder of Coptic children in Egypt.' At this, her voice failed her completely. She whispered, 'One little boy was only six years old and they dumped his ruined body in the family sewer.' There was a pause while Rana regathered her composure. She continued again in a stronger voice, 'My brothers said this is what happens to people who don't follow the true path, and it also happens to women who don't obey their fathers and brothers and who behave like sluts. I told them that I had done nothing wrong, that my friend was only helping me with my studies in chemistry. I tried to explain that there are always males in tutorial groups and lectures, that there's no segregation there. They said I must terminate my university studies and they burnt all my books.

'I was in my bedroom when I heard them speaking in loud and angry voices and went to my door to hear more clearly. At first, they were talking about places where drugs were being made – "cooked", they said – and about how someone had ripped them off, but then they started talking about me. They have recently bought a second-hand Ford. I don't have a driver's licence yet and a few weeks ago when I asked them who it was for, they looked at each other and laughed and said it was for me. From my bedroom door I overheard them talking about drugging me, taking me out of the city and pushing the car into a dam or river somewhere. I believe they are planning to murder me and make it look like an accident – or a suicide. That is why I believe I am in great danger for as long as they know where I am.'

I stopped writing and looked up at the beautiful girl. Our eyes met, and this time I saw something that hadn't been there in our earlier contact. Her face glowed with a new light and I recognised it as the beginnings of hope. She briefly closed her eyes before she went on. 'At last, I can be free. Free to decide what I want to do with my own life. It is terrifying and yet wonderful. You can't imagine what that feels like because you've taken it all for granted. God has given me this precious life and I must live it as *my* life, not as someone else's.'

'Rana,' I said, touched by the depth of her courage, 'I'll do everything I can to assist you in this. I'll get this statement printed up as soon as possible and back to you to sign.'

'There's something else,' Rana said, taking a piece of paper from her pocket and passing it to me. 'You might find this helpful.'

I looked down. Neatly written on the sheet of paper were five names and phone numbers. 'Whose are they?' I asked, raising my eyes to hers again.

'I believe they are the people who cook or distribute drugs. My brothers' garage is a safe place to store them. I've seen drums of chemicals stored in their workshop and also in the garage at our house. Sometimes they come back into the house carrying stuff in bags which I'm not allowed to unpack. Normally things like shopping, and putting groceries away, and cooking, are my work. But these packages I'm not allowed to touch.' Rana paused. 'But lately, they've been under such pressure from the police, constantly being watched and visited – you know what I mean, those welfare visits? Just to make sure everything is all right?'

I nodded. I'd made a recent 'welfare' visit myself.

'They had all this – this *product*. But they couldn't move it because the police were watching everyone. People owed them money that they couldn't collect. They were stressing out! They got careless because of the stress and I found these phone numbers on a table.'

In spite of the looming threat to my career, and my other worries, I felt almost jubilant. Rana had just handed me the best kind of information an investigator could want. Now we had names and phone numbers. I would send this information to Strike Force Raptor and the Gang and Drug squads. Combined with the evidence Rana had given us concerning a possible conspiracy to murder her, surely we would have enough to arrest the brothers, charge them, make sure they were no-bailed and get them off the streets so they could no longer menace their sister.

'Rana, thank you so much. It's very courageous of you, giving me this information about your brothers.'

Rana's beautiful mouth turned down in a bitter smile as she replied, 'What are they going to do – murder me twice?'

'I promise you I'll make sure no one ever knows where this information came from. It's strictly between you and me.'

Rana nodded her acceptance of my promise.

'I can't imagine what this means to you, leaving everything you know,' I added.

'I was undecided for a while, but something you said helped me to make up my mind,' she said, frowning in concentration.

I was curious, unable to imagine what wonderful words of wisdom I could have uttered that might have influenced the strong young woman before me. To me, Rana seemed mature beyond her years; compared to her strength and spirit I felt callow, insubstantial.

She looked at me. 'Debra, you said that I was a citizen of this country – a citizen of Australia – and entitled to the protection of the law like any other citizen. I'd never thought of myself like that before, that this protection was something I didn't have to beg and plead for, or fight for – it was my right. Those words just kept ringing through my mind, over and over. I belong in *this* country, not some other place, and I am entitled to protection under the law. For the first time I grasped what that means, that I have the same rights as anyone else, including the right not to be forced into anything. You don't know how important that was to me – for me to hear and take in.'

'You do understand that by doing this,' I waved the piece of paper with the names and phone numbers on it, 'you may have put yourself in more danger. As I've said, I'll keep your name out of it. But you must never have any more dealings with your family. They'll suspect it was you who gave the police this information. This is the end of your family relationships.'

Rana looked at me with something like indulgence, as if she were humouring a child. 'Debra, I understand that very well indeed.' She paused and then continued, shyly, 'Eshaq helps me and supports me. We read Psalm 27 together. There is a verse that says: "Though my father and mother have rejected me, the Lord will gather me in," and that comforts me.'

Her eyes filled with tears, and I was startled to find that her words had hit a hidden wound in me. To cover my emotional reaction, I put on a businesslike manner. 'Can I leave Rana with you now, Father Joseph?' I asked the priest, who had quietly re-entered the office. I put away my notebook and prepared to leave.

Father Joseph smiled. 'Rana will be safe with Mrs Fouad, Detective Inspector. She is one of our oldest converts but she's not known as a member of our community. She's very aware of what it means to be in Rana's position.' He turned to Rana. 'In that very psalm you mention, Rana, the Lord also promises to deliver you from the false witnesses gathered against you who "breathe words of violence".'

I liked the sound of that. 'Rana, call me the moment you're safely settled. I'll need to bring your statement around for you to sign, so I'll need your address.' I handed her another one of my cards just in case.

Rana hesitated, looking from Father Joseph then back to me.

'Okay,' she said finally, and wrote out the address on a piece of paper given to her by the priest.

'I'll guard it ferociously. I'll be the only one who knows it,' I promised. 'If that's all, let me wish you all the best, Rana. I'll check up on you from time to time – just to make sure everything's going well.'

I felt an impulse to hug her, but instead I put out my hand. She smiled and we shook hands.

'Would you like to see our church?' Father Joseph asked me after Rana had left the office.

'I guess so,' I said, not able to think of a good reason to refuse.

'You are not a religious woman?' Father Joseph enquired, noting my reluctance.

I felt uneasy about the direction this conversation was taking and just wanted to get out of there with Rana's information regarding the clandestine labs. I tried to be gracious. 'Nothing against it really,' I said as we walked across the walkway to the church. 'It's just not for me. God and I separated years ago.'

Father Joseph smiled. 'Impossible,' he said. 'You might have walked out on God, but . . .' He hesitated.

'God didn't walk out on me? Is that what you're suggesting, Father?' I asked, raising an eyebrow.

Father Joseph was smart enough to leave it there, and I didn't want to get into a theological debate just then. We paused together on the steps outside the entrance to the church; I sensed that the priest wanted to say something more, but the moment had passed.

He flicked on several switches near the entrance and I followed him into the fragrant interior of the church, glowing with gold and sumptuously decorated wall icons, lofty arched vaults and hanging lamps, blazing with light. It took my breath away. 'It's beautiful,' I said with sincerity, overwhelmed by its splendour.

'It *is* beautiful.' Then, as if he were confiding a great secret, he lowered his voice. 'The desire to dominate others is the essence of hell. Love is *freedom*. The spirit draws us by love and beauty, never by force. Perhaps one day you will discover this for yourself?'

'A happy thought,' I said, putting out my hand and shaking his. 'Now I really must go.'

'I will pray for you. That you come to see your fears are unfounded. That all will be well.'

I looked hard at him. Were these just clever lines from an experienced people-handler like the so-called psychics who do 'cold readings'? Or had Father Joseph read in my face something of my troubles?

'Thank you for supporting Rana,' I said, feeling uncomfortable under his benign, observant gaze. 'It's very good of you.'

'I'm just doing my job,' he said with a smile. 'Like you.'

I'd heard that comment twice today. I recalled the shrewd-eyed Detective Chief Inspector Fitzgerald. We're all just doing our job, but some of us do it better than others, I thought. Despite his attempt at catechising me, Father Joseph was in that group.

CHAPTER 20

By the time I got home, I was tired and hungry. Mark must have gone out, I thought. I made a quick meal of scrambled eggs and salad, then called my mother. 'Debra, you mustn't fuss about me,' she said, when she heard my voice.

'I'm ringing about Brad,' I said. 'He's been injured.'

'Brad? How? What happened? Where is he?' she asked, her voice high with anxiety.

I gave her a sanitised version, about a fight at the place he was staying. 'Brad came off the worse for wear and they've got him in hospital. He's okay.'

'I'd better go and see him now.'

'I can take you,' I said.

'I'm quite capable of driving, Debra,' she said, and I felt relieved. I was whacked and glad that I didn't have to go out again.

I rang off and was washing up when Mark rang.

'Darling, I'm really sorry. I'm ringing from the airport – I'm needed back at the mine urgently, something only I can sort out, apparently. I'll be back as soon as I can.'

My heart sank. There was so much I wanted to talk over with him, but now was not the time.

I sighed. 'It hasn't been the best week I've ever had.'

'If I was there, I'd give you a cuddle and pour you a G and T.'

I smiled. 'That would be nice. Especially the cuddle.'

—•—

Next morning, I called my friend in the drug squad, Geoff King.

'Debra,' he flirted. 'This is the best call I've had for ages.'

'It will be when you hear what I've got for you . . . five names and phone numbers, clan-lab activities: producers and locations.'

There was a silence, then, 'Who's your informant?'

'An anonymous source. But I can tell you the information involves the al-Sheikly brothers.'

—•—

I was checking my emails when Charlie knocked at my door.

'A call came for you, Deb, from a guy in the Federal Police. Then it was put through to me. It's about Kylie Mifsud.'

I tensed, fearing the worst. 'What's happened?'

'Hey, it's okay.' She must have noticed the fear on my face. 'In fact, it's all good news. George Hakan was arrested attempting to break into the friend's house at Leura. Kylie hadn't been there for some time but he wasn't to know that.'

'Cops attending a burglary in progress? I don't think that's ever happened in the history of burglary!'

'Don't be so cynical. And it wasn't a burglary. A squad car was driving past, keeping an eye on the address, and they did a rego check on a car – Hakan's car – parked nearby.'

I nodded, pleased that my request to the local cops had brought such good results.

'She must have good karma,' Charlie was saying, raising an eyebrow at the expression on my face. 'No, really, she must. Because Hakan's confessed to break and enter with the intention of killing Kylie Mifsud.'

'No way. How come?'

'MEOCS had some very damaging information on him, about him giving information to the police in a previous deal he did – he gave up a couple of very dangerous criminal associates to get out of a serious federal charge. They hinted that if Hakan didn't cooperate these criminals might get to hear who dobbed them in.'

'Then I think he made the right decision to confess. Terrible things can happen to anyone who betrays members of the gang brotherhood. Chainsaw amputations, that sort of thing.' Relief softened the muscles in my neck. Kylie's would-be murderer and the Massoud associate who'd been tailing me was off the streets. And if Massoud's associates were still after Kylie, that meant she must have found a safe place to hide. 'Time I had some good news,' I said. 'I just wish Kylie would contact me.'

Charlie cocked her head, frowning. 'What's wrong? What did that IA guy want? Can you talk about it?'

I shook my head.

'Please, like I said, if there's anything I can do.'

'Thanks, Charlie.'

She paused a moment in the doorway then walked off.

Feeling like a kid on detention, I started filling out the timesheet for Gavin, detailing what I'd done yesterday, the time I'd spent doing it, and my time out of the office.

Cecile called. 'Hey, you busy?'

'Always. Why?'

'I'm working from home,' she said. 'Why don't you come over and have some lunch? I've got some sensational French cheeses.' She paused. 'Are you okay, Deb?'

'Not really. Things have happened . . .'

'Things?'

'I'll fill you in when I see you. I won't come to lunch. I'll drop in after work.'

I went through the printout of the contemporaneous notes that Flash, Alex and Nadine had taken over the last twenty-four-hour surveillance period. No unusual activity had been reported. The brothers went to the garage and spent the day there. Several visitors had come and gone and all their registration plates had been recorded and photographs taken and forwarded to MEOCS and the Gang Squad just in case. The brothers left the garage at 7 p.m., had a meal at a local restaurant. No one approached them during the meal. They came home at nine twenty and the lights went out in the house at 11.06 p.m.

Dutifully, I added this activity to the timesheet that I would give to Gavin when he asked for it.

I buzzed Cecile's apartment and ran up the stairs, ignoring the lift. On the third floor, Cecile's flat door stood open for me and I went inside to find her pouring white wine into two long-stemmed glasses. 'You sounded like you needed a drink,' she said, passing me one of them.

I followed her out onto her small balcony and saw that she'd been working there, with her laptop on a table. The first red blush of a coral tree across the road softened the view.

'Okay,' she said, as I sat down opposite her. 'Tell me about the things. Good and bad?'

'Some good things, some bad. A girl I was worried about and who was being pressured by her brothers into a forced marriage is okay, has made a statement implicating her brothers in conspiracy to murder and involvement with the supply and manufacture of prohibited drugs.'

'Wow. She won't be popular.'

'She already isn't. She's the person they're conspiring to murder.' I sipped the wine, wincing at its dryness.

'Lordy,' said Cecile. 'So that's the first good thing. I can't wait to hear what the bad things might be.'

'And another girl who was under threat is flying under the radar, I hope – to start a new life. So she's off the immediately endangered list too.'

'Get to the bad things.'

'There's a line-up,' I said. 'It's Brad. And it's IA trouble – internal affairs.'

'Give me the Brad thing first.'

'Actually, they go together. Brad's put in a complaint about me. It's worse than just a paper file. He's got a tape recording of a conversation I had with him after that failed smash-grab. The man from IA played some of it. They must have acted immediately on getting Brad's allegations.'

Cecile was the only person apart from Mark whom I'd told about this and we'd excused my behaviour as misplaced kindness to a foolish young boy carried out by a very young constable.

'The little arsehole,' said Cecile. 'He deliberately provoked you into talking about it and got it on record? Those *Law and Order* shows on TV should be banned.'

There was a silence.

'So, Deb. What are you going to do?'

'I'm going to try and get him to retract his complaint. I didn't tell you he's been badly bashed by a dealer and just now he's in hospital. He was in a bad way when I found him. I'm going to take some special leave. At least I can use Brad for that.'

'You could always put a pillow over his face like they do in the movies.'

'Similar thoughts have occurred to me, don't worry,' I said. 'But no. I've decided to go bush. I'm going back to Garralong. I'll first make a visit to police records and have a look at the crime scene photos myself. Check out the old brief while I'm there, and the witness statements. Gavin's never going to cooperate in this matter now so I've got to get them myself. Maybe there'll be something in the other still photographs that will tell me something.'

'Like what?'

'Something I haven't noticed. Then I'll take a couple of days off and drive to Garralong. The fresh air will do me good. There are people I want to track down. And things I want to clear up.'

'The Smiley thing?'

'The Smiley thing. And then some.'

'Like?'

'Like seeing if there's anyone who remembers that night and might throw some light on the matter. I was only a little kid. There might have been things I didn't know about at the time – rumours about something missing from the crime scene. I've got to find out what Smiley's on about. Why he's trying to get me to re-examine the photos – and why he's chosen to stay anonymous.'

'Maybe he's the party who removed something from the scene?'

I nodded. 'That's occurred to me too. Smiley might have come across the scene before Craig Davidson discovered it the next morning and for some reason he's done something, taken something away. Something he shouldn't have. Or seen something no one else did. I just don't know . . .'

'Maybe Smiley just likes teasing you. He might keep sending you emails. If you wait long enough he might eventually reveal the answer.'

'I'm not prepared to wait for that.'

'But what are you going to do about Brad and Internal Affairs?' Cecile asked.

'Look, I might have to buy Brad off. Give him the money he wants to go to Bangkok on the condition that he retracts his allegation. Then I'll deny that's my voice and he'll back me up.'

'What if he doesn't? Are you honestly willing to perjure yourself over this? Have you really thought this through?'

'That's why I'm talking about it with you.' I shook my head, mentally striking through that thought. 'I can't submit to blackmail. Then he'd have that over me too, for the rest of my life. What's to stop him making me pay again and again?'

'Nothing, Deb. And he's an addict, so he would do that. Have you told Mark about this?'

'Not yet.' I felt some of the tension in my body dissipate and wondered if it was because I was talking through some of my problems or whether it was simply the effects of the wine. 'Cecile, the two cases I was preoccupied with are sorting themselves out. It's just a matter of time before the men who are threatening Rana are removed from her life and I'll have to be around when that happens. But before then there's a small window of time for me to go back to Garralong and try to figure out whatever it is that Smiley is pointing me towards. Every instinct tells me there's something wrong about my father's death – I mean above and beyond the awfulness of it. There's something else that's not right. It's a gut feeling and it won't go away. I've always been a doubter, and now with the Smiley emails I know that I have to go through with this.'

Cecile sighed and patted my arm. 'I hope it works out the way you want it to,' she said.

'Me too.'

'Let's drink to that.'

CHAPTER 21

I woke early in the morning, feeling alone and vulnerable, obsessing about the competing anxieties that tormented me – my mother, Brad, the looming IA investigation. I'd been singled out, cut out of the herd and brought to the attention of Internal Affairs.

At 8.30, I called work. Socrates answered the phone. Being an early riser, he was usually the first one to get to the office.

'Anything I need to know?' I asked. 'I'll be in late today.'

'If it's Gavin you mean, he's not here, boss. He emailed late last night. He's going to be away a few days. Big meeting on in the city over the next few days. There's a huge reorganisation going on, bringing all the specialist teams together – Apollo, Raptor, Talon and MEOCS – so they're streamlined. All the brass will be hunkered down there for days sorting it all out.'

'Okay,' I said, thinking of Gavin's demand that I account for every movement. I sighed. I'd put something down to give to him later, but right now I had more pressing troubles. 'I'll be out for the morning. If anyone wants me, I'm on the mobile.'

'You in some kind of trouble?' Socrates' voice was kindly.

'Could be. But I'm working on it.'

'Anything I can do?'

'No, but thanks, Socrates. I appreciate it.'

I checked my email account. Sure enough, there was Gavin's message. It was a small relief to have him out of my face right now.

— —

The storage system built recently to house New South Wales Police Records contains thousands of large brown cartons over several floors of floor-to-ceiling shelving. These are the recorded results of hundreds of thousands – possibly millions – of investigations, stacked in formidable ranks.

The archivist at the front counter took down my ID details and those of the case I was interested in. 'I remember that one,' he said, bringing it up on his screen. 'A police officer was murdered. Walked straight into a shooter?'

'Mm-hmm.'

He looked at me, curious. 'Why the sudden interest in an old case like that?'

'It's personal,' I said with a look intended to discourage further questions, then thanked him as I took the catalogue information he'd printed off.

I had to go up some metal stairs to the next level and felt the archivist's eyes on me all the way up. I walked slowly along the tiered ranks of cartons until I came to the area devoted to 1992. As I moved along the shelves, I squinted at the catalogue numbers, but it was the name that caught my eye – my father's name, *Peter Abel Hawkins*, jumping out at me from among the anonymous hundreds clustered around him on nearby shelves. My heart started pounding and my fingers were trembling as I lifted down the box.

Beside the levels of shelving was an L-shaped bench, well lit by fluorescent strips above it. I carried the box to the bench and pulled off the lid. Inside the dusty, stale-smelling container, several manila folders lay stacked on top of each other, some with smudged typescript labels on them. Carefully, I lifted them out. There was a major incident report written by Detective Inspector Larry Chisholm from Newcastle local area command; three badly typed witness statements, one made by Mr Ernest Cusack, another by his wife Kathleen of 'Little Plain', Garralong, and the other from Craig Davidson, the son; an autopsy report; a ballistics report; and a local police report. Beneath these was a rectangular white cardboard box with the name Martin Patterson and 18th April 1992 printed on it. I recognised it as one of the heavy white boxes in which old-style developed photographs used to be stored.

My heart was thudding as I took out the photographs. There were about a dozen of them, including the two that Smiley had sent me, but I knew it was common practice for several copies to be made of each one from a crime scene, so Smiley's copy could have been taken anywhere between Garralong and Newcastle. Two of them made me catch my breath: one was a close-up of the smear near the front door; the other showed the smeared mark on the wooden step leading up to the veranda. So, I thought, I wasn't the only one interested in those smears.

Martin Patterson had thought them worthy of preserving too. The words of the nineteenth-century father of forensic science Edmond Locard – words I'd learned off by heart as an eager young detective – played through my mind: 'Physical evidence cannot be wrong, it cannot perjure itself. It cannot be wholly absent. Only human failure to find it, study and understand it can diminish its value.'

My instincts had been right all along. These marks were worth close examination. They were literally facts on the ground. I pulled out my mobile phone and, after arranging the reports, documents and photos, carefully photographed them all.

Then, still feeling shaky, I returned everything to the box and replaced it in the gap on the shelves. I headed down the stairs again, feeling less miserable and hoping that I might have something valuable in the digital record of my mobile's camera.

'Get what you wanted?' the archivist asked as I headed for the exit.

'Maybe,' I said.

On the way to the office, I dropped by the hospital to see my brother. Brad just had to retract his statement. Somehow I had to get him to say that it wasn't my voice on the tape. That he'd made a mistake.

'He's with the specialist now,' said the young nurse at the front desk. 'But he should be able to take visits later. Try again after six this evening.'

I thanked him and was turning to leave when he said, 'Just a moment, Ms Hawkins.' He squinted at something on the admissions screen. 'There's a note here that one of the doctors wants to speak with you. I'll give her a call.'

'What's it about?' I asked, wondering if Brad had been misbehaving even in here.

'I can't really say, but Dr Wu will be here any moment. If you'd just like to wait a few minutes?' He flashed me a practised smile.

I waited near Reception, watching the visitors as they gathered near the lifts, patiently standing.

Finally, I looked up to see a slight Asian woman approaching me, sleek-haired and wearing pale pink lipstick. 'Dr Bernice Wu,' she said, shaking my hand, then she looked over at a closed door marked Staff Only. 'Look, can I speak to you privately for a moment?'

I frowned, puzzled, and followed her over to the staffroom. She stood back to allow me entry and I found myself in a small meeting room. Several discarded Styrofoam cups half-filled with old black coffee sat on the table.

'There's something I need to talk to you about, Ms Hawkins,' she said. 'You are next of kin?'

'That's correct. Is there something wrong? I mean, apart from my brother being an addict and getting himself beaten up?'

Dr Wu cocked her head to one side and said gently, 'We think there's an underlying condition, undiagnosed at the moment.'

'Hep C?'

'I'm not sure. I've ordered some blood tests. But have you noticed any changes in your brother's health?'

I almost laughed. 'Sure I have. He looks worse every time I see him, Doctor. But that's not very often. And he *is* a heroin addict.'

Nodding, the doctor said, 'We're aware of that.'

'So the only changes I've noticed in him are pretty predictable. Like I said, he's getting worse.'

'I'll let you know when the results of the blood tests come in,' said Dr Wu. 'I don't think it's hep C.'

'You think it might be something worse?' I could see from her manner that this was the case.

'Let's wait till we see the test results, shall we?' she said, giving me a reassuring smile. 'I simply wanted to forewarn you, I suppose. I'll be speaking with him myself soon.'

—•—

I thought about Brad all the way back to work. He'd been nothing but a problem to everyone in his life, not to mention the destruction of his own life. Still, I hoped for his sake that whatever condition he had could be remedied.

I worked at my desk for the next two hours, bringing my records up to date, recording our progress in the two cases – Kylie Mifsud and Rana al-Sheikly. I also dutifully wrote up my actions and movements for Gavin, omitting the morning's visit to police records.

An email arrived from Barry in Forensic Services. *Here's the result from your bottle*, it read. *We couldn't find a match. Sorry we couldn't be more help.*

There was no match on the prints left on the glass of the failed Molotov cocktail. So it hadn't been George Hakan or indeed any of the usual suspects in the CrimTrac database. Whoever had hurled that bottle into my backyard that night was a cleanskin. Someone else was gunning for me. Someone who wasn't yet on our radar. I sat staring at the screen for a few moments. I'd have to be careful and vigilant.

I tried to distract myself from this worry by opening email attachments to read reports from the other squads. Together with the Riot Squad and the armoured BearCat riot vehicle, a multi-agencies strike force of three hundred police officers had stormed dozens of households and businesses in raids on the Khaybar Riders that had netted a huge haul of illegal firearms and large amounts of cash. Thirteen men had been arrested, with more arrests pending as further information came to hand. I imagined the deals that were going on, the horse trading, men coughing up information to the investigators in exchange for less severe charges. I wondered if more links to the al-Sheikly brothers would emerge.

Once I'd caught up on my work I could focus all my attention on the crime scene photos and documents I'd photographed from police records. I uploaded them to my computer then printed out the documents and put them in folders, leaving the photographs in my photolab program so that I could edit them later, printed them out, and finally copied everything onto a memory stick. By the time I went home, I had everything I needed all ready for close textual examination.

Before I left, I filled out a leave form and put it in the internal mail, together with the account of my movements. I would be away for three days at least, more if I needed it.

I made a brief announcement to the others that I'd be away a couple of days or so, but I would be contactable on the mobile.

CHAPTER 22

The house seemed emptier and lonelier than usual without Mark. On the doorstep, I turned around to check the street.

After a quick meal of grilled salmon and salad, I cleared the table in the kitchen under the brightest downlights in the house, and sat down with my laptop and the pile of printed documents from police records. I read through the notes made by the first police officers at the scene, describing what they had encountered, and including a rough sketch one of them had made of the crime scene showing the position of the two bodies inside the house. I was about to turn my attention to the next document when a couple of final notes caught my eye: *All house light switches in off position. No sign of forced entry.* In those days, and in that area, I remembered, a lot of people didn't lock their houses at night.

Next, I pulled out Ernie Cusack's witness statement.

My name is Ernest Alfred Cusack and I live at 'Little Plain' along the Garralong road, adjacent to the property 'Loxley' where Frank and Betty Davidson live.

On the night of 16 April 1992, I was watching television with my wife Kathleen when at around 10 p.m., I heard some shots from a rifle. I think there were three, although there may have been more as I wasn't really paying attention. I didn't think much of it because people occasionally shoot rabbits and foxes in the area at night. To the best of my ability, I recall two shots fairly close together and then a third sometime later. The last shot could have been about five or ten minutes after the first two.

I stood up from the table and walked to the back door, unlocked it and stepped out into the cool evening air. The hum of the traffic formed a background to my thoughts as I turned on the hose and watered the broccoli seedlings, which were now growing into sturdy young plants. As I watered, I imagined the scene that made sense of the grouping of gunshots. The terrible argument escalates; in the heat of the moment Frank grabs the .303 and shoots his wife, but then hears a car outside the house . . .

A question struck me: why were they arguing in the dark? It wasn't impossible, of course, but was it likely? Curious.

I returned to my mental re-enactment. Enraged still, and fearing a witness coming onto the scene of his shocking act, Frank goes to the doorway, still holding his gun, and when he sees my father, he shoots him. Was it the headlights of my father's vehicle coming up the long driveway and hitting the windows of the unlit house that first alerted Frank Davidson to the fact that he wasn't alone?

I stood in the quiet garden as the awful scene played through my mind. I felt tears, old and too long suppressed, pushing against the back of my eyes, but I refused to release them. I refocused my mind on the crime scene at the Davidsons' farmhouse.

Perhaps it's at this stage, with two bodies now lying on his property, that Frank realises for the first time the enormity of what he's just done – he's murdered two people, his wife and a police officer, a man who was also a fishing companion. As the dreadful truth of his own actions starts to penetrate his surging rage, and reeling from the sight of my father lying in his blood on the ground outside, Frank Davidson staggers back inside. Still clutching the rifle, he stumbles back into the living room to be confronted by yet another horror, the bleeding body of his murdered wife. Perhaps he slumps onto the couch, desperately trying to think of a way out of this. Did he consider calling his son Craig? What is he going to tell him – that he's just murdered Craig's mother? Perhaps he thinks of taking the car and driving somewhere – anywhere – and hiding. But as the futility of this idea becomes clearer, he tries to think of something else.

Perhaps he is immobilised with shock and just sits there, staring blindly past the familiar objects in his living room. Perhaps he goes outside to check if what he thinks he did just then really happened, that he hasn't imagined it. But the collapsed body of my father only reinforces the terrible reality of Frank Davidson's actions. Maybe he goes back inside and tries to resuscitate his dead wife – maybe that's when he switches off all the lights, as if to hide the dreadful scene? Maybe he goes to the phone, thinking to ring the ambulance, the police? Maybe there is still some way out of this, he thinks. He could concoct a story about a crazy stranger who ran in and shot his wife and the police officer before Frank was able to wrest the .303 from the killer, who then ran out into the darkness and disappeared.

But as the minutes tick by, reinforcing with every passing second the unforgivable sins that his ungovernable temper has finally led him to, Frank Davidson realises there is no way out, or at least no way out while he remains alive. Turning the rifle towards his face, and stretching his arm as far as he can, his straining finger finds the trigger, and with some difficulty, he pushes it back.

The third shot rings out, and Frank Davidson joins his wife and my father in death.

—•—

I brought up on the laptop screen one of the photos in which the smeared mark just inside the front door was visible. I zoomed in on it but all I got was a pixelated mess of black and white. I did the same with the photo of the stain on the front step. Again, all I got was a hazy smudge with no detail.

Eventually, I went to bed but couldn't sleep. The crime scene photos had unsettled me. I kept 'seeing' my own re-enactment.

—•—

In the morning I felt like I'd scarcely slept at all, and my face in the bathroom mirror further convinced me of this.

I called my mother but it went straight through to her voicemail. 'Call me when you can,' I said to the recording.

Then I rang the hospital and was told Brad was sleeping. He was doing better than me, I thought bitterly. But I was about to wake him up. On the way to the hospital, I could feel my anger mounting.

I found Brad in a four-bed ward. He was still asleep, his heavily bandaged head turned to one side on the pillow. I stared at the cuts and bruising on his cheek and around his eye and felt no pity for him at all. Thoughts raced through my mind. Strictly speaking, years ago I'd been accessory to a crime. In DCI Fitzgerald's words, I had conspired to pervert the course of justice – I'd advised a juvenile on how to avoid the detection of his crime. I'd further compounded it by telling him to drive the car away and abandon it. I thought of Thomas Piper and Sons Jewellery with its smashed window and its stock scattered on the footpath as my useless brother panicked and drove off. No way was this a victimless crime. Mr Piper and his small business had been harmed. I recalled what Mark had said about the corruption of Corrective Services officers – how once a person takes a bribe, even if it's only something small, that person is then owned by the briber.

All the hospital beds appeared to be in use, although two of the occupants were missing, leaving rumpled bedsheets. The remaining patient was an elderly man lying on his back with his mouth open, and for a moment I thought he was dead. Then he snored loudly.

I grabbed a chair and dragged it over to Brad's bed, then poked his shoulder. 'Bradley? It's me.'

Brad grunted and turned his bandaged head in my direction.

His bloodshot eyes blinked at me. 'Huh? Deb? What are you doing here?'

'You little arsehole. How do you think you got to the hospital? Who do you think brought you in?'

'Fuck, I'm in all sorts of trouble. They bashed me bad. They only left me when they thought I was dead. Once they find out I've survived they'll be back again.'

'Listen, buddy, at the moment I don't give a shit. But I do give a shit about the fact that you've dropped me in it. I've had Internal Affairs talking to me. This could be the end of my career.'

'But you wouldn't help *me*. I was trying to get straight and clean. All I needed was a lousy three thousand dollars.'

So it was up from two thousand already, I thought, seething. 'And what did you think you'd gain by setting me up like that? Recording our conversation?'

Brad winced as he tried to move. 'I see now it wasn't a good idea. But I thought I might need to get in good with the cops, plus you'd fucked up my life by not giving me that money . . . It was the last thing I did before this.' He indicated his bandaged head.

'*What? I'd* fucked up your life? You've been doing a pretty good job of that since you were twelve! So you think you're going to fuck up *my* life in revenge. Clever. Really clever.'

Brad turned away. 'I said I realise now it wasn't a good idea,' he whimpered.

'Okay, tell me what happened back there at that vermin hole where I found you bleeding to death?' My anger surged, fuelled by my fear and frustration at how my life was turning out. 'I saved your life, you little prick.'

Brad was quiet for a while and for a brief moment I recalled the golden-haired baby whom I'd once adored. In a softer voice I asked, 'Who did this to you, Brad? And why?'

'Two guys from the Khaybar Riders. Jeez, Deb, they had orders to kill me.' He choked back a sob, which started a coughing fit; as he struggled to sit up, I instinctively went to help, lifting him higher in the bed. He cried out in pain, clutching his ribs.

When the coughing fit had subsided, he went on. 'The doctor said I mightn't walk for six months – if at all. They'll come back. Sami Allen has sworn to kill me. He was one of them. I don't know who the other guy was. Sami's broken away to make his own gang. He's started a new group – Deth2K. He needs to kill me to show how tough he is on people who owe him money.'

'He gave you the drugs without getting the cash up front?' I asked, incredulous.

'He gave me a chance. To collect what was overdue.'

'You're dealing these days?'

Brad didn't answer – as good as a 'yes'.

Sami Allen. A familiar name. But the name of this gang was new. 'Deth2K?' I asked. 'What does that mean?'

Brad smiled. 'Here I am, providing intelligence to the cops. You don't know?' I waited, irritated. 'Okay,' he said. 'It's probably "death to coppers".'

'You don't spell "coppers" with a *k*.'

Brad went to laugh, but then flinched in pain. 'You think those thugs care about spelling? Or it could stand for "death to kuffirs". Infidels. Unbelievers. You know, us.'

I suppressed my anger, even managing a smile for the nurse who had come in to check Brad's chart. Behind her, one of the other occupants of the ward shuffled in and sat on his bed, looking out the window, the picture of dejection.

'Here's the deal, Brad,' I said when the nurse had gone. 'You're going to retract what you said about that recording. You're going to tell the police that you're very sorry you were angry with your sister – angry and jealous – and that the female voice on the tape is someone who sounds like her, but is *not* her. Got it?'

'No way.'

'You're going to do this, otherwise Sami Allen will never stop coming after you. You're going to do this because I can get Sami Allen off the streets and out of your life. Think about it.'

I stood up, ready to leave, turned and saw my mother in the doorway. Great, I thought, a family reunion. The addict certainly brings the family together. For a moment, my mother stood there taking in the hospital room, her navy pantsuit hanging off her thin frame, her hair newly shortened and coloured. She nodded to me, then hurried to Brad, shaking her head.

'If you like, I can wait downstairs and give you some private time with your son. I can give you a lift home after that.'

My mother appeared not to hear me. She sat down in the chair I had just vacated, scrutinising Brad's injuries. She looked up at me, and I was shocked to see how strained and drawn her face was. But her words belied her evident agitation. 'Off you go to work, Debra. I'll call you later on. Pull that curtain along, will you? That way we have a little privacy.'

'Think about what I've just said, Brad,' I said. 'It's a life or death matter.'

My mother looked puzzled for a second, then turned back to Brad. 'What's she talking about? What do you mean, Debra?'

'Brad might tell you,' I said, knowing he wouldn't. I left them to it, pulling two of the curtains around the bed.

After leaving the ward I hurried towards the lifts with my head down, fuming internally. I almost bumped into Dr Wu, who was walking down the corridor towards me. 'So sorry,' I said, intent on getting out of the place.

'Ms Hawkins,' she said. 'I was going to call you later today but now that you're here . . . Please, may I have a word with you?'

The tone of her voice checked me, and I followed her into a small lounge room off the corridor, where a few visitors chairs and a hot water urn for tea and coffee offered a small retreat from the busy hospital.

Dr Wu indicated for me to sit down in one of the chairs against the wall, then sat next to me, turning the chair around a little. 'Ms Hawkins,' she began.

'Debra, please,' I said.

'I have some rather distressing news. About your brother.'

Now what? I thought.

'Normally it takes us much longer to get results on these tests, but we happen to have a visiting fellow from the US who's an expert in this field.'

I frowned, alarmed by the seriousness of her manner. She paused, then asked, 'Have you heard of a condition called Huntington's disease?'

It must have been obvious from the look on my face that I hadn't, as Dr Wu continued, 'It's a neurodegenerative disorder, and it has a wide variation in onset age, but the average onset age is around forty years. Your brother is unlucky in that it's showing up much earlier.'

I shook my head in confusion. 'What does that actually mean? In terms of what's happening to Brad?'

'I asked you before whether you had noticed any changes in him. What I was asking about were choreiform movements – jerky involuntary movements. Have you noticed those in your brother?'

I thought back to our meeting at the kebab shop and remembered his strange tic, the spasmodic movement of his hand across the table, his grimaces when he spoke. 'Is it something he's picked up from a needle?'

Dr Wu shook her head. 'It's a genetic disorder. In young people like your brother, mostly the disease is inherited from a father carrying a coding error on a particular chromosome. It's like a genetic stutter in the DNA at the end of a gene. It causes nerve cell loss in the brain.'

The shock silenced me for what seemed a long time before I stammered, 'B-but my father was perfectly healthy. He was —' I stopped. My father had died young. It was quite possible that the disease hadn't manifested in him before his death. 'You said mostly it comes from the father – does that mean it could be from my mother?'

'Also possible.'

I was struggling to take it in. 'What can be done about it?' I asked.

'Regrettably, nothing much can be done to stop the motor and other deterioration, but the mood disorders and the cognitive impairment can be managed somewhat with various drug regimes. Of course, new research is always happening . . . Are your parents still living?'

'My mother is. In fact, she's here right now – in the ward with my brother.'

'I'll wait here. Your brother should be told, too. Perhaps now is as good a time as any. Would you like to get your mother first?'

In a daze, I walked back into the ward to see my mother still standing at Brad's bedside, holding his hand. As if my mother didn't have enough to worry about, I thought. She looked up, surprised, as I approached.

'Mum,' I said, 'can we just have a word in private?'

My mother looked as if she was about to object, but seeing the expression on my face she patted Brad's hand and followed me meekly enough out of the ward. Once we were outside the door she turned to me. 'Debra, what's this all about?'

I took a deep breath. 'There's no nice way of telling you, Mum. It seems that Brad has some kind of serious degenerative disease. Dr Wu in here will explain more to you.' I gestured towards the small lounge.

My mother's gaunt face blanched and her voice was a wail. 'Explain what? He's an addict. This assault is a blessing in disguise. He'll be able to stop using now. He just needs to get well and strong again.'

It was clear my mother hadn't heard – or didn't want to hear – what I had just said. I took her arm gently. 'Let's hear what the doctor has to say, okay, Mum?'

Dr Wu went through it again with my mother, trying to explain incomprehensible details about triple repeats on chromosomes with names comprising strings of numbers and letters. My mother sat in one of the bucket chairs, knees pressed together, hands tightly clasped on top of her handbag in her lap. 'So it's just going to get worse and worse,' she said finally, her words more a statement than a question.

'New discoveries are being made all the time, Mrs Hawkins. We're discovering more and more about the human genome, the behaviour of chromosomes. We're learning slowly about how to deal with coding faults.'

'But there's nothing that can be done right now!' my mother cried, suddenly collapsing over her knees. I sprang to comfort her, putting my arm around her narrow shoulders, remembering that terrible day when she'd run screaming out of our house and onto the road. She was heaving uncontrollably, trying to say something. Eventually I made out what it was. 'It's all my fault, it's all my fault. I should have known that something like this would happen. How can I ever forgive myself? And I screamed at him to get out! I didn't see him for three years!'

'Mum, you can't go on blaming yourself like this. You had to do that. He was stealing money from you, becoming violent, don't you remember?' But she was inconsolable. Dr Wu waited patiently until Mum's sobs eased.

I helped my mother to her feet. As we left the small visitors' room, Dr Wu, her face soft with genuine concern, handed me her card. 'Ring me any time. Night or day. Brad will need a referral to a specialist. Someone who can answer all the questions properly, for him and for you.'

My mother and I walked back towards the ward in silence. Just before we reached the door, my mother stopped. 'I can't tell him, Debra. You'll have to do it for me.'

I took a deep breath. 'Okay. But you can't go home like this. Let me drive you home. There's no hurry to tell Brad.'

'I'll be perfectly all right,' she dismissed me. 'I need to be alone to think about this. I feel as if I'm being punished.'

'Of course you're not. You heard Dr Wu. If you want to blame anyone, blame Dad's chromosomes.' Recklessly I added a feel-good: 'It's got nothing to do with you.' Then I amended, 'Probably.'

She was adamant that she wanted to go home alone. Finally I gave in. 'Okay, Mum, I'll call you after I break the news to Brad.'

She didn't seem to be listening, but remained staring off into the distance.

'Mum?' I said. 'I'll tell Brad and call you later, okay?'

She looked at me as if she couldn't see me. She was somewhere else, alone in her unreachable place.

I waited with her until a cab arrived, and helped her into it. Thin as she was, her movements were still graceful. She looked so small and lost as she hauled her trouser-clad legs into the back seat of the cab that I had an impulse, quickly subdued, to fold her up in my arms like a little child and comfort her. I closed the door behind her and leaned down to the window. 'It's not your fault, Mum. I'll call you as soon as I can, okay?'

CHAPTER 23

Dreading what I had to do, I walked back into the ward, where Brad had hoisted himself up a little more in his bed and was looking at me expectantly, seemingly brighter after my mother's visit.

'God, Debs. I'm just hanging out to score. Anything would do. See if you can get me something from the nurses' station. Anything ending in — ' he lowered his voice and spelled out the letters – '-e-i-n-e?'

'Don't be crazy!'

'Where's Mum? She'll do it for me.'

'She's gone home. She had to leave unexpectedly.' I paused, regretting now my earlier harshness with this young man who was just about to receive news of a very hard life sentence. I sat on the chair recently vacated by our mother. 'There's something I have to tell you, Brad. And I'm afraid it's bad news.'

'What?' he asked, frightened eyes on mine. 'Sami Allen knows where I am?'

'It's got nothing to do with Sami Allen or any of that lot. It's concerning your health. Brad, blood tests show that you've got a very serious illness. No, not AIDS or hep C,' I said as he went to speak. 'It's something called Huntington's disease.'

He listened wide-eyed as I passed on some of the information Dr Wu had given us, keeping it fairly vague for now; it wasn't my place to be describing the increasing degeneration he would experience over his lifespan. 'You'll need to see Dr Wu and get a referral to a specialist. I'm sure there are things that you could do to help to improve your well-being.'

Brad remained silent after I'd finished speaking. Suddenly, something had shifted between us. The spite and anger that had fuelled his vengeful betrayal, and my fury over his stupid, malicious act seemed to fall away, and I was left feeling helpless and sad in the face of my brother's terror. I put my hand on his bruised arm.

At last he spoke. 'Is it because I'm a user? Is that what's caused it? The gear?'

I shook my head. 'Whether you'd used or not is irrelevant. It's a genetic thing. Most probably inherited from our father.'

'Are you going to get it?'

That thought pulled me up short. 'I have no idea,' I finally said, thinking that I'd probably need to be tested for it too, as would our mother.

'I'll bet they've made a mistake,' he said with a rush of bravado. 'They've mixed up some test results. I'm an *addict*. Not someone with Huntington's or whatever it is.'

But his denial didn't last very long. After a few moments of silence, Brad whispered, 'What am I going to do?'

'Contact Dr Wu, like I said. The hospital staff will have her details. She'll be able to answer your questions.' I paused. 'Brad, I'll get Sami Allen off your back. And I'll do what I can to help you in dealing with this diagnosis.'

His eyes filled with tears. 'Dibs. What's going to happen to me?'

'Let's just do it a day at a time,' I said, remembering one of Mark's sayings. 'First you need to recover from your injuries and I need to deal with Sami Allen. Okay? But you must withdraw that complaint you've lodged with Internal Affairs. Otherwise I'm not going to be any use to you or Mum at all.'

Brad mumbled something but I was insistent. 'You're going to sign a statement that I'll write for you saying that the voice on that recording is not mine but someone who sounds like me. This statement will say that you deeply regret bringing this fallacious complaint and that since being diagnosed with Huntington's disease, you've rethought your priorities in life. Okay? You've decided you want to live your life with more honesty.'

'But I wouldn't be,' he said, reasonably. 'I'd be telling a lie.'

'Noble cause, Brad,' I said. 'Sometimes a lie is the decent thing to do.'

As I was leaving the ward my mobile rang. It was Geoff King from the Drug Squad.

'I can't talk very long,' he said. 'And we never had this conversation, okay? But something's happening tomorrow morning. Those five contacts you supplied? Simultaneous raids on all of them. The briefing's at four a.m. My office.'

'Thanks, Geoff. Good luck with it. I want to lock in every scrap of hard evidence against those two men.'

'I'll do what I can to ensure that, Deb,' he said.

I rang off without enthusiasm. Once I would have been excited and made sure that I had some part to play in a raid like this, but today, with the double burden of Brad's illness and my mother's fragile capacity to cope, my spirit was weighed down with something close to despair.

Despite my mother's Greta Garbo–like words about wanting to be alone, I knew it was essential that we talk. I called on the way to say I was coming round to her place. Again, my call went straight to voicemail.

When I arrived, I let myself into her house with my key and found her sitting at her computer. She quickly finished the call she was making and stood up from the small cedar dressing-table stool that she used at the computer. 'I've just had a tremendous blow today. I'm still in turmoil about it all. I need to be alone. I wish you would respect that.'

'I'm sorry for going against your wishes, and I do understand that you've had a huge shock,' I said softly. 'But we have to talk, Mum. About Brad. About you. It's crazy to stay silent when all this is happening.'

'About Brad, you may have a point. But what's there to talk about concerning me?'

I stood there a moment taking in the way the tailored pantsuit hung off her, the gauntness of her face, the hollows from the depths of which her sad, tired eyes still seemed to defy my gaze. 'Look at you,' I said gently. 'There's nothing of you. What's the matter? I know there's something wrong – badly wrong. Please be honest. I know you're ill. What is it, Mum?'

My mother sat down again. 'It's not Huntington's, if that's what you're thinking.'

'Then what is it?'

My mother looked up from the small cedar stool. 'It's everything, Debra. My life, Brad. The past . . . Everything is hitting me all at once. I'm older, and frailer, and now I've got Brad to worry about. He'll be coming here when he's released from hospital. I don't know how I will cope.'

I blinked. I'd never heard my mother speak so openly, or express such vulnerability. But she still hadn't replied to my question about her own ill health. I let that go for the moment. 'Listen to me,' I said. 'It's a *progressive* disease he's suffering from. It'll be years before he needs care. At the moment, all he needs to do is recover from his head and leg injuries. Once those have healed, he can go out and get a job like anybody else. He could be working for years before the disease gets too bad. Until then, he can pay rent in a share house. Or a boarding house.'

'It's going to take a long time to recover from those injuries, and he can't afford to stay in hospital. And when your brother leaves the hospital, you can't have him living in a single room in a boarding house!'

'Why the hell not? It would be a great improvement on where he's been living lately, believe me. You should have seen the place I found him in. A filthy squat!' I could feel my anger rising, so I took a breath and made myself calm down. 'And Mum, you're in no position to be looking after someone else when you . . . seem to need care yourself.'

My mother didn't reply for a long time, but sat looking away from me. I knew the pressure of silence is a powerful tool in the hands of an interrogator. Finally, she bent her head, raising a hand to her forehead. 'It's cancer,' she said. 'It's inoperable. It's behind my sternum and all through my chest. God knows where else. I'm due for another scan next week.'

I sat down with a jolt on her favourite armchair, facing her. 'Inoperable? Surely there's something . . .'

'Nothing, Debra. I've known for a couple of months.'

'Why didn't you tell me?'

My question hung in the air, unanswered, although I already knew the answer. My mother had never told me anything of a personal nature over a lifetime. So how could I reasonably expect her to tell me about this?

Before I could utter the next question forming in my mind, she'd answered it. 'And if you're wanting to know how long I've got, it's not very long now – a few months at the most. Maybe less.'

'Only months?' Millions of thoughts jumbled in my mind. My mother would have to come and stay with me, or I'd have to move in with her so that I could care for her. At least that would put a stop to this crazy idea of Brad moving in and sponging off her.

I stood up, walked over and put my arm around her narrow shoulders. 'Mum, I don't know what to say.' I found myself trembling with shock, my vision oddly impaired. 'Surely there are treatments that —'

'Don't you think I've gone into all of that with the specialists?' she interrupted me. 'There are treatments that might give me a little more time. But they are very debilitating and, frankly, I'm not all that sure I want to prolong this – this business.'

I stood beside her, silenced and dismayed. Finally, as much for myself as for her, I said, 'Mum, you don't have to do this alone. I will do everything I can to support you.'

She looked up at me with a soft, loving expression and there were tears in her eyes. 'Dibs,' she said, making my heart jump – I hadn't heard her use my pet name in over twenty years. But she paused for a moment, looking down, and when she spoke again it was in her usual guarded manner. 'You're very kind,' she said, as if speaking to a stranger who'd helped her pick up some spilled groceries. 'Now please, if you want to help me, go home and leave me with my thoughts.'

I did something then that I hadn't done for many years: I leaned down and kissed the top of her smooth head. 'Can I pour you a drink, or make you a cup of tea before I go?'

She shook her head. 'I'll be fine.'

I wanted to scream, *No! You won't be fine! Stop pushing me away!*

'I'll call in the morning,' I said, standing by the door. 'Mum,' I began, but stopped again. I didn't know what else to say.

On the way home, I couldn't see the road properly and almost collected an idiot who swung out from the kerb in front of me without indicating. I swore, then pulled over, and sat there trying to calm my mind, vaguely listening to some man yelling until I finally identified him as being on the radio, the race caller at the Dapto dogs. I switched off the radio. One moment I felt like crying, the next like dragging Brad out of his hospital bed and beating some sense into him, or shaking my mother by her bony shoulders until she told me everything. Finally, my thoughts started to quieten down. I needed to do something ordinary, I realised, to stitch me back down into normality again. Something dull and mundane. Something life-affirming.

—·—

I stopped at the mall for some much-needed supplies: tomatoes, bread, butter, a bottle of good wine. On the way out, I noticed some nice clothes in the window of one of the chintzy little boutiques which I usually avoided because of the over-priced goods. But today, with the scene with my mother on high-rotation replay through my memory, I decided to distract myself by stepping inside the small shop. On a rack near the entrance I saw a beautiful dusky blue silk all-weather coat, three-quarter length with a hood. When I tried it on, it felt as though it had been made for me. It was a perfect light weight and the colour suited me. For once, I paid the exorbitant price without flinching. As soon as I walked out of the boutique with my new coat wrapped in tissue in a beautifully embossed bag, my obsessive thoughts resumed. My mother was dying, and my brother had a serious incurable disease that would eventually take him. Get a grip, Debra, I told myself. We're all dying. You're going to die too, like everybody else, you just don't know the date yet. I endeavoured to interrupt the relentless merry-go-round in my head.

It was hard to do. I practised concentrating on my next move.

I called Flash from home after putting the groceries away. 'Sami Allen,' I said. 'I need to contact him.'

Flash hesitated. 'What's the problem?'

'He almost killed my brother – and when he finds out that he failed, he's going to come back and finish the job.'

'Cripes,' said Flash. 'What's the story?'

I briefly told him the mess Brad was in, omitting my part in it. 'That's why I need to get Sami Allen off the streets.'

'There are three outstanding warrants which I'm currently in no hurry to deliver and they're the only reason he talks to me from time to time. MEOCS tagged and released him some time back and I fished him up again. He's terrified of going to prison and running into Adam Massoud's people. He heard what they did to Danny Malik.'

'None of that has stopped him from almost beating my brother to death and breaking away to form a new group. Deth2K – do you know them?'

'A bit. Some young guys have joined up who'd been knocking at the Khaybar Riders' and the Warlords' doors but not getting admitted as patched members. They're already getting a bad reputation.'

'What are Allen's usual haunts? I'll track him down and remind him about the warrants. Give him a nice surprise.'

'Debra. Be careful. The man's a snake.'

'Promise I will.'

Flash gave me some names and addresses where I might find information about Allen's whereabouts.

I spent most of the day driving around and asking reluctant people where I might find Sami Allen. He wasn't in any of his usual lairs. Finally, I hit on something helpful through Speedy.

'I hear he's waiting for some people to arrive from interstate for an important meeting,' Speedy told me when he called back. 'Hanging out at the Settlers Rest. It's a bloodhouse near Corella. Deth2K haven't organised a clubhouse yet.'

In minutes, I was driving along the freeway to Corella.

CHAPTER 24

Corella police station was a tiny sandstone and timber outfit built in 1888, when disputes over fences and a bit of cattle rustling were the usual problems. I found Constable Gary West, a smart young man with slicked-back fair hair and frank blue eyes, manning the fort by himself.

'My partner's called in sick,' he said by way of explanation. I told him that I was about to arrest Sami Allen and would be grateful for his assistance. I left my car at the station and joined him in his vehicle. We headed to the Settlers Rest.

—•—

I recognised Allen the moment I saw him through the glass pane in the swing door into the bar area of the nineteenth-century Settlers Rest Hotel. I could feel the music through my feet – the vibrations of a heavy metal band played way too loud. That was good. He wouldn't hear me. I stood a moment in the corridor, working out the best way to take him down. I knew he wouldn't come with me and Gary voluntarily.

Allen was standing by himself, one booted foot up on the brass footrest that ran the length of the bar a little way off the floorboards. He was a huge, hulking man, massively ripped from hours at the gym and with obvious signs of steroid use. A rat's tail swung from the back of an otherwise shaved head and tattoos wrapped around his upper arms, which burst out of the ragged cut-off sleeves of an old leather jacket. I imagined the fists at the end of those arms punching into my helpless, stupid brother's emaciated addict's body, and I hated Sami Allen for the brutal thug he was. He was leaning slightly across the bar, his enormous hand enveloping a shot glass, keeping an eye on the barman, busy at the register.

Years ago I'd trained with a Brazilian jiu-jitsu master. As I looked at Allen I hoped that my muscle memory was in good shape and that all the weight training I'd done at the gym would stand me in good stead. It had been some time since I'd had to floor an offender. Apprehension and adrenaline kicked in, surging through my arms and legs, right to my fingertips. I was psyched up, pumped, even eager to take him on.

Silently, with Gary behind me, I pushed open the swing door. The sound of the music was deafening. But Sami Allen had the finely honed instincts of a street fighter, and when I was almost close enough to reach out and touch him, he sensed my presence and started to swing round. But he was a moment too late. I'd already closed in tight behind him and blocked his right foot with mine as I yanked him backwards. Off balance, he fell heavily on his back as I quickly sidestepped his crashing bulk. He swore unintelligibly.

'Police!' I yelled over the music, stoked by the thrill of a successful stunt. 'Sami Allen, you're under arrest for breach of bail conditions and three outstanding warrants. Don't make this any harder than it has to be!'

Without taking my eyes off Sami, I yelled at the barman, 'Turn that noise down!'

I already had the cuffs in my hand. But Sami Allen was a fighter and, like any fighter, trained to stay off his back. In the split second it had taken for him to roll over, I threw myself on his back so he was pinned down with his face to the floor. Gary, too, threw his weight across the writhing giant.

I was in top-dog position, sitting astride Allen's shoulders, as he attempted to heave me off and get to his feet. Despite his bucking, I managed to grab his flailing right hand and double his arm back behind him. But it was like riding a wild bronco. Even with the savage come-along hold I had on his arm, Allen kicked and writhed, his studded boots scraping the floorboards, screaming at me, calling me every filthy name he could think of. I applied close to maximum pressure to the hold, and Allen shrieked in pain.

'Okay now, Sami,' I said. 'Nice and easy. Don't make me break your arm. Your left arm. *Now!*'

To encourage him, I applied some nasty carotid pressure. Sami swore and finally obliged, putting his left hand behind his back. Between the two of us, Gary and I dragged him to his feet, almost impossibly dead-weight heavy.

Now that Sami was safely cuffed with his hands behind him, it seemed time to introduce myself, even if it was only to the back of his head. 'I'm Detective Inspector Debra Hawkins, and you are not obliged to say anything but I must warn you that anything you do say could be used in evidence later. This is Constable Gary West, in case you're wondering.'

'You can't hold me, bitch. My boys will have me out of here before you can scratch your scumbag slut arse.'

'Shut up, Sami,' I said, delivering a little more carotid pressure. 'You talk, I squeeze. Got it?'

We were manhandling the big man out of the hotel and towards the police car, half-dragging and half-lifting him, when the distant sound of motorbikes heading our way made me pause.

'See? I told you!' Allen was sneering with triumph. 'My boys will fix you filthy dog coppers real good.'

The growling roar became louder, and within moments five huge motorcycles had skidded to a halt around us, kicking up the straggling lawn in front of the hotel. Their riders dismounted. What a bunch of ugly bastards, I thought as I scanned them. They were dressed to intimidate, to threaten violence without any word or action. Bearded, pierced and tattooed, one with a black spider web etched on his face, another with lacy Arabic lettering inscribed across his forehead; I had no idea what it meant, but I knew it wasn't a blessing. Yet another man, now looming closer, had four diagonal scars running across the left side of his face, as if the devil himself had clawed him. Beside him a glowering, thickset bodybuilder, with heavy, viciously studded rings on every finger, stepped towards us. Two against six; I didn't like our odds.

Beside me, I felt Gary move to draw his service pistol.

'Don't do that, dog.' The warning came from the bodybuilder. My gaze was now riveted to the ugly double muzzle of a sawn-off shotgun right in front of my face. I froze.

The bodybuilder was smiling as he pointed the gun at me, but his brutal features turned it into a snarl. 'Okay, slut. Let Sami go. He's our friend and we want him back.'

'I can't imagine why.' I hoped my voice sounded cool.

'Let him go!'

'I need the key,' I said, warily moving my hand towards my key ring and the small, simple handcuff key it held.

'Get it – nice and slow.'

It was hard to take my eyes off the shotgun levelled at me, but as calmly as I could I unlocked the handcuffs that held Sami Allen.

'You guys are in big trouble,' I said, memorising the plates of the bikes I could see.

'We own this city. You —' he spat '— just live here!' Sami Allen, now freed and eager to join his mates, barged into me, knocking me down.

I fell against the legs of the brute holding the shotgun, and swung away from the contact as fast as I could.

A huge explosion of noise erupted and I crouched on the ground, stunned into immobility. After the ear-shattering noise came a weird nanosecond of silence before the demonic yells, shrieks and curses started up. Sami Allen loomed over me. This is it, I thought, and as Sami Allen started falling on me, I closed my eyes.

He mustn't fall on me. I recoiled in horror, twisting away as he crashed onto the ground, one of his arms pinioning mine.

Blood fell like sticky warm rain. That's when I saw that half his face was missing.

'Get the fuck out of here!' someone shrieked. Cursing and yelling, they scrambled for their bikes. Someone started screaming, 'It wasn't supposed to happen, it wasn't supposed to!'

'Go! Let's go!'

The motorcycles roared away, skidded, then faded into a slow diminuendo. The Deth2K boys had abandoned their leader, who lay in a pool of blood and tissue.

Within seconds, there was just me and Gary left in the car park with Allen's shuddering body. My head was filled with a roaring vacuum. My ears were ringing. I threw off Allen's arm but it seemed to take me forever to get up into a crouch.

Gary helped me to my feet and I found I was barely able to stand on legs that felt like cooked spaghetti. Wiping bits of Sami Allen off me, I noticed the brain tissue dripping from the edges of a gaping hole in the smashed door of the bar. I looked down at the mess on my favourite T-shirt and jeans and gulped, stifling the urge to vomit.

'Jesus,' croaked Gary, looking at the bloody mess lying on the sparse lawn. 'What happened?'

'This is a crime scene,' I managed to say. 'That shotgun went off. Someone killed Sami Allen – it must have been that huge guy with all the rings.'

In the distance, I could hear the sirens. The bartender must have called the cavalry.

CHAPTER 25

I wasn't confident about driving, my body was still shaking, so I left my car at Corella police station and got a ride back into the city with one of the Sydney detectives who'd arrived and taken over the scene. The driver tried to engage me in conversation a couple of times but I felt too overwhelmed to talk. I couldn't stop the crazy action replays that kept going through my mind – flinching at the memories of Sami Allen's half-face. Eventually the driver left me alone and the rest of the trip passed in silence, apart from the low-volume chatter on the police channel.

I didn't feel guilty about Sami Allen's death – live by the sword, die by the sword – but I hadn't meant this to happen. I knew from talking to other cops who'd been involved in fatal shootings that action replays and post-traumatic stress disorder could be with me for a while. I'd told Brad I'd get Sami Allen off his back and that sure was the case. However, I also realised that it hardly mattered now whether my brother withdrew his allegations or not. I was in more trouble than Ned Kelly.

There would have to be a critical incident report, and once I was back at headquarters and had cleaned myself up a bit, changing into clean clothes, some spare trousers and a clean police shirt I made a statement. Gary and I were interviewed separately.

I found it difficult to speak. But I told them as much as I could, giving them the bike registrations I could remember. I described the big guy who looked like a weightlifter or a bodybuilder, with rings on every finger, and told them that he was holding a shotgun but that I hadn't actually seen him pull the trigger. It was possible, I said, that someone else had grabbed the gun when I'd been pushed over and caused one of the bikies to stumble against another. They showed me some photographs and I picked the man who'd been carrying the shotgun. His name was Bashar Qassab, unsurprisingly known to his confederates as 'Basher'. The officers told me he was not long back from Syria, where he'd been fighting with one of the jihadi gangs against his namesake, Bashar al-Assad. He was one of hundreds of young men who'd been looking for trouble and jihad in Syria. They said I was lucky that he hadn't shot me and Gary as well. The Federal Police had been after him ever since he'd slipped past border control on his brother's passport, returning from Syria.

Finally, I made a statement in which I said: *It is possible that when Allen pushed me to the ground and I knocked into the big man's legs, he could have stumbled and fired accidentally. It's also possible one of the other bikies might have grabbed the firearm during the melee.* Then I was allowed to go home. But when I got inside I couldn't sit still. I threw out the jeans and T-shirt. My mind kept replaying the incident and Sami Allen kept coming at me with his bloodied half-face. I walked around the house, pacing like a neurotic big cat.

I called Cecile and when she heard my voice, she ordered me to come straight over. 'I'm cooking ravioli tonight. I always cook too much.'

I couldn't eat the ravioli. The sight of its red sauce made me want to vomit. I finally managed to get down some bread and cheese. Afterwards, we stayed up late talking, and I told her about Brad, Sami Allen, and finally the situation with my mother.

'My God, girl,' said Cecile. 'This is unbelievable! The IA business will sort itself out, one way or the other. And even the Sami Allen incident will be taken care of by other people. But Deb, what are you going to do about your mother? Oh, that poor woman!'

She poured me a glass of wine and I let her fill it right to the top. 'You know how difficult she is,' I said. 'I'm just going to do it a day at a time. I've told her I'll support her all the way.'

'She'll need you as she gets weaker.' There was a silence. 'As for Brad,' Cecile said. 'That pillow-over-the-face idea is looking better all the time. He can't kill you.'

'He can kill my career. Cecile, how come this is happening?' My world was unravelling and there was nothing I could do about it.

Cecile gave me a hug. 'It'll be tough, but you will get through it. I know you, Debs. You're gutsy and bold. You'll win through.'

'At the moment I feel like a scared kid who's been sent to stand outside the headmaster's office.'

'Stand your ground, Debs. I love you and so does Mark Spicer.'

I spent the night at Cecile's apartment, in her spare bed, trying to sleep but without success. I was dreading what I knew was going to happen the next day. Gavin was already furious about me spending time on extracurricular work related to my family; now he would go ballistic. Next morning, as soon as I switched on my phone, I could see all the messages from him.

I went home and showered, then dressed in my uniform, putting it on slowly, making sure I was perfectly turned out. A bruise was starting to show on my forehead, almost in the centre. I had no memory of how I'd got it. I must have banged my head on something when I was pushed over outside the hotel.

I checked Gavin's phone messages: I was to report to the regional office, where I knew Acting Assistant Commissioner Gavin Bailey would be waiting for me.

'Christ Almighty! Have you gone completely insane?' Gavin shouted, his face maroon with fury, waving a newspaper over his head. 'Have you any idea what you've done? Have you?!'

'He'd breached bail conditions, so I —'

'I couldn't give a flying fuck what he'd breached! You are *not* part of the Drug Squad. You're no longer with MEOCS. You could have got yourself killed. Or got that stupid prick of a cop at the Corella police station killed! You might have totally destroyed some covert drug operations or some business with ASIO by going after this lowlife!'

My pulse was racing and my mouth had dried up. There was nothing I could say anyway. I dreaded what might be coming next.

'And that's not the worst of it, by any means!' He slammed a copy of the local newspaper down on the desk. 'Look at this! You can't even control your own security! It'll be in the national newspapers by tomorrow!'

Confused, I picked up the *South-West Courier*, and scanned the half-page article beneath the large heading: 'Disband Racist Unit, Community Leaders Demand'.

> Mr Nigel Mehta, spokesperson for the Community Cohesion Conference held yesterday at Daylesford town hall, said community leaders are calling for the immediate disbanding of RED-V, a recent initiative of the New South Wales police formed to tackle allegedly hidden violence in migrant communities.
>
> 'This unit demonises all our community,' Mr Mehta said today. 'We reject completely the suggestion that violence in our communities is any worse than that of non-migrant populations. Politicians have been calling me, saying their constituents are deeply offended and insulted by the existence of this unit. They're demanding it be shut down. The New South Wales Anti-Discrimination Board is examining the matter right now. We believe this unit is in breach of national anti-discrimination laws as well. I'm therefore calling on the police commissioner to disband this group at once. It is unnecessary and racist.'

Slowly, I put down the newspaper. As I did so, my eye flicked to the by-line: Alistair Lethbridge. Alistair. Nadine had a boyfriend called Alistair Lethbridge. I clenched my fists as I recalled an argument in the meal room between Socrates and Flash. Alex and Charlie had occasionally made comments too, discussing the over-representation of violent behaviour and forced marriage in certain migrant groups in comparison with the national average. Flash thought statistics should be published in the public interest. According to a recent UN survey, Sweden, since opening its borders, now had the highest rape rate in Europe. Socrates thought otherwise, suggesting that discretion in these matters was important for what the politicians call 'social cohesion'. I recalled a robust argument developing around this and Flash making several somewhat politically incorrect remarks. At that stage, I'd cut in with my contribution: just remember that we focus on criminal behaviour, I'd reminded them, not any group or ethnicity. Our job is to respond to crimes, not to groups. Let the statisticians do their job. Our job is policing the law.

Nadine alone had remained aloof from the argument, fiddling with a pearl earring, but I could see she was taking it all in.

'This is ridiculous!' I said. 'Our unit was set up to *protect* vulnerable migrant women and girls, people who might be too intimidated by the men who beat them to approach us. Why don't Mr Nigel Mehta and the constituents find *that* offensive? It's one of the core functions of the police force – *to protect*. How is it racist, for God's sake?'

I was furious at the leak. Furious with Nadine, the traitor, for talking out of school. 'And it's just too bad if that protection offends certain patriarchal control freaks! Was I supposed to tell Rana al-Sheikly, "Sorry that you're being threatened with death if you don't go through with this forced marriage where you'll be raped and beaten if you're 'disobedient'. I'd like to help you but I can't, because someone – some male somewhere – might be *offended*"?' I paused to draw breath. 'And you know as well as I do that violence in some groups *is* four times higher than the —'

'*I don't want to hear it!*' Gavin roared. '*I'm* in the firing line now because of you and your failure to control your team! I've had the commissioner on the phone, demanding to know what the hell's going on! I promoted this unit! I backed you up and this is how you repay me!'

'But be reasonable, Chief Superint —'

'I'm cutting you loose! I'm suspending you right now!' Gavin yelled. 'Hand in your appointments here, on my desk! And get out of my sight until further notice.'

I stood still in shock as his words penetrated the turmoil in my mind. Suspended. Then I slowly started removing my gear – my badge, my Glock, my handcuffs, my police mobile and my swipe pass. All the insignia of my position as a police officer, sworn to uphold the law.

'You will have no contact whatsoever with any serving member and you are not to approach any police premises,' Gavin went on. 'I'll be sending you the statement of your suspension conditions within twenty-four hours.'

I stared at Gavin. I'd never seen him as furious as this – flushed and grim-faced, his jaw set like a vice, eyes flinty with anger.

I turned to leave the office. As I did so, Gavin crashed down in his chair in disgust, as if I'd exhausted him. I turned back to attempt one more argument in my defence, but he waved me away, gesturing with a closed fist. 'Out! Just go! Get out! Get out now!'

I walked out of the building, not seeing or hearing the people around me. I felt as if I were in a long, dark tunnel, completely alone. Around and around in my mind spun the same words: *You're a bad police officer, just like your father. You'll be talked about because of your mistakes, just like he was.*

The unit I'd been so proud of heading seemed doomed to demolition. I couldn't imagine things getting any worse.

CHAPTER 26

As soon as I got home, I called Cecile again and told her what had happened.

'They're still paying you, I hope?' she asked.

'Yes. But I can't go near anyone at work and I can't call anyone.' I swallowed hard. 'If they talk to me, they can be in real trouble, too.'

'Good grief, it sounds like excommunication from Holy Mother Church! Or what the Vikings did when they branded someone an outlaw – cast out without protection.'

'It feels like it, too.'

'Have you told Mark?'

'Not yet. There's nothing he can do, and it will only make him feel bad for me.'

'He should know. He loves you.'

'I can't believe RED-V is in danger of being disbanded. It

makes no sense. Toss me out if they have to, but not the unit. There are women who need us!'

'I'm so sorry, Debs. So sorry all this is happening.' Cecile paused. 'Do you want to come over to my place again tonight? Dinner's pretty simple – Niçoise salad with tuna out of a tin. But maybe some company would be helpful.'

'Not tonight. Thanks, Cecile. There's work I have to do.' I knew that if I didn't keep myself busy, I'd go nuts with worry – about Mum, my job – or the end of it – and RED-V. Even my wretched brother. 'I'll call if I change my mind.'

'Okay. And call Mark. Tonight.'

I spent the rest of the day doing mindless domestic chores, still dazed by the events of this morning, finding myself standing at the sink staring out the window, in disbelief.

I called my mother and asked if she needed any shopping done and she declined the offer.

Later in the day, I checked that the CCTV was on. As dusk was falling, I went around making sure everything was locked up. I wasn't hungry but made myself a cheese and tomato sandwich and sat down under the bright light in the kitchen to go through the witness statements and crime scene photographs yet again. I told myself that the blow of being suspended at least gave me uninterrupted time to devote to making sense of Smiley's cryptic emails and to conduct a further close examination of the photographs. Silver lining? I didn't think so. But focusing on this old crime distracted me, even if momentarily, from the fact that my life was crashing down around me.

Slowly, I went back through all the photos on my laptop. The most poignant of the crime scene photos was an interior shot of the living room showing the old sofa, its crocheted rug covering up wear and tear, on which Frank Davidson, in his striped pyjamas and dressing gown, had finally taken his life, before toppling to the floor, where he lay with his bare feet spread. Some distance from her husband, Betty Davidson lay on her back in a black pool of blood, one fluffy slipper still on; above her was the trophy shelf with its collection of sporting trophies from happier times, and the photographs of the ones that didn't get away, Frank smiling hugely into the camera. Had my father taken any of those photographs? I wondered.

When I had looked through all the photos again, I read and reread Ernie Cusack's statement until I practically had it off by heart. Two shots close together and then, some time later, the third. I looked through Kathleen Cusack's statement, which was almost identical to that of her husband. Nothing new there.

The statement from Craig Davidson was even less helpful. Because he lived some distance from his parents, he'd heard nothing. He'd had to cancel dinner plans with them because he needed to work on his accounts until quite late. I reread the last two sentences: *I wish to God I'd had dinner with them that night. They might still be alive today.*

I sat down, thinking hard, remembering how he'd come around to our place in Garralong with his bunch of flowers and his awkwardness. It seemed that everyone connected with my father's death suffered the guilt of the helpless. I put down the printout of Craig's statement and took another look at the black and white photograph of the living room.

In the right-hand corner of the room, close to the open fireplace, stood the rectangular dinner table, covered in what looked like a crocheted tablecloth. The Davidsons had obviously cleared away the evening meal, but three glasses still stood on the table. I paused at that. None of the original investigators had made any mention of this, clearly presuming it wasn't important that there were three, not two, glasses. Maybe they'd set the table for Craig before he cancelled, I thought, and they hadn't cleared away the glasses when the fatal domestic argument began. But it niggled.

I read the ballistic report that connected the bullets removed from the bodies to the old .303 from the Davidson farm. I skimmed through the autopsy reports on the Davidsons and then slowly read the pathologist's finding regarding my father's death.

> *... A circular puncture wound 10 mm in diameter with a surrounding web of abrasion 2 mm wide inferiorly and 1 mm wide superiorly on the left lateral chest wall. Grey discolouration was noted within the rim of abrasion inferiorly ... The track of the wound passed from left to right, passing slightly downwards and slightly anteriorly between ribs seven and eight on the left lateral chest wall ... through both the upper and lower lobes of the left lung ... through the pericardial sac laterally on the right ... The exit wound was an 18 x 10 mm stellate lacerated puncture wound ...*

I was no medical expert, but the implications of the grey discolouration on the lower rim of the chest injury suggested that my father's killer had been close enough for particles of gunpowder to be deposited in the wound.

I raised my head and pictured Frank Davidson standing on the low veranda of his homestead, firing down at my father.

I read it again, trying to reconstruct my father's movements in my imagination.

The hours passed. Round and round in my head went Smiley's taunting question: *What's missing from this picture?*

Nothing came to mind. Restless, I stood up and went to the kitchen window, looking out into the dark garden. I unlocked the door and stepped outside. A cold wind lifted the branches of next door's palm tree, rustling the fanlike boughs, making me shiver. But my garden was safe from hostiles now, under constant surveillance by my CCTV system.

I stepped back inside, chilled by the wind, and went upstairs to put on something warmer. Opening my wardrobe, I saw my new jacket hanging on a coathanger from the doorknob, its outrageous price tag still dangling. I couldn't resist slipping it off the hanger and trying it on again, my beautiful silky jacket . . .

And that's when I got it.

Why had it taken me so long?

The *jacket*.

The jacket I'd picked up from the house that night, making my father late for work. The jacket I'd left in the car for him. *That's* what was missing from the crime scene photographs. It was a freezing night. Why wasn't he wearing it?

I ran downstairs and clicked through the photographs until I found the one showing the slumped figure of my father against the front passenger wheel. The dark stains showed up on his shirt. Why was he only wearing a shirt and cardigan on such a cold night? I looked again at the photographs of Betty and Frank

Davidson, Frank in his pyjamas and winter dressing gown, Betty with her fluffy winter slippers.

I brought up the photo that showed a detective bending over my father's body. He was rugged up against the cold in a heavy windcheater. And that was during the day. The night of 16 April 1992 had been the coldest April night on record in Garralong and my father had gone out to a job practically in shirtsleeves. Why? Why hadn't he worn the jacket that I'd left in the car for him? The absence of the jacket was important. But how, and why? One of the oldest laws of forensic science states: 'An absence of evidence doesn't mean that evidence is absent.' How could I apply it in this case?

I stood up and walked around the kitchen, attempting to come up with possible explanations for why he wasn't wearing his jacket. My father could have left the jacket in the car – but if so, it should have been visible in the crime scene photographs of the interior of the station wagon. He could have left it at work, hanging on a hook or on the back of his chair; later, it might have been piled into a box of his personal possessions when his drawers and locker were cleaned out after his death.

My mother might remember what had happened to it. I picked up the phone and called her. 'Mum,' I said when she picked up. 'Sorry for calling so late. And this question might strike you as very peculiar, especially coming at a time like this, but what happened to Dad's personal items from the police station after he died?'

My mother's sharp intake of breath was the only hint of her displeasure at this question. But eventually she answered, no doubt relieved that I wasn't calling to 'fuss' about her illness. 'Your father's personal things were all put in a box. I can't remember if I went down to collect them or if someone brought them to me. But I remember that box of his things coming into the house.'

'Was his jacket in it?'

'Debra, how on earth do you expect me to remember something like that? That's a crazy question.'

'You remember that his weapon was missing.'

'How could I forget? The whole place was in an uproar about that for days – weeks. As for his jacket, God knows where it would be now. Maybe someone threw it out at the police station. Why are you asking me this?'

'It could be important.' I could see I wasn't going to get very far with this line of questioning. 'When I'm not thinking about jackets, I'm thinking about you,' I said. 'I don't know how to help you. You won't let me. I meant to ask you, are you in pain?'

'I've got something to take for that. I don't sleep well, but then I've never slept well.'

'I'm thinking of you,' I said.

'Debra,' she said, hesitant, 'there's something you should . . .'

'What, Mum?' I prompted, when she trailed off.

'No, no. I'll be fine.'

I paused, waiting to see if she'd say anything more. When she didn't, I quickly said, 'I'll drop around in the morning and see how you are,' then called off before she could forbid it.

I realised I hadn't called Mark. I'd do it in the morning, I promised myself. I just couldn't face talking about my suspension and my mother's illness, and my fears for RED-V, right now.

Next morning, I drove to my mother's place, and walked up the path past the doggie cemetery, which now seemed unbearably poignant. I let myself in and found my mother resting on her couch, looking haggard and exhausted.

'Oh, I didn't mean to disturb you,' I said, hurrying over. 'Can I get you anything or do anything for you?' I sat down opposite her, waiting for her to respond.

'I went to sleep here on the couch last night,' she said weakly. 'I woke at about four and couldn't get back to sleep again. So I've just stayed here, thinking. Worrying about Brad most of the night.' She paused and added with a bleak smile, 'It takes my mind off worrying about myself, I suppose.'

In that moment, I felt nothing but pure love for her and it surprised me with its intensity. 'Would a cup of tea help?'

She smiled and nodded. I made the tea and brought it in to her on a tray, using her fine china pot and teacups. We drank tea in a companionable silence. 'How are you feeling today?' I asked eventually.

'Not too bad. I have the medication. It makes me a bit dopey.' Mum frowned, leaning forward to peer at me. 'What's that bruise on your forehead?'

'Not sure,' I said, touching it gingerly. 'I was involved in an altercation. Police work.'

'What happened?' Her tone had none of its usual spikiness in it – just genuine curiosity mixed with concern.

I shrugged. 'A difficult customer. I got a knock to the head. It's nothing.' I pushed the hideous memories of the ear-shattering, skull-shattering shotgun blast to the back of my mind, concentrating instead on the face of the woman in front of me, my mother.

'Last night you asked me about your father's jacket. Why?' My mother looked anxious, as if this question had been troubling her.

'I'm not really expecting you to remember something minor like that from such a long time ago. It was just on the off-chance.'

'His jacket,' she repeated, returning her teacup to its saucer and lying back down again. 'Yes, it was a long time ago. But I really can't remember what became of that jacket. I wasn't taking things in very well back then.' She paused. 'Debra —'

'Yes?'

'Pass me that little bottle over there?' she said, pointing to a plastic container with a chemist's label wrapped around it. I did so.

I left her dozing on the lounge with a rug over her legs, and took her shopping list with me – milk, eggs, bread, some chops, greens, fruit. Simple foods.

By the time I returned, my mother was awake and sitting at her desk, looking a little brighter, so I went home.

'I've got some bad news,' I said, when Mark answered the phone. 'Actually, it's a bit like a shopping list of bad news. Mum is sick. I mean, really sick. She has an inoperable cancer. And Brad's been diagnosed with a serious illness.'

There was a silence on the other end of the line. Then I told him about the diagnosis of Huntington's disease and its early onset in my brother's life. 'It gets worse. I've been suspended from work, and RED-V is under threat. Some community leader has denounced it as racist. Gavin is furious with me. Because I was involved in a critical incident.'

'Hey, not so fast. Start at the suspension and tell me what's been going on.'

I told him about Sami Allen and the accidental or otherwise shooting outside the Settlers Rest hotel and how I'd feared for my life.

'I'm so sorry, baby,' he said. 'That must have been horrendous – a man killed in that violent way – right in front of you.'

'It was pretty bad,' I said, my voice quivering at the memory.

Then I described Gavin's fury with me. 'Gavin suspended me because in his view, I'd exceeded my brief and it's true that I've been chasing up details about my father's death in police time. He'd been angry about that before the Sami Allen business.' I explained to Mark why I'd had to get Sami Allen off the street, because of Brad. 'He'd reported me to IA, he had my voice on tape advising him how to pervert the course of justice after his gang's stupid failed robbery when he was a kid.'

'What happens with a suspension? What does it mean?'

I told him.

'And how do you become unsuspended?'

'After there's an enquiry and it's cleared up. And I've been penalised in some way – if I've been found guilty – a fine, demotion. I'm not sure how long it might take.'

'So how are you going to handle this IA charge? Damn your brother. Is there some way that you don't have to perjure yourself?'

'Brad can perjure himself. He started this. He can finish it.'

'Your family seems to have had more than its fair share of life's shit,' Mark said. 'Are you going to be tested for that disease?'

'I will. But right now I have other priorities. Like making sure a young Iraqi woman is safe from her violent brothers, to protect her as I'm sworn to do, suspended or not.'

'But why is RED-V under threat? I don't understand.'

I told him about how sensitive material from a private debate in the meal room had been exposed. 'I'm almost a hundred per cent sure it was Nadine who leaked it to her journalist boyfriend. Now some community leader is waving the racist card and the local paper made it their front-page story. I can sense Nadine is resentful of me. Reckons my job should have been hers. I feel like saying: "You want my job? Here, take it."'

'But Debs, surely they won't undo RED-V? The same complaints were trotted out about MEOCS, remember? How it was "marginalising and demonising" and all that. But it's still going strong.'

'I hope you're right, Mark. Gavin was so furious with me and although what's happened to me is completely unfair and unjust, I can't help feeling I've let him down somehow.'

'Let *him* down? He's let you down, darling. Instead of backing you up and backing the great work you're doing, he surrenders at the first shot over the bows. He's gutless, I'm sorry to say. He is chasing a promotion and that's all he's thinking about. How to stay in good with the top brass. I'm sorry about your mother, and Brad too. But for a moment I thought something really bad might have happened to you – or that you might be kicking me out.'

'Mark, you are the only trouble-free zone in my life.'

After lunch, feeling restless, I drove around to the address where Rana was staying. At least she was safe for the time being, and that was one good thing I'd helped to do. Mrs Fouad, a short, curvaceous woman with large expressive eyes and a chiselled mouth, smiled when she opened the door. Rana was out, she said, but she ushered me inside, insisting that I have tea and offering me a pastry from a plate of them on a highly polished table. I asked her about Rana.

'Rana is . . .' Ereini Fouad paused. 'I think she is doing well. Even though it is difficult for her to be living with strangers. We do our best but we are not her family.'

That's just as well, I thought. You don't intend to kill her.

Mrs Fouad continued, 'She's making plans to move to Queensland. She's transferring her studies up there. You know she has a friend? Eshaq? A nice Coptic boy?'

I nodded.

'He's trying to find work there now. He will go up and join her, complete his studies. Also, there is another good woman up there, a friend of mine, and she's told Rana that she can stay with them until she finds her feet. Rana is a brave soul. I pray that she can make a happy new life for herself. She can leave the fear behind.'

'Please tell her I called,' I said. 'And that we need her to sign her statement. Also, I'd love to hear from her. We have to organise contacts for her in the agencies that can help her once she's made her plans.'

I noticed Mrs Fouad frowning, glancing over at the elaborate gold clock on the mantelpiece. 'I'm a little surprised she's not back already. She went out earlier with her friend Jamila, shopping for some new clothes. Father Joseph gave us some money for her. But they have been gone for a long time.' She turned anxious eyes to me. 'Too long, I think. But you know what girls are like. They've probably lost track of the time.'

'Ask her to call me as soon as she gets in, please,' I said. Something didn't seem right, my instincts were warning. I made polite farewells and returned to my car, then drove directly around to the address I had for Jamila. I knocked on the door, and was a little taken aback when a tall young woman wearing full black burqa with niqab opened the door and gazed at me through the slit. I was even more surprised when I recognised the golden streaks in those astonishing velvety brown eyes. I could hardly believe it.

'Jamila?' What had happened to the tight jeans, platform shoes and glorious free-flowing locks.

'What do you want?' Her voice still had its defiant edge, but this time the defiance was directed at me rather than her fate.

'Jamila! Is that really you in there?'

'What do you want?' she repeated, urgency as well as defiance in her voice now.

'I want to know where Rana is.'

'Rana? How should I know?'

'You went out shopping with her hours ago. Before you say anything, I've just been talking to Mrs Fouad, so there's no point in lying.'

The golden streaks were briefly eclipsed as Jamila blinked through the eye slit.

'So,' I repeated, 'where is she?'

'I don't know. She didn't tell me where she was going. I last saw her talking to some friends.'

'Friends? What friends? Where?'

'In the mall. Near the halal chicken shop.'

I felt like saying, 'You'll be a halal chicken yourself if you don't come clean with me right now.' With a struggle, I remained professional. 'Okay. When was that?'

The shrouded black figure shrugged. 'Maybe an hour ago? Two hours?'

'And the friends?'

'New friends of Rana's. People I don't know. People I don't want to know. They're not good for me to know. I want to be a good, pleasing girl.'

I couldn't believe what I was hearing. 'Jamila, what's happened to you?'

A torrent of words poured out. 'I've turned my life around. I was on a wrong path. You know what happened when Rana's cousin in Iraq heard that she had run away?'

'Who told him that?'

A strange, muffled laugh agitated the black fabric across her mouth. 'Only about a dozen people! He was furious. The al-Sheikly family has brought shame on him as well as on themselves. Everyone is laughing at him. The whole family is disgraced. They're all unclean now because of Rana. No one will want to employ any of the men. No one will want to marry any of the cousins and nieces here or back in Iraq.' Jamila continued, 'You know what her cousin said about Rana? That the only way he will ever see her again is if she's in a box for him to pray on! And now he wants compensation for the shame she has brought on him.'

'Shame? What shame? She didn't want to marry him! Jamila! You're supposed to be her friend! You understand why she didn't want to marry him. You told me!'

Jamila's voice trembled. 'I was wrong. I started mixing in bad company. Bad influences. Now that the imam's told me about the four poisons, and other things, I don't want to see Rana again. I have to go now. I can't talk to you any longer.'

'Just a moment. If she's such a bad character, and you don't want to see her again, how come you invited her to go shopping this morning? And were you looking like that –' I indicated the black robes and veil – 'when you asked her out? I'll bet it was all tight jeans and high-heeled boots this morning.'

Jamila started to close the door. I shoved a foot forward to block it. 'What's going on, Jamila? Tell me the truth! Why did you invite Rana to go shopping with you?'

'If you don't let me close the door, I'll call the police!'

'I *am* the police, Jamila. I want the truth. Now!'

'Go away! You'll get me in serious trouble! Please, please just go!' Her voice broke and she started sobbing.

I spoke more softly. 'Rana is your friend. Help me help her. Please, Jamila.'

The defiant voice broke through the sobs. 'Why? Why should I? No one helped me! No one's going to help me! Go away! Leave me alone!' She slammed the door.

―•―

I sat in my car outside Jamila's place for a few minutes, heart banging against my chest wall, wondering what I'd just witnessed. My fear for Rana ratcheted up another notch and I made a decision. Suspended as I was, I drove to the mall and raced up the stairs to the chicken shop. I quizzed the man and woman behind the counter, but they hadn't seen anyone of Rana's description with or without friends that morning. I called the Fouads. No, Rana had not yet returned.

Not knowing what else to do, I drove fast to the al-Sheikly house. There was just a chance that Rana was there. Maybe, inexplicably, she'd gone back to that place where I first saw her beautiful, pleading eyes through the glass.

But as I approached their street I saw that something was going on. Police cars blocked off the entrance to the road while neighbours stood around in groups, watching and passing commentary. I parked in the next street and walked up to a group of three middle-aged women. 'Hi,' I said, nodding to them, 'what's happening?'

'Some big police operation. But apparently the guys they're looking for aren't there. They've been doorknocking, asking if we know when they left.'

What had happened to our surveillance? Had Gavin pulled that?

And that's when I saw the al-Sheikly house taped off and people from Forensic Services coming out carrying objects in large heavy-duty brown-paper bags. My heart constricted. 'So when did they leave?'

'Late morning. The two men and the girl. The people next door said they drove away. The girl looked sick, they said.'

The two men and the girl. The girl looked sick.

I jumped back into my car and drove the short distance to the al-Sheikly brothers' garage. My worst fear had been realised: Talal and Samir had grabbed Rana. Jamila had set her up. What had they done to her? Had the brothers doped their sister with something or was she just sick with fear, knowing that she was in their clutches again and there was no way to contact anyone to help her?

Again, the laneway was blocked by police vehicles. Beyond them, though, I could clearly see the rolled-up door of the garage; there was no one inside. Maybe they'd made an arrest, I thought hopefully. I managed to slip past the police tape and ran over to a young woman loading files into the back of a police vehicle. 'Debra Hawkins,' I said, sidling over and doing a quick introduction. 'Used to be in MEOCS. Any arrests here?'

'No such luck. They must have been tipped off. They've gone dark. No mobile phone use.' She sighed. 'Means hours and hours of sorting through RTA footage trying to locate their vehicle.'

I hurried back to my car before anyone official spotted me. This was about as bad as it could be. Betrayed by her best friend, delivered into the hands of her violent brothers, Rana was in terrible danger.

I called Flash but it went straight to voicemail. Then Charlie. Same thing. I remembered Socrates was having a rostered day off and Alex was at court with his phone switched off. I called Nadine. I took a deep breath as she answered. What I wanted to say to her would have to wait. Just now, I needed her.

'I can't talk to you!' she said.

'You don't have to. Just put out an urgent missing persons bulletin on Rana al-Sheikly and add that the police have grave concerns for her safety.'

'I can't do that! You're suspended. You have no right to contact me or anyone else here. It's very unfair of you putting me on the spot like this. I'm going to terminate this call right now!'

'Please, Nadine! Please! This girl could be killed!'

'I'm terminating this call now,' she repeated, and my plea was cut off as she hung up.

Sitting in my car, I next called Mrs Fouad and told her what had happened at Jamila's place. Although I could hear the concern in her voice, Mrs Fouad didn't seem overly surprised to hear of Jamila's sudden conversion to religiosity. 'It happens quite a lot. Somebody's got to her and terrified her. She might have been threatened. Or some old cleric's been telling her about the punishments awaiting her in the next life – horror stories about the tortures of the grave and that hell is mainly full of disobedient women hanging by their breasts from hooks.' My mother's generation had been similarly terrorised by horror stories, although less sexualised or gender specific, of the eternal torments awaiting sinners.

'Please report her as missing,' I said. 'Call the police. Right now! Tell them you're very concerned about her safety.'

'I will. I'll do it now. And in the meantime, we must pray for her.'

I rang off, hoping that the woman's report would alert the police to act fast. I had no idea if Nadine would do as I asked, but there was every reason to assume she wouldn't.

I called a contact in the Australian Federal Police, Paul Ackroyd. We'd worked on a joint operation some years back. I felt sure that no one there would know of my suspension yet. 'Paul. It's Debra Hawkins. From the new RED-V team – the

Religio–Ethnic Domestic Violence team.' He remembered me well. 'I need to get three names onto a watch list for all airports.'

Paul listened while I gave him a fast review of Rana's case. 'We've lost her,' I said finally. 'She's one of my cases and she's in real trouble. Both of the brothers have warrants out on them, and if they get her out of the country she may be forced to marry a first cousin back in Iraq. And that's the best-case scenario.'

'RED-V? Isn't that the team that's in trouble for being racist?'

'Oh, come on, Paul. Please – Rana al-Sheikly. She mustn't leave the country. Make it an urgent priority?'

'It has to go through the right channels.'

'Just do it fast. They've got to be stopped, Paul. She mustn't be taken out of the country. God knows what might happen to her.'

'I'll get onto it now, although I'll need authorisation from higher up.' Paul sounded overworked, unenthusiastic.

'Just get it! Do whatever.'

There was nothing more I could do for Rana now so I drove home. What if Paul didn't get authorisation? What if my word had been so devalued by suspension and the taint of racism that no one would take any notice?

Where was Rana right now? My mind filled with thoughts of her being beaten, or, worse still, unconscious, being driven into a dam. With the watch list in place, she couldn't leave the country. But there are no watch lists on country roads, on dams. And my request might not have gone through at all. I felt sick with concern. And completely helpless.

All I could do to quieten the anxiety was try to focus my attention on the crime scene photographs. I forced myself to concentrate on two images: one that showed the front of the house with the mark on the veranda step and the other that showed the similar mark on the floor near the front door.

I zoomed in on the first smudge and then cropped around this so that I had an even closer and larger version. I did the same with the mark on the floor near the front door. Then I lined them up side by side on my screen. For reasons known only to itself and the photolab program I'd downloaded several years ago, the second image had loaded itself upside down. I was about to flip it right side up, but I paused a moment, thinking that the different orientation might give me a new perspective – using a different side of the brain or something similar. I increased the intensity of the contrast, darkening the faint stains, then looked closer. Both shared something I'd never noticed before: a series of faint ridges, with the first one, the stain on the veranda step, clearer and more intense. Maybe my eyes were playing tricks on me, maybe my brain was compensating, but as I looked at the images, they suddenly started to make sense. Now that I could see it, I wondered how I could have missed it before – it was impossible *not* to see it now. What I was looking at were unquestionably the marks left by part of the ridged sole of a boot or shoe. I remembered my previous conjecture that the muddy boots Frank Davidson had clumped across the floor had been the last straw for his unhappy wife. But Garralong had been caught in a savage drought, so where did the mud come from?

Despite everything that had happened over the last couple of days, this discovery brought a thrill of elation. I inverted the first image so that it too was upside down, and gasped with excitement. Now I could trace the similarity. What I was looking at were two separate partial shoe or boot prints; the outside edge of a left shoe, and if there hadn't been any mud, there could only be one explanation for the smear. Not mud, but blood!

I realised the implication of these marks. Neither Frank Davidson nor his wife could have made those prints – Betty because she was dead and Frank because he was barefoot. This was a partial boot or shoe print in two locations. They had to have been laid down afterwards, once the couple were dead, *when there was blood on the floor.*

My fingers shaking, I went through the rest of the crime scene photographs again, pulling out the four that showed Frank and Betty Davidson's bodies. I grabbed a magnifying glass, examining not the bodies but the surrounding blood. Slowly I circled around the areas close to the bodies of the dead couple with the magnifying glass. I knew what I was looking for. And there on the edge of the dark pooling around Betty Davidson's body, I found it. The corresponding disturbance on the edge of the blood; very faint but once studied closely, incontrovertible. I took a deep breath and jumped out of the chair, my head spinning. This changed everything. This changed the whole case!

I went to the door of the kitchen, staring sightlessly out into the garden. There was only one conclusion to be drawn: someone else had been there who was neither Frank nor Betty Davidson, and certainly not my father. Someone had been there after the killing of the couple; someone had trodden in blood that had already been shed. *There had been a third party at that crime scene.*

Someone had walked through the crime scene after the Davidsons were killed. When a case has been interpreted a certain way for twenty-two years, it takes a while for a new theory to settle. It hadn't been my father's boot print. He'd barely had time to get out of his vehicle. There was no mention of any blood except his own on his clothing or shoes. Who else might have been there that night? Was Craig Davidson lying? Did he go over that evening after all? And if he did, did he kill his parents? I tried to recall that time years ago when he'd come to our house with his bunch of tulips. 'I used to go to sleep thinking that one day I'd come back when he least expected it, and shoot him. And our bloody mother, too.' Had he been making some sort of confession to me? Or was it his brother Tim, filled with the rage to avenge his childhood suffering? There had been such cases, I knew.

I tried to sit down, but within moments I was prowling around, calling Mark. 'I've found something! In the crime scene photographs,' I told him. 'Somebody walked through blood on the night of my father's murder and left two partial footprints.'

'Are you sure?'

'As sure as I can be. I've just found the corresponding disturbance at the edge of a blood stain near Betty Davidson's body. I'll bet the house that there will be a perfect match between the slight impressions in the blood stain and the marks on the floor and the veranda step.'

In my mind's eye, I replayed the scene that I now believed had occurred. 'In the darkness, whoever it was didn't notice that part of their shoe or boot had come into contact with the blood around Betty Davidson's head. It looks like a left shoe because of the slight convexity of the partial print, then they take another step with their right foot, another with their stained left shoe near the inside of the front door, leaving part of a boot print, the right foot hits the veranda and it's clean, then that left shoe again connects on the step and once again leaves another mark, fainter of course than the first one. And it would've had to have been done when the blood was still fresh, and not yet congealed. So it couldn't have been the detectives the following day.'

'Have you been able to find any others?'

'Nothing obvious. I'll have a closer look. Someone was at the crime scene. I'm wondering if Craig Davidson lied about his whereabouts that night.' I grabbed up the copy of his witness statement, reading out the body of the text to Mark: '*I spent the day driving and knocked off at about six p.m. Mum had asked me to dinner that night but I declined because I had work to do. Because it was quiet, I knocked off and worked at home, bringing my accounts up to date. My ex-wife Valerie called me at around nine o'clock and we talked about the kids. I went to bed at about ten thirty p.m. I wish to God I'd had dinner with them that night. They might still be alive today.*'

'You think maybe Craig *did* go to his parents' place that night?' Mark asked. 'He hasn't got an alibi for the evening – apart from being home at the time of his wife's call.'

'How often have you read about sons who murder their parents? He told me what a bastard his old man had been towards him and his brother when they were kids. His younger brother, Tim has never been interviewed. Craig told me years ago how he and his brother used to fantasise about shooting their father one day.'

'And you think he might have been in the process of doing that when your father surprised him on the premises?'

'That's possible. There's a gap in his witness statement of an hour and a half between talking with his ex-wife at around nine and then going to bed around ten thirty. There would have been time for him to drive over to the old farmhouse. People prefer not to lie outright in witness statements. They just leave things out.'

I thought again about the grouping of the shots. 'The Cusacks are sure that they heard two shots close together and then, maybe five or ten minutes later, they heard the third shot. But they weren't paying attention so we can't be sure of the time lapse between the shots. It could be longer or shorter than five minutes.'

'So,' Mark said slowly, 'you're thinking . . .'

'I'm just playing with possibilities now. I'm wondering if instead of Frank killing his wife and my father in quick succession and then turning the gun on himself, those three shots can be interpreted to create an entirely different picture. The third party – let's say it's Craig for the time being – shoots his parents, and then hearing the police car coming up the driveway he knows he's in deep trouble. So, as my father gets out of his station wagon after probably hearing the two shots, Craig creeps to the front of the house, accidentally stepping in his mother's blood, then treads on the floor inside the house, then out to the top step, from where he shoots my father. That would account for the downward angle of the trajectory of the bullet.'

'And his parents?'

'In his mind, they deserved to die.' I recalled the awkward conversation on the veranda of our old house in Garralong and the flowers lying on the table between us. 'Craig told me how his father used to lay into them. He bullied them, and apparently their mother never intervened.'

'But what about the jacket? Where does that fit in?'

I considered awhile. 'I'm still no closer to finding out anything about the damned jacket,' I said finally.

'But you've found more of the truth. That's got to be valuable. That will have to be taken into account. You once told me how with cold cases, an investigator has to throw out all the conclusions that have already been arrived at – all the suppositions – and start again.'

'That's right. There are facts and there are presumptions. Nothing but the facts. Accept nothing. Question everything. Turn everything on its head – and start again.'

Finally, I told him about Rana, how I'd done everything I could and yet I'd let her down, failed her.

'You have to let go, darling,' Mark said, his voice kind. 'You've done everything you can – and more. Let the Federal Police do their job at the airport.'

'But what if it doesn't come to that? What if the brothers murder her?' I told him about the second car the brothers had bought, the conversations Rana had overheard.

'I don't think they'll risk that. They're already on the run. Think about it – they've got warrants out on them. Their plan would surely be to get out of the country as fast as they can – taking Rana with them. And that's not going to happen, okay?'

'God, I hope not.' What Mark said made sense. If I were the al-Sheikly brothers, with the fear of a long gaol sentence ahead of me, surely bolting overseas would seem the best solution. In several instances, criminals who thought they'd got away with it were dismayed to find the Australian Federal Police stopping their aircraft from taking off, coming on board and removing them from their flight.

CHAPTER 27

After my call to Mark, I continued to pace around the house, and when I wasn't worrying about Rana, or my mother, or the possible dismantling of RED-V, I was thinking of the farmhouse, the Davidsons, Frank, Betty and now Craig and Tim. At one stage I heard the kids next door yelling at each other, the younger one saying over and over again, '*This* one's yours! That big one is mine!', until their mother yelled at them to shut up.

Finally, unable to settle, I threw on the new blue silky jacket and, after locking the house carefully behind me, stepped out into the cool night. It was very late and the hum of traffic was softer now. In another few hours, the early morning truckies would start trundling through the road nearby, but until then it would be quiet.

I needed to walk to clear my head. If only the museum was open at night. That would have been perfect to prowl around during bouts of insomnia, checking out the hominids, the diorama showing the little troop leaving their footprints behind them, the volcano in the distance, belching ash, about to explode and destroy them, and, in the process, immortalising those footprints, the signs of their passage.

I walked through the backstreets until I came to the lights and buzz of Oxford Street and the places that never close. Muted doof-doof music from several different venues made a random mix as I strode down towards the museum and the swimming centre.

There were still a lot of people in the bars and cafes or strolling down the streets, men sweetly holding hands or in earnest conversation in doorways. I turned down into College Street and passed the grammar school and the museum, dark and brooding; I pictured how spooky it would be inside, with the dim lights turned off, and the figures of the hominids standing still in the darkness, the leopard on the bough above, waiting to strike. Lying in wait for its victim to pass by . . . Lying in wait.

Accept nothing. Question everything. Turn everything on its head and start again.

I passed the museum and was pressing the button at the lights to cross William Street when I did exactly that. I had been assuming that even if it wasn't old Frank who did the killings it was a third party who shot my father simply because he'd walked into a rage-filled situation at the wrong time. But now I turned my own assumptions on their head and asked myself: what if the Davidsons were not the primary targets? What if they weren't the people the killer was after?

What if someone had been lying in wait – *not to kill the Davidsons, but to kill my father?* What if the Davidsons had simply been collateral damage?

Riveted by this new interpretation, I stopped walking and stood for a minute beside the massive bulk of the gothic cathedral with its dark shadows under the top-lit buttresses, and replayed in my mind the three shots described by Ernie Cusack. The sequence of shots made perfect sense for someone who first murdered the Davidsons – one, two – and *then switched off the lights* and lay in wait, in the darkness, ready to pull the trigger on the .303 and shoot my father as he drove up with his headlights shining on the dark house. My father wouldn't have had a clue what was going on until the killer stepped out onto the veranda and levelled the .303 at him.

Shot number three – some minutes later.

Soon, with almost no idea of how I might have got there, I was walking fast down Macquarie Street, past Parliament House. My head whirling with this new interpretation, I almost stepped onto the road in front of an oncoming car. The horn blared and I jumped back just in time.

Who might have known that my father was going to check out a disturbance? The person who made the anonymous phone call. But who was that? I didn't even know if the caller had been a man or a woman. All I'd seen was the brief note on my father's running sheet: *9.34 p.m. – Caller reporting altercation at Davidsons' homestead. Will check out.*

I was almost on the downhill run to the Opera House before I turned back. This dark possibility had, perversely, filled me with enthusiasm. If someone had wanted to kill my father, there had to be a motive – a big one – to warrant the murder of two people as a by-product. Somebody must have hated my father to the point of triple homicide. I couldn't believe that my mother wouldn't have known about such a person. She must have heard something. It was hard to imagine somebody's hatred festering in complete silence until being released in such a deadly fashion. Somehow, I had to make her open up that vault she'd locked down almost a quarter of a century ago. Frail and ill as she was, she must talk to me. She *must* talk about these painful events, I told myself. Garralong was a small town. My mother must have some ideas about who could have hated her husband so much – and why.

I flagged down a passing cab and jumped in, pulling out my mobile and dialling her number. There was no answer. Of course, at this hour. Suddenly, I was exhausted. I went home and crashed out on top of the bed, fully dressed.

It was almost midday by the time I woke. My mouth was dry and I felt in need of a shower. I hadn't realised how drained and exhausted I'd been.

After my shower, and a strong coffee, I tried calling my mother again. Once again I got the message to try again later. By now I was starting to get really worried about her, so I raced to the car and drove to Mum's place. I parked outside and hurried to the back door. Without bothering to knock I opened the door and ran inside. 'Mum? Where are you? Why aren't you answering the phone?'

She wasn't in the living room so I went from room to room calling out. In the guest bedroom I found my brother, Brad, sitting up on a nest of embroidered pillows like the bloody Queen of Sheba. 'Why didn't you answer?' I asked.

'Thank goodness you're here,' he said. 'I was getting worried that I'd miss out on dinner. I haven't had anything except this.' He indicated a large block of chocolate, now half-eaten.

'Where's Mum?'

Brad shrugged and then winced. 'I don't know. She said she was going out to meet someone a while ago. I heard her getting a few things together and then she was gone. I yelled out after her but she just kept going. She'd been talking to someone on the phone before she went. She was very upset. She was crying when she left.'

'And you didn't ask her what was wrong?'

Brad shrugged gingerly. 'I didn't know what to say.'

'Who was she going to meet?'

Brad shook his head. 'Like I said, she didn't say. She just drove off.'

I pulled out my mobile and dialled her mobile. Switched off. I threw down my phone in frustration with her – and Brad. 'She must have said *something* about where she was going.'

'You're not listening to me. She didn't. She just said she was going out to meet someone. Do you think I like it? I shouldn't be left here on my own like this.'

I looked at him properly for the first time; his head was still bandaged and the bruising around his eyes was fading to yellowish green. It wasn't a good look. 'You seem okay to me,' I said callously. 'I need to find Mum. You'll have to get your own dinner.'

'Aw, come on, Deb. I'm off the drugs. And I'm remembering what being hungry feels like.'

'Good. Enjoy it. Get used to it. Have a look in the fridge. I've got better things to do than play nurse to a self-obsessed idiot brother.'

I went back out to the living room and over to the desk where Mum's computer sat, its screen blank amid a pile of papers that looked like they'd been in a storm. Hoping to get an idea of where she might have gone or who she might be meeting, I started looking through the papers. I sifted through medical reports, PET scan results, and two or three letters from ex-clients. I flicked through the desk diary, checking for meetings, but found only doctor, client and hair appointments. There was nothing to give any indication of where she was and with whom.

Then I recalled the phone conversation she'd cut short when I'd walked in a few days ago. 'I don't want to talk about it,' she'd said. The story of her life.

I started looking through another pile of client reports, then stopped my search in shock.

At the bottom of the pile was something that took my breath away. I pulled it out.

It couldn't be! But it was.

I was staring at the crime scene photograph from my father's death – the photograph of him slumped against the front wheel of his station wagon with the blackened hole in his chest.

The photograph that had been sent with the last Smiley email.

I straightened up, confused and frightened. What did this mean? Had she got hold of the photo from one of the investigating officers or the crime scene photographer all those years ago? Not possible, I thought. It would have been a gross breach of protocol: these pictures are protected species, and especially to be quarantined from a distressed family member. I ruled out that possibility. Where else could my mother have got hold of this photograph? What the hell was going on? I sat down on the stool in front of the computer and logged on, using her password which was taped along the top of the screen. I checked her emails, and when I looked in the sent box I took a sharp involuntary inbreath.

I stared at the email, addressed to me. Its subject was a question. As I read it, my brain did a slow somersault: *What's missing from this picture?*

There it was. The third Smiley email! Did she know Smiley? Were they friends? Was she meeting with Smiley now?

I searched vainly through her sent box for the two earlier emails until I remembered that they'd been sent from Broadway Library. But the third one had undoubtedly been sent from this very computer. I squeezed my eyes tightly shut and then opened them, shaking my head in an attempt to clear it, to make things comprehensible. There was only one conclusion I could draw. I swore out loud.

My own mother was Smiley.

I jumped up, disoriented with shock and disbelief, then walked around the room in a stupefied circle. I went back to the screen to make sure that what I was seeing was really there, not some stress-induced hallucination. My thoughts were a whirlpool of confusion, anger and fear; most of all, though, I had a leaden feeling of betrayal. My mother had been playing me for a fool. Why?

I was furious. I *had* to find my mother. I would use whatever means possible to get to the truth of what was going on. This silence and betrayal could continue no longer.

I dialled her number again. This time I left a message. 'I know you sent the third Smiley email and I have every reason to believe that you also sent the first two. I know that you know something about Dad's missing jacket. And if you know that, you know a whole lot more about what happened that night at the Davidsons' farmhouse. What the hell's going on, Mum? Where are you? Call me the minute you get this.'

Brad hobbled into the room as I was hurrying out. 'Where are you going?' he asked.

'To find Mum. And then I'm going to Garralong – want to come?'

'You're joking.'

'I sure am!'

I left my mother's house with Brad yelling after me, 'Hey! What about dinner?'

I ignored him.

I jumped into the car and pulled out angrily, forgetting to indicate. Realising I was lucky I hadn't collected anybody, I made myself calm down. I had no idea where my mother was and there was absolutely no point in driving around looking for her as if she were a lost cat. All I could do was go home and hope that she would contact me. Eventually, she'd *have* to come home. Brad would see to that.

On the way, I called in at the health clinic where Mum worked, but no one there could help me. 'I'm sorry, Debra,' said the receptionist, Norah. 'She didn't say anything to me. I've had to cancel her clients for today. We realise she's not at all well and we're concerned for her. If she contacts you, please let me know.'

I assured her I would. 'Do you mind if I take a look in her office? She might have her own appointments book that could shed a little light?'

'Of course. Go ahead.'

My mother's small office was very neat but there was one piece of paper on her desk. I picked it up and read 'Brother Lorenzo.' And there was a phone number.

Sitting in my mother's chair, I immediately dialled the number. A recorded message told me, 'You have reached the office of the Retreat House of the Benedictine monastery, Arcadia. No one is here just now to take your call, but if you leave a message and your number, we will get back to you.'

I put the phone down slowly, surprised. Is that where my mother was? With Brother Lorenzo, in a Benedictine monastery? Had she booked herself in on retreat? As far as I knew, my mother had turned her back on all things religious a long time ago. I briefly considered, then quickly rejected, the notion of driving there myself. I could hardly expect Brother Lorenzo to betray any confidences. And my mother might not welcome my intrusion. I got up and walked to the window that overlooked the roofs and chimney pots of the nearby buildings. I was very surprised by my mother's behaviour. But as I stared out the window, I understood that I knew so little about her, that she could be involved in gun running and I wouldn't know. It made sense to me that someone facing imminent death might well turn her mind to things of the spirit and feel the need of a retreat, some quiet place where she could reflect and organise her remaining time in the way that pleased her best.

—◆—

Driving home, the anger about her elaborate deception and the frustration I'd been feeling softened into something more accepting. After all, how could I know how I might react given the same circumstances? And I realised too, that I'd feared she may have gone somewhere to harm herself. At least she was safer talking to Brother Lorenzo. Was she telling him all about Smiley?

A confession?

As I watered the garden, the decision I'd almost made now hardened into resolution. My mother had hidden behind the Smiley emails. She'd alerted me to something that I didn't understand concerning my father's jacket, pointing me to the double murder–suicide that was supposed to have claimed his life. There was only one reason for this: she wanted me to investigate. She wanted me to reopen the case and take a closer look. My mother must have suspected that something was wrong but for some reason she couldn't – or wouldn't – come forward with her suspicions. If it wasn't a double murder–suicide, it could only mean that a third party – the third party I had conjectured in my reconstruction – had murdered three people that night.

I was suspended from my work until further notice. There was only one place for me to be right now. My home town, Garralong, the country town that had been the location of a vicious, premeditated and coldly executed triple murder. The sooner I got going, the sooner I'd get there.

Online, I checked out the Convent of the Holy Family where I used to have my music lessons, only to find that it was no longer a convent but a retreat centre with aged-care units now taking up what used to be the playing fields and the tennis court. I rang the phone number and left a message, saying I was hoping to speak with Sister Mary Aloysius if she was still living there. As I rang off, I wondered if she'd even be alive.

I packed a few overnight essentials because I didn't know how long I was going to be away. Then I called Mark. 'I'm going to drive up this evening,' I explained. 'As far as I can, I'm going to retrace my father's steps on that night. I'll spend tomorrow seeing what I can discover and tomorrow night, I'll set off a bit before ten o'clock, just as he would have done after he got that anonymous call about the domestic blue at the Davidsons'. I'm going to drive right up to the farmhouse and get out just where he did.'

'Is this some kind of pilgrimage?' Mark asked.

'It's a cold case investigation. I'll explain more when I see you.'

'It's only a little while now, Debs. And I'll be back in town.'

'We'll talk about it when you get here.'

CHAPTER 28

I was nearly packed when my mobile rang. 'Mum?' I grabbed up the phone without looking at the number. When I realised who it was, I almost jumped out of my shoes.

'Debra!' Her voice was strained with fear, the words tumbling out, running together so that they were almost incomprehensible. 'Stop them! Stop them! I won't marry him!' In the background I could hear a woman's voice raised in protest, then a man's voice shouting in agitated Arabic.

'Rana! Where are you?'

'EK413, EK413 – *please stop them.*' There was a harsh male voice close by, then Rana broke off into a choked silence, and a moment later the line went dead.

'Oh God, Rana,' I said out loud, fingers fumbling as I tried to call her back. But there was no option to call back, just a screen telling me it was a private number.

EK413, she'd said. A flight number?

I went online and found the airlines. My heart started thudding. Sure enough, EK413 was a flight to Iraq at 9.45 – in three hours' time. They were taking her back to the old country. The first cousin she'd been intended to marry had said that the only way he'd want her back was in a box for him to pray on. Once Rana was back in the war zone of Iraq, now tearing itself apart in civil war, she would be in terrible danger. She must have grabbed someone's mobile in a last-ditch attempt to alert me. She knew she would soon be beyond help.

I called Paul at the AFP. 'This is urgent. Is the al-Sheikly family definitely on that watch list at passport control?'

'The word is you're suspended,' Paul said. 'You have no authority to ask me this.'

'A girl's life is on the line. Life is bigger than police regulations, for God's sake! She's flying out on EK413 to Iraq tonight. She's facing a forced marriage over there. Or possibly death.'

He paused. 'I was going to call you about this. But then I heard about the suspension. I'm sorry to say there's been a glitch in our computer system. We got hacked last night. I did put them on the watch list, but I'm not sure if it went through. I was going to check it today.'

'Check it now! You've *got* to make sure it goes through!'

That was a mistake; he hung up and I cursed myself for my folly. I rang back but this time he didn't answer and all I could do was leave a message: 'I didn't mean to tell you how to do your job. But Rana al-Sheikly is in terrible danger. Please help her.'

I still had time to stop this. As I ran downstairs and out the door, I threw my mobile into my bag. I sent encouraging thoughts winging towards wherever Rana was being held. I would go to the airport. If necessary, I would stop the brothers myself.

— —

I was almost at the international airport when my mobile rang. I snatched it up. A male voice asked, 'Is this Detective Inspector Debra Hawkins?'

'Yes.'

'This is Simon Poole from the AFP, Sydney International Airport.' Simon Poole. The name was familiar. 'We are holding a young woman here who refuses to speak to us. She set off the alarm at security. She's in big trouble. Says she'll only talk to you.'

My heart surged with relief. Rana! Thank goodness. I swung my car off the road, stopping in a nearby bus stand. 'Is her name Rana al-Sheikly?' I asked, my voice shaking.

'That's correct.'

'Tell her I'm on my way. Tell her not to worry. That everything's going to be fine.'

'I very much doubt it. She was hiding a knife in her waistband. Airport security pulled her out of the screening line.'

'Where will I find her?'

'She's in number three interview room. Just ask for me at the AFP office. Someone will direct you.'

My spirits lifted as I pulled back onto the road. Rana would be okay. She would be safe in an AFP and Customs interview room, away from her brothers, who would now be arrested.

I parked in an area marked for security vehicles. I was already in so much trouble that a parking ticket would seem like a birthday card. Inside, I asked the way to the AFP offices, then ran in the direction I was pointed.

—•—

The first thing I saw when I was ushered into the interview room was Rana sitting hunched in a chair, draped in a burqa, only her pale face and hands showing. She jumped out of her seat the second I walked in and I was enveloped in black polyester and the scent of jasmine and orange blossom. Her body trembled in my arms and I wasn't sure if it was from fear or with sobs. Tears welled in my own eyes as I drew away.

'Thank you for coming!' she cried. 'I was so frightened. I didn't want to talk to anyone else but you. Jamila tricked me.'

'I know. I saw her.'

'How could she? She was my friend! We've been friends all through school. I can't believe she's done this to me! But I know how a twisted ideology can distort the human heart. I've seen it happen in my mother, but I never thought it would happen to my friend Jamila. Never!'

The other two people in the room – AFP officer Simon Poole, whom I immediately recognised from the joint operation I'd been part of in my MEOCS days, and a short, dark-haired woman in airport security uniform, whom I supposed had been brought in to search Rana – watched us in evident surprise. Now Simon Poole reintroduced himself, passing me his business card. 'Thanks for coming so quickly, Debra,' he said. 'We haven't been able to get anywhere with . . .' he glanced at the passport in his hands, '. . . Miss al-Sheikly here.'

'She was carrying this,' the woman explained. 'She was asked to step aside by the staff at the screening station and brought here. I found it tucked into the back waistband of her trousers.'

For the first time I noticed the object sitting on the table in a sealed AFP exhibit bag: a knife with a black hilt and a narrow four-inch blade lying beside its sheath.

'It was the only way to get away from them,' Rana cried, her eyes on me. 'To be separated from them! Please, Debra. You can make them understand. I didn't want to say anything until you were here. You are the only person I can trust.'

I appealed to the federal agent. 'Agent Poole, Miss al-Sheikly did this quite deliberately in order to trigger the metal detector. It was the only way she could get away from her relatives, who have been making death threats against her and are already the subjects of arrest warrants on other criminal charges. They'd gone dark, stopped using their phones and they are – were – attempting to take their sister out of the country for a forced marriage to a first cousin in Iraq.'

'I had no intention of using that knife,' Rana said to me. 'It was the only way I could think of that would get me away from Talal and Samir. The only way to stop them taking me back to Iraq and my first cousin.' She shuddered. 'They must believe me! They must! Please explain it to them. I am not a terrorist!'

'Please sit down again, miss,' Poole said to Rana, indicating the chair. Reluctantly she did so and I stood beside her with my hand on her shoulder.

'Agent Poole, I can explain this,' I said. 'You may not have heard of RED-V – a new initiative I'm running that aims to tackle hidden domestic violence, particularly in migrant groups. We've only been operational for a few weeks.'

Poole shook his head. 'I'm afraid I have to go by the regulations. It's not my job to adjudicate. I only apply the law, and the law has been broken. People other than me will have to examine the rights and wrongs of it.'

'But surely, under the circumstances . . . Rana's just told you that the knife was a deliberate ploy on her part to get her away from her brothers. Can't you use your discretionary powers to drop this? I have plenty of evidence to back up Rana's statements to you. It's on file back in my office.' Back in my office where I was forbidden to go, I thought, as I quickly continued. 'Rana – Miss al-Sheikly's made a statement in which she alleges that her brothers conspired to kill her if she didn't go through with a forced marriage they've organised back in Iraq. Miss al-Sheikly has been the subject of a missing persons bulletin which will need to be called off now that we've found her and we can organise a safe place for her where her brothers will never find her.'

'I'm afraid we're going to have to charge her just the same,' Poole said. 'It is a very serious offence. At this stage, the motivation for her actions is not our business. We have to charge her and take her into custody, pending a bail application.'

I started protesting, but Rana interrupted me. 'It's okay, Debra. It's fine with me if they want to arrest me. I'm safe. I don't mind spending time in a lock-up. I've been locked up for so long now! And this lock-up is only temporary. I can't imagine a safer place at the moment.'

I saw from her expression that she was sincere. After a pause I nodded in understanding. Another thought struck me. 'How did you make that phone call? We weren't able to track either of your brothers' phones, or yours. They were all switched off.'

'I went into the women's toilets and a kind woman lent me hers,' said Rana. 'She saw how distressed I was. But while I was talking to you Talal barged in and knocked it out of my hands.'

'And you knew my number?'

'It's here,' said Rana, touching her breast. 'I learned it and threw away your card.'

'Agent Poole, please call your superiors and ask them if it's possible for you to use your discretionary powers. I understand you'd have to get the okay from your boss. You can see for yourself that Rana's no threat. Desperation has driven her to do something like this – in order *not* to get onto that flight to Iraq.'

Poole hesitated and I pressed on, seeing that his position might be changing.

'Or if you feel you can't take this to a higher ranking, at least tell the bail sergeant at the police centre to bail Rana. I'll guarantee bail for her.'

'Oh Debra,' Rana breathed, touching my arm.

'She's hardly a flight threat,' I said. 'You seem to be holding her passport at the moment.'

Poole considered for a moment, then stepped out of the room. I strained my ears but couldn't hear what he was saying. I felt sure he was making a phone call.

We waited, me with my arm around Rana's shoulders, while the airport security officer fiddled with her pen on the table.

Finally the door opened and I held my breath.

Simon Poole walked back inside, slipping his mobile back into a pocket.

'Miss al-Sheikly needs to come with me to AFP headquarters where a full report will be made of the incident. She will be required to make a statement.'

'And then?'

'Then she's free to go. If we need her again, we'll contact her.'

'I can't go home,' Rana said, looking up at me with a worried face. 'I mean I can't go to where my brothers were living. Or to relatives. Not now.'

I exchanged a glance with Poole. 'I'll come with you, Rana,' I said. 'To AFP headquarters. After that, I'll take you to a refuge.'

Rana jumped up, panic on her face. 'No! Not a refuge. The people there might betray me! That's happened before at women's refuges. Someone contacts the husband or the relatives and the next thing, the place is surrounded by angry men demanding that the woman is released!'

'Trust me,' I said. 'I know a place where nothing like that can possibly happen.' From my time in MEOCS, I had the contact number and address of a very safe house. 'You've trusted me so far, Rana. Okay?'

She nodded warily.

'Only a few people know about this place,' I said, to reassure her. 'Even most of the police don't know about it. You will be safe there.'

I turned to the airport security officer. 'Rana will need her luggage.'

'Send it through to the office,' said Simon Poole to the officer, who made a note.

'I'll meet you at headquarters, Rana,' I said as I was leaving the room. 'You're safe now.'

I watched as she disappeared from view through a door marked 'No Entry. Police Only' with Simon Poole.

I hurried back to find my car with an envelope under the windscreen wipers. I shoved it in the glovebox and called my contact at the covert women's refuge, letting her know that I'd be bringing Rana around later in the evening so she could start the paperwork.

I then headed off to AFP headquarters.

—•—

Two hours later, I accompanied Rana, now dressed in jeans and a striped T-shirt, together with her suitcase, to a squat brick house with bars on the window and a strong security door in a suburb not far from the central business district. She had been given a Crisis cash payment from Centrelink and allocated a single dwelling place.

I'd bought a bunch of lilies on the way and walked in with her as she opened up the security door and the front door. She breathed a sigh of relief as we walked down the hallway and into the kitchen–living area at the back of the two-bedroom house.

I found a tall glass and filled it with water for the lilies, putting them on the table near a barred window at the rear of the living room.

'I can never thank you enough, Debra,' she said, turning from arranging the lilies, tears magnifying her large eyes. 'This is the beginning of a new life for me. I'll call Eshaq and we can really start planning our future together. But first I'm going to enjoy this precious solitude and peace.'

'I'm just so happy that I could help,' I said. 'Call me if there are any problems.'

We hugged and said goodbye and Rana wasn't the only one with tears in her eyes.

CHAPTER 29

Next morning, I checked my overnight bag, ensuring that I had the prints I'd made last night of all the photographs I'd taken of the old case file, including the witness statements, crime scene photographs and the enlarged copies of the footprint smears. I planned to use these to keep the re-enactment as accurate as possible. I packed my new blue jacket too. After some toast and tomatoes, washed down with coffee, I set off around eleven-thirty.

As I drove west, the trees changed and so did the landscape. Apart from the occasional green paddock growing feed, the countryside looked sunburnt. But the landscape wasn't my concern. I tried calling my mother again. She was still not taking calls.

I imagined her walking through the grounds of the retreat house, somewhere in the semirural landscape of Arcadia. Maybe by the time she got back, she would have found some peace and be willing to talk with me frankly and intimately. That's what I hoped for, that's what I longed for. Maybe there was a partner I didn't know about – somebody with the nickname Smiley. How would I know? She kept her life completely hidden from me – and, I presumed, everybody else. Brad would know even less about her than I did, having been out of her life for years.

I called him on the handsfree as the rolling sunburnt hills gave way to granite country. 'Just checking to see if you're okay.'

He saw straight through me.

'No you're not. You're wanting to know if Mum's here.'

'That too.'

'She isn't.'

'When she does come home, tell her I'm on my way to Garralong.'

'What am I supposed to do? Mum's not here, you're going bush. I had to hobble up to the shop. I didn't have any money. I went through her wardrobe and checked all the pockets. I managed to get together eight dollars fifty – well, fifty-four, to be exact. I found two of those little brown coins on the floor of her wardrobe.'

'I thought you couldn't walk! See – you're coping really well. You've got a nice house to live in, and money.'

'Yeah. Sure.'

I rang off, smiling in spite of everything.

Around 4 p.m. I took the turnoff to Garralong and drove the few kilometres from the main highway, noticing the new 'Hidden Hills' housing estate on the outskirts of town, the big advertising billboards showing happy young families and promising 'a slice of real country living with real city convenience'. I left a message on Mum's phone telling her I was in Garralong and to call me asap.

Driving into town I passed the Soldiers Memorial Hall, and my eyes burned with tears as I remembered that night from over twenty-two years ago, my father dropping me off, his face stern and angry in the streetlights – that anguishing last image I have of him.

Blaxland Street, the commercial centre of town, was almost unrecognisable to me, except for the Victorian-era post office and a number of the old bank buildings, which had been turned into cafes or the offices of local businesses. Too many shops had for lease or for sale signs in their windows. From what I could see, country living was losing large sections of that promised 'real city convenience'.

I pulled over next to the low stone wall that surrounded the Botanic Gardens and got out to stretch my legs. I walked over to the War Memorial, a statue of a First World War soldier, his head bent, his hands resting on the butt of a Lee Enfield rifle; on the plinth below were inscribed the names of the locals who had fought and died in the two world wars, and a few more from the conflicts in Korea and Vietnam. Names familiar to my girlhood sprang out: Mitchell, Onion, Sinclair, Cusack and others.

I booked into the Garralong Motel situated in a side street running off the main drag. It was a classic country motel, unadorned bricks inside with the main window looking onto the car park. In the small, plain room I unpacked and hung up my clothes, putting my toiletries in the bathroom.

I'd factored in enough time to visit both the Cusacks and the ex-convent, so I drove the short distance out of town to the Cusack farm. I called from the road. Kathleen Cusack answered. She was home and would be happy to talk to me.

Minutes later, I was driving into the large front yard of the Cusack house, past the home paddock where Taffy and Ringo had once grazed, and parked near the large double garage. Kathleen Cusack, stouter and more weatherbeaten than when I'd last seen her, had come outside to welcome me. 'Fancy seeing you again, Debra, after all this time. Come in, come in.'

I followed her through the house until we came to the living room with its large plate glass window opening onto the back garden and beyond this, the low hills in front of the mountain range that surrounded Garralong.

Briefly, as we stood together looking out at the mountains, I told her why I was back in the town of my childhood.

'I believe there was a third party there, the night the Davidsons and my father were murdered.'

Kathleen's face registered surprise at this bald statement. She turned away from the window and indicated a comfortable lounge chair for me to sit on. 'Take a seat, and I'll make a cup of tea.'

'Thank you,' I said. 'I was wondering if you or your husband might have remembered anything more from that night.'

'Debra, Ernie died seven years ago. I'm alone now.'

'Oh. I'm sorry, Kathleen.'

'And I don't think I can add anything more to what I told the police at the time,' she continued. 'We both heard gunshots, two fairly close together and then a third shot after some minutes. Such a dreadful business.'

I waited while she boiled the jug and made tea in the kitchen. I thought of the happy days I'd spent here with Kiera and that I hadn't been back to ride since my father's death.

Kathleen brought the tea tray out and put it on a low table near the window. 'I thought it was an open and shut case,' she said, perching on another chair. 'It was all wrapped up. And now you're thinking differently? That could open a whole can of worms. Do you have any proof?'

I told her about the bloody partial footprints. While the tea was drawing, I asked, 'Did you notice any change in behaviour in the Davidson boys at that time?' As I asked it, I realised it was an impossible question. The murder of one's parents would necessarily affect behaviour.

'Tim left the country and Craig started drinking very heavily. But that's hardly surprising.'

'I was thinking of dropping by Craig's place after visiting you,' I said.

Kathleen poured the tea, passing me a generous mug. 'Well,' she said, 'you'll have your work cut out for you. I'm not sure where that would be now. He was living in an old caravan down near the river last I heard of him, drinking himself to death. He used to rave on, saying crazy things.'

'Such as?'

'He became an embarrassment. He'd buttonhole you on the street and ramble on saying, "I might have done it! I could have done it!" No one really took any notice of him.'

'What did people take that to mean? What did you think he meant?'

'Maybe he was feeling guilty about the bad relationship he had with his father,' she said. 'But he might have been referring to the murders.'

Thoughts flashed through my mind; the tulips and his apologies, drinking to blot out the memory . . .

Mark had told me about alcoholic 'blackouts' – periods of time when a person is so under the influence that the brain either doesn't record or entirely fails to remember, sometimes quite large lapses of time. 'I did an illegal Harbour Bridge climb apparently, according to the mates I was drinking with at the time,' Mark had told me not long after we became serious. 'To this day, I have absolutely no memory of doing it, apart from waking up very stiff and puzzled on the grass near the base of the south-east pylon with a hangover right off the Richter scale.'

Had something like that happened to Craig Davidson? His witness statement might have been fiction. Was it guilt that had driven him to apologise to me and bring tulips all those years ago? But if Craig Davidson was the guilty party, it blew apart my theory that my father was the prime target and the Davidsons merely collateral damage.

An hour later, I'd said goodbye to Kathleen Cusack and driven down to the popular picnic spot near the brown river where my family used to go. A few people sat about on rugs. Two kids threw a Frisbee. I turned my attention to the entry in my notebook. Craig Davidson could be anywhere along the banks which went for many hundreds of kilometres and I wasn't planning to chase him up right now. But he would need to be re-interviewed and the question should be put to him: *Did you shoot three people on the night of the sixteenth of April in 1992?*

I turned the car around and drove the six kilometres to the ex-convent, passing a large billboard that welcomed visitors to 'The Old Convent Retreat and Conference Centre'.

Where the old established gardens had once lined the driveway, low blond-brick units now stood behind small box hedges – the aged-care facility, I presumed. But despite the modern additions on the left-hand side, the nineteenth-century dark-brick convent building at the top of the drive was instantly familiar, with its cloistered verandas and squat bell tower topped with a cross.

I parked outside the old building and headed for reception, indicated by a small sign that was still visible in the dusk. Nobody came when I rang the doorbell, so I retraced my steps, hoping to find someone.

In a circular rose garden near the convent building, a small woman in modified nun's habit was busy with secateurs, nipping off the deadheads in the fast-fading light. One of the old nuns, I thought, put out to pasture.

'Excuse me, Sister,' I said. As soon as she turned around I knew who it was. She hadn't changed much – a little shorter, her face a little thinner, her eyes as keen and alert as I remembered. 'Sister Mary Aloysius! Did you get my message?'

'Debra Hawkins. Well, fancy that.' The old nun put the secateurs in one of her voluminous pockets and hurried over to greet me.

A few minutes later, armed with a second pair of secateurs, I was nipping off the deadheads alongside Sister Mary Aloysius in the twilight. 'So why exactly are you here?' she asked. 'I know you didn't come to see your old music teacher.'

'That's not quite true,' I said. 'But the main reason is that I want to go back to the Davidson farm and take a look around.' I gave her a brief outline of my reason for returning. 'I believe now that there was a third party at the farm that night. Someone who killed them and then killed my father.' I hesitated before adding, 'I wonder if you ever heard of anyone who might have had it in for Peter Hawkins – my father? For all I know, he might have been involved in a scandal of his own. I was just a kid then.'

Sister Mary Aloysius straightened from her pruning. 'I never heard anything at all like that about your father,' she said. 'And as far as I know, Peter Hawkins had no enemies hereabouts. He was well liked.' She thought for a moment. 'The only police officer from that time who's still in the area is Alfonso. He married one of the Quimby girls. Lenore Quimby.'

Fonzy. 'What about the young constable?' I asked. 'Carleen Gilder? Whatever happened to her?'

Sister Mary Aloysius reviewed the rose bushes with a critical eye before answering. 'She ran away with one of the teachers from the high school. *She* caused a scandal for a while. Her husband was arrested for assault, too. Took matters into his own hands.' She nodded as if satisfied with her gardening work. 'There, that should do it,' she said, decapitating one last, almost hidden, rose crown.

Fonzy had been rostered off that night, I remembered, the night my father went out to the Davidson farm. And Gavin Bailey had been away in Derby. The scandalous Carleen had been on leave. My father had been alone that night in the police station.

Sister Mary Aloysius took the secateurs from me, and started walking towards a low building of blond bricks, a recent addition adjacent to the old convent.

'So you want to visit the scene of the crime?'

'It's more than that,' I said, following her. 'I want to walk through it, retrace my father's last steps.'

'You'd better be careful then. It's been derelict for ages. The Cusacks eventually bought the place but they haven't done anything with the old farmhouse except store hay and agricultural machinery in it sometimes. But lately there's only been vandals and hippie people there. Goodness knows what you might find.'

We'd reached the corner of the last of the aged-care units and an automatic light came on, lighting the old woman's face as she stopped and turned to me. 'Let me make you a cup of tea. I've got a little unit around the back of these dwellings. Another day or two and you'd have missed me. As it is, I'm in the process of packing up. I'm moving to live with my sister in Derby.'

She led me to her small unit then ushered me inside. Sister Mary Aloysius boiled a jug and got out two cups. 'Sorry about the mess,' she said, surveying the stacks of boxes and zipped-up bags. 'I'd ask you to stay for dinner except there isn't any, and we've missed the dining room over at the main centre. But I can offer you a biscuit. Only made them yesterday.'

I was hungry and tired and gratefully accepted her offer of a very respectable Anzac biscuit, full of oats, coconut and golden syrup, chased down with a cup of black tea. Sister Mary Aloysius asked questions and I told her something of my cases, without mentioning names, of Kylie Jane Mifsud and Rana al-Sheikly. The old woman listened intently, topping up my teacup with water from the electric jug.

When I was leaving, Sister Mary Aloysius walked with me towards the door. I noticed several framed paintings leaning against the wall ready to be packed. 'Isn't that the Madonna that used to hang in the parlour over the piano?' I asked, recognising it. 'I always loved that painting. I used to think the baby was looking at me.'

'You're very welcome to take it if you'd like. I was going to drop them off at Vinnie's tomorrow. I can't take all of them with me. I'm already taking too much to my sister's place.'

I picked up the painting in its narrow gilded frame, pleased to have it – one memento of my childhood days that didn't cause me pain. My old teacher pressed a couple more Anzac biscuits on me, wrapped in plastic. 'For the road.' She smiled.

'Thanks. I hope Derby is a good change for you,' I said. 'I only remember its name because of the fire the day before my father was killed.'

'That was arson, for sure. They never got to the bottom of it. It was never properly investigated. Henderson's big general store was quite close to where my sister lives.' She sighed. 'Derby's very different now. Just tearooms and cafes and hairdressing salons.'

She followed me outside, looking at me with her ageless grey eyes. 'It's good to see you again, Debra. I always knew you'd be successful in spite of everything that happened to you. Some people have that touch of steel even when they're kids. You always stood out as an original soul. Be careful. You're going to need your steel, every ounce of it. Because whoever that third party was at the Davidsons' house, it is someone very dangerous. Tough enough to kill three people to get something they wanted very badly.'

'You would have made a good investigator,' I said.

'All it takes is listening with attention,' she said, 'and seeing with clear eyes. Oh, and caring for roses.' She paused, continuing to look at me intently. 'You've chosen to oppose the bad, not collude with it or pretend it isn't there. Protecting those young women. It's God's work you're doing, Debra.'

'It's *police* work, Sister,' I corrected her gently. 'But I must try that idea on my chief superintendent. Though I doubt it'll get me out of the mess I'm in.'

She raised an eyebrow enquiringly and I found myself almost about to spill the whole story of the death of Sami Allen, my suspension, the probable dismantling of my unit. But I decided against it. It was not really appropriate. 'I must go, Sister,' I said, walking towards my car.

With the Tempi Madonna stashed in the back of my car, I headed back towards the town centre, keeping an eye on the time. It was after eight o'clock and I wanted to grab something to eat in town before driving out to the Davidson farm. No alibis had been checked in 1992 because the case was wrapped as a double murder–suicide. As far as I knew, there hadn't even been the whisper of another party possibly being at the Davidson farm that night. There'd been no suspects to give alibis, checkable or not, and the only helpful witness statements were from the Cusacks, who both mentioned the approximate time they'd heard the shots. That first investigation had been hasty and slack. But what did I think I was going to be able to do, twenty-two years later? It occurred to me that I was on a fool's errand and that because of this – combined with some misdirected family loyalty towards my kid brother – I'd very likely lost my career. And precipitated the end of RED-V. Whatever happened twenty-two years ago was still shadowing me, still damaging me. Like some ugly low-grade infection simmering along all the days of my life.

I couldn't resist driving a few blocks out of my way to see our old home. I slowed down and crept past the house, now almost invisible behind the trees that my father had planted a quarter of a century ago along the front border – grevilleas, bottlebrushes and tall eucalypts, spreading out so that the house, never a big place, seemed even smaller, huddling down behind them. As I slowly cruised past I recalled the night I'd run up the driveway and inside to get a jacket, keeping my father waiting, making him late. I shivered as different emotions struggled together in me: sadness, loss, anger and regret – regret for what had been, and for what had been lost.

In town I grabbed a hamburger from a fast-food outlet. When I'd finished eating I looked at my watch. It was time to start my re-enactment. At nine fifty-five, I began the drive out to the farm, leaving from the corner near the police station, just as my father would have done twenty-two years ago. Compared to my feelings back at the house, I was surprised at my lack of reaction when I passed the entrance to the police station building. Now I was intent on the job, tense with anticipation, ready to retrace my father's footsteps. I made one last, unsuccessful, attempt to contact my mother, then put my phone away.

Okay, Dad, I thought, as I drove away from the police station. This is for you.

CHAPTER 30

I had no clear memory from my childhood of the Davidson farm entrance because whenever we drove past I'd always been keen to get to the Cusacks' and the horses, so I almost missed the driveway, with its painted four-gallon drum on a post and the faint lettering *F & E Davidson, 'Loxley'*, still just visible in my headlights. I braked at the last minute, grateful for the lonely road and no chance of a rear-end collision, and slowly turned in towards the cleared area where a long iron gate stood wide open, pointing in towards the corrugated driveway. Beyond this, on a slight rise and almost hidden by trees, the old farmhouse squatted, about fifty metres from the road, a deeper blackness against the night sky.

I remembered an old crime scene examiner telling me years ago how the crime scene will open up to you if you just let it – 'Observe,' he used to say, 'and let what you observe tell you its story.' Now the thought struck me: how had the anonymous caller been able to hear raised voices from such a distance, especially from inside a house? Not impossible on a clear night, but how likely?

I parked my car at the gate, took a torch from the glove-box, got out and looked up towards the house, then turned to scan the area. Further along the road some distance ahead was a school bus stop and what looked like an abandoned shop. I walked along the roadside to the old shop. It was a mess, with graffiti covering its walls and door, and rubbish and long grass blocking the recessed entrance where the old door rusted on its hinges. Above it hung a faded sign, *General Store & Post Office*. Presumably in 1992 there'd been a public phone booth outside the post office, where the anonymous caller had made his or her call.

I walked back to the car and gaping front gate, peering up at the darker shape on the rise, the old farmhouse. But maybe, I thought, giving the caller the benefit of the doubt, it had been a still, clear night and the sound had travelled easily and unhindered from the small farmhouse to the road. Almost as I thought this, a bullock or heifer made a series of trumpeting bellows from an adjacent property. A chill little wind lifted the leaves above me and I shivered. Something was niggling at the back of my mind, something that had arisen during my conversation with Sister Mary Aloysius, but I couldn't for the life of me recall what it was. I swung around, paranoid, feeling that someone was watching me. But all was still and silent except for the very occasional passing car and the sound of cattle stomping in a nearby paddock, hidden by brush.

I climbed back into my car and, keeping the headlights on, just as my father had done before me, I drove carefully up the rutted driveway.

I pulled up a little short of the house, where my father's station wagon had stopped; checking the position from the crime scene photograph, I felt my estimation was fairly accurate. As I got out of the car, a shiver went down my spine and some atavistic instinct growled a warning deep within. The niggle that I'd experienced down by the gate grew stronger. Something about Derby. Something about that fire. Spooked, I swung my head around to look behind me. Of course there was nothing, just the increasing darkness and the occasional rustle of night creatures in the brush, and beyond that only the dry, rolling hills silhouetted black against the moonless sky. From out of nowhere came a flash of memory, the kitchen table with my mother's shopping list on it. And a question arose: I'd always assumed she'd simply forgotten to take the list, but what if she hadn't gone shopping at all? If so, where had she been that night?

The old farmhouse – derelict now for many years, according to Sister Mary Aloysius – was in darkness just as it had been twenty-two years ago, when all the light switches had been in the off position. I remembered that the brief police report had also noted that there had been no forced entry.

I had left the car's headlights on as my father had done, so that he could see where he was going. He *knew* these people, he'd been fishing with old Frank, and the house was dark and quiet when he'd arrived and there was nothing to indicate he was in any danger. Because if my father had suspected danger of any sort, why would he have left the headlights on, providing a well-lit target? And yet suddenly it had all changed. *What happened?*

I stood near the car, leaving the driver's door open, just as my father had done, and stood looking at the old farmhouse, its outlines lit up in my headlights, the sagging timbers of the veranda where broken cane chairs and a dusty old iron boot scraper rusted away, the dodgy-looking front step where that boot print had been deposited all those years ago, the front door now out of alignment with the door jamb so that it didn't close properly anymore, broken windows at the front and the remnants of a filthy lace curtain visible behind the jagged glass. I shivered again, chilled both inside and out. I reached into the car and pulled the enlarged image of the boot print out of my briefcase. I walked up the stairs to the front door and placed it down on the timber, then stood back. Someone had stood here in the dark, with a shoe or boot that had picked up blood from the awful scene inside, holding the .303. Goosebumps erupted along my neck and arms and I wished I'd brought a warmer coat with me. I was only wearing the new expensive silky number. I'd definitely brought the wrong jacket. Had my father thought the same about his? Why hadn't he been wearing it?

I was standing right in front of the door. Hidden frogs had stopped croaking as I ascended the stairs. Now a sound from inside the house broke the perfect silence of the night, startling me. Just a possum or a feral cat, I told myself. But then it happened again and I recognised it for what it was – the creaking of floorboards.

There was someone in the house, a stealthy tread. Human footsteps.

My heart was racing with fear. Take it easy, Debs, I told myself. It's probably a tramp or squatter. Someone availing themselves of some shelter, rent-free. But at the same time, my investigator's mind was telling me: *This is what happened to your father – exactly this.* He saw something or heard something in the house. But what? Or who?

It was eerie standing there, near to where my father had done when I was twelve years old. There was only one answer to my question: my father had seen or heard the third party who'd been there that night.

The house fell silent again. Observe, I told myself, and let what you observe tell you its story. Observation didn't only mean looking, it also meant listening. Listening with attention. The fire in Derby. Sister Mary Aloysius had said they'd never got to the bottom of it. Obviously, the investigation had been futile.

I put a foot up onto the wonky wooden step, avoiding the piece of paper that demarked the killer's boot print, but the step gave under my weight, falling sideways, and my right ankle twisted painfully. I grabbed the door handle to steady myself, swearing under my breath. 'Hello?' I called, now that there was no chance of stealth. 'Who's there?'

No answer.

I felt fearful and ridiculous as I stood there, nursing my twisted ankle, calling into a dark house in the middle of nowhere, late at night. But I repeated my question. 'Who's there?'

A horrible, rasping whisper hissed from inside, 'Why – don't – you – come – in – and – find – out?'

My blood froze. Crazy ideas of wandering psychopaths came into my head. But I reminded myself that even without my sidearm I wasn't completely defenceless. I was confident I could handle most situations, despite a twisted ankle. And the whisper seemed somehow familiar. I took another step, wincing at the pain in my left ankle. 'Who are you? What are you doing here?'

The horrible whisper came again, dark spaces of silence between each word: 'Come – in – and – find – out – for – yourself.'

If my mother hadn't gone shopping that night, where was she? The question forced itself once more into my reluctant consciousness. But she couldn't have . . . Not her husband. Not my father. It wasn't possible, was it? My racing mind threw up other questions. The fire at Derby. They'd never got to the bottom of it. Why? Who was the police officer investigating the suspicious fire, lending his skills to the local firies? But what if he'd never turned up? What if this oversight got lost in the confusion that followed the terrible events of that night? The fire investigation unit might have been very rudimentary in a town the size of Derby . . .

No! My mind refused to accept the conclusion that was forming. It couldn't be. I was hoping against hope that I was wrong – that the person in the house wasn't who I suspected.

A whirlwind of scattered pieces of information came together, spinning themselves into a terrifying inevitability. I swore under my breath. Why the hell hadn't I seen this before? Now I knew who it was inside the Davidson farmhouse – the same person who'd been there twenty-two years ago.

I realised instantly the real danger of my situation. *You are walking into a trap, just like your father did!* With my twisted ankle there was no way I could storm the front door and take down the whisperer.

'Come out here,' I demanded. 'I want to see who I'm dealing with.'

No answer. No way was I going to walk in through that door, into the fatal doorway position, all nicely framed up for my father's killer to take me down. Time to back away, as quickly as I could, and get back into the car. Stop this crazy re-enactment and return to Sydney with my allegations.

Trying to quell my rising panic, I took a cautious step back, then another, but it was too late. A huge black shape, like an enormous bat, flapped out of the front door. I crashed to the ground, fighting back even before I hit the veranda, years of training kicking in, fighting for my life. But my assailant was strong and I was fighting blind, my elbows and knees constricted. Terror gripped me as I felt something tighten around my neck.

'It's no use fighting, Debs. I wish I didn't have to do this.'

Now that it was so close, I knew that voice intimately.

I had to fight to live. I tried to get a hand beneath the rope around my throat, but it was too tight. Images flashed through my mind, realisations and understandings, way too late. I tried to speak. If I could have formed the words, if I'd had the breath, I would have said: 'I should have known it was you who killed my father. I should have known that you had a debilitating disease. I should have recognised the symptoms of Huntington's disease when the cup of coffee fell out of your hands in the kebab shop. Or when your body twisted on the staircase in the police building and practically fell on top of me. Or when you lost all your strength and crashed back down into your chair after suspending me. You weren't at Derby that night. You were somewhere else.' Now I understood the jacket. And why it was so important.

It was important because it was the *wrong jacket.*

Too late I grasped the real reason for my father's cold anger in the car that night as he looked across at me, rugged up in the jacket that I'd grabbed from where it had been thrown over the banister. I'd asked him if he'd been wearing perfume. But my father never used aftershave. Alerted by my remark, he'd taken a closer look at *the jacket that wasn't his.*

The noose tightened and now I was dragged roughly and painfully across the veranda, banging my head on the door jamb. I attempted to inhale, a long rasping whistle as it became impossible to breathe.

For a confused moment, I thought he was hauling me up to my feet. But no. Still blinded and bagged, I was lifted completely *off* my feet by the rope around my neck. The pressure on my neck and in my chest became unbearable. I couldn't have screamed if I'd wanted to. Hopelessly, I kicked, but the tips of my toes barely scraped the floor. *This is it, Debra.* I was slowly being strangled by my own body weight. I'd never know exactly what happened to my father, because the same thing had happened to me: I'd been set up, just as he had been. My killer had been waiting for me, just as he had waited for my father. The same killer. I had re-enacted my father's last moments to lethal perfection.

That was my last logical thought before the bursting pressure in my ears and behind my eyes blacked out everything else.

My chest heaved crazily, straining for oxygen, and as I started dying, a terrible sound deafened me.

I crashed to the ground.

Blackness.

CHAPTER 31

Coughing, choking, my breath came in shocking rasps, the oxygen being dragged over raw and scraped tissue in my windpipe. As the pumping of my chest gradually eased, somewhere I could hear a hoarse screaming. I knew it wasn't me because all I could do was wrench air from the top of my throat into my aching chest.

Then came the hallucinations. I heard my mother's voice saying, 'Talk to me, Dibs.' The screaming continued behind her. Bright light shone in my eyes and I blinked, wondering if this was the tunnel people said you saw in near-death experiences.

But my mother's voice continued, begging and pleading through her tears, and slowly I realised it was no dream. The stinking blanket had been pulled off my head, and in the light of a strong torch now lying on the ground nearby I saw that it wasn't a blanket at all but a large doubled-meshed sack. Disoriented, too bewildered to feel anything except immense gratitude for each breath, I concentrated on inhaling and exhaling, while my streaming eyes took in the scene around me. In the old plaster ceiling above me was a large hole, revealing an exposed rafter from which a rope still hung. He'd been hauling me up over that rafter like a sack of potatoes to hang me. My mother knelt beside me, and next to her was a bloodstained heavy object I recognised as the iron boot scraper.

Gavin Bailey lay heaving against the wall opposite us. Beneath him, a darkly glistening pool was spreading. His harsh screaming had subsided to grunts. As I watched, his flailing arm connected with the corner of the wall where it turned into the kitchen. Clutching this, he began to pull himself to his feet, and as he raised his head I saw the murderous rage on his distorted face. With blood still streaming down one side of his head, he started lurching towards us.

'It was your jacket!' I croaked at him, struggling to get to my feet, weak and dizzy. 'The one I grabbed from the banister. It was *your* jacket and you were upstairs with my mother! And when I got into the car with that jacket, my father recognised it. Another man was in his house, upstairs with his wife. He knew who it was!'

Mum had half fallen against me, no doubt exhausted by the effort of landing that heavy blow on Gavin. But I couldn't help her up just now. I was fighting for our survival, mine and hers. Gavin Bailey would deal with me, and then he would deal with her. We were both done for unless I could pull something out of my drained, oxygen-starved body.

Gavin was almost upon me, dragging a leg, but relentlessly getting closer. I kept talking, hoping to find a way to distract him, never taking my eyes off him while my mind scrabbled around desperately for a plan.

'Your partner! The person you were supposed to protect!' I hissed with what was left of my voice. The words came out of my crushed larynx in harsh, staccato rasps. 'You betrayed him! You killed two other human beings to set up a trap to kill my father! You set up a non-existent domestic dispute and my father walked straight into you. He never had a chance.'

By now I was upright, swaying on my feet. Gavin made a low snarling sound like a wild animal as he fell forward, grabbing me around the neck. I attempted to put my fighting training into action but there was no conviction in my muscles. I was spent. My body shook with strain and weakness. I tried to push him away. I fought with everything I had left in me, ignoring the pain in my ankle, but it was no use. Those hands tightened around my already damaged throat. Useless fingers tried to prise his away, but it was hopeless. As the last of my strength ebbed I made one last attempt to get him off me, throwing myself to one side. Gavin stumbled after me, off balance and tripped over my mother, hunched on the floor. He took me with him, and as we crashed down his fingers loosened a fraction and I managed to jerk free.

Adrenaline surged through me in a final explosion. As I pushed myself back up to standing, a primitive growl in my throat shocked me. Gavin was halfway to his feet when I managed a kick to his groin. My other foot skidded in a puddle of his blood, and I crashed down again onto my back. Gavin staggered backwards, swaying and cursing, regained his balance and charged towards me. As I was frantically pushing myself back up, my mother crawled between us and threw something dark and heavy, which hit him hard in the face before falling to the floor with a loud thunk.

'Take it!' she screamed to me. 'I don't know how to use it!'

Gavin roared in pain, clutching his face. Blood now pouring from his eye, he kicked her aside with one boot. He seemed immense, like some swollen genie, powered by rage and hatred.

My feet slipping in the slick blood, every muscle depleted, I kept scrambling to get up. Registering my mother's words, I looked down at the heavy dark object on the floor at Gavin's feet.

Even though I hadn't seen one of these models for a while, I knew exactly how to use it. I threw myself forward, snatched it up with shaking hands, prayed it was loaded, and fired. And fired again.

Gavin Bailey, now immediately on top of me, toppled backwards. Shot through the upper chest and neck with Sergeant Peter Abel Hawkins' long-lost service pistol, .38 Smith & Wesson, serial number 67823. Someone was screaming primal berserker shrieks of triumph as I shot him again and again with my father's weapon.

Gavin slumped to the floor, arterial blood pumping from his neck. Dazed and shaking uncontrollably, I turned around to see my mother trying to get up. Tears streamed down her face, mingling with the blood running from her nose from Gavin's kick. Wordlessly I crawled to her.

I don't know how long it was that we held each other in that dark and bloody place, with the torchlight skittering shadows on the walls and roof and the still-quivering body of Gavin Bailey, dying, turned away from us.

'I hope you can forgive me for my years of silence, Dibs,' my mother whispered, tightening her arms around me. 'I tried to tell you a number of times. I just couldn't.'

I had barely enough strength to hug her back. We rocked together for what seemed a long time, as the sounds from the dying man finally turned to silence.

Eventually I said, 'We need to call an ambulance, and the police.'

CHAPTER 32

We stayed the night – what was left of it after the police and ambulance arrived – at the Garralong Main Street Motel, and Cecile came up the next day on the early train to drive my car plus my mother and me back to town. We'd work out something later to retrieve my mother's car. But first we spent the rest of the morning with the police, filling out statements and answering questions. The shooting death of an assistant commissioner by a suspended junior officer would require a huge critical incident enquiry and report. Exhausted and damaged as I was, I gave as accurate an account as possible of what had happened at the Davidson farmhouse the previous night. My mother did the same. The red and purple bruising around my throat, photographed from every angle by one of the detectives, was clear evidence that I'd been fighting for my life and the life of my mother when I shot and killed Gavin Bailey. His body still lay on the floor of Frank and Betty's living room and I felt there was some synchronistic natural justice in that – that he should be shot down in the same room in which he'd perpetrated three murders. I dreaded the additional attention that would be focused on me once the family relationships were exposed. I couldn't think about that right now. All I wanted to do was take my mother home and get her settled. Go back to my house. Call Mark and hear his voice.

My twisted ankle was badly swollen but I'd been able to get excellent first aid from the ambos who'd attended me, after pronouncing Gavin Bailey dead. They'd also examined my mother's nose; it was bruised but not broken. My mother had grasped my hand. 'That's us, Dibs. Bruised but not broken.' I squeezed her hand back in acknowledgement.

Flash rang while we were still in the car with Cecile. 'I'm ringing from an outside line,' he said, 'but the word's got around. The rumour mill's going full speed. I know you'll tell me all about it when you can. Any idea when you'll be back?'

I felt like I had tonsillitis, and swallowing was painful. But even though every muscle ached and protested when I moved, I was alive. 'Thanks, Flash. Not within the next few weeks. I'll need to take leave while the incident is investigated.'

'Are you okay? Were you injured? Your voice sounds strained.'

'Just a dodgy ankle. Nothing too serious.' I flinched at the memory of the stifling fabric over my head, the noose tightening around my neck.

'And by the way,' Flash was saying, 'I don't think that suspension will be mentioned again, somehow, now that the person who ordered it is not only dead but disgraced. But what about the man from IA?'

'The guy who made an allegation against me seems to have made a mistake.'

'You know this guy?'

'A little. So what's been happening your end?'

'It's crazy round here. You've no idea how the shit's hit the fan since Sami Allen got himself whacked. Cockroaches running all over the place trying to hide. The Drug Squad and the Gang Squad and MEOCS have been racing around, rounding them up. They've pulled in all the ones they'd tagged and released and made a whole new batch of arrests. The raids on those five clan labs resulted in a massive amount of intelligence. The counter-terrorism guys took away truckloads of files – records of money transfers to Hezbollah and the Syrian jihadis, illegal arms shipments, you name it. There's so much material that we've been called in to assist the other squads sift through it. By the way, just how did you get those five addresses? Your informant?'

'A very special informant,' I said, thinking of Rana, safely hidden away, 'Where are the al-Sheikly brothers?' I asked.

'Safely no-bailed in remand.'

I felt a sense of completion. I'd done my job in this instance, at least.

'Nadine has asked for a transfer,' Flash went on, 'but I know Charlie's dying to catch up with you.'

'What about RED-V? Are they going to dismantle us?'

'Can't really say. There's been some talk about it. And the usual people hissing and spitting. They did the same about MEOCS, but it's managed to keep itself together – and keep its name. We live in crazy times where speaking the truth gets you labelled as some sort of hatemonger.'

'I'll come in and sign a leave form in the next few days. So I'll see you all then.'

'I'll be taking some leave very soon, too. Going to Surfers Paradise for a week or so. With a friend.'

I smiled. 'Well done, Flash. I knew it was only a matter of time before those ties of yours aroused female interest.'

'Hey! She says it was the tie with the stripy-tailed lemurs that first drew her attention. How did you know that?'

'Check out who topped the detective course in 2003.' I laughed.

—

Cecile briefly came in with us as I hobbled into my mother's place, holding her hand. There were so many questions I wanted to ask, but I knew I'd need to be gentle, let her tell me the answers in her own time. In spite of everything, a new sense of peace was seeping steadily into my consciousness, flowing and spreading out, underpinning all the mess and muddle that was still jangling around my head.

It was mid-afternoon and the house was silent. 'Brad?' I called in my hoarse new voice, repeating the call as I limped into the spare bedroom. There was no sign of him, just the rumpled bed and a couple of dirty plates on the floor. I picked them up and took them out to the kitchen, catching a glimpse in the hall mirror of the angry red marks around my throat.

My mother was resting on the lounge when I went into the living room. 'How's your brother?' she asked. 'I didn't hear him.'

'He's not here.' I limped over and perched on the edge of the lounge. 'He must be feeling better. He's probably gone home.' He was the least of my worries at the moment.

Cecile made tea. My mother poured herself a brandy but then left it untouched and accepted a green tea instead. My stomach was still in revolt and I wasn't sure that anything I drank or ate would stay down. We sat in a tired, companionable silence.

Her drink finished, Cecile got up and kissed both of us on the cheek. 'I'll get a cab outside,' she said. 'I'll call later to see if you need anything. You look after yourselves,' she added.

'Piggy,' I said as she closed the door behind her.

I sprawled on the floor, elevating my throbbing ankle on a little footstool near the lounge where my mother reclined. Although she looked exhausted there was a light in her eyes that I hadn't seen in a long time, and some colour in her cheeks. Seeing her looking so well, I felt encouraged to start a conversation. 'What did you know about Gavin Bailey? I mean concerning Dad's death? I know you went to Arcadia the day before yesterday,' I said. 'I went into your office and I saw the note about Brother Lorenzo. I'd already been here and found a copy of the crime scene photograph you sent. That's when I realised you were Smiley. I didn't do it just to pry into your private life. You'd gone missing and I was very concerned about you, worried that you might be going to do something – something stupid.'

'I'm in no rush to get to the end of the story,' said my mother with a half-smile. 'It will come soon enough.' She frowned. 'I needed to talk to someone. I needed to talk about things that had been troubling me for a long time. I needed to go somewhere quiet and decide what to do. I knew I couldn't die in peace without telling the truth of what happened. I'd met Brother Lorenzo at a meditation group.'

I was surprised at that. Another aspect of my mother's life that I didn't know anything about. 'He came to mind so I called him and drove up to the retreat house. I had to tell someone.'

'Can you tell me?'

She put down her teacup deliberately and carefully before she spoke. I noticed she was wearing her wedding ring again. I hadn't seen that for many years. 'I always suspected him, but I had no proof,' she said quietly. 'He put pressure on me the night your father died, to talk to Peter, to talk him out of what he was going to tell his boss the next day.'

The meeting with the inspector from Newcastle, I remembered. 'What was that all about?'

'Your father had evidence of Gavin verballing one of the local thugs. Your father knew the guy was innocent of this particular charge, but Gavin wanted to clear up the books by hanging this extra charge on him. Gavin pressured me to talk to Peter about it, make him change his mind. He said that it would destroy Peter's career too and that we would all suffer because of what he called your father's stupid white-knight mentality. We had a huge fight. He stormed out not long after you came in and picked up the jacket.'

'That must have been a moment for you both,' I said, imagining the lovers upstairs, immobilised by the sound of my voice, wondering if I was going to walk in on them at any moment. 'And when Gavin left, he must have realised his jacket was gone.' I kept working on it. 'So that must have been the moment he resolved on killing Dad. He knew Dad would recognise his partner's jacket. And he knew that his career was over, his engagement would be over, and he would lose everything unless he eliminated Dad that night. That was the only way out for him. Everyone knew the Davidsons had been blueing for years. He used that.'

'You think he must have taken your father's jacket with him when he left the house?'

I nodded. 'Maybe he dumped it in a bin, threw it in a dam. He got rid of it somehow. Then he drove out to the Davidsons' a little while later, making the anonymous phone call from the public phone at the post office on the way.'

My mother nodded. 'It would have been so easy, Debs. He could have just dropped by and they would have made him welcome. He must have used some excuse like checking the gun licence, or making sure the rifle was in good order, fiddling with it, loading it and then suddenly swinging it around, aiming it —' Her voice faltered.

'The third glass!' I remembered. 'It was for him! Then all he had to do was switch out the lights and wait.'

We both fell silent, stunned by the pure evil of it.

'I know I was weak, Deb,' Mum said at last. 'After your father's murder, I should have told somebody what I suspected, but I was pregnant with Brad. And I had you to consider. I felt that things were already bad enough without me being revealed to you and the whole town as an adulteress. I didn't want you and my little son growing up with that. Everyone talking. You will never know how deeply I have regretted my stupidity in falling, even briefly, for a man like Gavin. But I was young and foolish. Restless and discontented and feeling trapped in a small town. I hadn't realised what it meant to be a police wife. And your father was very preoccupied with the job. So I stayed silent then and I've been silent ever since – in too many ways. I couldn't talk about that night because of my own guilty knowledge, and I never knew what I might say that would give the whole thing away. And so I said nothing – about anything important. Closing down the truth in one area of my life had a knock-on effect on everything else. I became guarded. My silence became habitual.'

'And Brad?'

'Gavin's son.' My mother's face looked stricken. 'It was dreadful when you told me about the Huntington's disease. I felt that I'd inflicted it on him by my infidelity – that it was my fault.' I placed my hand on her thin arm as she continued. 'Can you imagine growing up in Garralong, with all the gossip and the judgement? People looking at Brad and whispering? Maybe taunting him at school? Silence became my way of life. I know that's hurt you terribly. But once I got my diagnosis, I thought of a way where you might be tempted to reopen the case and I could stay hidden. I became Smiley. Years ago I'd snatched up a couple of crime scene photographs from someone's desk down at the police station when I was there finalising some paperwork. I'm not sure why. I used those, and I found a picture of a similar jacket online . . .'

The strange peace that I'd felt as we came through her front door seemed to settle between us. The ice splinter of shame, remorse and regret that I'd thought was lodged forever in my heart, melted as I realised that I hadn't been the cause of my father's anger the last time I saw him. I was about to ask Mum another question but she answered it before I'd framed the words.

'I took your father's pistol that day after the police came. I'm ashamed to say that I even thought of killing myself. But then I thought of you and the baby I was carrying. I knew where he kept it in the drawer and so I took it and wrapped it up carefully in waterproof material and buried it down in the backyard. My suspicions of Gavin were only circumstantial. I vacillated between sometimes believing that old Frank Davidson had gone crazy and shot three people and then suspecting that Gavin might have somehow had a hand in it. But I had no proof and I didn't dare say anything that might endanger you or me.'

'But how did you know to go to Garralong yesterday?'

'I followed Gavin. I'd called him from the monastery, telling him about Brad, that he had a son who'd inherited a deadly disease from him. I felt I had to do this. That he should know.'

'What was his reaction?'

'He was very quiet, actually. He told me about you – that you'd been suspended. He told me that you'd received some strange emails with crime scene photographs attached and did I know anything about that. I told him I'd sent them – and that if he had anything to do with my late husband's death, he should take responsibility for it.'

She paused. 'That's when he hung up. On the way back from the retreat house, I called Brad. He told me you'd come round looking for me and that you'd said something about going back to Garralong. He said some big cop had come round, wanting to know where I was.'

'Gavin,' I said.

'Brad must have told him about you, too.'

'Not necessarily,' I said. 'He could have tracked me via my mobile. That's what I'd do if I wanted to know where someone was going and their location.' I thought of something. 'Just as well he didn't have your mobile, too. You could have been in danger, Mum.'

'I'm already in that state, darling,' she said, but there was no bite in it. 'So on the way back home, I called in at his house. There was no sign of him, but his wife Amy – do you remember her from when we lived in Garralong?'

'Not really. I remembered he'd married one of the Sheffield girls.'

'Amy told me that he wasn't there. But that he was very concerned about a young detective he'd recently suspended – that he feared she might harm herself. He wanted to talk to her urgently.'

'He wanted to do a whole lot more than that,' I said, shivering at the memory.

'I've learned a few tricks from you,' she smiled, 'about how to keep a car under surveillance. I lost him well before the turnoff to the highway. But I knew he was heading for the Davidsons' farm. I parked off the road and in the dark, I crept up to the house. I saw your car. I couldn't see his car and wasn't sure he was there. But then I heard the struggle inside the house. I picked up the boot scraper from near the door and I had brought Peter's gun along with me. I've kept it all these years. I had some ammunition with it. I knew how to load it – your father had taught me. You know the rest.'

I was reluctant to leave her, although I longed to go home. I made a salad with some smoked salmon that I found in the fridge, and we sat down together to eat, although my mother only picked at hers. 'Come on,' I said. 'Try and eat a little more.'

When we were finished I cleared up, hobbling around awkwardly. 'Would you like me to stay with you for a few days?' I asked.

My mother smiled at me, a benign and beautiful smile that I hadn't seen since I was a child. I felt tears burning behind my eyes. She shook her head. 'Drop in on me every day, if you like. But you have your own life to lead, Deb.'

'I feel – this might sound a bit pathetic but – I feel like I don't want to lose you again.'

'You can't lose me. I'm your mother and now, instead of all the silence and hiding, I'm finally here. Many, many times I went to talk to you about all this – but I feared your judgement of me.'

I finished my tea, hugged her, promised to call later, and went home.

The fact that I'd killed a man – my mentor, my boss – didn't seem to have penetrated my brain yet. I'd barely processed the shocking death of Sami Allen. The events at the Davidsons' old farm still felt unreal. I wondered when it would hit me. I hoped word of his father's innocence would bring some relief to Craig Davidson somewhere in his caravan.

Just do boring routine things like housework, I told myself as I opened my front door. Noticing the mess I'd left in my haste to get to Garralong, I went around gathering up washing that I'd neglected for days. I leaned the Tempi Madonna near the long window. I'd hang it as soon as I could.

I was loading the washing machine with my blue police shirt when I suddenly thought of my poor father, having just discovered his wife's unfaithfulness, alerted by my childish remark about perfume, then driving out, with his broken heart, to walk into his sudden, violent death.

'Oh Dad,' I whispered. 'I'm so sorry.' I leaned against the laundry wall, sobbing.

―――

My mobile rang just as I was hanging out the last of the towels on the line in the backyard; as always, my spirits lifted at the sound of Mark's voice.

'Dear detective. How are things?'

'Hang on till I get inside again and settled with a drink. I'll tell you about everything. There's a hell of a lot to tell.'

And so I did, curled into the corner of his black leather chair, with the baby from the Tempi Madonna levelling his steady eyes on me.

I told Mark everything that had happened at Garralong as well as my mother's revelations. Then I told him about Rana. He listened in silence, then asked many questions, which I answered as fully as I could, and then there was a long moment as we both wordlessly acknowledged the tumultuous events of the last forty-eight hours.

Finally I spoke again. 'But the best thing, Mark, is the sense that my mother and I have bridged that deep chasm that used to lie between us. It's hard to describe – it's as if things have fallen into place somehow.'

'No more secrets, Deb. Secrets make more secrets.'
'I miss you. I want you home.'
'Careful what you wish for,' he said teasingly.

CHAPTER 33

'The phone hasn't stopped ringing,' Charlie said, calling from work a week later. 'Not just enquiries from individuals, but also other government agencies. We've had visits from Immigrant Women's Health and the New South Wales Domestic and Family Violence Council. Families and Community Services are arriving any minute. Everyone's after you.' A press release about the work of RED-V, combined with news items about the brilliant ploy of an unnamed young woman who had concealed a weapon on herself to alert authorities and prevent being taken overseas and forced to marry, had brought a load of interest. It also seemed to have brought a reprieve from the threatened dismantling of the unit.

'You're more than up to the job, Charlie,' I laughed. 'You and the team. I'll be back soon.'

'How's your mother?' she asked.

'Surprisingly good,' I said. 'She seems to have a new lease on life. It might just be the new drug regime she's been trialling. She's even talking of getting another dog.'

'We miss you, Debra. Come back soon.'

'Promise,' I said. 'I want to organise a hotline when I get back, where people who have information about suspected child brides or FGM happening can call in anonymously. Also I've mailed a little package to Maryam, care of you, Charlie. It's a gift for her, to show her my appreciation of her help. She was instrumental in getting Rana and me together.'

Maryam had admired some gold and turquoise earrings in a jewellery shop at the mall and I'd bought them last week, now pleased to give them to her.

'I'll call her the minute the package gets here,' Charlie promised.

I brought in the mail and a postcard, forwarded from work. It was in the form of a photograph of a dark-haired girl posing in a crocodile park – and as it was written in an unfamiliar hand it caused me to pause mid-step to read.

Hi, Kylie had written. *I'm living in Darwin now. It's a crazy town but I love it. Gone back to my natural colour and have a job with a small tourist business. New name, new life. All good. Thanks for your help. I owe you fifty bucks. Next time you're in town, I'll take you to lunch.* It was signed 'Shayla'.

I smiled and put Kylie's card up beside the wedding invitation propped up on the shelf near the fridge – Rana and Eshaq inviting me and a guest to a 'small, private wedding' to be held in a small private chapel next month, where my presence was very much desired. They were living temporarily in a flat above a shop, belonging to a relative of Eshaq's. A wedding calls for a new outfit, I thought with a smile. A fabulous new dress to match the pink diamonds in the new earrings. A brand-new pair of shoes. I'd seen a stunning pair of suicide heels in nude patent leather . . .

Mark called. 'What are you doing?'

'Just tidying up. Thinking of what I'll wear to a wedding.'

'Is this a proposal?'

I burst out laughing. 'What would you say if it was?'

'I'd say hell yes!'

'Oh, I miss you.'

'Miss me no longer, detective. I'm calling from the airport. I'll pick up the car and be off shortly. I'll be home later tonight in time to tuck you into bed.'

I felt a surge of joy and gratitude for his presence in my life, and as I rang off, I thought that in spite of the shock and terror that I'd endured recently, things were turning out well at last. I'd come through the fire almost unscathed and so had my mother. As for Brad . . .

I gave him a call. 'What's happening, bro?' I asked, as kindly as I could manage. I could hear voices in the background. 'Hope you're out of that filthy squat?'

'I'm at Lennox House,' he said, sounding offended. 'I've been clean and straight for five days, seven hours and thirty-three minutes.'

I'd heard about Lennox House, a drug and alcohol rehab centre in Darlinghurst. 'Good for you,' I said. 'After you've settled down, we'll come and visit you. Mum has some interesting things to tell you. And so do I.' Like the fact that our mother is dying, that the man who was your father is now dead, that the man you had always assumed was your father wasn't, and that there are shocking circumstances surrounding his violent death. But I was in no hurry.

'Bring me something decent to eat? I can't eat the slop here. And we're not allowed to drink coffee for some crazy reason, so bring me some good coffee, too.'

'On second thoughts,' I said, 'it might be better if we left our visit for a while.'

He didn't miss a beat. 'Just drop the things at the office, Debs. And for goodness' sake bring a carton of fags. I'm practically out of them.'

I rang off and swung myself to my feet. As usual, he'd asked no questions about me or anyone else. But I was used to the self-absorption of the addict and the way I was now feeling, I couldn't be angry with anyone. Especially not Brad. After testing my ankle I walked across the room to where the Tempi Madonna rested against the wall, tenderly holding her plump and twisting baby. Gently, I lifted the framed print up onto my last empty hook, then stepped back to check how it looked. It was definitely in the right place. If I sat on the floor opposite, that baby looked straight down into my eyes.

I was eating my supper of toast and Vegemite, sitting on a stool at the kitchen table trying not to think of the events at the old farmhouse, when I heard Mark's station wagon approaching the sliding gate. A big grin spread across my face and I hobbled as fast as I could to the back kitchen door, ready to throw my arms around him.

I spent a lot of time over the next two weeks visiting my mother; remarkably, her condition was continuing to improve. 'The physician told me to keep on doing whatever it is I'm doing,' she said on my latest visit, smiling. 'The tumours haven't grown at all since my last scan. The new drug regime is having a good effect.'

We spent hours, talking, talking, talking; we had half a lifetime to make up for. Sometimes we'd walk together, in Centennial Park, Hyde Park, or along a beach. Woman to woman, we understood and accepted each other's lives. How could I blame or judge her now? We all make mistakes that have life-changing consequences, I'd learned that the hard way. As I sat with her on the beach, hearing of her struggles as a young mother, watching the eternal waves move in and out, the breathing of the ocean, old resentments and sadness were simply washed away.

—•—

Mark had resigned from his old job in Western Australia and had since accepted a position in a flourishing manufacturing workshop in Homebush, starting in November.

A couple of days after he'd secured the job, he looked up from where he'd been tying young tomato plants to stakes. 'I've got a surprise for you tonight, Debs,' he said.

'Oh, I've seen it all before.' I laughed and Mark just grinned.

The surprise turned out to be a night in the most luxurious penthouse in a bijou hotel down at The Rocks, with a view to the Opera House and Circular Quay. Breakfast came in on a trolley covered with starched linen, plus champagne for me and sparkling non-alcoholic cider for Mark in an ice bucket.

'This is a Thanksgiving breakfast,' Mark said.

'But we don't do Thanksgiving in Australia.'

'Yes we do. You're alive. You've saved your father's reputation. You've wrapped up a couple of tricky cases. There's a hell of a lot to eat eggs Benedict and drink champagne for.'

We sat up in bed, with the glories of Sydney Harbour displayed through our window, and devoured the breakfast, which also came with extremely fattening pastries.

'Are you ever going to tell David about you and Juliet?' I asked.

'What makes you ask that now?'

I shrugged, and took a sip of champagne. 'I'm not sure, but it might have something to do with feeling that things are starting to fall into place. Like a wrap at the end of a case. Even though I've never found out who threw that Molotov cocktail into my backyard.'

'I'd have to speak to Juliet first,' he said. 'I'm not sure if it's the right thing to do after all this time.'

'Mark,' I said after a pause, looking into his blue eyes, 'I'm so glad you're here.'

'Me too,' he said, picking out a feather-light pastry and waving it in front of my mouth. 'And I'm never going away again. Look what happens the moment I turn my back on you.'

'You've never turned your back on me,' I said, pulling him down to me, accidentally tipping over my glass. Champagne splashed on my face and I laughed. 'Hey! I'm drowning!'

'I'll save you,' he said, pouncing on me.

I was enjoying being saved when my mobile rang. 'Let it go to voicemail,' I said, drawing back from a kiss.

But Mark had already reached over and picked it up. 'Hello?' he said.

'Tell them I'm not here,' I whispered. 'I'll call them back.'

But Mark was frowning. A chill went through me.

'I think you'd better take it.'

I signalled 'what is it?' with my eyes as I took the phone. 'Deb Hawkins speaking.'

At first I had no idea who was on the other end of the line. Choked-back sobs interrupted his words as he struggled to speak. Finally I made out what he was saying and my blood ran cold. 'It's Eshaq. Eshaq Boutros. My heart is breaking, Ms Hawkins. I'm calling to tell you about Rana. My beautiful Rana.'

My heart squeezed with fear. Somehow I already knew what was coming. 'What happened? Eshaq, what is it?'

CODA

A few days later, Mark and I drove through the lower Blue Mountains, headed towards Katoomba, the late afternoon sun in our eyes. I was happy to let Mark drive. I wanted to be free to remember Rana without the distraction of driving. I also needed time to reflect on what lay ahead for my family; whether I'd be up to the challenges facing me – the future deterioration of my brother, the progress of my mother's illness.

I would also be facing official enquiries at work when I went back. These could and would be overcome, and they were problems in my *life*, my future. They were proof of living, part of life. Whereas Rana al-Sheikly, gifted, intelligent and beautiful, with her whole life ahead of her, was gone – no life, no future.

On the back seat lay a huge sheaf of white oriental lilies and roses that I'd purchased on the way.

As we made the Katoomba turn, I broke the sombre silence. 'Eshaq told me that the autopsy report indicated she'd been dead for a number of days,' I said. 'Her body had hit a rock ledge that's not easily seen from the walking track. Her injuries were catastrophic, to quote the doctor's report, and consistent with falling from a great height. It's thought she somehow got too near the edge and slipped. It's easy enough to do. The guard railings protect people on the lookout, but anyone can easily walk around through the bush and get to the edge of the cliffs in front of the rails.'

Mark threw a glance in my direction. 'Is that likely?'

I gazed sightlessly at the passing bushland, my mind preoccupied with a shy, beautiful and intelligent young woman who had asked for my help. In the short time I'd known her, Rana had revealed herself as daring and resourceful, with a soaring spirit and a steel will beneath her gracious manner. Although I didn't have her graciousness, I felt we had other, crucial qualities in common. She had wanted a different life than that dictated for her by her family. Being navigator and pilot of my own life had always been non-negotiable for me; I'd charted my course since I was twelve, and I couldn't imagine why this should be less important to a woman like Rana.

'Is it likely Rana al-Sheikly would be wandering around up there outside the railing?' I said, rephrasing Mark's question. 'No. It's not likely at all. Everything about her indicated prudence and sharp intelligence.' I hesitated before adding, 'The saddest thing is that no one from her family or clan claimed her body. She lay unclaimed at the morgue until Eshaq organised her funeral. Her family have completely turned their backs on her.'

We parked some distance away from Echo Point. The sun had just set behind the sandstone ridges as we took the path that led to the lookout across the Jamison Valley and over to the Three Sisters, the uneven trinity still glimmering gold in the afterglow. Beside me, Mark carried the huge sheaf of flowers.

'Eshaq can't stop blaming himself,' I said, blinking back tears. 'He says he should have gone with her that day to say goodbye to her aunt Sarah and the cousins. According to what Sarah told the police, Rana was upset and crying when she left the house after saying goodbye. She disappeared somewhere between Sarah's house and the flat where she and Eshaq were living at Bondi Junction. Eshaq is adamant that Rana didn't kill herself. He says she would never do that. They were planning their new life together in Queensland, where they hoped they'd be safe from any interference.'

I paused, no longer needing to shade my eyes from the fading glory of the sunset. 'But remember, we only have Sarah's word for what happened at her house. What if things didn't go the way she described? What if she'd set Rana up – told her all was forgiven and that she was welcome back in the family? There've been many cases overseas where that's happened. It's a well-known deception, mothers saying to their daughters, "Come back home. Your father and I have forgiven you. We miss you. We love you," and then standing by while the men of the family murder their daughter. Perhaps Sarah wept and pleaded for Rana to come back, and all the time someone organised by the brothers was waiting in the next room, ready to grab the disobedient girl.' My foot lurched on the uneven path and I winced, stopping for a moment.

'There's so much talk about human rights,' I said, as we resumed our walk. 'Surely the first and most basic human right is the right of an individual to live their *own life*, in their own way, and to be able to walk this path unmolested in whatever way they choose – even if,' I thought of my mother, of Brad, of Kylie Mifsud, 'their choices are often difficult for others to understand.'

Mark squeezed my hand. 'I'm trying to find a gentle way to say this, but there really isn't one,' he said. 'What's your conclusion? Did she jump or was she pushed?'

We were nearing the lookout with its expansive viewing deck and strong steel railings as I considered his question. Behind us, the bus shelter was empty. There was no traffic around. 'There's no evidence of her travelling up here by train,' I said. 'She doesn't show up on any of the CCTV footage – Charlie had a look for me last week.'

'She could have driven up?'

'She doesn't even have a licence, Mark.' I told him about the conversation Rana had overheard in which her brothers discussed making her death look like a suicide. 'If Rana came up here by car, someone else was driving.'

'But her brothers are in remand,' Mark said. 'They're out of the picture.'

I shrugged. 'I don't know. It's quite possible that other parties also felt dishonoured by her actions. It's a tribal thing, remember. Relatives of the jilted fiancé in Iraq might have taken it upon themselves to execute the correct penalty for a disobedient woman who brings shame upon the family. Or got someone to do it for them.' I thought of something else. 'Or on the other hand, maybe it was just all too much for a young woman like her, not entirely at home with Aussie Skip culture, to cut herself off completely from her community, and to look ahead and realise that she could never go back to her family. Putting all her trust in this young man. Leaving behind everything she knew. It could have overwhelmed her, made her feel powerless and helpless.' I paused. 'I know a little of how she feels. I failed Rana. I'm even thinking I'll resign – get out of the job.'

Mark put his arm around me as we arrived at the guard railing. Ahead of us, ancient, untouched Australia opened up like a fourth dimension, ridge after ridge connecting invisible valleys, mountain sequences fading into the famous misty blue of distance and refracted evening light. I peered over the railing and down through the still, cool air into the valley, the shadows lengthening beneath us and darkening into purple. My breath caught at the back of my throat and my perineum tensed as I imagined falling off this escarpment and tumbling down hundreds of metres. Or the terror of being manhandled and dragged to the edge and pushed over. I shivered. Taking the beautiful flowers from Mark, I hurriedly ripped open the cellophane encasing them. I had to press my lips together to stop the threatening tears.

'Remember what you said to Eshaq on the phone,' Mark said, his arm still firm around me. 'That it's not possible to keep a person safe twenty-four hours a day, seven days a week. Unless you lock them in a cage. Or spend hundreds of thousands of dollars on rotating shifts of bodyguards. That's what you told him.' He drew me closer. 'Can you apply that comfort to yourself?'

I pushed my face into the warmth of his chest. 'I think I need a break next year. I've got heaps of long service leave.'

'Okay. Take a break for a while,' said Mark. 'But I can't imagine you ever really leaving the job. There are too many other Ranas who need the help and support of you and RED-V.' He kissed my forehead, pushing back a strand of hair that the evening breeze had blown across my face. 'You've done an amazing thing, salvaging the memory of your father. Dealing with his killer. Doing everything in your power to assist an Australian citizen under threat. No one could have done more. Don't sell yourself short, Debs.'

His words brought some comfort, and I pulled out a long stem of white lilies, fresh and barely opened, like Rana herself, and hurled it like a javelin over the edge. It fell soundlessly, vanishing into the tree canopy. Slowly, I scattered the rest of the lilies and white roses over the edge – a shower of blooms to float to the bottom of the valley.

'It's done,' I said. 'Rest in peace, beautiful one,' and the words caught in my throat.

―――

As we walked back to the car, Mark pulled a small black velvet box out of his pocket. 'I've been carrying this around ever since I got back,' he said. 'I was going to present it to you at our champagne breakfast – but then Eshaq called. It's not a conventional engagement ring, but I'm hoping you'll accept it – and the man who comes with it.'

I opened the box and gasped. A magnificent South Sea pearl, silvery white with rainbow hints, dangled imprisoned in a delicate net of fine gold, sprinkled with diamonds, the whole radiant orb suspended on a diamond-flecked gold chain. I lifted out the glorious jewel and held it up in front of my eyes.

'You don't have to say anything right now,' Mark said, 'but if you were thinking of taking a break next year, let's plan an adventure. You've got heaps of long service, I've got a pile in the bank. We could hire a skipper and a yacht, go cruising. Diving in the Whitsundays. Eating red pawpaw under a coconut tree. You might even find another one of these washed up somewhere and make earrings.' He gave the pearl in its diamond net a gentle push. 'If there's any change for the worse in your mother, we can come straight back. What do you think, Debs? Will you give it some thought?'

Slowly, I nodded. Saying 'piggy' would be all wrong in this situation. Instead, I kissed him. Time to live more and work less, I thought. Time for Mark and me. 'I promise. But first I have to do what I can to find out what happened to Rana. I can't just forget about her life – and her death.'

'You do what you have to do. I'm content if I know that we can take off together sometime not too long away.'

In that moment, I felt a huge surge of love for him, for his understanding and patience. 'It won't be a long wait, Mark. I've already got Charlie and Socrates putting a brief together for me. Once I've done that —' I broke off and turned back towards the lookout and the darkening ridges. Something had caught my attention.

From the depths of the hidden valley a soft hum had started, as if millions of insects were rising, but this was a wider, deeper sound, with several different notes, reminding me of the spinning tops of my childhood that sang as they whirled.

'What's that sound?' I asked, turning to Mark. He was also listening, his head cocked. The sound deepened, wrapping us in its plangent hum, as if an orchestra of a million strings were softly vibrating a major third.

'Must be the music of the spheres,' said Mark, smiling and bending to kiss me. When I came up for air and opened my eyes, I saw that the first stars had appeared behind Mark's head. As we stood there, the humming faded until there was only silence and the calling of a late currawong.

I climbed into the car, my heart not quite as heavy as when we'd arrived.

'Okay,' I said. 'Let's go.'

Also by Gabrielle Lord

THE GEMMA LINCOLN NOVELS

Death by Beauty

Young, beautiful and dead

'Grimacing with horror, she saw what he was flicking with his fingers. She tried to move, to scream. A strangled sound escaped her throat, her mouth gaping in her frozen body, immobilised, as his face loomed closer.'

A 'vampire' is stalking the streets, attacking beautiful young women; some are murdered days later, others aren't touched again. Gemma Lincoln, PI, begins to see a pattern and predicts which girl will be targeted next. But can she convince the authorities to take action?

Meanwhile, at the salubrious Sapphire Spring Spa, a private cosmetic surgery clinic that boasts the latest breakthrough in the search for eternal youth, post-operative clients are experiencing sudden onset depression and worse. Is the exclusive clinic involved in a lethal cover up?

While dealing with her most brutal and baffling case yet, Gemma's ex, Steve Brannigan, the father of her son Rafi, desperately needs her help as he faces career destruction from the vengeful woman who also wants Gemma dead.

As she inches closer to discovering the appalling truth about the murders, Rafi and Steve disappear. Confronting a mother's worst nightmare, Gemma discovers what she is prepared to do to save her son . . .

'a writer at the top of her game'
Sydney Morning Herald

Shattered

A young boy runs down the hallway stairs as his family are shot, one by one, at the front door. His eyes catch those of the killer. For a split second they stare at each other – *Hell, what's the kid doing here?* – before three shots tear into his body.

Private investigator Gemma Lincoln and Detective Sergeant Angie McDonald take on the case, tracking down the brutal killer and piecing together fragments of evidence which hint that the shooter might have been a cop.

Meanwhile, Gemma is dealing with a runaway schoolgirl, searching for a young woman who does not want to be found, and grappling with the biggest question of her life.

Who is going to help her find the answer? Or is this something Gemma has to decide on her own?

'keeps readers turning her pages'
Bulletin

'delivers novels of criminal excellence'
Weekend Australian

Spiking the Girl

PI Gemma Lincoln is brought in to investigate the disappearance of a missing schoolgirl by the principal of Netherleigh Park Ladies' College. The day after Gemma takes on the case another teenager from the exclusive school goes missing. Detective Sergeant Angie McDonald is the investigating officer, but she is overworked and distracted. And Gemma's got her own problems . . . She has no idea her life is about to get a whole lot more complicated.

Gemma discovers the missing students were messing about with web cams transmitting from their bedrooms and that they had links to a hardcore pornography site. She pushes hard to uncover deadly secrets. But will Gemma be able to catch the murderer before they kill again?

'superbly written psychological thriller . . .
Gemma fans should fasten their seatbelts'
Australian Women's Weekly

Baby Did a Bad Bad Thing

Gemma Lincoln has never been busier. She's investigating the disappearance of Benjamin Glass; she's trying to discover who killed her old friend Shelly; and she's also closing in on a serial killer who targets sex workers.

But at the same time some unknown person seems determined to destroy Gemma's business. And she suspects her boyfriend is two-timing her. Always haunted by the insecurities of her past, Gemma struggles to pull her life together in increasingly sinister circumstances.

'Harrowing . . . and irresistibly readable.'
Jeffery Deaver

Feeding the Demons

Gemma Lincoln, ex-cop and owner of a security and surveillance business, has more than her fair share of skeletons in the closet. Gemma and her sister Kit's childhoods were haunted by their mother's murder and their father's conviction for the crime. Thirty years later he is released from prison, causing conflict between the sisters, who have different opinions about their father's guilt.

At the same time a series of gruesome incidents involving slashed women's clothing escalates into serial murder. Both Gemma and Kit become caught up in a terror linked to past secrets.

In a gripping climax that threatens both their lives, demons from the past return to haunt their present.

'A complex, masterfully paced story peppered with memorable characters and superb dialogue'
Sydney Morning Herald

www.ingramcontent.com/pod-product-compliance
Ingram Content Group UK Ltd.
Pitfield, Milton Keynes, MK11 3LW, UK
UKHW041228200426
11947UKWH00034B/572